Chasing Cherry

ALSO BY JILL BROCK

Pennywise
Drop Dead Delicious

Semisweet

Chasing Cherry

A Maggie and Odessa Mystery

Jill Brock

DEDICATION

Always to my family and friends who love me in spite of myself. Especially to Kam, who gives me a reason to laugh and reminds me how much I love her.

CHAPTER

1

I stared down at the plate. A grayish mass of something that resembled meatloaf took up much of the dish. Mixed into the ground meat were large, unidentifiable white chunks. A thin layer of burnt crust held most of it together. I recognized the asparagus only by their shape and faded green color. I took a precautionary sniff and straightened as the assault on my senses told my sensitive stomach the unwelcome news: I'd located something awful.

I collected my thoughts, corralled my stomach and tried to answer the question the confused diner asked moments ago. He repeated it, maybe believing the fumes from whatever masqueraded as food had overwhelmed me.

"What is this, Odessa?" he said. The customer was a regular, often eating at the restaurant twice to three times a week.

I worked my mouth into a fixed smile, which was no easy feat considering I didn't have a clue. "What did you order?"

He shook his head and pointed to the offending plate. "Not this."

My family's restaurant, the Blue Moon, in Queens, New York, was famous for its excellent home cooked favorites, and the best desserts in town. We pride ourselves on making our clients feel at home. The customer's expression of confusion reminded me of one of those parallel universes moments, I knew we were in trouble. You know the feeling, where you step into your favorite eatery, everything seems normal, but something is off, especially the food. The staff tries to convince you otherwise, but the warning in your head blares like a three alarm fire, telling you to run like hell. This guy had the run like hell look written all over him.

"Sorry." I picked up the plate. "Why don't I suggest a juicy steak and the house salad—no charge."

"Okay." The alarm on his face eased a bit, perhaps appreciating I'd gotten the offending plate away from him. I turned, lost my smile, and headed toward the kitchen and the source of my current problem, my sister Candace. I hadn't taken three steps when my best friend Maggie Swift entered the restaurant. I groaned remembering our lunch date.

Standing just less than five foot four, with red hair and pixie features, Maggie reminded most people of a grown-up Tinkerbelle. Her usual cheery demeanor faded as she cut through the dwindling lunch crowd, and caught sight of me in the Blue Moon apron, which covered my pink chef's jacket. She'd expected to find me next door in my little cake shop, *O So Sweet*, making specialty cakes and desserts for the restaurant and my own customers. I should have been finishing Mr. Hirsch's birthday cake: double chocolate, with pale yellow sugar miniature sunflowers, but instead one of the Blue Moon's waitress begged me to come to the restaurant to deal with the impending disaster.

When Maggie's bright blue eyes narrowed in confusion, I just shook my head. "Don't ask," I said, exhausted from the Herculean task of dealing with complaints about the food.

"What is that?" Her nose crinkled. Like a car accident you

couldn't believe or ignore, I read the doubt.

"Meatloaf." I tried to sound convincing, but my heart wasn't in it.

"That's not meatloaf." Maggie shook her head. Besides being the mother of my godson, a housewife, and former secretary to the Hicksville chapter of the P.T.A., Maggie aspired to be a private investigator. She worked part-time for a retired New York City detective as a receptionist, secretary, and researcher. She had dreams of opening her own investigation office one day. So, when I shoved a nondescript piece of graying mass in front of her, I trusted her to know it wasn't meatloaf.

"Who cooked that?" Maggie arched a quizzical eyebrow at me.

"Candace."

"Oh my God!" Maggie covered her mouth, realizing she'd drawn the attention of several of the restaurant's customers. I smiled at their concerned faces and prayed they didn't order the meatloaf.

"George is at one of his ex-marine weekend retreats in Atlanta and Bebe hasn't shown up for work. Candace insulted the temporary cook so badly the man threatened to join the priesthood to pray for her soul. I need to stop Candace before we get shut down by the board of health and Homeland Security for domestic terrorism," I said between gritted teeth. We headed toward the kitchen and a confrontation with my sister.

"Bebe's never late," Maggie said.

She was right. Eighteen-year-old, Bebe Dunn, former wannabe juvenile delinquent and current sous chef wouldn't miss an opportunity to be in charge of George Fontanne's kitchen. Bebe had come to us from the Queens County Family Court. As a first-time offender, he participated in a work program. It kept him out of trouble and washing dishes. He started off as a bus boy and graduated to food prep and sous chef when the head chef discovered Bebe had a talent for food. At the moment, I had bigger concerns than Bebe's whereabouts. Before I had a chance to deal with any of them, my phone rang.

"Dammit." I handed the plate to Maggie and fished the phone out of my pocket. My fiancée Lee's name and image displayed on the small screen. Though a pleasant interruption to my day, Lee's phone call postponed the much-needed confrontation with my sister.

"Hey honey, I'm a little busy." I almost dropped the phone when another waitress exited the kitchen carrying a plate of meatloaf. I commanded Maggie to stop her.

"Odessa!" Lee's tone begged my attention.

"Can I call you back? Candace is trying to put us out of business," I said.

"Huh!" My declaration had surprised but not deterred him. "I have a problem. In fact, we have a problem," he said.

I recognized the panicky hitch in his voice. Typically, calm under pressure as a civil lawyer, it took a lot to faze him. Something had knocked him off his center.

"My sister!" He declared as if this explained everything.

I hated when he thought I could read his mind. Growing impatient at his lack of details, and needing to deal with my own sister-drama, I wanted him to get to the point before Candace killed someone. "What's wrong with Allie?" Lee's sister lived in California with her dentist husband.

"She's coming in on the afternoon flight out of Kennedy. I can't pick her up because I'm trapped in court all day. I need you to get her."

This got my attention, and I stopped worrying about mass food poisoning and focused on the conversation. Whatever drama happened at the restaurant couldn't compare to an unexpected visit from Lee's sister. My only contact with her had been sociable, but short, phone conversations. Why was she coming to New York City unannounced?

Was it because I was about to marry her only sibling, whose first marriage ended in divorce? Now, he wanted to tie the knot again with someone who had more differences than a Texas prom queen and a Chinese jockey. Lee, an even-tempered white Scot-Irish lapsed Catholic, jazz lover, climbed rocks for laughs and giggles. I was a black, Baptist, ex-advertising executive, a dessert chef who believed shopping should be listed as a form of therapy by the American Psychiatric Association.

"Sure, no problem," I lied as my stomach churned.

He gave information about Allie's flight. I took a deep breath, and then another as a headache formed. If I were lucky, it would be the beginning of a stroke, which would force me into a coma, and then everyone would have to deal with their own mess. I waited a beat, and nothing happened. So, I shoved the phone in my pocket and headed for the kitchen with Maggie close behind.

"Remember Odessa, she's trying," Maggie implored. Always the voice of reason, moderation and denial, my friend hated my confrontations with my sister. She ranked my fights with Candace next to nuclear fallout and reality television. Maggie failed to realize that, without these familial altercations, Candace would take over the world, especially my life. I braced myself as we entered the kitchen. I zeroed in on Candace, who barked orders at a helpless kitchen helper. Luckily, he barely spoke English, so the tirade coming from her mouth must have sounded like loud condescending gibberish.

"Candace Wilkes," I shouted.

The entire kitchen staff spun in my direction and took an

involuntary step back. One worker covered his privates with a large pot. Another stepped into the kitchen, assessed the situation, turned on his heel, and left.

My older sister by several years, Candace was under the delusion I was still that thirteen-year-old girl she took care of when our parents died and left her in charge of the family restaurant and me. She was bossy, opinionated, and I loved her. Tenacious when it came to her family, and the Blue Moon, her take-no-prisoners attitude developed the moment she stepped out of diapers.

My sister was an attractive woman. She had the Wilkes women's height, but my mother's pale honey-brown coloring. She had incredible eyes the color of amber. Her hair, thick and black, was always worn up, or tied back. While I stood tall and lean, Candace had curvaceous lines. All this loveliness was deceptive. Someone once described my sister as one of those Greek Sirens that lured sailors with their beauty and song, ultimately smashed against a rock and died. Get on the wrong side of my sister and chances were you'd walk away bruised and bloody.

"I'm busy," she snapped, her attention focused on the unfortunate kitchen helper. His pleading eyes fastened on me.

"Meatloaf? Really Candace, really!" I held up the plate just above a trash can. I tipped the plate slightly, hoping its contents would fall off in dramatic fashion. They didn't. I had to shake the thing. The asparagus went, but the meat and potatoes clung on for dear life. I gave another solid shake, and the meatloaf and stiff potatoes thumped in the can like a body in the Hudson River. Candace gasped in horror. The same way Doctor Frankenstein did when the townsfolk killed his science project.

"Stop cooking." I pointed to a petite woman in an oversized white apron. "Terri is suppose to cook, not you."

"I can cook," she said.

An audible groan went throughout the kitchen. She silenced them with a fierce glare. My sister had been trained at the Medusa School for Young Girls. She'd mastered the ability to shrink men's souls and their man parts.

"What were those white things in the meat?" I circled my finger over the offending objects.

Candace jutted her chin out at me. "They're apples. I got the recipe from Martha Stewart." Knowing my sister, I'm sure she confused this with a recipe for apple pie.

"Give Terri the spatula and step away from the stove." I didn't have time for Candace to find her inner Julia Child.

"You haven't even tried the chili." She turned to a pot on the stove and stirred its contents. Terri's eyes widened in terror, like some trapped rabbit too scared to leave. She shook her head, possibly warning me not to eat whatever my sister served. Candace poured something chunky into a bowl and headed my way. Maggie slipped behind me. I presumed her support of Candace ended at taste testing.

As Candace's sister, I've been the victim of her forays into the culinary arts. When we were kids, she blew up my Easy Bake Oven. She tried cookbooks and lessons—nothing improved her ability to make something edible. Macbeth's witches had a better chance at concocting something I'd eat. Facing her, I had two choices. Refuse to taste, which would embarrass her. She would respond by making my life a living hell for a few days. Or I could be a grownup, taste what was in the bowl and do my best to convince her she would better serve the restaurant out front as manager. This would stroke her ego and possibly get her out of the kitchen. I inspected the contents as she held it in front of me. Large dark chunks floated in reddish black sauce, the unmistakable smell of sewage floated upward.

"Hell no." I shook my head.

As expected, Candace erupted. Her diatribe lasted a full three minutes as she brought up our deceased parents, her unappreciated sacrifices, Moses and the Israelites. This speech would have been moving if I hadn't heard it for the umpteenth time. She took my lack of response as an insult and stomped out of the kitchen. Someone clapped.

"That went well," Maggie said, impressed.

I stared at my best friend since high school as if she had lost mind. "She's going to make me pay for that." I had no doubt.

"You're exaggerating." She seemed clueless of the havoc my sister could throw my way.

I ran my cake shop next door and Candace managed the Blue Moon. We share a common storage area, and some suppliers. I made the restaurant desserts and sometimes her staff helped me with deliveries and special events. Better at managing money, Candace did the accounts of both places and paid the bills. If she stopped doing any of these things, I would have to close my shop and sell pencils out on the street. My rumination on how horrible the rest of my week might be was once again interrupted by my phone ringing. I didn't recognize the number on display this time.

"Hello!" I'd reached my limit of lousy news for the day. What was next, the Four Horsemen of the Apocalypse wanting a reservation?

"Hi Miss O, it's me." I barely recognized the voice.

"Bebe?" He didn't sound like himself.

"I'm at Queen Central Hospital. I'm in trouble." His words came out in an excited rush.

"In trouble for what?"

"They think I killed someone," he blurted.

Before I responded, we were disconnected.

CHAPTER

2

A lot of things go through your mind when you're hyped up on fear and panic. I had a complete Spielberg directed end-of-the-world 3-D movie running in my head with Bebe's frantic phone call playing like some bad soundtrack. I drove my cake shop's pink delivery van as if it were the Bat Mobile through the streets of Queens. I didn't put fear in the hearts of men, just a few pedestrians foolish enough to cross against the light.

A grim-faced Maggie sat next to me. Desperate for her optimism, I kept glancing at her as if she might bestow some happy words of wisdom as she always did. She didn't. Instead, she sat quietly stewing in her own worst-case scenarios.

"Tell me what he said again," she said, finally breaking the silence.

I repeated my conversation with Bebe.

"You didn't recognize the number so he must have used someone else's phone. This means, he doesn't have his with him because it's lost or someone took it."

Good, she was thinking logically, unlike me.

As we pulled up to the eighty-year-old hospital undergoing a massive renovation, I recklessly parked behind a large dump truck and didn't care. Temporary signs gave confusing directions; within minutes we'd gotten lost. Maggie finally stopped someone to ask for directions. This delay only heightened our concerns when these directions took us back to the entrance. I checked the time. An hour had gone by since Bebe's call.

"Christ," I said when realization hit me. "I forgot about Lee's sister." I checked the time again, knowing I couldn't go to the airport and deal with Bebe.

Maggie held up a hand and pulled out her phone. "I'll take care of Allie. You find Bebe. I'll catch up with you."

"Are you sure?" I didn't want us to split up, but I didn't want to wait.

She pointed to a sign hidden behind a large linen cart that showed the way to the emergency services department. I left Maggie and prayed I'd gone in the right direction. A few minutes later, I found myself in an open area filled with poor lighting, minimal seating and a small reception desk manned by a girl wearing headphones and texting on her phone. She never acknowledged my presence as she asked me whom I wanted to visit.

"Bebe. I mean Benjamin Bernard Dunn. He's eighteen, black, about so high." I had my hand just above my head, before realizing the Blue Moon sous chef might not have been vertical when he came to the hospital. The smug expression on the girl's face said she'd come that conclusion before I did. She picked up the phone, and for reasons I couldn't fathom, gave someone a brief but accurate description of me.

"Yeah, tall, black, skinny, if you ask me." The girl gave me a quick, dispassionate once over. "What's your name?"

"Odessa Wilkes." My wariness deepened.

"Someone wants to talk you. Wait over there." She pointed to a row of chairs filled with people. The girl's snarky attitude didn't improve my mood, and I had a mind to tell her so. Maggie's appearance at my side stopped me.

"Did you find him?" She asked.

The receptionist gave her a perusal before returning to her texting.

"Someone's coming out to talk to me. What about Allie?"

"I got Frank to pick her up." She seemed proud of this feat. In an instant, I forgot about the rude receptionist, Bebe, and the reservation for the Four Horsemen of the Apocalypse as I digested Maggie's news. I would have preferred a stranger selected at random than Frank McAvoy.

"Why in the hell would you get Frank?" I said.

Frank was Maggie's boss, and owner of McAvoy Investigation. I wouldn't let the man babysit a houseplant, let alone my boyfriend's sister. Our contentious relationship had to do with the fact that he cursed like a sailor, dressed as if he never left the seventies, ate and drank like a college freshman. Also, I didn't think he appreciated Maggie's investigative skills.

"Frank will be okay. He's close by. I told him to take her to the Blue Moon. Candace will take care of her."

"Candace," I said in disbelief, "whom I just reminded that she was the worst cook in the world. She barely tolerates my relationship with Lee, you think she'll be inviting to his sister?"

"Candace has things to worry about other than tormenting Lee's sister." She dismissed me with a wave.

Annoyed that Maggie didn't share my concerns, I groaned in frustration. "My sister torments me just to break up the monotony of her day. She's not crazy about Lee because he's not Will Smith, Denzel Washington, Barack Obama, or my ex-boyfriend. His sister just widened her strike zone." I took a deep breath because the headache that formed threatened to turn into an aneurysm.

"Let's worry about Bebe and deal with Candace later." She used her inside mommy voice, which I hated. Physically bigger and taller, I could take her in a fair fight. When she used her mommy voice, I crumbled. With an eight-year-old son,

Maggie mastered the art of dealing with both real and imaginary disasters. Unless an asteroid was about to strike the earth, everything else was good.

"Fine, if this person ever shows up." I scowled at the receptionist, who remained on her phone and oblivious to me and the world around her. The place could be ravaged by flying monkeys, and it wouldn't stop her from texting.

"Odessa." Maggie's wary tone pulled my attention. I followed her line of sight to a man dressed in green hospital scrubs emerging from a pair of swinging doors. Before we got our hopes up, he veered left down another corridor and disappeared.

"I think you want me," a deep male voice said.

We turned. A broad shouldered, black man with salt and pepper hair and mustache approached. His full lips were set in a tight line, and his eyes were intent on us.

"He's a cop," Maggie whispered. "I better try Lee again." She'd been around enough of Frank's old cop friends, to recognize their demeanor.

"We've been calling since we left the restaurant," I said in frustration. Then I remembered Lee wasn't the only lawyer I knew. "Call Aaron."

Aaron Boyer was a divorce lawyer and a senior partner at Lee's law firm. He loved my desserts and lived off of George's roast pork sandwiches. He knew Bebe and wouldn't refuse to help. However, from the expression on the cop's face, Bebe might need more than a divorce lawyer who liked my key lime pie, but you go with what you have.

Maggie took a few steps away and made the call. The cop gave Maggie a momentary glance before zeroing on me. I tried to put on my best game face, but it was hard dressed in a pink chef's jacket.

"Odessa Wilkes? I'm detective Maddox." He had a deep,

authoritative voice that made my knees go a little weak. He reminded me of one of those actors who did the voice over of God in the movies. Then he pulled out a small, worn wallet and showed me his gold shield and identification. "You here for Dunn?"

I nodded.

"What is your relationship with him?"

"He's my friend." My words came out weak and spastic. I wanted to kick myself.

He seemed transfixed by my pink jacket and cocked up one eyebrow. "How'd you know he was here?"

"He called me." This seemed to surprise him. His dark brown eyes examined my every gesture. I felt vulnerable. I searched for Maggie for support, but she was too far away talking on her phone.

"Ms. Wilkes!" His upraised voice made me regain my focus.

"Is he alright?" I asked. "Can I talk to him?"

"He's okay, doctors working on him." Maddox pulled out a small pad and pen. "When was the last time you saw Dunn?"

It took me a while to process this; I translated his words through a haze of confusion and concern. "Why?" His question made me pause, and I said nothing more. Lee always told me never to lie to the police but also never volunteer information.

Bebe's last words played back in my head. They think I killed someone.

"Do you have a problem answering the question, Ms. Wilkes?" A curt sounding Maddox's asked.

Suddenly annoyed by his attitude, I stiffened. He told me nothing about Bebe and expected me to answer his questions as if nothing had happened.

"No, but I'm trying to find out why Bebe is in the

hospital and why the police would care about when I saw him last."

Maddox visibly bristled. "Murder, Ms Wilkes. The murder of Linwood Rovell, in fact. Your boy Dunn is in deep shit, and I need answers. So tell me." Maddox's face had gone hard around the eyes, and little veins on his temple doubled in size. Maybe Detective Maddox was working on his own aneurysm.

"Is he under arrest?" My voice broke when I asked. I didn't know who Linwood Rovell was, or why anyone would murder him. I did know without a doubt Bebe hadn't killed anyone.

"Perhaps, if you answer a few questions, it won't go that far." Maddox's tone softened and held a glimmer of hope. I wanted to believe it and tell him everything I knew just to talk to Bebe, but I wasn't born on the Planet Stupid. Dressed in my pink chef jacket with the floating cake logo, I'm sure Maddox thought I had. First, I lived with a lawyer. Second, most of the patrons of the Blue Moon worked at the nearby courthouses. They were cops, lawyers, and their clients, and the only thing they talked about between stuffing their faces with food, was the law, every day, all day. Last and most importantly, I've watched enough episodes of *Law and Order* to set up my own practice.

"I got hold of Aaron, and somehow he reached Lee. They're sending someone," Maggie interrupted as she joined us. Her eyes went between the detective and me. She started to get that wide-eyed happy face when faced by anyone in law enforcement. Most mistook this expression as alarm; I knew it for the hero worship it was. With Frank McAvoy as a daily reminder of what an investigator was not, anyone with a shiny badge seemed golden to her. I glared at her. If not only to remind her that Maddox was the enemy, but to be on her guard.

"You are?" Maddox barked.

"A friend," I said, not giving her a chance to answer.

Maddox turned to me. "I'm still waiting for the answer to my question."

"Let me talk to Bebe," I demanded.

Silently, we stood for several heartbeats, waiting for the other to speak. Obviously, Maddox didn't appreciate my new attitude because he flipped his little pad closed and shoved it and his pen into his pocket. I put my hands on my hips, and Maggie tried not to show her adoration too much.

"I'll talk to the doctor and find out when that might be," he said with little enthusiasm, obviously not pleased with my lack of cooperation. He turned to leave.

"If you're not back in fifteen minutes, I'm going to find him on my own," I yelled as he pushed through the swinging doors. Take that you underpaid civil servant, I mentally cursed.

The clock above the receptionist desk passed time slowly. I watched the clock above the receptionist desk, and Maggie watched at me. She expected me to blow. My growing anger was tempered only by my uncertainty as to what to do next. I could make a scene, demand to talk to Bebe and hope my tantrum didn't make the situation worse. I didn't want anyone to throw Bebe in jail because I had a fit. I'd wait.

This decision was taken out my hands with the arrival of a handsome, impeccably tailored man into the reception area. His appearance garnered everyone's attention. Like a beacon in the dark, he glowed with an aura of authority. In his late thirties or early forties, white, lean, dark hair and eyes, he strode up to us like a man who expected to be noticed and listened to. I caught a hint of his cologne, a familiar light scent of wood, spice and a floral hint of bergamot. The cologne reminded me of a mistake I'd made once with a man call Davis Frazier, an investment banker. A mahogany god, whom I thought I loved and wanted to marry, only to find out he loved his tailored suits and himself more. Davis glowed too. He taught me to recognize the significance of a well-tailored suit, Italian loafers, a fabulous silk tie, and an overblown sense of self-importance.

"You must be Maggie and Odessa." His thin smile didn't quite reach his eyes. His aloof manner irked me as he kept an arm's length distance between us.

"Who are you?" I asked.

"Thaddeus Ziemann, attorney at law and your personal savior." He gave me a wink. Was this guy for real, or was he trying to be funny?

"We don't need saving, Bebe does," a confused Maggie said. "Did Aaron send you?"

"I've met all Aaron's lawyers and you're definitely not one of them," I said. No one in Aaron's firm could afford the man's socks, let alone his three thousand dollar suit.

"I'm sure if this were a dispute over a pig, Aaron Boyer would have sent one of his minions. But to correct you, Aaron didn't send me, Leland did." He wagged his eyebrows at me as if we shared some hidden secret. The fact he knew Lee's full name told me Ziemann must know him well.

"Lee sent you?" I searched his face for some inkling of recognition I couldn't find it.

Ziemann seemed to read my unease. "Don't worry about it sweetie, he didn't tell me about you either."

CHAPTER

3

I didn't like being called sweetie by a man I didn't know, let alone someone who oddly smelled like my ex-boyfriend. Lee had sent him to help. All Ziemann had done from the moment he arrived was irritate me. He seemed to take perverse pleasure in it. He took equal pleasure in bullying his way passed the receptionist and the emergency room head nurse to confront the two New York City detectives. When we found Maddox with his younger partner, Detective Russo blocked entry into Bebe's room, Ziemann clarified that since the detectives hadn't charged Bebe with murder, or even jaywalking, they had no right to bar anyone—especially his lawyer—from seeing him. By the time he finished, Maddox was seething, Russo wanted to strangle him, Maggie seemed awestruck, and I had already shut my eyes from Ziemann's verbal onslaught about the first amendment, due process and the rights of man. My aneurysm kicked into high gear.

"Does this mean I can talk to Bebe?" I asked, exhausted.

"No, it means that I speak to Mr. Dunn and you wait here." Ziemann pointed to the spot where I stood as if I might have some confusion of where I should be. Without asking permission, he stepped inside Bebe's examination room and shut the door firmly. Maddox, Russo, Maggie and I stood silent, too stunned or stupid to respond. Russo made a move to follow, but Maddox stopped him. In an odd sort of kinship, Russo and I acknowledged our frustration at being kept from Bebe. This didn't last long of course.

"Thanks for the help, Ms. Wilkes." Russo snapped. His face turned an odd shade of red. My head still ached, I hadn't talked to Bebe, and I had a New York City detective with a burr up his butt because I wouldn't play nice with him. I sighed deeply, shut my eyes and wished Russo would go away.

"Bebe is our friend. His family," a heartfelt Maggie said. "You've known him only a few hours, detective, we've known him longer. So when you say he's done something horrible, I'm sorry if I don't believe you."

Despite the fact that the detectives towered over her in height and girth, she glowered at them with the ferocity of a mother protecting her child. She saw Bebe, as her family as well as a friend. His mother was in another state, unable to protect her son, and she didn't mind filling the role.

"We're doing our jobs and you may be disappointed by what you find out about Dunn." Maddox sounded as if the idea of destroying her illusion were the last thing he wanted to do.

"We're gonna talk with Dunn, and you just made it harder." Russo seemed less concerned with Maggie's feelings than his partner. She turned her cold azure eyes on him, almost daring him to say something worse. My headache grew as Maggie got into a staring contest with Maddox.

"These walls are thin, detective, I can hear you, so please don't threaten anyone," Ziemann interrupted as he emerged from the room. "I spoke with the doctor confirming that my client is dealing with serious injuries and recommends he stay overnight for observation. Until he gets a medical clearance, there will be no discussion, so goodbye."

"We're not done," Russo said.

Ziemann's eyebrows did a little hitch before the lawyer narrowed his gaze on Maddox. He held it until the detective blinked.

"What if we charge your client?" Russo said hastily.

Maddox's hand went on his partner's shoulder, indicating they had no such plan.

"With what?" Ziemann crossed his arms and waited.

Maggie mimicked Ziemann's indignant stance and acted as if they were comrades in arms. Her admiration for all things legal was now directed at Ziemann. Maggie was a law whore!

"Let's go, Mickey." The older detective pulled Russo away. When Ziemann gave them a finger-wave, I thought Russo might break free and punch him. I knew I wanted to.

Thankfully, Russo left with his partner.

"So much for Shaft and Serpico." Ziemann shrugged.

"What if they did charge him?" I complained. I didn't particularly like Ziemann and the detectives' testosterone game of chicken.

"Either they don't have any evidence, or what evidence they do have isn't developed yet. We have some time." Ziemann had a mommy voice of his own. How cute.

"Whatever!" I tried to get passed him, but he blocked me, and wagged his finger.

"Ask him how he's feeling. Promise some chicken soup but nothing more. Because whatever he says to you can be brought up when those nice little detectives haul you down for questioning." His intensity obliterated all hint of playfulness.

"Fine." I huffed.

Ziemann waited a beat before he stepped aside, allowing me into the small room with Maggie close behind. The sight of Bebe made me stop short. Thick bandages covered his head. His mocha-colored skin seemed ashen and drained of blood. Dark bruises peeked out from beneath bandages on the right side of his face. I hadn't realized I'd begun to tear until a hot wetness rolled down my cheek.

"Don't cry." His voice cracked.

Maggie and I went to flank his bedside. A moment later, I had my tears under control, but Maggie had gone full-blown. The woman couldn't go to Disney's movies because her crying jags have been known to set an entire theater sobbing. The harder she tried to stop, the worse it got.

"Just let her go, or she'll sound like a strangled pig," I joked as I touched his shoulder.

"I think I'm in trouble, Ms. O," he whispered.

I nodded. "Don't worry. We'll take care of it. Just rest."

Maggie grabbed some tissues from the bedside table and blew her nose.

"My mom… George…" Bebe closed his eyes, one of which was swollen.

"Candace contacted your mother and told her to wait until we had more news," I said.

Bebe's mom had recently moved to West Virginia for a new job and a better life for his two younger siblings. A single mom, Mrs. Dunn had a chance to take her children out of the rough neighborhood Bebe barely escaped. It had been hard for her to leave her oldest child, but he'd made a decent life for himself at the Blue Moon. George Fontaine, the head chef, had become a strong father figure in his life. Under his tutorage, Bebe had become an accomplished cook. Maybe one day he'd be an excellent chef.

"I don't want her here." His soft voice was surprisingly demanding.

"Okay," I said, not sure I could keep that promise.

"We'll figure this out." Maggie's reassuring smile vanished as she ran her hand along his shoulder, and finally his hair. Recently, Bebe had allowed his hair to grow out into neat little dreadlocks that had reached passed his shoulders.

"Maggie, what are you doing?" I cocked an eyebrow as she continued to touch his hair and hospital gown.

"You're wet." She fingered one of thick locks.

"Why are you wet?" I touched his hair too.

"When I woke up my head hurt. My wallet and phone were missing, and everything was wet. I thought I'd been mugged, or something," he said.

Maggie's expression of curiosity mirrored my own.

Our visit lasted another fifteen minutes before Ziemann, and the doctor kicked us out. They moved Bebe to a private room, and wouldn't let us follow. I complained. Ziemann ignored me as if I were a ready-made suit from the Sears discount rack.

Two orderlies put him on a gurney and wheeled him away, with Ziemann and the doctor following. Maggie started crying again. Having known her since high school, I'd become immune to it and waited for the storm to pass. This didn't stop several people passing from tearing up at the sight of her. The woman was like a freshly-cut onion.

We stayed until Ziemann emerged from an elevator in the main lobby. He stopped at one of those automatic disinfectant dispensers that hung from the wall and cleaned his hands thoroughly. He used the elevator's reflective facade as a mirror and straightened his tie. When he finally acknowledged our presence, his smirk had returned. "Still here ladies?" he said.

"We want to talk about Bebe," I said.

His response was interrupted by his cell phone ringing. "Mr. Dunn is my client, not you. So, Little Miss Cupcake no can do." He engaged the phone and turned his back on us.

"Did he call me Cupcake?" I asked Maggie. She nodded in confirmation.

"Yes she is." He turned to grin at me. "I'm playing nicely,

I just don't think she likes me much." He laughed and handed the phone to me.

"Lee?" I said, pleased yet surprised to hear his voice.

"You okay?" he asked.

"Bebe…" The image of his bruised face flashed back to me, robbing me of my words.

"Thad will work this out," he reassured.

"Why can't you?" I urged.

"He's better, trust me." The certainty in his voice was hard not to accept. I wanted to trust him, but Ziemann's smug expression glared back at me. I took a deep breath and tried to find my happy place, unfortunately, Ziemann was there sitting in my seat.

"Okay," I huffed.

"Is Allie okay?" he asked.

Guilt slammed into me like a brick wall. I'd totally forgotten about his sister.

"Allie… no problem, someone is picking her up," I said much too quickly. My desperation must have shown because a pleased Maggie returned an enthusiastic thumb up. She had more faith in her boss than I did. "Gotta go, sweetie."

"Who's picking her up?" Lee wouldn't be dissuaded.

I hesitated. "Frank. He took her to the Blue Moon."

A long moment of silence followed. Lee liked Frank the same way people like other people's crazy drunk uncle. He's a lot of fun, but you're happy he's not related. Lee didn't want crazy Uncle Frank with his sister. Nor did he want her around Candace. Lee wasn't under any delusion that my sister tolerated his presence in my life.

"I'll meet you at the Blue Moon." He hung up.

I handed Ziemann his phone.

"Am I invited to the wedding?" He wore a wicked grin.

"I wouldn't invite you out of a burning building." I

snapped. Now I had to deal with a confrontation between Frank and Lee. My aneurysm grew.

"Oh, Ms. Cupcake, I want us to be friends." Ziemann held out his arms.

I took a step away and glared at him. "You better get Bebe out of this mess," I warned.

Ziemann dropped his arms in mock defeat. "I will. It will be fun, trust me. I haven't had a compelling case…" He tapped his chin with his index finger.

"If you don't do this right, you'll be a compelling spot on the floor." I meant every word. Someone I cared about was in serious trouble, and I had a jerk thinking this a great way to have fun.

He laughed and gestured toward the front entrance. We reluctantly followed.

Outside, the late afternoon air was thick and warm, and I couldn't shake off this sense of dread or my annoyance with Ziemann. He walked out of the hospital whistling and pleased with himself. Maybe this was just a game to him.

"It's been interesting ladies," he said. As if on cue, a black town car pulled up in front. He stepped in and was gone.

"What a prick," I mumbled as Maggie and I headed for our own transportation. So preoccupied with the day's events, at first I didn't register the sight of the tow truck maneuvering in front of my pink van. When I did, I ran across the street shouting like a crazy woman.

Ten minutes later, it took all the money Maggie and I had, a little begging, and Maggie threatening to cry a river to get the tow driver to back off. The parking ticket that decorated the window amounted to another two hundred dollars. When I examined the ticket, there was a note written on the back. It read.

Thanks for the help, Russo.

"How the hell did they know it was my van?"

Maggie pointed to the logo design on my chef's pink jacket, which matched the same logo on the van. I groaned, shoved the ticket in my pocket, got in the van and drove to the Blue Moon. I gripped the wheel tight, trying to figure out how I was going to tell Candace the news.

My trepidation evaporated on my arrival at the Blue Moon. The sight of Frank and a woman I recognized from Lee's family photographs as his sister, sat at the bar taking turns doing tequila shots.

CHAPTER

4

Allie Mackenzie Danbury was a lousy drunk. She laughed too loud and pawed Frank as if he were Brad Pitt's cuter brother. She shattered any illusions I had of her. I ignored the family resemblance, the wide-set mouth, hazel eyes, and dark auburn hair and convinced myself this wasn't the soft spoken dental assistant I'd conversed with over our long distance phone calls. During those calls, she sometimes had a reserved politeness that came off as timid.

Lee, the younger of the siblings, acted as if he was the oldest. With less than a year between them in ages, Allie seemed to defer to her brother in most things. The Mackenzie family joke had been that Lee and Allie were meant to be twins but Allie got impatient.

"This is what you're marrying into." Frank wore a sloppy smile as he pointed at me.

"Frank!" Maggie admonished.

"And this is my better half, professionally speaking." Still dressing like an extra in a 1970's police show: dark polyester suit, thin tie, and rubber soled shoes, the portly private investigator tried to grab Maggie into a hug. She expertly sidestepped him. Frank moved like a beached whale.

"Odessa." Allie offered up her hand to shake, and nearly toppled off her stool. I caught her just before she fell. She smelled of tequila and fading perfume. Her familiar voice made my heart sink. This was Lee's sister and drunk beyond the ability to stand. I just had enough time to pick my heart off the floor when the sight of Lee coming through the front door made me grab Allie off her stool.

"Allie, why don't we go to the ladies room, and freshen up." My desperate cheerfulness seemed to propel her. I grabbed her pocketbook off the bar and gave a gentle push toward the back of the restaurant. Getting there wasn't easy. She had about thirty pounds on me and had the coordination of a wet noodle. For some odd reason, she wouldn't stop laughing. Obviously, some joke Frank had told her kept running in a perpetual loop, in her head.

"You're so friendly." She giggled.

Inside the bathroom, I propped her against the sink. Her resemblance to her brother unnerved me a bit. They had the same coloring, hazel eyes and dark auburn hair. She was Lee with lipstick.

"That's me… helpful." I grabbed a bunch of paper towels and wet them.

"We're going to be fast friends. I just…" Allie froze in mid-sentence when she caught sight of her reflection in the small mirror. Her makeup and clothing hadn't traveled well. "Oh my," she exclaimed.

I handed her the towels. "Your brother just walked in."

Allie's eyes widened. This wasn't what she wanted to hear as her face twisted in panic. She began to hyperventilate. "I shouldn't have had those drinks on the plane. I hate flying, honestly I do. I thought I might lose my nerve." Her lower lip trembled as she dabbed at her face with the towels.

"Freshen up, and I'll stall him." I took a deep breath.

She kept thanking me before I left her in the bathroom. When I entered the dining and bar area, things hadn't improved in the least.

"No, I didn't drive like this," Frank shouted at Lee. Both men had faced off. Maggie stood between them like a pixie sandwich.

"Frank would never drive drunk, Lee," Maggie said. Lee seemed unimpressed.

"Trust me, it took a while to catch up with her, but I think I did." Frank grinned.

"Okay everyone, take a step back." I pulled Lee away from Frank, who was about to get an earful from Maggie.

"Where is she?" he asked. Beneath his suit jacket, I felt his muscles tense. Lee could possibly take Frank in a fight, but Frank wouldn't fight fairly.

"Slightly embarrassed. She's in the ladies room cleaning up. Please take a breath," I said.

We'd already made a scene. Maggie dealt with a boisterous Frank; I handled Lee's righteous indignation, and familial problems. All I needed was Candace getting into the mix, annoyed that we were disturbing someone's appetite. I pulled Lee into the back of the restaurant, away from curious eyes. "I've been dealing with Bebe, so please don't make my day worse by killing Frank," I pleaded. "Maggie needs him."

Lee growled. "If she wants to get her investigator's license I'm sure I can find someone besides Frank to mentor her."

Considering how angry he was, I wouldn't put it passed him to try. Maggie worked with Frank for the experience, and on-the-job training. She needed to apply for her New York State investigator license. Not many P.I.'s would have taken on a housewife, and part-time soccer coach as an associate.

"But she likes Frank, and you liked Frank until he became your sister's drinking buddy." I smiled at him.

"This isn't funny Dessa." He ran his fingers through dark auburn hair, leaving small spikes in his wake. He snatched off wire-framed glasses to rub his temples allowing a full view of his dark hazel eyes. They were a golden brown, flecked with greens and blues. Almost hidden by his anger, they appeared exhausted. He'd struggled with a challenging court case most of the day. Now he would come home to find more drama with his sister. Normally, Lee radiated a practiced inner calm I always appreciated. I've seen him maintain his cool when opposing counsel tested his last nerves; when witnesses lied on the stand and the defendants were more problems than they were worth. Now his sister pulled at it and threatened to throw him off his center.

"Okay, honey." I placed a soft kiss on his cheek and wrapped my arms around his six foot two frame. Beneath his suit, I felt the lean and tense muscle of a rock climber.

"She calls me out of nowhere saying she's on a plane to New York. I haven't talked to her in weeks, and she pulls this?"

"Pulls what?"

"I don't know. One minute, everything's okay, and the next she's here." He sounded a little disheartened and rested his head on my shoulder and wrapped his arms around me.

"Well, let's deal with it like adults," I said unsure on how to find a common ground between the two siblings. I understood his familial distress. I had sibling issues of my own.

"You're right." He slipped his glasses back on, his anger far from gone. "Just keep Frank away from my sister."

All I could do was smile, promise world peace, and end global warming. It would be a lot easier than getting Frank to do anything I wanted. I needed Maggie for that. I turned around to see her shake a finger at him, and saying something that made him wince. I knew she was using her mommy voice. What she lacked in height, she made up in heartfelt intensity.

Turning back to Lee, I gave him a tight hug in the hope

that a little body contact would distract him. It didn't. Lee caught sight of his sister emerging from the restroom, and he tensed again. I had just enough time to wrap an arm around his, and hope it didn't come to blows.

"Hi." Allie gave her brother a feeble wave.

A stone-faced Lee glared at his sister. Frank opened his mouth, but Maggie had elbowed him hard in the stomach before anything came out.

"I'm taking you home," Lee said. "Get your bags?"

A wobbly Allie gave him a weak smile and held up her pocketbook. An oversize purple handbag and the clothes on her back were the only things she brought from California. Her common sense and her luggage were probably sitting by the door at home.

Lee rubbed at the crease that formed at his temple; drained all emotion from his face before he turned and walked away. He had that ability to shut down his feelings, lock them away in his little man cave somewhere in his head. The ability served him well as a lawyer, but as a friend, lover and future husband, not so well. At the beginning of our relationship, there were many nights I had to bang on his man cave door and beg him to come out and play.

Allie stood silently. She seemed unsure of what to do, go with her angry brother or stay and drink until she was numb enough to take the next plane home.

"You better go," I encouraged.

Her fixed smile seemed a little apprehensive as she followed after her brother. I took my own deep breath and turned my eyes on Frank, who was about to order another drink. "Oh no you don't. You're cut off." I glowered at Trevor the bartender, who slunk away.

"I'll take him home." Maggie sighed.

"She's married, Frank." I poked my finger into his fleshy

chest. He was a broad man, who dressed like Joe Friday from Dragnet and thought social media were a bar that had all the sports channels.

His crooked grin widened. "She just wants to have a little fun." He stood against the bar a little unsteady.

"Be silent, Frank," Maggie said. Though I wanted to talk to Maggie longer, I was happy to see Frank go.

With Maggie and Frank gone, I sat at the bar and poured myself a shot of tequila. Before I had a chance to place it to my lips, Candace came out of nowhere and took the glass from my hand. She dumped the contents into the tiny sink behind the bar and glowered at Trevor. It was remarkable how she did that, like some black ninja.

"I need you sober, and the dessert case filled," she said.

"I'm tired, Candy." I leaned against the bar and rested my head on my hand.

"Cry me a river. I had to deal with a restaurant with no cook, Bebe in the hospital, his mother wanting to leave her new job in Virginia to save her son, your boyfriend's out-of-control sister, and Maggie's freeloading boss." She hadn't taken the news of Bebe's situation well and found the only person she could take it out on.

Candace would never admit how much she cared for the sous chef. He had been dumped on her by one of her patrons, a judge at the nearby family court. Overtime, Bebe had endeared himself the only way possible with my sister. He worked hard, had a healthy fear of her, and understood his place in her world – three steps behind.

"Fine."

Resistance was futile. I hopped off the barstool and headed for my shop. Three hours later, the dessert case was filled with pies and cakes. By the time I closed up the dessert shop and left the Blue Moon, I was truly exhausted.

When I approached my house, all the lights were off except a faint glow coming from the living room. I had no doubt Lee sat there stewing about his sister. I found him alone on the couch, shoes off, but still in his suit. On the end table sat a half finished bottle of beer next to an empty one. The television played with no sound. I came up behind him, wrapped my arms neck, and kissed him on his cheek. "Sorry I'm late."

He leaned back, pulled me over the couch in one fluid movement, and placed me in his lap. He kissed me full on the mouth.

"Do you want to talk?" I pulled away to catch my breath.

"No." He continued to kiss me, planting kisses along my shoulder. Before I knew it, he had his hand up the back of my t-shirt trying to work off my bra. His touch had an urgency about it that made me realized his need to replace his current feelings with something else. When I pulled away to ask about Allie, he ignored me, and continued about his business, having trouble with the clasp. I yanked his hand away, and glared at him, demanding an answer.

"Asleep in the guest room," he said flatly.

Her proximity got my focus enough to slip out of Lee's grasp and off the couch. Lee frowned as if someone had taken away his favorite chew toy. Why is it, when men get upset, they want sex? Why can't they go shopping like normal people?

"Don't you think we should talk about this?" I gestured to the room down the hall.

He closed his eyes, sighed, and pushed himself off the couch. "No." He walked passed me to the stairs that led up to our bedroom. Too tired to argue, I followed, shutting off the television and lights as I went. When I got upstairs, he was already in bed, his arm lay across his face covering his eyes and blocking out the light.

"I can't talk about Allie right now." He sounded tired as if he spent most of the evening fortifying his man cave perimeters.

"Okay." I went to the bathroom to shower. I half expected to find him asleep when I returned. Instead, he stared at the ceiling as if it had the answer to this problem. When I slipped between the sheets, he pulled me close. "So Thad is still an asshole," he said quietly.

I felt as if I'd missed half the conversation he'd been having in his head. "He's a jerk," I said, ready to get off the subject of his sister. I knew a minefield when I saw it.

"He's an excellent criminal lawyer. Dessa, he's one of the best. He'll sort this out."

"He impressed Maggie. By tomorrow, she'll have a dossier on him an inch thick." I knew my friend's penchant for finding out things.

"How long have you known him?" The question I truly wanted to ask was how these two different men knew each other.

"We worked at the same firm for a while and became friends."

I expected more, but he didn't elaborate.

"He's kind of full of himself, but the police seem impressed."

We slipped into our usual position when conversing in bed, his arm around my waist, and our legs entwined, his pale skin snuggled against my dark.

"This is just the beginning," Lee said, willing to engage in a less stressful subject.

"I still can't believe someone thinks Bebe murdered some guy named Linwood Rovell."

Lee propped up on his elbow. "Linwood Rovell, it can't be."

"You know him?" I said.

"Yeah, I do."

CHAPTER

5

The next morning, I sat in the kitchen drinking coffee and reading an article about the murder in the newspaper. When Lee said he knew Linwood Rovell, I didn't believe him. I tried to guess how a murder victim became the common denominator between an eighteen-year-old sous chef and a lawyer. The brief news story about Rovell didn't clarify anything for me.

"You remember the jazz group I took you to see at a club downtown near Waters Street?" He sat across from me at the Formica kitchen table putting too much butter on some cranberry scones I'd made the day before. I watched him as he did this absent-mindedly. I couldn't help but smile. When I'd first met Lee, he'd been slightly underweight, no doubt living off his own cooking. Between meals at the restaurant, my desserts, fresh muffins and bread, he'd filled out nicely. Thankfully, an ex-jock from his school days, he kept fit. I eyed the butter dish again, before reaching over and pulling it to my side of the table.

"Ted Mozee Quartet," he continued.

I vaguely remembered a claustrophobic hole in the wall he dragged me to Manhattan in the dead of winter. An ancient jazz trio out from Chicago left the Windy City to get warm in

New York by playing in a small group of jazz freaks in the East Village. The drinks were watered down, the food inedible, and the octogenarian group leader couldn't find a beat if he paid for it. In all honesty, not being a jazz fan I couldn't tell if he could find a beat or not.

"I had a wonderful time," I lied. Why hurt his feelings? Lee enjoyed himself, and I survived the night.

"The guy playing the bass once belonged to an R and B group in the seventies called the Sweet Intuitions. I think they had one top one hundred hit or something. The bass player's name is Ted Mozee. All his recording biographies said he sang for this group in the seventies called the Sweet Intuitions."

I twirled my finger in the hope he'd speed up the process. He smiled at my impatience. "One of Mozee's group members was a guy called Linwood Rovell. A baritone, I think." Lee pointed to an old publicity shot in the paper of the three black men dressed in matching seventies leisure suits. Linwood was a big guy. He seemed more like a football player than a seventies R & B singer. The paper drew a circle around the face of Rovell, indicating him as the murder victim. The guy next to him was identified as Mozee, renowned jazz bassist and finder of elusive beats.

"What about Bebe?" I asked.

"What about him?"

"How does he know Rovell?"

"Haven't a clue. You'll have to ask him, that's if Thad lets you."

I huffed at the idea of Ziemann trying to stop me.

"Babe, it's his case," he said, doing his mind reading thing with me.

"Sure." I gave him my best contrite smile. The fact I planned to pump Bebe for information shouldn't interfere with Lee's delusions of my self-control.

"The cops must have found something," he said.

Images of Maddox and Russo came back to me like a 500 hundred pound headache. I sipped my lukewarm coffee and sighed. "Ziemann is picking him up from the hospital. He promised to bring him around to the Blue Moon afterward for lunch." I got up, grabbed my breakfast dishes and put them in the sink. "I'm going to be at the shop all day and catch up with Maggie later."

"What about Allie?"

He joined me by the sink and put his coffee cup into the soapy water. "What about her?"

The question confused me. The last discussion we had before we fell off to a fitful sleep dealt with Rovell, not his sister. Unless he talked in his sleep about her and I'd missed the conversation.

"I can't take her to court with me." I stopped washing the dishes and faced him, unsure of his meaning. "You have to take her."

"You make her sound like she's ten and we've forgotten to arrange for a babysitter," I said. He didn't seem to appreciate my sarcasm. Then I realize he was serious.

"I don't want her sitting all day, with anything to do. She had no plans or even luggage." His voice did that hitch thing it did when he got stressed. I hadn't yet figured out why his sister's surprise visit bothered him. I surprised him all the time, and he didn't turn into a grouch.

"There's always Frank," I teased.

"Not funny." His jaw tightened. His hazel eyes went dark. He had a wide expressive mouth that got tight when he got serious.

"What's going on with you two?" I said.

This time everything on him constricted, and I sensed he was about to shut down, go into his little man cave, and hunker down, refusing to say a word. I wrapped my arms around him and laid my head in the crook of his neck. A few heartbeats later, he seemed to relax, but not by much. I gave him a soft kiss, which he pushed deeper. Suddenly, he was all hands, and Allie was the last person on both of our minds. By the time, we stopped and he'd left for work, I was willing to give Allie keys to the cake shop.

Our early morning groping session left me horny and frustrated. Add on the babysitting duty with Allie, Bebe's predicament, and two wedding cakes to finish before noon just added to my irritation. Needing a long hot shower to focus myself, I trotted up to the upstairs bathroom. When I returned twenty minutes later to the kitchen dressed and ready for work, I found Allie waiting. She wore the same clothes from the day before, slightly rumpled but presentable. The temptation to ask why she'd left California gnawed at me, but I restrained myself. She smiled sheepishly, embarrassed about the night before. She clutched a half finished cup of coffee, like a lifeline.

"Morning," she said. Her freshly scrubbed face now absent of makeup made her appear younger and made it easy to catch the family resemblance. Not being twins by any stretch the imagination, I always sensed Lee had a close and playful relationship with his sister. So their present situation disturbed me.

"How are you feeling?" I poured a cup of coffee for myself.

"I want to apologize," she began, but I held up a hand to stop her. I didn't want her apology. I just wanted her to make peace with Lee. "No worries." I joined her at the table

"Thanks, I appreciate everything. Coming to New York on a whim isn't as easy as you think." She chuckled, but it held no humor. A night's rest didn't remove the drained expression on her face.

"There's nothing wrong with whims." I shrugged. "I believe in whims."

Her smile strengthened but wouldn't make eye contact with me.

"Also, I know my brother asked you to babysit me."

Surprised by her admission, I almost burned my mouth gulping coffee. If she heard that, she heard everything else, especially the moaning and groaning. Now it was my turned to be embarrassed.

She laughed again, and this one seemed genuine. "I can't wait to see the shop. Lee said he proposed to you there."

The memory made me smile. It had been weeks since the engagement and I still hadn't wrapped my mind around it. Allie gazed at me wistfully as I recalled how her brother asked me in front of my family and friends for my hand in marriage. She thought the whole thing romantic. In all honesty, Lee's unexpected announcement shocked me. I came close to ruining everything when I almost pissed my pants.

Lee had become a part of my life during a time when I hadn't expected much of anything. I'd recently lost my job, my boyfriend dumped me, and I found myself trapped in perpetual servitude to my sister at the family restaurant. He wasn't what I'd expected, but I was glad he was in my life.

Allie and I sat for a while, finishing our coffee, talking about her job as a dental assistant and working in her husband Phil's office. She didn't sound enthusiastic about her chosen profession. She asked how I got into baking. I told her I started out in advertising, first as a graphic designer and later as project manager. I explained how I used baking as a form of therapy for an anxiety disorder I developed. A disorder I'd gotten on the same day my job and my boyfriend went south and had the misfortune to end the day in a subway fire.

"Not a good day for me." I put a sarcastic tone in the

words. "There were days I didn't want to get out of bed, but when I did, I baked. It relaxed me. So now here I am."

Allie smiled genuinely for the first time since I met her. The tension seemed to ease from her face. I asked her if she didn't mind spending the day at my cake shop. Her smile widened and said she didn't mind in the least. A half an hour later, we were at the front door O So Sweet cake shop.

The place was small, decorated in pink and cream in a shabby-chic style. A long glass antique counter filled with cupcakes, pies and cakes divided the front of the shop from the back. The smell of sugar, baked goods and freshly brewed coffee from the large coffee maker permeated the air. Esperanza, my employee, was boxing up a dozen muffins for an early morning customer.

"Ms. O," she greeted warmly, with her expressive black eyes, moon-shaped caramel-colored face. A recent culinary student, Esperanza often opened the shop on her own. Hired by George when I was desperate for help, she turned out to be a godsend and an excellent baker. She greeted Allie as if she was an old friend and gave her a quick tour of the small shop.

Allie spent much of the morning watching Esperanza, and I tended to customers, take orders, and worked on various specialty cakes in the small, work area in the back of the shop. At one particular harried moment, I came back from loading a large cake in the walk in-refrigerator to find Allie on the phone, taking an order. She began calling out selections to Esperanza, who filled a large box with a variety of cupcakes. Allie waved me away when I offered to help. I hesitated for a moment, knowing this wasn't what Lee expected when he asked to keep her busy. Before I knew it, a more relaxed Allie chatted up the customers, and rang over the counter orders, freeing Esperanza and I to finish up a particularly challenging wedding cake.

Late in the morning while Esperanza and I worked, sounds of uncontrollable laughter came from the front of the shop. As the laughter continued, my curiosity got the better of me. I went to investigate. I found Allie at the register finishing an order of cupcakes for a group of officers from the nearby courthouse. One guy laughed so hard, his face had gone red, and he held his sides.

"Hey Odessa," one of them said.

I recognized him from several visits in the past. He pointed at Allie and broke out laughing again. At first, I thought they were laughing at her, but she seemed unfazed by the attention.

"Do it… oh God, do it again." Another officer could barely speak between bouts of laughter.

"Oh, I can't…" Allie said, suddenly shy.

The officers pleaded, and she relented. I couldn't imagine what would have some of the most serious people on the planet almost laughing in hysterics.

She sighed, closed her eyes for a moment. "Darling, you don't know how to cook the borscht. You have to have the good beets," she said in perfect Russian accented English. One of the officers laughed again.

"Do mine," an officer named Sanchez said.

Without warning, Allie broke into Spanish accented English with perfect inflections, obviously mimicking one of the court officers' mother's. It wasn't parody or a disparaging mockery you often found in bad movies, her dialect and diction were perfect. If I closed my eyes, I'd imagined someone's Puerto Rican mother complaining why they don't visit her enough. I must have had my mouth open because she stopped.

"That's amazing," I said in total disbelief.

One of her eyebrows rose, and her lip lifted in a crooked

smile. "You make her sound like she's ten and we forgot to arrange for a babysitter," she said in an exact copy of my voice.

"Stop that." I pointed at her playfully. I wanted to peek down her throat and see if any little people resided there.

"She's good, huh?" one of the officers said, clearly amused. "She could get into trouble with a trick like that."

Everyone laughed, including Allie. Her doubt and nervousness had vanished and been replaced with almost a childlike enjoyment.

"Yeah," I said with some unease. I wondered who'd I been talking too all those phone calls ago, not this woman with an infectious laugh, odd little talent, and a few secrets.

CHAPTER

6

At around three o'clock, I put Allie in a cab with a box of white chocolate mint cookies, and my thanks. She'd been on her feet most of the day, and I felt sorry for her. I gave her a spare key, and told her to go home, and put her feet up. She reluctantly agreed. Also, I wanted to limit Allie's contact with Candace. Every time the two women came near each other, Candace gave her the evil eye. Clueless to my sister's dislike for her brother and her by association, Allie asked if Candace wore glasses because of the constant squinting. I guess they have a different version of the evil eye in California. In all honesty, she'd arrived on the arm of Frank McAvoy, drunk as a skunk. This didn't improve her standing with my sister. She had a better chance showing up with the Grand Master Wizard of the Klu Klux Klan.

With Allie safely at home, I left Esperanza to mind the shop, and went over to the Blue Moon. An access door between the two businesses always stayed open, but my sister and I had an understanding about the separation of the businesses. O So Sweets was like Cuba, a no Candace fly zone. We provided the Blue Moon with desserts and nothing more. If I wanted to close the shop or rent it to gypsies, she had no say short of throwing biting remarks at me. The Camp David

Peace Accord was a pinky swear compared to this. With exception of Candace cooking or doing a striptease on a tabletop, I tried to keep to my side of the line that was first drawn across our shared bedroom when we were kids.

I found Candace in her usual position at the front, seating guests and guarding the door like a pit bull. I checked the wall clock for the third time in less than a minute. Ziemann had promised to deliver Bebe to the Blue Moon for lunch. They were late. I didn't have the lawyer's number, and Bebe's phone was still missing in action. I didn't want to be a nuisance and call Lee, so I waited. I took a seat at the bar and ordered an iced tea. My feet hurt, and I needed a moment to myself. When Candace caught sight of me, she stomped over, and invaded what little personal space I had.

"Where is he?" she barked.

"Who?" I leaned away from her.

"Bebe. Who else? You can't think I'm talking about your boyfriend. Or even that freeloader, McAvoy."

Before I said anything in defense of my boyfriend, or even Frank, my phone rang. Maggie's face appeared on the display, and I silently thanked her for the interruption. Unfortunately, the phone call didn't deter Candace from hovering over me. I had to turn my back on her to get some privacy. Most people would take that as a sign to back off. Not my sister. She just walked around to my other side to face me again.

"Hey, how's Bebe doing? Rocket asked about him." Maggie asked.

"Missing." I tried desperately not to make eye contact with Candace. This didn't work because she pulled the phone away from my ear, and got in my face. Normally, I wouldn't tolerate this behavior from any other person, I would have gone all King Kong on them, but this was Candace, her

Godzilla could beat my King Kong ass any day of the week.

"Bebe. Where is he?" she yelled. She came close enough for me to see the tiny little veins in her eyes. I pried her fingers away, and told Maggie to hold on.

"I don't know, Candy. But if you give me a minute, and some space, maybe I could find out."

Her golden brown eyes narrowed, and appraised me. She seemed pleased I hadn't backed down. She often complained hanging out with Maggie made me soft, but she would say the same if I hung out with the Marines. For half a minute we had a traditional Wilkes Woman, see who blinked first, contest. I did before she huffed and walked away with her sense of superiority intact.

"Candace's is freaking me out," I whispered into the phone and kept an eye on my sister. Fortunately, one of the busboys crossed her path and she let him have it. He responded appropriately by shaking like a leaf. Content with putting the fear in the heart of the unsuspected, happily she went back to the front desk to greet a new customer.

"Do you want me to check if they left the hospital?" Maggie offered.

I told her yes and disconnected. When the phone rang again ten minutes later, I picked it up on the second ring.

"He's been discharged for over three hours. Maybe you should call Lee," she suggested.

I didn't want to sound like a pain, but I called the law firm, and got bounced between the two secretaries before they handed me off to his law clerk. The clerk promised to have Lee call the moment he got off the phone. I said I'd hold.

By the time Lee got on the line, my stomach was in a royal fit. I couldn't find Ziemann, and had no way to contact Bebe. Another worst case scenario movie ran in my head again.

"Hello, Dessa." Lee's solemn tone didn't ease my

mounting nerves. "I just got off the phone with Thad...."

End credits... world explodes!

"Where's Bebe?" I almost shouted, getting everyone's attention, including Candace who abandoned the customer, and walked over to me.

"They've arrested him," he said in a neutral attorney's voice he sometimes used.

"What!" I clutched my forehead as if the aneurysm might return.

"Thad's with him now. He's too busy to call. He's trying to sort everything out." His matter-of-fact tone annoyed me somewhat. I wanted him to feel as disjointed as I did.

"Where is he?" I finally sputtered.

"Wait a minute, Dessa," Lee warned.

I ignored him. I wanted to find Bebe, choke Ziemann for not contacting me, and get this damn movie out of my head. I'd disconnected the call and dialed Maggie.

"I'll try to find out where they are holding him. I'll come get you." She sounded amped up, feeding off my frenzy. When my phone rang again, Lee's image appeared on the display. I didn't want to talk to him. He'd talk me out of whatever I was planning. My only plan had been to find Bebe, and no one would talk me out of it. My sister stood before me, her face tense, and her eyes soft, and moist. Like Lee, my sister hid her feelings most of the time. She didn't have a man cave but a condo, at least. For her to get so emotional, said a lot about her feelings for Bebe.

"They've arrested him," I said.

"Oh my God. They can't do that. He's a baby." She slapped a hand to her mouth as if to hold in any emotion she might be having. Wilkes women did not do hysterics. They coped, gathered the wagons in a circle, stocked up on bandages and fortified their perimeters.

"They can. He's eighteen, and no longer a minor," I said.

"What's that lawyer of his doings? We need to find him a better lawyer," she said much too loudly. Half the patrons in the restaurant were lawyers. I expected them to pull out business cards, and offer their services.

"Lee said Ziemann is good," I said, and she sneered in disgust.

"As if I'd take his recommendation," Candace said. An old argument I didn't want to debate.

"Listen Candace, Maggie says she can find where they are holding Bebe. It's okay?"

She took a deep breath and steadied herself. "You better!" She pointed a finger at me. Eerily, she resembled our mother, whose no-nonsense declarations became edicts.

You will go to college.

You will not date Larry Shipmen.

You will find Bebe, and bring him home.

When Maggie finally arrived at the restaurant and I got into her minivan, my mission seemed clear. Determined to either find Bebe or never return home—at least those were Candace's choices. Through a friend of Frank, Maggie had found out which precinct they had taken Bebe. With the address locked into the GPS, we arrived at the solemn nondescript concrete structure within fifteen minutes. We parked, took deep breaths, and entered. Maggie politely asked the desk sergeant if we could speak to Detective Maddox. She batted her baby blues at him, quirked her perky lips into a playful grin and watched as he melted at her sincerely. I would have offered to wipe the drool from his lips but I restrained myself. He made a phone call and sent us to the second floor to the detectives' room.

"What we are doing?" Maggie asked as we climbed the stairs.

I shook my head and pushed through the door labeled Detective Squad. Inside, Ziemann stood with Maddox and another man I didn't recognize, an older man, distinguished, with graying hair, and a tailored navy suit. When Ziemann did notice our presence, his face went from surprised to displeasure. He turned his annoyance on Maddox, who somehow approved our visit to the detective squad.

My attention went to where a door stood ajar. Inside the room, Bebe sat with Russo standing just to his left as if some avenging angel. I made a beeline to the room until Ziemann derailed this by blocking me.

"What the hell are you doing here?" Ziemann nearly growled.

Maddox trailed up behind him. The other man got pulled into a conversation with another detective and walked away.

"When Bebe didn't show up at the Blue Moon, we worried. I called Lee, and he said he'd been arrested," I said.

Behind Ziemann, Maddox watched. "Hey ladies." His tone pleasant and welcoming. I should have been suspicious.

"You can't see Bebe right now. Go home." Ziemann had lost his playful air as his face tightened with barely controlled irritation.

I wanted to say something, but Ziemann put up his hand to silence me. Though I'd been hushed by better people, I kept my mouth closed. Our sudden arrival might have interrupted something he had in the works. Suddenly, I wondered if coming to the precinct had been a brilliant idea.

"She can answer a question for me, can't she? Or is Ms. Wilkes your client too?" Maddox asked, stepping in front of Ziemann.

"I need a lawyer?" I said, alarmed at the suggestion.

"No… just a yes or no will do." A slight smile grew on the detective's lips. He turned to the desk behind him filled with paper, folders, binders, and a large box. Several photographs laid spread out there. He searched, pulled something out from a stack, and waved it at me. My stomach churned again as bile rose in my throat. Maggie took a protective step closer. I felt reassured with her nearness.

In the past, I'd had debilitating bouts of anxiety brought on by the Perfect Storm of disasters, I fondly called the worst day in my life. Therapy, little blue pills, and the Blue Moon, saved me. I found purpose in baking, helping Candace run the restaurant, and realizing it wasn't the end of the world. Lee helped a lot. However, an anxiety disorder wasn't like mending a broken bone. You learn to manage the symptoms as best you can. Somehow, I'd been successful in the last year or so. Unfortunately, when I got into a situation where my stress level kicked into high gear, I worried the problem might return like a mad gorilla. I took a deep breath, and another, keeping the beast at bay.

"I have a copy of a credit card receipt for the purchase of an expensive set of chef knives, engraved with the initials BBD on them, charged by you." He handed me the copy of the receipt. I didn't have to read it. I'd purchased the chef knives as a gift for Bebe on his eighteenth birthday.

Unceremoniously, Ziemann took the paper and examined it before handing it back to Maddox. The detective returned the paper to his desk and held up a photograph of the exact set of knives I'd purchased for Bebe. I turned to Ziemann, hoping for some help. He gave away nothing, offering me no support. I wanted more from him than his best Mr. Spock impersonation. Understanding, maybe for the first time, he came to save Bebe, not me. I was on my own.

"A gift to Mr. Dunn, I presume?" Maddox said. "Expensive, very expensive."

The engraved initials I'd had insisted be put on the

professional knives were damaging. No one could question who the knives belong too. I sorely regretted the impulse now. My stomach tightened when I noticed one of the knives was missing. Bebe normally left the knives at the Blue Moon. He started taking them home when Candace hired the temporary chef. He didn't want the knives used by others or worse, disappearing. When Bebe left the restaurant the day of Rovell's murder, he had them on him. I remembered him holding them in a unique carrying case. Bebe had decorated the tan canvas case with graffiti-like doodling.

"Don't worry about the missing knife, we found it." Maddox's smile widened. "Guess where?"

Ziemann glared at the detective, sighed, and offered me only an expression of resignation as it this truth couldn't be avoided.

"In Linwood Rovell."

CHAPTER

7

"Early Thursday morning, can you tell me where you were?" Maddox asked.

I blinked at him. As fuddled as my mind was, I understood the implications of the question. Did he think I helped Bebe kill someone? My eyes widened like some cartoon character in surprise, but Maddox took this for something else, possibly fear or even guilt. I'd been accused of a lot of things, but murder has never been one of them.

"Did you know Linwood Rovell?" he said.

"No," Maggie interjected in my defense. Maddox repeated the question giving little deference to Maggie's defense of me.

"You're joking, right?" I took a step back. The idea of running out of the squad room crossed my mind for half a second. You'd get a little squirrelly too if people accused you of killing someone. Alone in the room with Maddox and a naked bulb, I'd crack. I'm not that brave. Even Snow White would have given up every single dwarf under the same circumstance.

Maddox picked through a pile of photographs and shoved one in my face. He wanted a reaction, and he got one. I grabbed it. Maggie came closer for a better view.

"Bebe!" I gasped. His prone body lay on wet asphalt as

EMS workers knelt beside him. Someone had turned out his pockets, maybe the police searching for identification. The cold light of day illuminated his almost dead features. My throat tightened, and an involuntary squeal escaped.

"Where is that?" Maggie took the photograph.

Maddox ignored her question. "Maybe you, and he had a little disagreement, and you clocked him in a fit of anger. You seemed to care a lot for the boy."

"Don't say anything," a voice from behind us said.

We turned to see Ziemann and the gray-haired man we had seen before, approaching. Behind them, an angry Russo brought up the rear. I didn't remember Ziemann leaving; too occupied with Maddox's accusations, and my future life in prison.

"Stay out of this, Ziemann," Maddox barked. Within seconds, Ziemann and Maddox squared off.

"My client won't talk to you, and you try and tap the next best thing. That's sad, and pathetic, even for you," Ziemann said.

"Hey, back off." Russo put a hand on the lawyer's shoulder.

Ziemann glared at the offending hand, as if he knew several ways of removing it, none of which were pleasant or painless.

"Redmond, tell your detective to find a better place to put that." Ziemann's voice was low, and dispassionate.

The gray-haired man named Redmond stepped between them.

"Take a breath, Russo," Redmond demanded. Russo didn't move at first but eventually stepped aside.

"I just asked her where she was…" Maddox began, but Ziemann held up his hands, and chuckled.

"Let me get this straight, you're asking Ms. Cupcake if she

helped my client kill someone? You've been watching too much television," Ziemann said, dryly.

I started to say something, but he held up a finger to silence me again. Trust me, people have tried the finger thing on me, and it rarely worked.

"Don't call me that," I said, but the two men ignored me, caught up in some kind of macho volleyball.

"Maybe he had someone help him," Russo said.

"That's your new theory? So, you think she did it. Held the door for Dunn, and knocked him in the head in a fit of premenstrual rage," Ziemann huffed.

"I think Ms. Wilkes cares a little too much for some busboy at her restaurant." Maddox cocked an eyebrow at me.

"What!" I said indignantly at the implication.

Ziemann winked at me.

"I'm sure she was playing foot-warmer with her fiancé at the time of the murder. You can ask him. I'm sure he'd love to talk to you. He's a lawyer too. His specialty is civil suits." Ziemann put an emphasis on the words *civil suits*. Maddox sneered at me as if my market valued had taken a hit.

"I'm sure he'd give her a juicy little alibi." Ziemann aimed a crooked smile at me.

It was official: I hated Thaddeus Ziemann. I wouldn't let this man get me off death row. His need to belittle and mock me at every opportunity went passed his lawyerly duties.

"Well, did you play slap and tickle with your boyfriend?" Russo asked with a straight face. I stood with my mouth agape as the men awaiting an answer.

"You can't be that stupid!" My mouth overshot my brain when I said this of course, but I didn't care. "Do you actually catch criminals or do they just wander in lost off the street? I'm sure you would have cuffed Mary of Magdalene at the crucifixion just because she was there."

“Hey!” Russo exclaimed, touching a small gold cross that hung around his neck.

I spun on Maddox. “I expected better from you,” I accused.

“Why, because I’m black?” he said.

I shook my head. “No, because I thought you were the grown up. You try to intimidate me, and accuse me of messing around with Bebe, now you want to know if I had sex on Thursday.”

"Ms. Wilkes," Ziemann began in a contrite tone, which I refused to buy.

My chest heaved, I felt hot from annoyance, and embarrassment. "I don't like you, Ziemann. You’re a son of a bitch, so don’t say anything to me. I want you to help Bebe, not throw me under the bus to do it.”

“Okay, enough,” Redmond barked. “Everybody calm down. The D.A.’s office is loaded down with cases, and I have to listen to this?”

“Where’s the redhead?” Russo asked suddenly.

Maggie had gone. Had she abandoned me to these men? It took a bit, but we all turned in the direction of the room Bebe had been sitting. As if on cue, Maggie came out, giving Bebe a smile and wave as she went.

Christ! This wasn’t good.

“Had a nice visit,” Maddox said between clenched teeth as she came to join us. He glared Russo. Obviously, he’d been assigned to guard Bebe. Ziemann rubbed his temple, Redmond sighed and Maggie smiled at them all.

“What the hell were you doing in there?” Maddox asked.

“Talking to Bebe,” she said.

I'd known Maggie for a long time, and she can play dumb with the best of them. What she did better than anyone else was playing innocent. She worked those wide, azure eyes, alabaster complexion, and pixie face like a pro. Compared to her, Bambi seemed like a serial killer.

“You weren’t supposed to do that,” Redmond sounded like a school principal.

“No one told me not to, and you all seemed busy accusing Odessa of murder,” she said, flatly.

“Mrs. Swift, they can call on you in court on anything he might have said to you,” Ziemann said.

“Not really." Maggie said, unperturbed by the accusations. "I told him to repeat everything he told the detectives."

“You want us to believe that?” Russo said, raising doubts of his own.

Maggie opened the large saddlebag pocket book she always carried and pulled out a small pad. She flipped through the pages until she got to the one she wanted.

“She took notes,” Redmond said, surprised.

“She always takes notes,” I said.

“He said he was invited to Louis Mackie's party by his brother Jermaine Mackie the day before. He'd got the temporary cook to take the last of his services at the restaurant, and left there around ten. He caught the Q23 bus to Queens Village and arrived between 10:17. He remembers this because Jermaine called asking where he was. He arrived at the party, which was being held at RTM's building on Koch Street. He left before the party ended because he had worked the next day early. The party ended around 12:30.”

“He argued with the victim,” Maddox said.

“No.” She sighed and crossed her arms. “You said he argued with the victim. He only admitted he argued in the victim’s office with someone, but not Rovell. He had gone to the office because Rovell allowed him to leave his knives in there. They were a gift and he didn’t want them lost or stolen. You just assumed he fought with Rovell. And you know what they say about making assumptions," she scolded in the voice she reserved for her son. Maddox blanched.

"Witnesses said they argued when he arrived. Rovell refused to allow him inside," Maddox said.

"A misunderstanding. Rovell came around and let him inside."

"We found him at the goddamn murder scene," Russo added.

"Mary Magdalene," I said beneath my breath, but loud enough for Russo to hear. He responded with a grumble.

"He left the party and took the bus home. After at the third stop, he realized he'd left his knives in Rovell's office. He couldn't leave them. He needed them to work the next day. He went back." Maggie continued to read through her pages.

"When he returned the front security gate was down. He saw a light in the back of the building, went and found Rovell's car still in the lot. He knocked on the back door, but no one answered. He decided to wait. He couldn't be sure, but he thought he heard something, and then someone hit him from behind. He doesn't remember anything else until he woke up in the hospital."

"That's a convenient story," Maddox mused.

"His knife was found in the victim," Redmond added.

"Anyone at the party had access to those knives in Rovell's office," Ziemann said.

"Also, he was found unconscious. Who hit him? And please don't say Odessa." Maggie rolled her eyes.

"Maybe he tripped and fell," Russo said.

I laughed so loud at the total stupidity of the detective's response; I had to cover my mouth. Ziemann cleared his throat in an attempt to call things to order.

"I called the doctor who treated Bebe, and he swore Bebe couldn't have done that to himself. Seems like that's a question you should've asked."

"It would be easy to find another expert to say something different," Redmond said with confidence.

"Yeah, but then there's the rain thing," Maggie said.

Everyone stared at her as if she'd spoken Chinese. "When we visited Bebe in the hospital. His hair was wet. I got curious and checked the weather service for that early morning."

"The forecast predicted an early morning shower. But I checked because I wanted to be sure. It left the ground wet the next day when they found Bebe in the lot. You showed us the picture, remember?" She went to Maddox's desk and returned with the photograph. We huddled around her like students at their teacher's desk.

"So what? It rained," Redmond said.

"See, in the picture, and the ground." She pointed to the spot where EMS workers were aiding Bebe.

"What the hell am I looking at?" A frustrated Maddox searched the photograph.

"The ground is wet." Maggie pointed to another spot where the EMS had turned Bebe onto his back after applying a neck brace. A large dry area remained, in the shape of his body. "Not there."

"Bebe was attacked, and fell before the rain started, and stayed in that position until he was found the next day. They forecasted a light steady rain. His clothes were soaked, but beneath him remained dry. If someone killed Mr. Rovell around between two, two-thirty, then Bebe lay unconscious outside at the same time while it was still raining," she said.

"No one can tell exactly when the rain stopped or started," Russo said.

Maggie cocked an eyebrow up at him. "Well, you can, because I located 24 hour drug store a block over. I called the manager, and asked if he could play the security tape for that night because they're time coded. One camera is always aimed at the front door and parking lot. I asked him to view the footage to see when the rain started. The surveillance footage has a time and date stamped. He was sweet about it. Another thing you should've done." Maggie smiled.

"Why would he tell you?" Russo asked.

"I gave him my name and where I was calling from, you know… this precinct, and it had to do with a murder. He was helpful."

"You said you were a cop?" Redmond questioned harshly.

"Of course not. He just made the assumption, and we know about those," Maggie said with a knowing nod.

"What time?" I asked, impatient.

"Rain began exactly at 1:35 a.m. and didn't stop until 6:05 that morning."

Maddox inhaled deeply, repeating the action a few times before returning his searing eyes on Maggie. She wore her best I'm just waiting for your *catch up* face. The same face she used when her husband refused to read the instructions to the new weed whacker, or when her son, Rocket found a new use for his grandmother's hair dye. It took a week, several baths for the family dog return to his natural color. I loved that look.

"Let him go," Redmond announced.

"What, because of what she said?" Maddox nearly screamed.

Redmond shook his head. "No, because when she says it, it sounds ridiculous." Redmond pointed at Ziemann. "But when he says it in court, it will sound like fact and it will put doubt in the jury's minds. Get something more, detective, get something better. Talk to the drug store manager, get the security footage to make sure." Redmond left us to deal with more pressing matters.

"You've been busy, Mrs. Swift," Ziemann said with

reluctant admiration.

Maggie smiled at the compliment; she hitched her thumb toward the room Bebe sat. “I'm going to tell him the good news." Without waiting for permission, she left.

I smiled in her wake. I knew she loved good news.

CHAPTER

8

Twice we'd pull Bebe from the clutches of Russo and Maddox. Our names would go down in the annals of cop lore as Ms. Cupcake and the Weather Girl, evildoers who thwarted justice, and the American way. To the chagrin of Russo, and Maddox, Maggie practically skipped through the detective squad as if she just picked a bowl of strawberries. We were persona non grata at their precinct. Even the desk sergeant, who'd been so agreeable earlier, grumbled disparaging remarks on the way out. Ziemann remained tight-lipped, and obviously angry with us. We'd interfered and he didn't like it. Thankfully, I didn't care what he thought. I cared Bebe was free.

"I'm really hungry," Bebe, said to no one in particular and rubbed his stomach. He still resembled the walking wounded, but his skin no longer appeared ashen. The large bandage had been removed from his head and replaced with a smaller one.

"We'll take you to the Blue Moon." I grabbed his forearm. I had him; I didn't want to let him go.

"Don't you think you should ask his lawyer where he's going next?" Ziemann's mood had gone south the moment we left the precinct. He said barely two words to us.

"Are you hungry too, Mr. Ziemann?" Maggie dug in her

bag for her car keys.

"I wouldn't mind serving you a double helping of Humble Pie," I added, just to see him sneer at me.

"What I would like is for you two to stop interfering and let me do my job." Ziemann crossed his arms as his dark eyes zeroed in on Maggie and me.

Bebe gave him a gentle pat on the shoulder. "Listen Mr. Z, you are a righteous dude, but my butt was headed for lock-up, we all know that. You would have gotten me out but not before I spent the night in jail. Ms. Maggie saved my ass… I mean, my butt, so I'm going to the Blue Moon for a while and have a bite, call my mom, and tell everyone I'm okay. You need to chill, okay?" Bebe used his usual low-key matter-of-fact way he had of speaking. The kid just avoided being sent to jail, and he acted like it was any other day.

"You need to take this seriously, Mr. Dunn," Ziemann said.

Bebe shrugged, his wide shoulders lifting slightly, and he inhaled deeply. "I will," Bebe reassured, but I guarantee his empty stomach had priority.

Ziemann's manicured hand rubbed his forehead. "Fine, just go home afterward, and give me a call. Don't talk to anyone else." He gave Maggie and me a disconcerting sigh before he engaged his cell phone As if by magic, a dark town car appeared from around the block, and stopped in front of us. Ziemann stepped inside.

"That's so weird," Maggie said as she watched him go.

"Wait till you hear about Allie." I hadn't told anyone about Lee's sister's voice gymnastics.

As we walked to Maggie's car the sound of loud rap music stopped us. Everyone in front of the precinct turned in the direction of the approaching sound. A large, shiny, cream-colored SUV drove up and stopped by Maggie's car, blocking us in. The monster car with tinted windows, chrome trim, shiny wide tires, and elaborate hubcaps, dwarfed the minivan. A uniformed officer took a step toward the vehicle, and suddenly the music stopped. My ears rang in the silence.

"Oh shit," Bebe said beneath his breath.

"Oh shit what?" I sensed his body tense next to me.

My question was answered seconds later when the door opened and a young black man stepped out. Buzz-cut hair, cocoa-colored skin, loose-fitting jeans, a graphic t-shirt, and designer sneakers; his handsome face was twisted in a sneer. The object of his loathing seemed to be Bebe. If trouble could be embodied in a human being, it walked toward us with the menace of a junkyard dog.

"Is something wrong?" In many ways, Maggie could be brilliant, but sometimes she missed the obvious. I didn't know who this guy was, I recognized him as someone with anger issues, a dash of psychopathic tendencies, and a swig of impulse control for garnish.

"Maybe you and Ms. O should go to the car." Bebe took a step away from me. "I'll be a minute."

"Okay." An obedient Maggie obviously wanted some distance for whatever trouble she sensed. She reminded me of a zebra who happened across a lion and an alligator, at a waterhole, facing off over a dead carcass. She didn't want to be the next thing on the menu.

"No!" I didn't move from Bebe's side.

Though Bebe's expression hadn't changed, the stranger's angry facial features seemed to heighten. Bebe didn't need a confrontation with this guy in front of the precinct, or anyplace else, for that matter. A group of officers standing around the precinct took notice of us.

"Ms. O," Bebe complained when I didn't move.

"I'm not going." A little ball of nerves formed at the pit

of my stomach, and I tried to ignore it.

"Nigga, they said you were under arrest." The young man growled the words out to Bebe, his dark brown eyes narrowed with hatred.

Bebe slowly shook his head. I sensed his emotions mounting behind his composed facade. I envied his control.

"You ain't got no right to be out, you son of a bitch." The stranger leaned forward.

Bebe flinched and the stranger took this as a cue to take a step toward him. Without thinking, I slipped between the two men. Stunned by my recklessness, Maggie stood wide-eyed and silent. Though I had the height, I couldn't match their strength or sheer bulk. I started to feel like that carcass. To my surprise, the stranger backed off, treating me as if I were some impediment to his purpose.

"You need to back up, bitch," he said his voice low and guttural.

"Odessa," Maggie squeaked, her eyes wide with fear.

"Move, Ms. O." Bebe put a little more edge in his voice.

"No."

"Tell your moms here she needs to step aside and shut the fuck up." The stranger jabbed a finger at me. "This ain't your business."

Again, with the finger. Did they think the damn thing magical? I didn't know or care who this guy was anymore. I'd had it with the bad language, hostility and disrespect.

"Oh no," Bebe said beneath his breath, perfectly reading my change in mood. I had shifted from concern to let's get off the insult Odessa bandwagon.

After my dismissal from my advertising job, my life as a dessert chef has been anything but sedate or mundane. I had to blame Maggie for some of this. In her newfound career as a P.I. wannabe, she's gotten me involved in some pretty hairy stuff. I've been chased by kidnappers, threatened by police and the FBI, and people of various shapes and sizes have tried to put an end to my cake-making career. So if, this guy expected me to be intimidated, he had to get in line. Russo and Maddox had first dibs.

"He's my business," I raised my voice, and pointed at Bebe who stood behind me. "You being in his face become my business. So unless, you plan to remove me, then I'm your business too." I said this with the bravado of a woman standing in front of a police precinct.

He scrutinized me, possibly assessing how much I weighed. The lean muscle beneath his skin hugging t-shirt removed any doubt he could toss me aside like crumbled paper. His lips curled in amusement, and he took a step toward me.

"You've only been out a few days. You don't want to go back in jail, do you?" Maggie interrupted her voice a little shaky. The young man lost his smile and turned to her. I followed Maggie's line of sight to the man's exposed arms. A rough tattoo on the right lower forearm had the word Freedom and a date. The date was a week ago. Maggie had deduced he'd just been released from prison, and commemorated the event by inking his release date. Her mental leaps could be astounding, if not exhausting.

"I bet you're on parole." She smiled up at him. "This is a terrible way to start a new life."

A little doubt flashed in his eyes. He had been pulled in by her concern, but his attention switched back to Bebe, and the fire returned. "You killed Wood!" He cursed.

"No, I didn't, Louis," Bebe said.

"Sometimes the cops make a mistake," Maggie said in a voice that was supposed to convey confidence, but came off as unsure. Despite her unease, this seemed to resonate with him, and the fire that had been burning, went out as if someone had thrown a switch.

"Everything alright here?" One of the police officers, possibly sensing the mounting tension, finally walked over. "We're okay?"

"Everything is fine," the man called Louis said unconvincingly, his face still tight with anger.

"We're good, thank you sir," Maggie nodded.

Louis stepped away, never taking his eyes off Bebe. He swaggered back to the SUV like a prize fighter going to his corner. He got into the passenger seat, and a moment later the window slid down. A large white man sat on the driver's side and turned on the ignition.

"This ain't over," Louis yelled as the SUV drove away, and the music went on again, drowning out any other sound.

"It's never over," I said, relieved no one threw a punch. I waited for the two officers to leave before I confronted Bebe. "You know that guy?" I asked.

"Louis Mackie." Bebe's calm demeanor had returned.

"We should go to the car now before someone else shows up." Maggie surveyed the street for more potential threats.

"Was Maggie right about the jail thing?" I asked as Bebe and I followed her to the car.

"How'd she do that? Know about Louis in prison?" he asked.

"I don't know, it's some kind of Jedi Mom trick," I said. "What was he in prison for?" I hated to piss off a mass murderer or something.

"Gun possession," Bebe said.

I stopped, blinked a few times to process my thoughts, or corral my panic. I hadn't decided which. "Did you hear that?" I said, as I got into the passenger side of Maggie's car.

She pulled out into the street to take us to the Blue Moon.

"How many years did he get?" She eyed Bebe through the rearview mirror.

"Three, but got out in a year, and a half," he said softly. "You were right, you know."

"About what?" I asked, turning around to face him.

His attention pulled by the world outside his window. He closed his eyes and rested his head against the glass. He seemed terribly young at that moment, and the image took me back to the fresh-faced sullen boy who appeared at the Blue Moon for the first time. Quiet even then, his maturity shone through, understanding his situation and dealing with it. He'd put on the apron someone had given him and started busing tables without complaint. Eventually, curiosity won out over his taciturn mood, when the fast pace, sights, and sounds of the kitchen intrigued, and excited him.

Without opening his eyes, he said, "Sometimes the cops do get it wrong."

CHAPTER

9

We managed to get Bebe to the Blue Moon without incident. Maggie had to leave the moment we arrived. Her call home to the Swift residence to check-in had sent her into a panic. She gave Bebe a quick hug and she dashed out the door saying something about her husband and son, and a stove. The idea of those two and an open flame would trouble anyone. The last time Roger cooked something without Maggie's supervision left him with no facial hair and a first degree burn. Roger looked like a sunburned newborn for days.

Bebe and I retreated to my office at the cake shop, away from the prying eyes of the kitchen staff, and Candace, who asked a thousand annoying questions. Inside the small office, he seemed to relish the peace and quiet. The confrontation between Louis and Bebe made me uneasy, knowing the issue hadn't truly resolved itself. Even more so, when he explained that Louis lived two blocks from him. Growing up, he'd been close friends with Louis' younger brother, Jermaine.

None of this explained Louis's hatred of Bebe, or Bebe's almost forgiving reaction. Despite Ziemann's warning, I planned to find out over a turkey sandwich, ice tea, and a slice of my chocolate fudge cake. I wanted answers.

"Tell me about Louis," I asked. "Why was he so angry

with you about Rovell?"

Bebe sat back in his chair and pushed a half eaten plate of cake aside. "Rovell used to be in the music business back in the day," he said.

I remembered Rovell's singing group.

"Jermaine and Louis always did music, even when we were kids. They even got into making their own CDs, and selling them on the street, and clubs." Bebe picked at the cake with his fork.

"When did Rovell get involved?" I asked.

Bebe shrugged. "Suddenly he was there listening and talking to them. By then, Jermaine and I weren't as close anymore. I got into trouble, and you know the rest."

"But Rovell and Louis were close?"

Bebe nodded. "Jermaine and Louis' dad ran out. Rovell stepped in and does all right by them."

This explained Louis' anger and Bebe's self-restraint. He'd understood what Louis had lost by losing Rovell. Bebe had been raised by a single mother, as well.

"If Rovell supported him, what happened to the gun charge?" I asked.

"Rovell couldn't be on him twenty-four-seven, and Louis always liked hanging with a hard crowd. Wrong place, wrong time, I guess. But Rovell stood by him, took care of Jermaine and his mom until Louis got out. I guess he planned to pick up where they left off." Bebe pushed the plate away.

"Louis really hates you." I tried to measure his reaction, which was hard with Bebe.

"People tells him I killed Rovell, yeah he's angry." He shrugged.

"You think he might go after you?"

Bebe said nothing, which was answer enough. He had a sense of inevitability about him. As if, Louis was a storm he couldn't avoid, and his only plan was just to survive it. This didn't make sense. When the weatherman warns me about an approaching thunderstorm, I don't stand in the middle of an empty field with a lightning rod in my hand, and hope for the best.

"You can't go home," I insisted.

"What choice do I have? If George was here, maybe I could stay with him. Everyone I know, Louis knows, or could find out about," he said.

For a minute, I thought about taking him home with me but with the drama with Lee and his sister, having Bebe lurking around wouldn't improve their discord.

"What about Candace?" I said.

Bebe's usual stone facade cracked. "I hope you don't take this wrong, Ms. O, but I rather go back to jail than move in with Ms. Candace."

"Yeah, she might be a bit much." I gave him an understanding smile. I've seen my sister in the morning, and no amount of strong coffee prepares you for it. "She would keep Louis away, just by opening the front door in the morning, in her fuzzy bathrobe, house slippers, a cup of coffee in one hand, and I'll eat you whole expression on her face."

Bebe laughed, and I pushed the cake plate back in front of him.

"Don't insult me, and finish it." I went to the front of the shop and checked on Esperanza. As expected, she had everything well in hand. To take my mind off of Bebe, I began reviewing orders with her when the phone rang. It was Maggie.

"Hey girlfriend," I said.

She greeted me with a tired hello, and the reassurance the Swift house remained smoke free. She called to check on Bebe. I told her about my apprehension regarding his safety.

"Louis will find him. Right or wrong the outcome won't

be suitable for Bebe," I said.

"Well, the answer is simple," she said.

"It is?"

Just like Maggie to think everything was straightforward. She would have preferred if Louis and Bebe sat down with glasses of milk, and cookies, and talk things out. This only worked with the under ten set. Staying with Candace seemed the best solution. He'd survive, barely. However, I wouldn't put it passed my sister telling him to pull up his baggy pants, change the music on his iPod, and insist he attend church with her this Sunday.

"He can stay with me," she said.

I said nothing because the idea of Bebe staying with the Swifts didn't seem easy at all. Maggie lived in the middle of suburbia with her insurance salesman husband and a mischievous eight-year-old son. She had a dog and a picket fence. Every street was named after some tree, birds, or a dead president. The only diversity in the neighborhood was the color of the houses, or when I showed up.

"I don't know, Maggie." I politely hid my reluctance of this idea.

"Trust me, he'll be okay. If anyone shows up out of the ordinary, half the neighborhood will call the other half, including me," she said.

I'm sure Louis's arrival on Sycamore Lane, with his hip hop music blaring would get half the neighborhood's attention while the other half dialed the police.

"I know you like to think I live in a place that hasn't seen a black person since the Nixon administration, but we have," she said annoyed. "You're such a city snob, Odessa. You think everything outside Brooklyn, Queens, Manhattan, Staten Island, and The Bronx is a vast wasteland," she joked.

"We don't count Staten Island, but yes," I teased.

She was right, of course. Maggie's house was an excellent place to stash Bebe. No one would think to search for him there. I didn't ask Bebe how he felt about being dumped in the middle of the suburbs, my sister being his other alternative. So, I went and presented Maggie's offer.

"I'll go to Ms. Maggie's," he said before I even finished.

We headed for Hicksville, Long Island. We took a quick detour by his small apartment he once shared with his family. Thankfully, Louis was nowhere to be found.

We arrived at Maggie's a little after seven. As I pulled up to the familiar ranch style house on the neat tree-lined street, I nearly made a U-turn and headed back to Queens. Parked in the Swift's driveway, behind Maggie's minivan was her mother-in-law's car, a pristine 1989 tan Coupe de Ville.

"What's wrong?" Bebe said, expertly reading the dread on my face.

I put on a quick smile, hoped for the best, and prayed that Mrs. Swift's visit would be short, and painless. I parked the car and we walked to the front door. Rocket must have seen us from the window because the front door flew open and the kid raced out.

"Hey Rocket man," Bebe said in greeting as Rocket nearly jumped on him. The boys playfully tussled a bit before Rocket pulled Bebe into the house.

"Mom says Bebe's staying. That's cool, right?" Rocket seemed to finally notice my presence.

Small for his size, Rocket had his mother's coloring, reddish hair, and large blue eyes. His perpetual inclination to get into trouble was uniquely his. Sweet natured, curious to a fault, my godson gravitated toward chaos. At six, he crawled into the house's crawl space, and had to be rescued by police and the fire department. Once he allowed a squirrel into his grandmother's house because he thought it looked hungry.

Again, the police, fire department, and animal control were called to save the day. At day camp, he and a few cohorts released the camp's petting zoo animals. The police refused to take the call, passed it on to the fire department, who called animal control. I'm sure the town of Hicksville has to allocate money in its budget just for him.

"Where's your mom?" I asked.

Rocket pointed to the backyard then pulled Bebe towards his bedroom to play some game on his computer. I found the rest of the Swift clan in hot debate in the backyard. Roger, Maggie's husband stood between his mother and wife, trying desperately to buffer the obvious hostility the women had toward each other. Rarely did Maggie openly express her dislike of her mother-in-law. Mrs. Swift had no such restraints about giving her opinion about every, including her son's choice of wife. I stepped through the patio glass door and braced myself.

"Hey everybody," I said as cheerfully as possible.

Mrs. Swift glared at me. "Is she moving in too?" Mrs. Swift spat out. I wasn't on Mrs. Swift's family and friend list.

"A problem?" I directed my question to Maggie because asking doughy-faced Roger wasted my time. He would agree with his mother or his wife. Either way, he was screwed.

"There is no problem, because he's staying," Maggie said firmly.

"Mom, we promised," Roger added without much conviction. The man had the spine of a noodle.

"Rocket is impressionable. That Bebe boy has been arrested. You told me so yourself." Mrs. Swift said in a terse tone because her mind was set in concrete.

"That was a long time ago, Mrs. Swift," I interjected.

"Olivia, this is a family matter." Her tone insinuated more. "And he stole a car."

I sighed because yet again the woman refused to remember my name. Whether she did it by choice, or it was just the early onset of dementia, I didn't know.

"He got caught riding in a stolen car, and he was only fifteen," I clarified. This didn't make an impression on Mrs. Swift.

"He needs our help, Lenora." Maggie insisted. Roger stood next to her terrified.

I wanted to feel sorry for Roger, but it was difficult. The smartest thing he'd ever done was marrying Maggie. Unfortunately, Roger came with an overbearing mother with separation issues. I swore, if the woman could share a bed with them, she would.

"Now he's in trouble again. Say something Roger. You're the head of this household, aren't you?" Mrs. Swift said.

Roger's round, smooth face flushed. His mouth moved like a fish tossed on land. Nothing came out.

"You have criminals coming into the house. Dammit, Roger, say something." Mrs. Swift stomped her foot.

Roger gave off a pained expression. It seemed the only response to the two women before him. "Mom…" Roger pleaded, with his hands upraised in submission or maybe he was he praying for divine intervention. Nothing short of a lightning strike would deter Mrs. Swift when she got on her holy horse. She'd been riding that nag since I first met her.

"And now you have some hooligan living with my grandson." Mrs. Swift clutched her chest as if in the throes of a heart attack. While her face gyrated into a multitude of comedic facial expressions, we all watched. I took my cue from Maggie, who seemed unmoved. Roger looked a little wishful, but I couldn't be sure. It began and ended with one of Mrs. Swift's eyes opening, and staring back at us. Maybe she had gas.

"Mom, he's a good kid," Roger said beneath his breath.

I sighed, disappointed he didn't stand up to his mother. In truth, he always reminded me of chicken breast: pale, plump, and boneless.

"Shut up, Roger," Mrs. Swift snapped. Roger flinched and out popped his spine again.

Luckily, Maggie had one. "He stays, right, Roger?" Maggie glared at her husband.

Roger's brow furrowed as a low moan emanated from him, as if the act of choosing was painful. A choice of making his mother happy or having sex again with his wife again, didn't seem fair. Angered at her son's indecision, Mrs. Swift's face flushed. She pointed a stubby finger into Roger's chest.

"If that boy stays here, you won't see me visiting this house until he's gone," Mrs. Swift threatened.

Unexpectedly, Roger gave his mother an apologetic grin before patting her on her shoulder, and guiding her toward the pathway at the front of the house. Mrs. Swift protested as Roger helped his mother along.

"I'll be vigilant Mom, I swear," he said.

We watched a disbelieving Mrs. Swift, and her stoic son round the corner of the house. A few moments later, a car started and its tires squealed on the pavement as she drove off. Roger reappeared smiling, spine, and all.

CHAPTER 10

Maggie and I stood in the Swift's small den setting up a makeshift room for Bebe, who sat on the floor, petting the family's five-year-old dachshund called Mr. McGregor's Grand Endeavor. Mr. McGregor, as we called him, was a retired show dog whose previous owner realized the dog hated the limelight. A sweet animal with large black eyes and auburn coat had a temperate disposition, which often helped counteract Rocket's often extreme behavior. The dog's large head and floppy ears rested on Bebe's leg as Bebe stroked behind the ears. Whatever tension brought on by the day's events, including Maggie's mother-in-law rant, was drained from Bebe's face. Rocket had distracted him, and now Mr. McGregor helped him toward some inner peace. The dog was better than Prozac.

"The cop said you argued with someone?" Maggie tucked a bed sheet into the small day bed against the wall.

"Cherry," he said. The dog had rolled onto his stomach, giving Bebe access to a tender spot.

"Who's Cherry?" I shoved a pillow into a pillowcase that had a picture of fire trucks on it. Before Rocket was sent off to bed, he helped his mother select the bedding motif for Bebe. To Rocket, Bebe has been just a brother from another mother, a black, five-foot-eleven, dread-wearing brother, but a brother all the same.

"Trouble in high-heels," he said with a surprising bite in his voice. He absent-mindedly stroked the dog, and Mr. McGregor's back legs twitched in delight.

"Stop doing that, you'll make him go blind," I said.

Bebe smiled and gave the dog a reassuring pat.

"Why trouble?" Maggie asked, finishing off the bed with an Elmo bed sheet.

"She shouldn't have been there," he said, and for the first time. He sounded a little angry.

"Why would you say that?" I asked.

"No one invited Cherry anywhere, she just showed up. The party was winding down, and I went to Rovell's office to get my knives before I went home." He clenched his teeth and hesitated briefly.

"But you didn't get them," Maggie said.

"Cherry distracted me. I wanted her to leave. I made sure she left," he said.

"Why was that so important?" I asked.

"Like I said, she's nothing but trouble, especially for Jermaine, and Louis. Things were finally right for them. And then she shows up."

"You're very protective?" I teased.

A smile escaped his lips. "I guess…" He bashfully looked away. "My life is good, you know. Because of George and the Blue Moon, and all, even Ms. Candace. I'm okay. Things for the Mackies should be good too. If you have people who keep you from trouble or keeps trouble away from you, then thing can stay good."

I nodded knowing this was how Bebe imagined his life. Things could have gone terribly wrong if the judge had decided to send him to jail instead of insisting he be a part of a first time offenders work program for juveniles. With a little help from his friends, he turned out all right. He wanted to do the same for the Mackie brothers.

"Maybe she can tell the police you were arguing with her and not with Rovell. It might help," Maggie said.

Bebe shook his head. "No way Cherry would go to the police."

"She doesn't have a choice. She's going to have to tell," Maggie demanded.

"Yeah, says who? First you have to find her." He didn't seem too hopeful.

"We'll give her name to the police or to Ziemann," I said.

"I told the police. They think I made her up, and Mr. Zee didn't seem to care about my fight with her. All he cared about was what the police had on me, which was the knife and me being there." Bebe shrugged.

"You call him Zee?" I didn't hide my annoyance at his familiarity with the lawyer.

"He's a cool dude." From the expression of Bebe's face, this issue was not negotiable. He rarely revoked his cool card once given out.

I thought Ziemann's coolness rated up there with a rectal exam, necessary but not cool. Telling Bebe I didn't like Ziemann wouldn't help and it might even undermine his confidence in the lawyer.

"Zee was more worried about the thing that happened when I first arrived at the party. At the front door, Rovell has an issue about letting me in until Jermaine showed up and told him everything was okay. People saw that, but they remember the fight," he said.

"Was it a bad scene?" Maggie asked.

"Kinda, the guy at the door didn't have me on his list. Thing got a little loud."

"Why was Cherry in Rovell's office?" I asked.

Bebe shrugged. "Probably to steal something."

"Did you think she might have seen something?" Maggie said.

"Ms. Maggie, Cherry could have seen the murder and still wouldn't say a word to anyone, unless she got something out of it."

This made Maggie and I pause. "You're serious?" Maggie asked. From the expression on his Bebe's face, he was dead serious.

"Maybe we should talk to her," I suggested.

"Got to find her first. I couldn't tell you where she lives or tell you anyone who could," Bebe said.

"If you had a difficult time getting to the party, how did she?" Maggie asked.

Bebe thought about it for a moment. "Knowing Cherry as I do, she probably got one of the security guards to let her in or something. She probably promised him a blow—" Bebe stopped. Maggie's pixie face usual ingenuousness façade, made it hard to be blunt around. She always looked like she should have gossamer wings, toss fairy dust or something. I'd long since become immune to her fairy glamour.

"Blow what?" a clueless Maggie asked, confirming Bebe's suspicion of her guilelessness.

"Nothing," Bebe said and kept his attention on Mr. McGregor. I didn't hide my amusement when Maggie realized what Bebe had been referring to.

She cleared her throat and made a face. "What's her full name, and where is she from?" Maggie asked.

"Well, her real name is Sherrilyn Turnbull, but everyone calls her Cherry," Bebe said.

Maggie asked a few questions about her appearance, age, and possible place of work. Though she use to live in the neighborhood, and she worked as a hairdresser, off and on,

Bebe didn't know much. Roger interrupted the twenty questions with an invitation for Bebe to watch the Yankees/Red Sox game. He jumped at the invitation. He and Mr. McGregor left us for some chips, soda, and midsummer baseball.

"Maybe we should talk to Mr. Ziemann about her." Maggie laid out some towels and a brand new toothbrush on a small table next to the bed.

"Get real, Maggie. Ziemann doesn't want to talk to us, let alone about Bebe's case. We should find this Cherry on our own. If we have something, then we tell Ziemann."

"You don't like him much, do you?"

"He called me Ms. Cupcake," I said, snidely.

Maggie laughed. She and I finished up the room and headed back to the kitchen to work on how to find Cherry. Maggie thought if she were a licensed hairdresser, tracking her down might not be so hard. While Maggie pulled out her laptop to do a search on the web, I made some coffee. I got interrupted when my phone rang. It was Lee.

"Hey hon." I checked the time on my mobile phone display panel. It was a little after nine.

"Is Allie with you?" I caught a hint of trepidation in his voice.

"No. I sent her home hours ago."

"Shit!" He growled something beneath his breath.

"Did she leave a note or something?" I said, and tried not to get swept up into Lee's rising panic.

"Just she'd be home later, and she had the spare key you gave her," he said.

"She's fine then." I tried to reassure him, but he didn't seem mollified.

"I like to know where she is, considering all her friends are upstate."

This was true, born in a small town, near Saratoga in upstate New York, Allie had little if no connections in New York City. Allie went to school in California where she met, and married her husband. Since her arrival, she never mentioned she had friends in the city, but then something occurred to me. Recently, she made a new one. He had a closet filled with bad suits, a love for greasy burgers, cheep beer and a libido the size of Texas. Frank.

"Don't worry, she's okay." I hoped my suspicions weren't true. Lee seemed to be appeased for a moment, but he wouldn't be for long if she didn't arrive soon. When I got off the phone, I turned to my friend, who seemed engrossed with her laptop and the search for Cherry.

"Allie went out and hasn't come home yet. Lee's worried, and so am I," I said.

Maggie kept one eye on me, and the other on her laptop. "You didn't sound worried."

"That's because if Lee had any idea what might make me worried, he'd go ballistic."

"You know where she is?" Her eyes momentarily pulled toward the computer screen again.

Without reservation, I closed the laptop shut.

"Odessa." She slid the laptop away from me.

"I don't know where she is, but I might know who she's with."

This seemed to get Maggie's focus, and she gave me her full attention. "What do you mean?"

"You can become fast friends over tequila shots," I said.

Maggie connected the dots quickly. "He wouldn't." Maggie always wanted to think the best of people even when they were at their worst.

"Call him. If she's with him, I'll kill him, I swear."

"Maybe she's not."

Maggie's expression seemed hopeful, but I didn't have the luxury of thinking Frank would do the right thing, and leave Allie alone. Maggie made the call. Right away, from the expression on her face she'd found him, and confirmed Frank McAvoy was a complete idiot.

I snatched the phone from her. "Where is she, Frank? Is Allie with you?" I barked into the phone. I heard loud talking, and maybe a television set on a sport channel. "Are you at a bar?"

"Christ Odessa, you're not even married yet, and already you're acting like somebody's wife. The answer is yes, and yes," he barked at me. Then he hung up.

I held the phone and glared at it in disbelief. I was going to kill him. "He took her to a bar," I screamed. "She's going to be my sister-in-law, and he's treating her like some hoochie from around the way."

"Calm down, O. You know Frank wouldn't let anything happen to her," Maggie said, trying unsuccessfully to placate my growing anger.

"Frank has happened to her. What am I going to tell Lee?" I threw up my hands. "Sorry, but your sister is bar hopping with the likes of Frank McAvoy. What is his problem?" I wanted to wring Frank's fat neck. Why can't he act like other responsible adult? No, Frank wanted to revisit his teenage years, and decided to take Allie along for the ride, and what was with Allie? Had she lost her mind, or were the voices inside her head starting to talk back to her?

"I think I know where they are," she said.

I read a little displeasure on her face, and knew Frank had disappointed us both. She turned off the laptop, grabbed her handbag, and told Bebe and Roger that we had to run an errand. Roger waved back with his eyes clued to the television set. No doubt, he believed we were off to buy milk or something domestic like that. I guess for Maggie and Roger's relationship, ignorance was bliss, and you don't tell your husband you about to pull your drunken boss from a bar. You certainly don't tell him this.

CHAPTER

11

The Stone Parrot Bar sat on the corner of Hempstead Turnpike and Brewster Street, and on the border of Nassau County and the New York City. Sandwiched between a boarded up paint store and a Chinese takeout, the bar's garish neon sign of a parrot flashed with a few lights missing just above the door. Its worn clapboard exterior had seen better days. From the disheveled appearance of the patrons hanging outside, a motley collection of low-lifers, this wasn't your typical fruity mixed drink crowd. Book Clubs didn't discuss the latest from Oprah's book list. You'd find no veggie platter or tofu salad on the menu. A dive in every sense of the word, Ms. Cupcake and the Weather Girl didn't belong.

We'd parked across the street. Maggie got out of the car first. On the drive over, her displeasure with Frank had built into white-hot fury. I had to listen to a verbal condemnation of Frank's numerous shortcomings, and there were aplenty. Maggie's recent frustration of getting her boss to tend to business had fallen on deaf ears. Lately, the ex-New York City Detective has been courting several divorcees and thinking himself a neighborhood Romeo. The rotund, poorly dressed, rude, social inept and twice-divorced Frank discovered telling women he used to be a hotshot homicide detective turned him into a sex symbol to the over fifty crowd. I had no doubt this crowd had to be desperate, dumb and blind.

"He's so busy trying to get his groove on, he's too tired to do anything else. He drags into the office half dead and hung over. I'm done with it." Maggie slammed the door to the car and stomped off.

"You've been to this place before?" I asked with trepidation.

"It's one of the few places that allow Frank to have a running tab."

I could imagine Maggie coming here on her own trying to drag a reluctant Frank back to work after he had one of his liquid lunches.

We crossed the street and maneuvered between small groups of the bar's patrons standing outside the door. Like a UFO sighting, everybody stared at us because we washed daily and believed in oral hygiene. Maggie wore a t-shirt she'd gotten from a recent blood drive. It expounded on the benefits of blood and marrow donations. I didn't think she'd get any takers at the Stone Parrot, unless you liked your blood pickled. I stood out mainly because I was black. There would be no NCAAP rally held at the Stone Parrot.

Inside, the place reeked of stale beer, cigarettes and male funk. I instinctively held my breath for a moment but realized I should be more afraid of getting cooties than contracting Black Lung. Maggie made a beeline to the bar and the bartender. My eyes immediately went to a large parrot on a perch. It didn't move, or talk or anything. Someone had stuffed the poor thing.

Maggie had to squeeze between two large men leaning against the bar, whose matching leather vests indicated they belonged to the club with a flaming skeleton riding a motorcycle as its logo. They parted only slightly, and ogled Maggie as if she were a treat.

"Hey Buck, a Lilliputian," one guy said, pointing at her. The other biker ogled Maggie's rear end and for a moment, I thought he might grab it.

She slapped her hand on the bar to get the bartender's attention. When that didn't work, she grabbed an empty beer bottle and rapped it on the bar. The bartender turned to see a very annoyed redhead waving an empty Corona at him. The bikers stopped ogling.

"Ain't you a tall drink of hot cocoa," someone said behind me as a large white, sweaty arm wrapped around my shoulder. The offending arm belonged to a man who surprisingly had all his teeth, thick, dirty-blond hair, and the bouquet of beer and gym socks. I twisted away and bumped into someone large, wide and fleshy.

"Where's McAvoy?" Maggie asked the bartender.

Busy trying to find Frank's whereabouts, she was ignorant of my plight as I had become the curiosity of one or more of the bar's patrons. I apologized to the man I bumped, and tried to avoid the advances of the Sweaty Guy. I put my hands to my chest, not wanting to touch anyone or anything.

"Come on, Odessa." Maggie disappeared into a sea of bodies without even looking back.

Before I could follow, Sweaty Guy grabbed my wrist. "Come dance with me, sweetheart. Give me some of that jungle love," he said with a sloppy slur of words.

It took all my effort to push off him, hold my breath, and get some distance. "No." I held up a finger to stop his approach. Of course, this only worked with children and extremely small dogs.

"I want to dance." He did a little swivel with his hips. Everyone laughed.

I searched for Maggie and found the top of her red head hair way in the back of the bar. Allie stood next to her. The women were in deep conversation, but I couldn't hear over the noise of the music blaring out of a jukebox. Maggie started pointing and waving her hands, turned and headed for the door. Allie followed.

I sighed in relief until I realized they were leaving without me. When Frank scrambled after them, I called his name and tried to push through the press of people. "Frank," I repeatedly yelled to get his attention.

By this time, Sweaty Guy grabbed me again and started swaying and grinding his hips against mine. I had enough and pushed hard to try to dislodge myself. Sweaty Guy had a grip like a vice and breath as rank as day old potato peels.

Frank must have seen my plight and reluctantly headed my way. For half a minute, he appraised the situation and cocked an eyebrow. "Why you always got to ruin my fun?" he complained, ignoring the fact I remained in the clutches of a man who didn't believe in deodorant.

"Frank!" I exclaimed, trying to get free.

Frank seemed to ignore this, or thought Sweaty Guy was my problem. "I'm going to find Allie." He pointed to Sweaty guy. "I'd be careful, she's a ball buster." Then little the weasel left me. I stood there with my mouth opened in disbelief and horror.

"That's okay," the Sweaty Guy yelled after him. "Mine are made of steel." He grabbed his crotch with his free hand and jiggled. The place erupted with laughter.

I lost my patience. Finding some leverage, I whirled on him, yet still embraced in his clutches. Face to face, I glared into his bloodshot eyes. "If you don't let me go, I'll knee you so hard in your steel balls you'll be wearing them for earrings."

Sweaty Guy stopped jiggling. I channeled Candace's inner most bitch and twisted my lips into a wicked smile as if I might enjoy rearranging his man jewels. Sweaty Guy let go. I turned, walked away, and prayed he wouldn't follow. He didn't.

I found Maggie, Frank and Allie by the car arguing. In reality, Maggie did most of the yelling, reiterating Frank's list of faults. A contrite Allie stood off to the side acting invisible.

"Most days, I'm in the office by myself waiting for you to come, Frank. Our clients think I made you up," Maggie scolded.

I took the opportunity to pull Allie to the side. "Allie, what are you doing?"

"I was at the house bored, and Frank called." She swayed a bit.

I caught the whiff of alcohol. I sighed because I didn't have the energy to get into an argument in the street. I told her to get in the car, like some petulant child.

"I can't run this business by myself!" Maggie stood before her rotund boss, pissed off and fed up. There was a time Maggie would have never confronted Frank on his behavior. Genuinely sweet nature, even tempered and always forgiving, Maggie had changed. I'd like to take credit for her newfound confidence, but she'd accomplished that on her own. Working at the detective agency allowed her natural talents of organization, inquisitiveness and problem-solving shine through. Anyone who knew Maggie would say she was a great mom and wife, but who'd have thought she could crack Frank's nuts with the best of them? I should know, I tried to crack them every chance I got. By the time she finished and joined Allie in the car, Frank seemed dejected. Now it was my turn.

"You left me," I yelled.

"You seemed all right," he said with a satisfied grin.

"You're a jerk, Frank. And stay away from Allie."

"She wanted a little fun," a grinning Frank said in his defense.

It was kind of like the Twinkie defense. Instead of high sugar content as something to blame for his irresponsible behavior, Frank used intoxication and poor judgment as his.

"If she wants fun, I'll get her tickets to the Lion King." I climbed into the car and drove off, leaving Frank in the street cursing my name.

By the time I dropped Maggie off and reached my house in Queens, the car clock read 11:15. Allie and I hadn't said a word to each since we left Frank. I was still too angry. At home, Lee opened the front door the moment the car pulled into the driveway. We appeared relatively intact, so his expression of deep concern softened a bit.

"You okay?" he asked as I stepped inside.

I mumbled something, said nothing to Allie as I passed her to go upstairs to my bedroom. Brother and sister said nothing to each other as Allie made a quick escape to the guest bedroom and shut the door. Lee's expression of complete understanding surprised me. Had he reacted to his sister's behavior or my frustration? I didn't have the strength to ask. I peeled off my clothes, slipped on an old t-shirt and crawled into bed like the walking wounded.

Moments later, the familiar weight of Lee slipping in next to me made me sigh. I curled into him, burying my head into his chest and entwining our legs and said nothing. I listened to his heartbeat, and fell into a deep sleep.

***

Refreshed and renewed with a good night's sleep, the next morning, I concluded the best way to keep Allie away from Frank and sober was to put some distance between them. So when Maggie called and said she had an address on Cherry, I brought Allie along. Taking Maggie's cue that ignorance was bliss when it came to your spouse, I told Lee we were running a few errands, which might take up most of the day. He translated this as girls going shopping. Allie liked the idea of coming with us. Hanging out with Frank at bars and tracking down a reluctant witness told me so much about my future sister-in-law. She was a crazy as hell, and I had to worry that it might be genetic.

We drove to Brooklyn, taking Linden Blvd from Queens to an area called East New York, a working class neighborhood of semi-detached home, two to four family houses. As I drove, Maggie scanned for the address that said Devine Diva Hair and Nail Salon. A few blocks before Pennsylvania Avenue stood a small storefront beauty shop. Through the large plate glass window, two customers sat in chairs being attended to by a short round, dark skinned woman.

"Why are we here again?" Allie asked.

"We told you, to find this woman called Cherry," Maggie explained. "This is her last known mailing address and place of employment."

"And you have to find her for your friend who works at the restaurant, right?" Allie's said. "Shouldn't your friend's lawyer get his investigator to do that?"

"We're just asking a few questions and anyway, Bebe's lawyer is really busy with stuff." I skipped the small detail about Ziemann forbidding us to get involved.

In the rear view mirror, I saw Allie's brow crease in concern. "So this isn't illegal, or anything?"

This coming from a woman I had to pull away from a twice-divorced overweight playboy made me wonder about her moral center.

"No." Maggie turned around to smile at her. "We're fine."

We got out of the car and stepped into the familiar setting of a black neighborhood hair salon. The smell of hair being processed, blow dried and hot combed made the place smell like stuffy science project. By the door, an older woman sat at a manicure station doing her nails. In one chair, a woman was getting her roots relaxed. Parted in several sections, chemical relaxant coated much of her hair. I didn't envy the woman, who seemed to squirm a bit. Getting your hair relaxed could be at best a torturous process. If not done properly, you can walk away with no hair and first-degree chemical burns. Beauty could be painful.

Before I had a chance to open my mouth for introductions and questions, a beautician working at a hair washing station eyed us and had stopped what she had been doing. Even though the customer's hair was filled with soap, she walked over to us. She went right passed me and stood in front of Maggie, who seemed a little intimated by the plump woman examining her. The fact that Maggie was white and standing in a traditionally black salon wasn't the beautician's point of interest. I knew that right away because the woman showed little concern for Allie. It was Maggie's hair. Coppery red, thick and long, the woman were transfixed by it. It must have seemed like the Holy Grail. Without asking, she took several strands in her hand, she pulled out a pair of pink reading glasses to get a better look as Maggie stood petrified.

"Where you get this done and who did it?" the woman asked, in an accent that was a mixture of Caribbean and Brooklyn.

"What?" Maggie said wide-eyed.

I noticed Allie was taking a few steps toward the front door. I sighed and intervened. I pulled Maggie away. "Discount shampoo and God," I said.

CHAPTER 12

As owner and proprietor of Devine Diva Hair Salon, Vesta Winston refused to take no for an answer. The only thing she wanted was a sample of Maggie's hair, a large sample. Maggie politely refused. Vesta persisted, promising everything from styling service for a year to her grandmother's recipe for chicken croquettes. The next time Vesta asked, Maggie refused less politely, and glared at the scissors clutched like a weapon in Vesta's hand.

I took in the cluttered shop with is dated pink and black seventies décor, the small manicurist station by the door and the signs listing price and the week's special. My eyes stopped on several neat rows of locks of hair tacked to the wall behind Vesta's workstation. They were about six inch strands dangling from pretty pink ribbons. Maggie caught sight of the hair as well and took a step behind me.

"Odessa," Allie whimpered.

Behind us, another beautician blocked the front door.

"I just want a small piece." Vesta held up the scissors and snipped at the air.

Only slightly taller than Maggie, she wore purple house slippers and a floral printed apron that covered ample breasts. Her hair was done up in elaborate interwoven twists, piled high and tight on her head. Her broad face, the color of dark chocolate, had small, serious eyes as black as tar. Her ample mouth sported bright red lipstick.

"Why don't you put down the scissors before someone gets hurt," I said.

"It will grow back, and I'll give you free manicures. All of you." She tried to sound reasonable. You couldn't be reasonable with human hair tacked to your wall. Allie's eyes went wide with fear. I'm sure images of a massive black cast iron pot in the back with the last white missionary still boiling in it played in her head.

"Let's get out of here. We'll find out about Cherry some other way," Maggie backed away from Vesta.

The mention of Cherry's name seemed to knock Vesta out of hair-scalping trance. "What about Cherry?" She laid one hand on her hip and pursed her lips.

"Put the scissors away and I'll tell you," I offered.

"Vesta!" the woman in the salon chair yelled. She was fanning her head. Obviously, the processing chemical had been on a little too long. Being the professional that she was, a reluctant Vesta went to the woman and walked her over to the rinse station in the back of the salon to neutralize the relaxing crème.

"She wasn't serious, right?" Maggie whispered to me.

I didn't answer. I noticed behind one of the styling stations, several awards for best colorist for the year 2010, 2011 at the Beauty Best Hair Show in Chicago. The awards were given to Ms. Vesta Imogene Watson. I guessed Vesta wanted a trifecta.

"Yeah, honey, I think she was." I went to get a better view of Vesta's wall of fame. "I told you one day your hair would get you in trouble."

Maggie's brow furrowed deeply. We turned to find Allie

chatting with the manicurist, who suggested a treatment. For Allie, I guessed, the danger was over.

Vesta busied herself with trying to save her client's hair. Maggie and I took a seat in a small waiting area. We pretended not to listen as Vesta reassured her client a little hair lost was no problem. From their conversation, Vesta's hair rescue might take a while. I picked up an outdated gossip magazine and Maggie pulled out a softbound book from her oversized shoulder bag. She always kept something to read. As I read through the usual trials and tribulations of this year's celebrity, I quickly bored of the latest gossip, I noticed Maggie's book. "What the hell is this?" I snatched it from her.

"A gun book," she said, as if the obvious weren't apparent. I waved the book at her; the obvious was as clear as mud. What would my peace-loving, happy-ever-after girlfriend want with a book on guns?

"Why are you reading this?" I said.

Maggie held out her hand and waited for me to return the book. I did, reluctantly.

"I have to get my investigation license. Lately, Frank's no help. Every time I ask a question, he just grumbles and walks away. So I'm learning as much as I can on my own. The library is incredible." Her anger with Frank was still palpable.

"A gun book? Really Maggie." I'd known she was determined to get her P.I. license and her strange area of studies have delved in surveillance techniques, wiretapping and my personal favorite: disguises. One weekend we wasted an entire afternoon trying to find ways to conceal her appearance. Once, Frank had her follow a client's wayward husband. With flaming red hair and a dead ringer for Tinker Bell, Maggie found being in incognito difficult.

"I need to understand these things. It could be part of an investigation or something," she reassured me. Naturally intuitive, Maggie had a knack for retaining information like a sponge. If I needed to remember the boy I dated in high school, she'd remember. Such details tended to go through me like a sieve.

"You don't want one, do you?" I asked.

She made a face and shook her head. I felt a little relieved she wasn't going Rambo or Dirty Harry on me.

"Sometimes, Frank lets me clean his gun," she said proudly.

That sounded wrong on so many levels, but I didn't have the heart to tell her. Frank had a habit of using Maggie as his office wife, to do his laundry, grocery shopping and general go-fer, now gun cleaning. She needed to set boundaries for that man. Though I had to admit, dealing with the rotund ex-detective had given Maggie more confidence. If she could deal with Frank, everyone one else was butter. I let her go on about gun types—and which were preferred by the Israeli Military—until Vesta reemerged with her client, who seemed quite content. She put rollers in the woman's hair and set her beneath a large hair dryer. She walked over to us, a little exhausted from her efforts.

"Whew!" She fanned herself with her hand. "Girl, you almost cost me my favorite client."

"I'm not letting you cut my hair." Maggie patted the book that she'd been reading. This got Vesta's attention.

"Why don't we compromise?" I offered, watching the two women faced off.

"What kind of compromise?" an interested Vesta asked.

I smiled.

A few minutes later, a tentative Maggie sat in the chair at Vesta's station for an examination. In exchange for Maggie's cooperation, Vesta would answer questions about Cherry. While all this was going on, Allie had moved on from a manicure to a pedicure to a facial. I was gratified to know someone was enjoying Vesta's Devine Diva treatment.

"When was the last time you saw Cherry?" I asked.

Vesta made a quick sucking sound and sneered. "That girl, she owes me money. She rented out that booth there. She pointed to an empty station. "Hasn't paid me my rent in two months now. I haven't seen her since last Wednesday."

"She has your place listed as her last known mailing address?" Maggie kept a close eye on Vesta. She shouldn't have worried, I held Vesta's prize scissors in my hand.

"Didn't realize she did that until I started getting her bills here at the shop. I won't tell you what she owes me for that."

"You got a phone number for her?" I walked over to the workstation Vesta had pointed to and once belonged to Cherry.

"It's disconnected. What you want with Cherry, anyway?" Vesta lustily ran her fingers through Maggie's hair.

"A friend of ours needs her help." Maggie cringed as Vesta unceremoniously pulled Maggie's hair out of its ponytail and began to brush. Maggie protested for a moment then stopped, resigned to the fact that the woman wanted to play with her hair.

"What's in it for Cherry because, she won't do it for love," Vesta said with certainty. "In fact, if she does it for money can you make sure I get $553.98 out of it?"

As Vesta complained about Cherry, I picked through some of the clutter on Cherry's abandoned work station. I'd been around enough hair salons in my time to recognize that many of Cherry's professional tools, and supplies remained. They were poorly kept, dirty and neglected. Taped to a mirror behind the station were dozens of photographs. Each one of her and customers shot from the reflection of the mirror. Cherry Turnbull's big alluring eyes stared back at me from dozens of photographs.

I held up a picture of a pretty woman on the down side of twenty five, with a heart-shaped face, cafe au lait skin, with wide set brown eyes, and a shock of unnatural red hair. In every photograph, the smile remained the same, wide, tight and practiced. The truth seemed to lie in her dark almond-shaped eyes, tired and played out, and no amount of eye shadow or mascara could return her youthfulness and innocence. I peeled one off and slipped the picture into my pocket. Also, taped to the mirror were several business cards. Most were typical of the hair care business except one, a card for Tania Rovell Coffey, Vice President of RTM. I slipped it in my pocket too.

"She's always saying about how her payday was coming." Vesta threw up her hands in disgust. "That girl has been waiting for her payday since I met her."

"You've known her a long time?" Maggie asked.

"Long enough to know you don't leave your pocketbook open around her. She ain't great at her, either."

"Why did you hire her and let her live with you?" I asked.

Vesta shook her head. She seemed disgusted with her own lack of judgment. "I thought we were friends, but that girl can talk you into more shit that you can shake a stick at." This sounded like a confession.

"Odessa, do you think I have time enough to get my hair done?" Allie sat in a hairstylist's chair. The woman behind her ran a comb through Allie's dark wavy locks.

"Sure, why not." I shrugged. I asked Vesta if Cherry's stuff still remained at her house. She said no, she'd boxed up what little belongings she left and put them in the salon's storage room. I asked if I could go through it.

"Why? You a detective or something?" She laughed but stopped when I didn't laugh back.

"Maybe we can find out where she went," Maggie added,

trying to get up from the chair. Vesta gave her hair tug. Maggie promptly sat back down and grumbled something.

"And get you closer to that $553.98 she owes you," I said.

"You think you can get me my money?" This piqued Vesta's interest.

"We can try," Maggie said. "I work for McAvoy Investigations." She pulled out a card to give to Vesta who, after reading seemed intrigued.

"Oh, what the hell." Vesta shrugged and held out a set of keys from her apron pocket. "There, a box in the corner with her name on it. You can have it whatever's in the thing." She held out a key to me and pointed to a door in the back of the shop.

Inside the small room, I found Cherry's box filled with more photographs, small cameras of various designs, costume jewelry, hair products and dozens of music CDs. Some of the jewel cases were opened. Most remained still wrapped in plastic. Did Cherry sell music on the side? I read a few of the titles; most were rap, dance and techno music from artists I didn't know, an eclectic mix. I returned to the photographs and found a picture of Louis Mackie with an arm around Cherry in a tight embrace. In the photograph, he seemed younger and hadn't yet discovered his anger. I slipped this picture in my pocket and continued to search in the hope I could find a clue to Cherry's whereabouts. I didn't.

When I exited the small storage room some time later, I found an exceedingly different Allie sits in the chair. I'd lost track of how long I'd been in the room, but now her shoulder length brown hair had been replaced by a short, blonde bob cut.

"Allie?" I gasped.

I'd promise Lee I'd take care of his sister. I swore she would be fed, watered and changed regularly. Being the lawyer that he was, would our agreement include an extreme makeover by Ms. Vesta? I didn't think so. My mouth opened but nothing came out. Shock tended to do that to me. I turned to Maggie who struggled to keep a smile on her face.

"Why didn't you say something?" I complained.

Maggie shrugged. "She wanted to keep it a surprise?"

I glowered at her.

Surprise?

If surprises were a feeling of shock, wonder, or bewilderment produced by an unexpected event, then yes I was surprised.

CHAPTER

13

Vesta didn't have any clues as to Cherry's whereabouts. After leaving Brooklyn, we took our only lead I got from the business card at Cherry's work station. Besides being there the night Rovell died, what other connections did Cherry had to Rovell? Bebe alluded to some bad blood between her and the Mackies. Was there more? As always, the tight-lipped sous chef seemed reluctant to elaborate.

RTM stood for Rovell Talent Management Company. Former R & B singer, Linwood Rovell established the business in the late nineties. From what little information Maggie found on the business, RTM's main purpose was to promote and manage local artists in the entertainment business. Revenues reported by the business were meager, yet showing a steady climb each year. One of their biggest assets was a converted furniture store that housed their offices and recording studio in Queens Village, a mostly residential area in the borough of Queens.

We called the number on the card and gave Tania Rovell Coffey a deliberately vague introduction. Surprisingly, she agreed to a meeting. We found the accommodating thirty-something woman had only a slight resemblance to her once-famous father. Slightly taller and fuller than me, she had a round face the color of cinnamon, and large almond-shaped eyes. She wore minimal make-up, which didn't lessen her attractiveness. Despite working in the entertainment industry, she dressed rather plainly, with little adornments, save large gold hoop earrings and a wedding ring. She could have been an office manager or sales representative. I kind of expected something more flamboyant.

She greeted us at the door and apologized for the lack of a receptionist. The girl had gone missing leaving her to manage the small office on her own. Our arrival had interrupted a meeting, and she asked us to take a seat in the waiting area by her office.

While we waited, Maggie perused her gun book, Allie touched up her make-up, and my attention went to the closed door only a few feet away from Tania's office. The nameplate read Linwood Rovell, President. She'd been left to run his business on her own. I'd wondered where the rest of the RTM employees were. The place was cavernous, with a high ceiling and large storefront windows that hinted back to the building's commercial history. RTM would never be mistaken for a multimillion dollar music empire, but someone put considerable effort to make the place comfortable, clean, and professional. There were posters, pictures, and community award plaques decorating the walls of the small reception area. Linwood Rovell must have been proud of this place.

The sound of hurried footsteps shattered my mild contemplation. We turned in unison at the appearance of a slight, black man in a blue Oxford shirt, tan khakis, and brown loafers. He reminded me of an accountant.

He burst into the reception area precariously carrying a cardboard tray of coffee cups. Surprised at our presence, he almost dropped the tray. He seemed unsure of how to respond to our presence and settled on an uneasy smile. He glimpsed at

Tania's closed office door, and back at us.

"Hi," Maggie said, breaking the discomfort we all felt.

The sudden opening of Tania's office door stopped the man's reply. Out stepped two of the largest men I'd ever seen outside the NFL, and pro wrestling. One was white with closely cropped hair so blond he appeared bald. His round head, small ears, and acne-scarred skin detracted from his startling pale gray eyes. His dark suit accentuated his muscles but washed out the rest of his features. He seemed familiar, but I was unable to place where I'd seen him before.

The other man was black and broad with a trimmed beard, shaved head, dark down swept eyes, and had permanent scowl. Dressed neat but casual in loose-fitting clothes, which contradicted the ostentatious thick gold chain, Rolex, and diamond studs he wore. He had a slight resemblance to the coffee guy, same broad nose, and down-turned mouth, but no fullness in the cheeks. They had to be related.

"You kinda of late, Gerald," the black man said brusquely.

"There was a line," Gerald said and took on the demeanor of a disobedient puppy who'd displeased his master and pissed on the rug. He held out the coffee under the disapproving gazes of the two men.

"Thanks for coming." Tania stepped between them.

"I'm here to help." The black man's face softened somewhat, but it didn't seem to reach his eyes.

For some reason, I developed an instant, almost primal, dislike for him. He took up too much space and crowded too close to Tania, who seemed ill-at-ease in the presence of the men. Tania's awkwardness was saved by a loud, intrusive buzzer. The sound propelled her from her immobility as she went to the receptionist desk and pressed a button on a small intercom. She explained to a deliveryman about the loading dock at the back of the building.

"I'm sorry about this, just let me take this order, and I'll be right back," she said hastily to Allie, Maggie, and me.

"Please, don't rush on our account," Maggie said.

Tania seemed grateful for our patience. "Thanks for coming Lamar,"

The man called Lamar grasped her hands. Meant to be a comforting gesture, Tania seemed trapped in the man's embrace. She inelegantly pulled away.

"If you need anything…" Lamar began, but an apologetic Tania offered a quick goodbye before dashing toward the back of the building, presumably toward the loading dock.

We all watched her go, leaving an uncomfortable silence in her wake. Maggie went back to reading her gun book. Allie admired her nails, and I found a particular nice spot the wall to examine.

"Hello ladies. I'm Lamar Jones." He waited a beat for some reaction from us. There were none. We didn't know him from a hole in the wall. Gerald stood behind the two men still holding the tray of coffee like some offering these gods had forgotten.

"Hi," Maggie said.

Allie went back to her nails, and I didn't say a word. My dislike for the man seemed irrational, but I couldn't ignore it.

"You here to see Tania on business?" His tone remained affable but probing. "I only ask because I thought I was familiar with all her business associates."

I felt my eyes widen in mild skepticism. Tania and this Lamar character didn't seem like fast friends. It was clear he was fishing for information. Equally, we didn't want to give it. Maybe he foolishly thought we were a girl group hoping for an audition.

"We're here for the receptionist's job." I expected no reaction at all, but Lamar's mouth twitched in displeasure.

"I thought Jeanette was only out sick for a few days," he said to the blond man next to him.

I caught an almost imperceptible lift of Maggie's brow. She'd picked up on the same thing I had. Tania told us her receptionist had been a no-call, no-show, and said nothing about an illness. Obviously, Lamar knew a little more about Tania's employee than she did.

"I think Jeanette's coming back, so there isn't any opening," he said.

The blond man nodded and locked eyes on Maggie.

"And you are?" I said to Lamar's hefty friend. I ignored the comment about my employment prospects.

"Oh, this guy, we call him Bear, he does my security." He gave the man a slap on the back, which sounded as if he'd struck a brick wall. Bear appeared preoccupied by Maggie.

"Hobby," he said in a mocking tone.

Everyone took notice of the book on her lap, its cover decorated with a shiny silver handgun. He gave her an odd little smile before unbuttoning his suit jacket, and letting it hang open. I didn't have to guess what was hidden. Maggie's wide-eyed reaction seemed clear enough as well as the telltale shoulder holster strap peeking out of his collar. Bear had a gun. I had no doubt Maggie could probably tell him the make, and model. To her credit, she recovered nicely. I didn't.

"Profession," she said.

Bear smirked before he and Lamar exploded in laughter. From the flush on Maggie's face, and the narrowing of her eyes, she didn't appreciate their reaction.

"Yeah, what profession is that?" a bemused Bear asked.

I knew Maggie wanted to whip out her investigator's license, but she didn't have one. She wouldn't have one for a while if Frank had his way. At best, she could manage a library card, and her supermarket membership. Thankfully, Tania saved us with her reappearance. She seemed surprised the men had remained, but quickly read our discomfort. "Ladies why don't you go into my office." She gestured toward the open door, and a means of escape.

"Do you want me to stay out here?" a wide-eyed Allie asked. Clearly, she didn't want to be left alone.

"No!" Maggie pulled Allie out of her seat, took her passed the two men, and into Tania's office.

Lamar and Bear grinned. I lingered back. Protective of Maggie since we began our friendship in high school, the men's attitudes toward her annoyed me. Often picked on for her size and sweet demeanor, she rarely stood up for herself. I gladly took that role.

"Touchy little thing?" Lamar joked. My initial dislike morphed into red-hot loathing.

Before I even wanted to stop myself, I turned to face them. "She's been a little touchy since she left the agency," I said apologetically as a wild scenario played in my head.

"What agency?" Lamar wore a bemused grin.

I kept my expression non-committal. "She has a nondisclosure clause at her termination… I mean her… retirement." I said it with as much seriousness as I could muster. This seemed to get Bear's interest.

"Retire from what, the Girl Scouts or F.B.I.?" he teased. Inside Tania's office Maggie glowered at him.

"Please, don't mention the F.B.I. The last time she got involved with them, they put her on the no-fly list. She wants a normal life, you know." My concern seemed genuine, if not theatrical. This gave the men pause.

"You're telling me…" A disbelieving Lamar pointed at Maggie.

I held up a hand to stop him as if that would send the diminutive housewife and mother in an uncontrollable rage.

"Hey, I'm not saying a thing. You think everybody has to dress like the secret service or him?" I pointed to Bear. "Listen, she can't talk about it, I can't talk about it, but I try to give people the heads up, you know? With her anger issues, she could seriously hurt someone. I think she overcompensates because of her size."

"N.S.A?" Bear said in a conspiratorial whisper.

I inwardly smiled.

"Bull shit," Lamar said in disbelief. Now both men seemed intrigued by the five foot nothing redhead. Maggie's brow furrowed at the increased attention. I read the expression for what it was. Her confusion over why we were staring at her, but I imagined that Bear and Lamar read it as menacing, or at least, Maggie's version of menacing.

"C.I.A?" Bear asked.

I huffed in exasperation. "Just back off a bit, she'll calm down, and forget you."

"Forget me! You expect me to believe—" Lamar began but I stopped in with an upraised finger. "Is it possible?" he asked Bear. The bodyguard's appraising eyes lingered on the small form. Then he shrugged.

"Had a Philippine martial art instructor the size of a turd kick my ass every which way and Sunday," the large man said in a half-wistful remembrance. It would be just like him to have fond memories of someone kicking his butt.

My inside smile grew wider. I felt a little guilty about misleading them, but not much. Chances were we'd never cross the paths of Lamar and his overgrown guard dog again. I left them with the thoughts of Killer Maggie, the super agent, entered Tania's office, and took a seat by her.

"Why were they staring at me?" Maggie asked. Lamar and Bear remained just outside the door. "They wondered why you were unfriendly. I said you recently got thrown out of the

P.T.A., and you're still pissed about it," I whispered to her.

Maggie huffed and scowled at the two men. "I didn't get kicked out, I quit."

This time a little doubt registered on their faces. When they finally left, my grin widened.

"You called the chairman a jerk, and announced he'd embezzled money," I reminded her. A week ago, she'd gone Gonzo on the chairman at the local P.T.A. during a budget meeting. She displayed copies of receipts to the Golden Palace Restaurant, airline tickets, and his wife's liposuction, all paid for by the organization slush fund.

"I had the evidence to prove it." Maggie crossed her arms and jutted out her tiny chin.

I grinned knowing her super powers of investigation weren't limited to cheating husbands or thieving employees. In all honesty, her righteous indignation, non-reaction to Bear, and an inability to see herself as less than capable or small in anyone's eyes, made her fearless—at least to me. I believed big things sometimes came in small packages. I had Lamar and Bear believing this too.

CHAPTER

14

Cherry started to rank up there on the elusive creatures list, Big Foot came in a close second. Tania had little to say on the whereabouts of Sherrilyn *'Cherry'* Turnbull. She'd met the woman through Louis Mackie when the young singer became enamored with her. Her father thought the girl too distracting, but Louis wouldn't listen. He was in love, or lust, she hadn't figured out which. So, Cherry became a fixture at the RTM studio. When Louis got into trouble, she disappeared. So far, in my book, Cherry wasn't winning any merit badges. I'd never met the woman, but based on her interaction with Bebe the night Rovell died, her unproductive work employment at Vesta's hair salon, and now her brief romantic, or should I say opportunist relationship with Louis, my opinion about her had solidified. I didn't like her.

"She wanted to star in Louis' music video," a bemused Tania said, shaking her head. "We barely had the deals with the record labels, and she'd already planned her wardrobe. She actually thought we should pay for it."

"Obviously she meant a lot to Louis," I said, sarcastically.

Tania wrinkled her nose. "Louis liked her because she never said no, and told him how famous he'd be, like Jay-Z or some silliness."

I'm sure the sight of Cherry in a push-up bra won him over, as well.

"She's not one for staying around, is she?" Maggie said.

Tania shook her head. "She'd been there the day Louis got arrested. The next day, no one could find her. I told my father good riddance, we had enough to deal with getting Louis out of trouble."

"But he still went to jail," Maggie said.

Tania sighed and picked up a picture of her father off her desktop. "Dad never saw that one coming. Louis was wild, not reckless. He liked running with a fast crowd, but deep down he stayed a terrific kid. Afterwards, the record deals we had lined up vanished. I think it hurt Dad that he couldn't keep Louis out of jail. He took that as a failure." Her eyes began to tear.

Maggie pulled some tissue from her purse, and handed them to her. Tania waved them off and wiped her face with the back of her hand. "I need to stop this." She took a deep breath and then another. "Daddy worked so hard, and I can't let the place fall apart."

"These are difficult times for you. People would understand if you weren't ready yet." Maggie's voice was calm and reassuring.

"Daddy used to be part of this group in the seventies. Not bad, but mid-level talent he'd say." She smiled at the memory. "Their manager stole from them, and left them nothing, not even their royalties for the music they wrote. The group broke up. Dad learned a trade as a plumber. Did all right, but his heart never left music. He'd perform on the weekends, singing with some of his former group members, finding other talent. He had a dream about this place, representing artists and protecting them from the people who might take advantage of them."

"Artists like the Mackies," I said.

She nodded. "Dad had some serious music companies interested in doing a two-record deal with them. Then the arrest happened and everyone backed off. They wouldn't take Dad's calls." Absentmindedly Tania straightened out the picture of her father on her desk.

"When Louis got out, he went back to your father," I said.

"Yeah, everything seemed to get back on track. Daddy never lost faith in Louis, and promised him the moment he got out he'd be there for him. The party had been for Louis," Tania said.

"With him back, did Cherry show up? Someone said she came to the party," I said.

Tania shook her head. "Daddy wouldn't have invited her. After what happened, Louis hated her."

"So you didn't see her there?" Maggie asked.

"To be honest, I stayed for about an hour, and then I had to go home. One of my daughters took ill. When I left, the party was in full swing."

"She might have come after you left," Maggie suggested.

"I doubt it. Jermaine or Louis would have told me. You could ask Les Henry, our studio engineer. He stayed until the end. He always closes up with Dad." She held up a finger and pressed the intercom on her desk.

"Hey Les, can you come into my office for a moment?"

Five minutes later, a white, middle-aged man with a bald spot walked into the room, wearing Bermuda shorts, a Hawaiian shirt and sandals. His russet brown hair was dry and in need of a wash. It matched the color and condition of his oversized handlebar mustache. Massive headphones hung around his neck. He wore tiny shaded glasses, which made judging his eye color impossible. He appeared as out of place at RTM as my churchgoing Auntie Renne at a Satan for President Rally.

From the music playing over the loudspeakers, photographs and posters on the walls, I had no doubt that R & B, Hip Hop, and Pop music were RTM's style of choice. However Les reminded me of a salesman who tried to sell me a timeshare in Florida. His Lynrd Skynrd Concert t-shirt didn't help. Were my own prejudices showing?

"I hear you're trying to find Cherry Baby," he said in a wacky western twang. "Walls are pretty thin."

He wiggled his eyebrows at an awestruck Allie, threw her a hundred yard smile before taking a seat. I wondered what kind of mojo my future sister-in-law had, that attracted, overweight, fashion-challenged men.

"Cherry Baby?" Maggie questioned.

Les shrugged. "After a while, everybody is a baby to me… or sweetie, or honey," he said with a large, toothy grin. He gave Maggie the once-over as if to contemplate what to call her.

"Tania said you were at the party the night her dad died," I said.

Les lost his smile and nodded. "Great party, good food, good times." His gaze drifted away and fell on Tania. They shared a moment of mutual sadness before he focused back on us.

"You stayed the entire party?" I asked.

"Yeah, me and the boss man always locked up. We had an early recording session with the Mackie brothers. He said he needed to work on a few more things in the office, and then he'd go. Should have stayed around, but I shut the front gate, and drove home." He shook his head.

"Did Cherry make an appearance?" Maggie asked.

Les laughed. "Trust me, if Cherry was in the building you'd know. She'd be snapping her damn camera in everyone faces, and asking for favors. She wasn't there."

"You're sure?" I asked with some doubt, knowing Bebe

wouldn't lie to me.

"Trust me Honey Buns, Louis would have sniffed her out. I've been around long enough to smell trouble," he joked.

"You've worked here long?" I asked, curious about his history. The whole southern boy, Hawaiian shirt, and 1970 mustache had me intrigued and somewhat confused.

"Hell yeah. Been in the business for almost thirty years. Started with a band in high school, did a little managing, and about everything else until Wood called me with a sweet gig. I wanted to keep my ass in one place, anyway."

"Wood?" I asked.

"Linwood. Everyone called him Wood—at least the ones he liked. Anyway, back in the day, I produced some Bluegrass act in Nashville. Got sick of that real fast. Went into trucking for a steady paycheck. Got sick of that even faster. Wood gives me a call about setting up a recording studio for him. I said hell yeah, be like old times."

"What old times?" Maggie asked.

"When Wood ran with his group. The head singer turned into some tight ass jazz freak now. Always changing the arrangement, a damn pain. When the manager ran off with the money, Wood found out he didn't have a pot to piss in. Had a house, a mortgage, a kid, and nothing to show for working in the business." Les gave Tania a quick smile.

"Daddy built a small studio in our basement. He always had people hanging around making music. He found a few artists to work with, promoted them, and got a strong reputation. He found this place, put on a second mortgage, and the rest became history," Tania said.

"He worked hard, real old school. Wood recognized raw talent." Les ran his fingers through what little hair he had left.

"What's going to happen now that your dad's gone?" I asked Tania.

She bit her lower lip and seemed unsure.

"We're good," Les announced. "If we can keep those sons of bitches away."

"Who might they be?" I asked, surprised at his intensity.

"Those vultures trying to get a free ride. Take advantage of Tania Baby here. Ain't gonna happen." Les shook head.

"You mean Lamar?" Maggie had jumped to the same conclusions I had.

"He came by to give his condolences," Tania said, but no one believed her.

"He's just scratching for a way in, like a rat, and Wood recognized a rat, even if it wore fancy clothes." Les's anger was still palpable. Lamar wouldn't win any popularity contest at RTM.

"They knew each other?" I asked.

Les huffed. "Name's been in the papers enough, more for trouble than anything else. Thinks he's a big man, all hardcore, and all asshole. He gets one talented artist and some play on the charts and he thinks he's a big time music rep. He wants to get into clothing and merchandising wanting to be the next Russell Simmons. First, he needs some real talent, instead the old school hardcore crap that's been played out. All his good artists jumped ship if they had a chance, and the rest ain't been seen from. He treats his talent like dirt, steals their money, and dumps them when they're numbers tank," Les said.

"Lamar has a reputation of finding a lot of street talent. Local kids. Most of these kids are naive. He promises them the world and leaves them with nothing once the parties are over," Tania explained.

"He sounds like a terrific guy," I said acerbically.

"Daddy didn't like him much. They had different styles," Tania said, but she sounded too diplomatic.

"Wood didn't trust him. Be honest, Tania baby. He

wanted the Mackies, and Wood knew it. Wood was class. He wanted to teach those boys this was a business, not some candy land," Les said.

"Lamar wanted to merge with us. He thinks there was strength in numbers when it comes to us independents. At least that's what he always told my dad. Daddy never took him up on the offer. He played nice, but wouldn't turn his back on Lamar. Dad still had some decent contacts and a solid reputation in the industry. People didn't mind doing deals with him." Tania shrugged.

"Lamar wasn't at the party?" Maggie asked.

"Hell no. You don't let a jackal into your house. Lamar liked to throw money around, and some of these youngsters confused that with caring," Les huffed in disgust.

"After Daddy died he came around asking about how I was doing. But before long, he's asking about my artists, especially Louis, and Jermaine. I know what he wants," Tania said.

I knew what he wanted too. I finally remembered where I'd seen Lamar's bodyguard before. He'd been in the flashy SUV that had brought Louis to the precinct to confront Bebe. I debated whether I should give this news to an already-troubled Tania, who was struggling to hold onto her father's dream. Now, Lamar had begun to court Louis with fancy clothes and a new ride. Had he aimed Louis at Bebe like a loaded gun? If so, for what purpose?

What also unnerved me a bit was Bear. Had he remembered seeing Maggie and me with Bebe? If he had, I believe he would have told Lamar. This explained Lamar's sudden interest in us. Did I like the idea that we were on Lamar's radar? Not particularly. I understood nothing of the of hip hop producer's world, and wasn't too keen in getting drawn into it. I would have preferred that he was a classical loving techno geek who didn't need a bodyguard.

CHAPTER

15

After following Maggie and me around Brooklyn searching for Cherry and filling herself with one of Bebe's best dishes—oxtail stew with sautéed greens—Allie ensconced herself in the cake shop with Esperanza. Esperanza insisted on teaching her how to make pink fondant roses. After the twelfth attempt, a frustrated Allie decided to work in the front with the customers. She liked being around people, and they seemed to like her. The moment she got behind the register her inhibitions vanished. Her quick change of temperament jarred me at times, but I sympathized with her uncertain state. I'd been left of center myself some time back. I wanted to help her, but I couldn't get her to talk to me. As she served customers with a smile on her face and not a care in the world, I held off grilling her like a suspect in a murder investigation. I went in search of my other murder suspect.

I found Bebe in the middle of the Blue Moon kitchen directing kitchen traffic and filling dinner tickets. The tension and the stress of the investigation were absent. He was in his element, like a fish in water. Despite the small bandage hidden behind a white bandana, he seemed unfazed by his circumstance. Since Rovell's murder, this had been his first full dinner service. I thought he might not be ready, but Candace insisted he work. For her, work cured all ills. When I lost my advertising job and a little bit of my sanity, she insisted I come to the restaurant. She literally dragged me out of bed one day, dressed me and sat me in a chair in the corner. The first day I cried. The next day she threw me in the kitchen out of sight of customers who might not want to watch my meltdown over lunch. In the kitchen, under George's watchful eye, I busied myself making cakes. The same cakes I made with my mother as a little girl. The simple act of baking saved my life. Certain the American Psychiatric Association didn't recognize baking therapy, it helped me. Watching the sheen on Babe's forehead and his purposefulness in his motion, cooking had become his therapy of choice. If Bebe was a fish, the kitchen was his ocean.

"Has the great Ziemann spoken to you?" I sat at the end of one of the large prep table eating a plate of spicy grilled shrimp on a bed of creamy grits.

"I called him, told him where I'm hanging and stuff," he said. The dinner service had quieted down, and he had time to talk. "He doesn't like it, me at Mrs. Swift's house."

"Why? Didn't you tell him about Louis?" I asked.

Bebe nodded. "I think it has more to do with me being at Mrs. Swift's house and you."

I rolled my eyes at Ziemann's problem with Maggie and me. We were on the same side, weren't we? "Tell him to get over it," I said dryly. This elicited a rare smile from him.

"He said the cops won't drop me as the guy they're looking for." He turned away and surveyed the kitchen, possibly measuring what he might lose if the police arrested him again.

"We'll find Cherry, and she'll clear everything up." At least I wanted to believe this. Bebe didn't seem confident.

Before I said, say anything else, one of the waitresses, named Gloria came with a dinner ticket. He took the ticket from her and began calling orders to the kitchen staff.

"You got more faith in Cherry than anyone I know," he said.

I wanted to finish my conversation with Bebe, but the waitress caught my eye. "I need to speak to you." A worried sounding Gloria pulled me over to the kitchen's slightly opened double door and pointed at a table near the far wall. My breath caught at the sight of Lamar, Bear and Gerald.

"They were asking a lot of questions about Bebe, and they weren't talking about his cooking."

"Like what?" I asked.

"When does he get off and stuff." Gloria's worried express mirrored how I felt. .

"What the hell are they doing here?" I pushed through the doors and headed for their table. How had Lamar found me? I slowed a bit when I remembered the conversation Maggie had with Bear about guns. I took a deep breath, weighed my options, realized I had none, and stormed toward the table anyway.

"Why are you here?"

Lamar's disingenuous smile beamed up at me. Men who smiled too much always worried me. They either didn't have a care in the world or didn't care about the world.

"Ms. Wilkes," he said.

Bear's lips twisted up in a sneer. Gerald seemed to shrink away at the growing tension. He wanted to be somewhere else. I didn't blame him; I wanted him and his friends someplace else too.

"This is a surprise," I said, trying hard to hide my apprehension.

Lamar shrugged. "Oh, Gerald said you had some cake

shop nearby and had the urge for something sweet. We saw the restaurant and stopped for lunch."

"I Googled the name and the Times gave you a great review," Gerald chirped.

I didn't need a compliment; I needed him and his buddies to leave.

“Shut up, Gerald, sometimes you talk too much,” a dispassionate Lamar said. Gerald seemed to melt away. This made me wonder about the dynamics of their relationship.

"Where's your little friend?" Bear asked, scanning the dining area.

"Home cleaning her guns," I snapped. I didn't like his growing interest in Maggie, considering I'd been the one to make him curious.

"I can never tell if you're serious or not." Lamar lost a little of his smile and the lines around his eyes deepened. "How’d your visit with Tania go? You get that receptionist job?"

I said nothing as he held his gaze on me, maybe to intimidate, or maybe trying to read me. I began to understand how Gerald felt. The anticipation of someone lashing out at you would demoralize anyone.

"I wonder what she'd say if she knew you were connected to a boy who killed her daddy. As a friend, I should tell her." His soft tone didn't suppress the threat.

I swallowed hard and tried not to show my unease. "A friend?" I mocked and putting on the best game face I could.

Lamar sat back in his chair, arms crossed, too pleased with himself.

"We didn't go there to talk about her father's murder anyway."

"Then what?" he asked.

"None of your business," I snapped.

"Won't say." His body tensed with restraint as he clenched and unclenched his hands. "So you're telling me this has nothing to do with Rovell's death?"

“I'm telling you, it's none of your business.” I prayed I didn't sound as shaky as I felt. I wished Maggie were here, she would have said it nicer but the message would have remained the same. I wouldn't willingly tell Lamar anything and it was the unwilling part that had me worried.

"Why don't we enjoy our dinner?" Gerald offered, his face pleading for calm against the mounting tension.

"Shut up, Gerald." Lamar's raised voice caught the attention of the nearby diners. "Sometimes my brother don't know when to keep his damn mouth closed. Thinks he smart, but not so much, huh bro?"

Gerald's eyes fixed on the center of the table. He clasped his hands together and sat like a third grader on punishment. Lamar smiled. Bear remained indifferent to the family drama. I bet Gerald wished he'd been adopted.

"I've got to go.” I wanted distance between Lamar and his entourage.

"We're not finished, Ms. Wilkes," Lamar barked.

As if on cue, Bear stood up as if to emphasize how much space he took up in a room. I took a step back. Lamar pulled out an empty chair and patted it as if I were some pet. I shook my head. I'd rather be dropped down a rabbit hole head first than spend time with the man.

"George!" someone from behind me yelled.

I turned to see the imposing figure of the Blue Moon chef, George Fontaine standing in the doorway getting a hug from one of the waitresses. Candace frowned at the open display of affection between her staff, but this didn't hide the smile forming on her lips. With everyone's attention pulled to the commotion at the front of the restaurant, I took the opportunity to walk away from Lamar's table. I sensed his eyes on my every step.

"God, where the hell have you been?" I wrapped my arms around George's hulking frame.

"Hey there." He gave me a hesitant pat on the back. A large man, it was hard to get my arms around his broad shoulders, but I tried. I took in his warm brown face, with its day-old stubble, and tired eyes before I let him go. He felt as comfortable as a safe harbor in what appeared to be a growing storm.

"Now where is my boy?" he asked.

"I'm so glad you're here." I smiled.

"Christ Odessa, you act like he just came home from the war," Candace complained.

I ignored her and pulled George toward the kitchen, passed Lamar's table and watchful eyes.

Inside the kitchen, the world stopped as Bebe and George hugged the way men did, brief and intense. Bebe brightened at the sight of his mentor. George placed a firm hand behind Bebe's neck and let it linger.

"I'm okay," Bebe said, but his voice cracked a bit.

"Is someone going to tell me what the hell is going on?" George turned to me.

I walked over and tried not to smile too much, seeing them both together. "The police believe Bebe killed someone. He has an asshole for a lawyer, and Maggie and I are trying to find out the truth."

George's eyebrows slowly rose with a hint of incredulity. "And that truth is?"

"Someone killed a talent agent, and they used Bebe's chef knives to do it," I rattled off.

George rubbed his large face with his hands as if wiping off the dust of travel and disbelief. "This is a mess." He sighed.

"I'm staying with Mrs. Swift," Bebe said.

This confused George.

"Bebe's not safe in his neighborhood right now, and you weren't here," I accused.

"I'm here now." George still seemed unsure of the situation. "Right now, I'm exhausted. Flew in from New Orleans and I had a three hour layover."

"I thought you went to Atlanta," I said.

"I was, but ended up in New Orleans. Sorry I didn't leave word. Hopefully, the world won't turn to crap tonight, so I'm going to head home and get some sleep. I just wanted you to know I'm here now, okay." He placed his large hand on Bebe's shoulder and squeezed.

"Okay," Bebe said.

The sight nearly brought me to tears until George glared at me. No one cried in George's kitchen and lived to tell about it. He gave Bebe a reassuring pat on the back and headed toward the dining room. I followed, and half expected Bear to jump out at me, but they were gone. Their table was cleared and reset.

While George grabbed his suitcase, he'd left by the front desk, I asked Candace about Lamar. When she smiled at me, I began to worry.

"Oh, they decided to take it to go. They said something came up. But guess what?" She rubbed her hands together excitedly.

I didn't want to speculate, but asked anyway.

"He has some kind of launch party or something next Monday, and he wants you to do a cake for three hundred people." Pleased with herself, she smiled broadly.

"What!" I exclaimed.

"His brother… I can't recall his name, but he paid in full," she said. This of course was the reason for her happiness.

"Candace, don't you think you should have talked to me about it?" I tried to hold my temper.

"I checked with Esperanza and your schedule is clear. You seemed chummy with him at his table." Once again, Candace jumped to conclusions. I'm sure Lamar's credit card made us real good friends. I wanted to explain to her I distrusted this man and was a little fearful of him.

"What's wrong?" George said, reading my discomfort.

"Nothing." I'd worry about Lamar later.

"Sure?" George tried to suppress a yawn. He wore a light jacket and beneath a brand new t-shirt with an illustration of Key West.

I pulled open the jacket to reveal more of the shirt. "I thought you went to New Orleans?"

"New Orleans?" Candace questioned, eyeing the shirt a while.

"By way of Key West," he said, carefully pulling my hand away. He wiggled his eyebrows at me and grinned. I shook my head knowing if I asked a thousand questions, I doubted he'd answer any of them. George has had several professional incarnations, marine, taxi driver, boxer and now chef and those were the ones he told us about. Right now, I was glad he was home.

CHAPTER

16

The next morning I woke to an empty bed and utter silence. Usually, Saturday morning began with the sounds of Lee rummaging through the house as if he were Indiana Jones in search of the Ark of the Covenant. An ex-jock from his high school and college days, he and other like-minded professionals played basketball at the local high school—men playing contact sports meant for athletes ten years younger and in better condition. They geared up with knees, wrists and thighs wrapped for support and a generous coating of some sport gel that stank to high heaven. Afterward, Lee dragged his tortured body home, and stood in a hot shower as long as he could tolerate before becoming human again. Once I asked him why he put himself through the abuse. From his scornful scowl, you have thought I'd asked him to withdraw his Man Card, or something. I never asked again.

Instead of the sound of kitchen cabinets slamming in search of power drink or bottle water, I heard silence. Normally, I would enjoy this peace and roll over to sleep for another hour or so, but the quiet felt deafening. My Spidery senses tingled at the unnaturalness. I forced myself out of bed and headed downstairs.

In the living room, I found Lee's open gym bag on the

floor, the contents hung out like guts. I found him standing in the kitchen doorway. He appeared normal, dressed in a t-shirts and shorts, but he remained stone still. Approaching, I peered passed him, to find what held his attention so thoroughly.

Oh Christ!

Allie sat at the table, blonde hair and all, with a bowl of cereal in front of her. Thankfully, she'd washed off the makeup, which didn't diminish the dramatic effect of her new hairdo. Adding to the shock value was the oversize black t-shirt I'd given her to sleep in. The shirt had been purchased at a food convention, meant as a gift for George. I never had the courage to give it to him. With the confectioner's slogan of, *Bite Me* on the front, poor, pale Allie took Goth to a whole other level. Now all she had to do was recite lines from some radical manifesto, and Lee would have fainted. No wonder he stood dumbstruck; he didn't recognize her. This wasn't his married sister from San Bernardino.

I would have preferred the siblings deal with their issues right then and there, but I guess my expectations were too high. I felt frustrated. Seriously, how hard was it for two grown adults to sit down over a cup coffee and discuss their problems without reverting to their prepubescent state? They were the opposite of Candace and me. The Mackenzies went to their separate corners and never came out. Candace and I never even wasted time going into the corners.

"Hey." I slipped passed Lee and into the kitchen. An expression of total mystification and growing irritation grew on his face.

"Hey honey, you're going to miss picking up the guys." I plastered on a smile that almost hurt to maintain. He said nothing, took a deep strangled breath, and then turned his hazel eyes on me—the glaring gaze he reserved for criminals, difficult judges and annoying prosecutors.

"You were there when she did this?" He pointed at his sister, accusingly.

I turned to Allie, whose saucer eyes were like a deer in headlights. She had her hand on the carton of milk and a spoon in the other. Obviously, Lee had surprised her. I turned back to him.

"Tell me you didn't encourage this?" He'd gone icy on me.

His quick temper turned me a little frosty, as well. I huffed. The last time I checked, Allie was a grown, married woman with constitutional rights of her own. I was not her keeper, or jailer or her fashion consultant. I sighed deeply, hoping to find my inner Buddha, or Mother Theresa, or at least Reverend Al Sharpton.

"Lee, you have two choices." I stood in front of him, blocking his view of Allie. "You can go to your game and not think about why your sister has been body-snatched by some teenage girl, or you can sit down, have a real conversation and ask her."

His eyes flickered between his sister and me as if he was a mouse caught in a trap. Sitting around the kitchen table sharing his feelings wasn't what he had planned for a Saturday morning, or maybe any morning. He'd rather be knocked around by a few sweaty men than deal with his sister. He leaned away from me, turned and left.

Coward. The familiar sounds of him gathering his things, slamming the front door and driving away made it seem like my usual Saturday morning.

I shook my head, disgusted. Since they weren't going to talk, I opted to eat breakfast. I went to the cupboard, got out a bowl and spoon from the drainer. I took a seat next to Allie and poured cereal for myself. She remained a little shell-shocked. I had to take the milk carton from her hand to pour over my cereal. This seemed to jar her into the present.

Her eyes glistened with tears.

"No you don't." I pointed my spoon at her. "I haven't had a cup of coffee yet."

"I'm sorry." Allie gulped air between sobs.

I set down my spoon. I couldn't eat. Who could? She sounded like a strangled whale. She cried worse than Maggie. I wanted to tell her to snap out of whatever funk she'd found for herself before my cornflakes got soggy. But snap out of what? Was she depressed, suicidal or just demented? I didn't have an answer but the next best thing. I poured milk into her bowl.

"You better eat. We have to talk to Maggie," I said as if her brother hadn't abandoned her. Her crying subsided to an occasional sniffle.

"You still want me to come with you?" She seemed uncertain.

"Sure. Maggie has something to do at the office this morning, and she wants to talk about the case." I handed her a paper napkin, and she blew her nose thoroughly. We ate our cereal in relative quiet, with an occasional sniffle from Allie.

Later in the morning, a dry-eyed Allie and I drove towards Hicksville, New York and McAvoy Investigation Office. Located in a small strip mall fifteen minutes from Maggie's house, she spent all her free time there. I hoped Frank would be out. Usually, he spent his Saturday morning sleeping in and recovering from Friday nights, Thursday nights and Wednesday nights. Thankfully, Frank's late-model death trap wasn't in the parking lot. We did find Rocket and the family dog sitting at Frank's desk.

"Isn't this usually, Rocket and Roger's bonding time," I asked. Recently, Roger had complained to Maggie that he didn't think his son thought he was interesting. Considering Roger sold insurance how could you blame a kid? Maggie's recent incarnation as a private investigator in-training won brownie points with her son. So given the choice of whether Rocket wanted to learn about insurance actuary tables or how to do a background check on a potential spouse, Maggie won hands down every time.

"His father is playing golf," she said with some annoyance.

"Roger doesn't play golf," I said.

"He does now." She shook her head. "One of his clients took him to his country club and introduced him to the game. He brought some clubs and now he's talking about joining the club.

"I thought he was into fly fishing." I couldn't keep up with Roger's hobbies.

"He hates sitting around waiting for something to happen." Maggie shrugged.

"What about that thing.... huh, that bird watching thing?"

Again, she shook her head. "Still waiting around and too much nature, grass and trees."

"I guess he doesn't realize a golf course is nothing more than an over-manicured park."

Maggie closed her eyes and shook her head solemnly. She had lived through many of Roger's hobbies. Much of the time spent in the emergency room. I enjoyed the time he took up cycling. A torn Achilles tendon, two dislocated fingers and a lot of friction burns in spandex.

"How dangerous could golf be?" I said.

"Don't do it!" Allie cried suddenly.

I nearly jumped out of my skin. I checked to see if there was a fire or a meteor heading toward earth before I told my heart to calm itself. "Don't do what?" I asked.

"Join those horrible clubs." She exclaimed.

"Why?" Maggie asked.

"Trust me, before you can say who's in charge of the Mariachi Band, and the refreshment committee for the holiday dance, the teaching pro has already gone through half your liquor budget. It's a terrible job, and they gave it to you because you're new. They promise to be on your committee, but no one shows up. They invited you for a girls' weekend, but made fun of your sensible shoes and Super Cut hairstyle and your clothes from Target," Allie said almost in one breath.

Rocket put down his Nintendo Game. Even at his young age, he was assessing Allie's level of sanity. Mr. Macgregor sniffed the air as if crazy had a smell.

"Oh that's reason enough," Maggie said giving Allie a warm and sympathetic smile. "Most likely, Roger will become bored. Anyway, there's nothing wrong with shopping at Target. I love Target, and J.C. Penny and Sears."

"So, do I," Allie said, happy to find a comrade in style. They waited for me to add to the retail lovefest.

I shrugged. "I'm more of Niemen Marcus or a Saks kind of girl." I took a seat on the worn sofa Maggie found at a secondhand store.

"Are we getting anywhere with this Cherry thing?" I said, now that Allie and Maggie had bonded over their fashion sense. "The hair salon was a bust. Bebe couldn't wait for Cherry to show up and confessed she was with him the night Rovell died. No one will even admit seeing her."

"What about Lamar's alibi?" I asked.

"I checked. He was on that party boat and didn't return until the next day. He got a ride in some famous guy's helicopter. There were pictures of them on the gossip page and a few blogs. It couldn't have been Lamar."

"I kind of liked the idea of Lamar being our number one suspect." I sighed.

"He still isn't innocent," Maggie said.

"They won't arrest Bebe again, will they?" a concerned Allie asked. She hadn't been around the Blue Moon sous chef long, but I thought she liked him. She loved his food.

"I still think Rovell's death is tied to Lamar. I just don't know how." Though I didn't have a clue and from the blank expression coming from Maggie and Allie, neither did they.

"Maybe Cherry knows," Allie said.

"The woman doesn't file taxes. She has no credit cards, and she has no place of residence." Maggie retied her ponytail several times, a clear sign of her frustration.

"She's like a ghost, an irritating ghost," I said.

"Someone must know something about her. She has to live somewhere," Allie said.

"It seemed Cherry likes to make friends, exploit those friendships, take whatever monetary goods are available and then disappear," I lamented.

For an hour, we considered where an ex-hairdresser opportunist might go. She had no family to speak of, or any we could find. Maggie found a high school picture taken some time ago. Even then, the woman seemed as if she wanted to start trouble. Reduced to watching Mr. McGregor clean his hindquarters, while Allie preoccupied herself with some of Maggie's library books on investigation, and Rocket with his video game; I realized Maggie kept staring at me.

"Would you say Davis knows a lot about you?" Maggie asked.

"What?" Why would Maggie bring up my ex-boyfriend from hell? Did I ever bring up the fact she practically stalked Jimmy Welks in high school. She came close to tattooing his name on her chest, if I hadn't stopped her. I did not bring up these things because they were embarrassing and showed poor judgment and a great amount of stupidity.

"Who's Davis?" Allie asked. She'd been reading one of

Maggie's books on how to do wiretapping at the mention of my ex-boyfriend.

"A jerk and an asshole." I wanted to make sure everyone was clear on this point.

"How well did he know you?" a deliberate Maggie continued.

I glowered at her. There was no way I would talk about my ex-boyfriend in front of my current boyfriend's sister. "Why are you asking?"

"I mean, if someone asked him about you, what would he say?" From the expectant expression on her face, she was serious. She wanted me to speculate on a man who I thought I loved and who dumped me on the most miserable day of my life. I didn't care about Davis Frazier's opinion regarding me. I'd heard enough when we were dating.

"He'd have a lot to say, don't you think?" Maggie continued to push the point.

"Why would I care? I snapped.

"I wonder what Cherry's ex would say. I bet he could guess her likes and dislike. Where she'd like to hang out," she said smugly.

We knew of only one ex in Cherry's life, and that would be Louis Mackie. I smiled back at my friend and cocked an eyebrow at her.

"Who's Davis?" Allie repeated.

CHAPTER 17

Sometimes I worried about Maggie. Her rosy viewpoint on the human condition didn't suit her current aspiration to be a serious, private investigator. Sam Spade never worried if we all got along. To Maggie, life was a Hallmark card waiting to be read. As an ex-criminal before the age of twenty, I didn't think Louis Mackie had many Hallmark moments in him. Yet, Maggie expected to hold a civil conversation with a man who believed Bebe killed the closest thing to a father he'd ever had. Louis' anger engulfed him and all in his proximity. Possibly, he had a reason, given his past situation, but if he didn't lighten up, his social calendar would be free. I tried to explain to Maggie why Louis wouldn't talk to us. This didn't dissuade her.

"He'll want to know the truth about Rovell's death, won't he?" she asked. Only in Maggie's mind did this sound like a reasonable question. I wondered if she'd ask him before or after he took a shot at her.

"In his head, he has the truth," I said with equal certainty.

"But he's wrong," she said.

"At the precinct he wanted to kill Bebe," I said.

Only the presence of police outside stopped any confrontation. If Louis had laid a hand on Bebe, he would have broken a land speed record for the fastest arrest by the

NYPD.

"Odessa, you always exaggerate," she said, dismissing my concerns.

Was I the only in the room beside Mr. McGregor who had a realistic view of the world? Maggie's denial didn't help. Allie seemed firmly on Maggie's side since they bonded over fashion, and got no support from her. Anyway, she seemed busy keeping Rocket amused with funny voices, and pig jokes.

"What do pigs get when they're ill?" she said.

"Oinkment!"

"What do you call a pig that does karate?"

"Pork chops!"

Rocket laughed. Maggie laughed. I realized their appreciation of horrible animal jokes had to be genetic. After the fifth one, I tuned out; Mr. McGregor yawned, licked his privates, and went to sleep. I didn't have the luxury of such social ineptness, though I wouldn't mind a nap.

"What's worse than a male chauvinist pig?" Allie said. This got my attention because her voice went a little tight.

"A woman who won't do what she's told," Allie, sounded like a pissed off Daffy Duck.

Rocket didn't laugh.

"Why can't men get mad cow disease?" she continued. "Because men are pigs." Daffy seemed to have issues.

Rocket's confusion mirrored my own. We didn't get Allie's humor or her underlying hostility. She'd done an emotional shift thing, from happy to sad in under a minute, which left me a concerned. Candace's words bounced in my head again, about Lee's sister being a little left of center. I sighed, and wondered if my future children would answer back to the voices in their heads. I shook my head slowly, urging her to stop scaring the crap out of my godson. Rocket's dumbfounded expression must have confirmed her suspicion something was off. She plastered on a weak smile and moved on to jokes about chickens. I thankfully turned my attention back to Maggie.

"So, let me get this straight, you want to talk to Louis about Cherry. What makes you think Louis want to talk to us?" I said.

Maggie seemed undeterred by this problem. "Jermaine."

I blinked. My mind did this when Maggie made enormous leaps of deduction without giving me a road map. "Huh?"

"You ever wonder why Bebe got invited to Rovell's party?"

"Jermaine."

I knew that much.

"Bebe and Jermaine grew up together. Best friends until they had a falling out."

"What falling out?" I asked.

"Something." Maggie shrugged. "They renewed their friendship before Rovell's death and after."

"How do you know that?" I didn't think Bebe and Maggie sat down over cocoa and chatted. Bebe was as talkative as a log.

"Rocket's baby monitor," she said.

I still didn't have a map to this conversation and didn't have a clue as to what she was hinting at. I crossed my arms and waited.

"Rocket has been driving Bebe crazy using his old baby monitor as a walkie-talkie. He thinks he and Bebe are Special Forces or some silliness."

"We are." Rocket announced.

"Bebe has been sweet about it, but after an hour of it, I'd had enough," Maggie said.

"So." I gestured her to hurry up, Bebe might be in prison before I'd hear the end of the story.

"He left it on, and I heard Bebe call Jermaine. I meant to turn it off, but I thought it was odd considering how Louis reacted to him. Now his brother and Bebe are talking like he didn't believe Bebe murder Rovell."

"You spied on Bebe," I said, stunned.

"I overheard. Bebe doesn't go out of his way to express himself unless he's locked in an interrogation room. I can barely get a hello or goodbye from him. Though, he did have a lot to say to Jermaine."

"Like what?" I asked.

She frowned and set her lips in a tight line. When she refused to tell me, I huffed in response.

"You can spy on him, but you won't tell me?"

"I like to think of it as professional confidentially," Maggie said.

No doubt, something she read from one of her many library books written by Lars Putterman, a former Swiss intelligence agent, now an expert on anything that had to do with private investigation. He'd become one of her favorite authors. I had my doubts about Putterman: a secret agent from a country whose only major claims to fame had to do with banks, chocolates, a multipurpose knife and minding their own business.

"How convenient."

"He'll tell you when wants to," she said, giving me no clue.

We had a staring contest for half a minute before we got back on topic. Still a little surprised at Maggie's intrusion into Bebe's privacy, I wondered what went on in my friends' heads. For Bebe, who kept a secret better than the Pentagon, and Maggie who crossed a line I'd never thought she'd cross.

"Don't act so shocked. It has to do with the case," she insisted.

Still not pleased with being excluded, I settled back for the rest. "You're going to ask Jermaine to talk to Louis about Cherry? A woman he hates and hasn't spoken to in years." I had doubts about this.

"If I asked Davis about you, I'm sure he'd have some little tidbits. Maybe about where you like to eat, or your favorite hangout, your friends, and family," Maggie said.

"I wouldn't ask Davis for a bucket of water if my ass was on fire." Davis remained a sore point in my life.

"Who's Davis?" Allie said, her eyes wide with curiosity

"Auntie O's stupid boyfriend," Rocket said, and giggled.

"You have another boyfriend?" Allie's eyebrows lifted in surprise, and concern.

"No. I mean yes. I mean no. I mean Lee is my boyfriend." I gave Rocket a menacing look of my own.

"Rocket!" Maggie admonished her young son. "He's Odessa's ex-boyfriend, and don't call people stupid. It's not nice."

"He was stupid, and an idiot, but can we forget about Davis and get back to Jermaine?" I didn't want to regurgitate all my failures, bad judgment, and poor taste in men. I preferred to consider what would happen if we involved ourselves with another Mackie. Jermaine might be as hotheaded as his brother, and shoot us just for asking. Or he might tell his brother, and Louis would shoot us for asking. Either way didn't work for me.

"We talk to Jermaine, convince him to get Louis to help us find Cherry," Maggie said.

"Yeah right." I had a better chance convincing Louis to sing Broadway show tunes. However, Maggie persisted, and I caved.

"This morning I called Tania to ask if she could have Jermaine talk to us, but she was out doing some promotional thing. They still hadn't found a receptionist, and Les picked up. He said Jermaine was working at the studio, and we should stop by."

"You'd decided to do this even before you talked to me," I said, surprised at her determination. Maggie often threw caution to the wind if she found the answers to questions. Sometimes she needed a reality check to say she shouldn't put her hand in the lion's mouth, cross against the light, or piss off angry men just out of prison. Despite my misgivings, she'd been hard at work tracking down Cherry. She'd used a baby monitor as a listening device, and uncovered a relationship Bebe secretly kept. I decided to trust her decision to connect with Jermaine, though I wanted to stay as far away from the other Mackie as possible.

Maggie closed down the office, left a note for Frank, and we piled into the car, and headed for RTM in Queens Village. An hour later, we arrived at the small brick building and parked in the lot in the back. A dented pickup truck with Georgia plate, and a faded Doobie Brother Concert sticker on the bummer was the only other vehicle in the lot. This had to belong to Les. He met us by the front door, and guided to a small lounge area, and a promised Jermaine would come talk to us. Much to my consternation, he flirted with Allie and talked with Rocket for a while before Jermaine appeared in the doorway of the lounge. As he stood there, I didn't know what to expect, a hostile Jermaine or Bebe's friend. Surprisingly, we got a combination of both, receptive but guarded.

"Hey little man, want to see how we make records?" Les said to Rocket.

Rocket's eyes brightened for the first time all day. "Can Mr. McGregor come?" he asked. From beneath the table the dog perked up at the sound of his name. His tubular body waddled from beneath the table, and headed for the door. I guess you didn't have to ask him twice.

"How about you darling," Les asked Allie.

From the ear to ear grin on Allie's face, you didn't have to ask her twice. I thanked her. Rocket with the unsuspecting Les was just asking for trouble. His mother couldn't afford if he broke anything. Knowing my godson, he'd find something expensive.

"Can I come?" Allie asked.

Les's smile broadened. "Two is company, and three's a party. I'm sure you'll like what you'll find." I groaned. Allie had become a magnet for men with large egos, and nothing else. The three of them headed toward a set of stairs that led to the RTM basement recording studio.

Unlike his brother, Jermaine had none of the outward hostility. He appeared younger than his eighteen years and still dressed as if he were still in high school. While Louis played and dressed the role of an urban music star, Jermaine's attire seemed oddly bohemian, with his tight jeans, argyle socks, vest, and vintage Rare Earth t-shirt—a funky, eclectic style. Physically smaller and leaner of the two Mackies, he had a mature aloofness about him his brother lacked. While Louis' hostility seemed always front and center, it was hard to tell what the younger Mackie was thinking. He took a seat across from us.

"Les said you wanted to talk to me." His eyes danced between Maggie and me.

"Do you know who we—" I began.

"Bebe told me."

"What exactly did he say?" I asked with some trepidation.

"He said you make a coconut cake better than his mama, and your mouth should be registered as a lethal weapon." His mouth twisted into a sly grin. He turned to Maggie.

"He says you're too forgiving but smart, and if anyone

hurts you, he'd break their legs."

"How sweet," Maggie said, pleased Bebe had become her avenging angel.

"Yeah, that's our Bebe, sous chef, enforcer, and murder suspect," I said dryly. I didn't think I appreciated being assessed by someone several years my junior.

Jermaine lost his smile. Despite his youthfulness, you couldn't deny the intelligence behind his dark brown eyes. "He also said you two have a better chance at finding out who killed Wood than the cops." He gazed at us both. "Is he right?"

"Yes," Maggie blurted.

"Good, I want to hire you."

CHAPTER

18

A delusion is your mind telling your body it can fly. A catastrophe is your efforts to prove the point. In all honesty, I didn't think Maggie was delusional, but when she told Jermaine Mackie she'd take his case, a hint of crazy came into play there. The fact that she wasn't licensed and her boss would never agree to take on a case that didn't involve him sitting in a car eating stale donuts and drinking coffee. Frank McAvoy's skill set included finding wayward husbands, not murderers. Lately, though his mind hasn't been on work, period, he still had the credentials. This didn't deter Maggie, who had Jermaine believing she was the new and improved version of Sherlock Holmes.

I'd asked Jermaine to check on Rocket when Les started piping music through the sound system of my godson rapping a Kanye West song and Allie doing backup as Marilyn Monroe and Betty Davis. His absence gave me the opportunity to give Maggie another reality check.

"You can't," I said.

"It's just an extension of what we're already doing."

"No it's not," I said, annoyed with her selected view of reality. "We're trying to clear Bebe, not search for a murderer. Because, trust me girlfriend, I rather hunt for some low rent groupie than a guy who put knives into other people's backs." Maggie rolled her eyes and dismissed my concerns.

"Okay, we find Cherry and get her to tell the police Bebe's argument was with her, not Rovell. But she's going to answer another question too."

"Which is?"

"How she got into the party and what was she doing in Rovell's office?"

"She probably went to steal something." In truth, I didn't want to know how Cherry got into the party. I was afraid it had something to do with the exchange of bodily fluids. I just wanted Bebe off the police's radar. I wanted things to go back to normal. Trying to find a killer wasn't normal in my book.

"Who let you in?" a familiar voice said from behind us.

The sight of a disheveled and angry Tania left us flabbergasted. Next to her stood a pretty, young black girl who seemed to have gone through the same maelstrom as Tania. The girl plopped on a nearby chair shaking and sobbing.

"Are you all right?" I said.

"Do I look alright? How the hell I'm I alright?" Tania's strained face; wide eyes seemed on the verge of hysterics.

Maggie and I remained silent.

"What the hell are you doing here?" She gathered herself a bit, walked to the small refrigerator, retrieved a bottle of water and handed it to hand to the distraught girl. Tania cocked her head as she listened to Les' latest creation, which now included Jermaine, who added a sweet R & B vocal to the mess.

"Has everyone lost their goddamn mind?" she screamed. "What is that?"

"My son," Maggie croaked.

"Has something happened Tania?" I took a step closer, but stopped when she turned on me, her face twisted in a mixture of anger and frustration. "You've got some nerve coming here." She pointed at us.

"Excuse me." Maggie's confusion matched my own.

The last time we'd spoken to Tania, she had been warm and welcoming. Now her revulsion at the sight of us, made me wonder what happen since then.

"Hey, Tania," Jermaine said, nonchalantly as he entered the room. He froze at the sight of her appearance, and then his eyes fell upon the girl. "What happen to you, Keisha?"

The girl began to weep.

"You want to know what happened to Keisha?" Tania pointed passed him. "I'll tell you if someone turns that damn noise off." As if on cue, the speakers went dead, and Rocket's singing ended.

"Thank the Lord Jesus." Tania threw her arms in the air and rubbed her forehead. Her small shoulders heaved, then took in breath in an attempt to find calm.

"He wasn't that bad," Maggie murmured. Tania scowled at her.

"How did the signing go?" a tentative Jermaine asked.

Tania's scowl deepened. "There was almost a riot." Keisha's weeping intensified. Tania sat next to her and put an arm around the girl's shoulders.

"They went crazy," Keisha said between sobs. "I thought I was going to die."

Tania gave her a disingenuous smile and patted her shoulder. She was about to turn her fury back at Maggie and me when Rocket burst into the room. Tania narrowed her gaze on the small redheaded boy as if she didn't recognize the species. Her eyes registered the similarities between mother and son.

"I made a record." Rocket held up a CD case to his mother. He did a small dance with his hips, but stopped when he realized everyone was staring at him. Maggie smiled at her son, but her eyes kept their sense of concern.

"I didn't break anything," he declared. Following him, came a chatty Allie and Les, and getting along famously. Mr. McGregor brought up the rear.

"What the hell is going on?" Tania barked.

Maggie stepped in front of her son protectively.

"What happened to you?" Les said when he took notice of the condition of the two women.

"The signing Les, the damn signing for Keisha's new CD, remember? At the mall. Everything was going perfect before those thugs showed up."

"They were so mean." Keisha wiped at her tear stained cheeks. "They ripped my new blouse." Her hands pulled at the tear on her shoulder.

"They went crazy, and security was nowhere to be found. They manhandled Keisha and me before someone in the crowd stopped them."

"You should have taken someone with you," Les said.

Tania threw up her hands in frustration. "Who Les? Dad used to do it, and I couldn't get hold of Richie. I thought I could handle it myself. This office use to be filled with people, but where are they now." She rubbed her temple hard.

"Was anyone else hurt?" a concerned Maggie asked.

Tania's eyes narrowed on her as if she remembered we were there. "You need to leave," Tania said between clenched teeth.

"No," Jermaine said.

Tania glared at him in disbelief. "You know them?" She nodded toward us.

Jermaine didn't respond, but we all knew what was coming next, and it didn't take long. "They're helping that boy who killed daddy."

Bingo!

"No," Jermaine insisted. "They're helping my friend."

Tania's face tightened. She pointed at the young Mackie. "Your friend killed my father!" she screamed, close to hysterics.

"No he didn't," Maggie said.

"Lamar called and said you got that Bebe kid out of jail." Tania turned her fierce eyes on me. "The police had him, and you made them let him go."

"Yes." I wouldn't deny it. I just needed to defend it. "He didn't kill your father. He wouldn't kill anyone."

"The police had him."

"And released him. They didn't have enough evidence to hold him," Maggie interjected.

"That doesn't make him innocent!" she yelled. Keisha's cries got louder.

"It doesn't make him guilty," I snapped back. If another person wanted to jump on the let's throw Bebe under the bus bandwagon, they had to go through me.

"Bebe's innocent," Jermaine said, his voice low and determined.

"No, he's not," Tania eyes glistened with tears. "Dad told me how the kid almost got you arrested."

Tania's statement surprised me. And from Jermaine's reticent expression, she'd struck a chord. Bebe never spoke of getting Jermaine in trouble. Not that the young sous chef was a library of information about his life. Considering we're trying to help him, I would have thought he might have mentioned this little tidbit. I waited for the story.

Nothing. In fact, he had difficulty making eye contact with me. I realized Maggie refused to make eye contact, as well. She knew something.

"I don't care, I don't want them here." She pointed to the

door. The facade of calm and control she'd shown us on our first meeting was gone. Maybe she hadn't dealt with her father's death, or been able to handle the responsibility of a struggling business. Being assaulted at the publicity event, and now our arrival at RTM didn't help. Tania was a woman on the verge of exploding.

"I've got artists who want to jump ship because they don't think I'm up to this. All the deals Daddy put together are unraveling. My staff is missing. Now this with Keisha, I can't even protect my own artists." Her rant was to no one in particular, maybe verbalizing her inner struggle. We listened.

"We'll manage." Les reached out to her, but she stepped away.

"How?" she spat at him.

Maggie and I stood powerless to help. I knew Maggie wanted to explain more; mercifully she didn't. Rocket and Allie remained silent. Tania's grief and frustration were painful to watch as tears streamed down her face.

"It hasn't been alright since Daddy died." Her voice heavy with resignation, cracked. She sat onto one of the couches and covered her face with her hands and sobbed. Les came to sit next to her and wrapped an arm around her small shoulders. A stunned Jermaine remained silent as whimpering sound came from Keisha.

"I'm sorry," Maggie said.

I knew she meant it. She pulled Rocket towards her and wrapped an arm around his tiny shoulders. His little face confused by the anguish of the adults around him. Allie appeared on the verge of tears.

"I'm sorry, Tania," I added as I followed Maggie, Rocket and Allie out of the lounge.

Outside in the parking lot, we remained silent for a time. Rocket slipped into the backseat, the dog nestled close to him.

Allie joined them, looking as if she'd finally met someone worse off than her. Maggie and I sat there, unsure what to do.

"I want to help her," Maggie said.

I wanted to help her too, but I didn't know how.

"Then help her," a voice from behind us said. Jermaine stood in the doorway.

"Her problems are bigger than just finding Cherry," I said.

"You promised to find out the truth." His dark brown eyes set on Maggie. He'd believed her promise to him, the way kids believed in Santa Claus and the Easter Bunny.

"I'll do my best," Maggie said before I could stop her. You can't promise a kid the moon or a murderer, but Maggie had.

"Have you two lost your minds?" I said. They both needed a reality check.

"Somebody's got to help. All I can do is stay and not walk away like everybody else," he said.

An image of Louis in the Bear's car came to me, and I wondered how long Jermaine would continue if his older brother jumped ship. His young face held such hope. The idea that Maggie and I were the answer to Tania's problem depressed me.

My depression deepened at the sight of Lamar's car pulling into the building's parking lot. The sight should have surprised me, but it didn't. I expected vultures landing on a dying man, why not him at the demise of RTM. Jermaine scowled at the sight of the large man stepping out of his car with Bear in tow. Gerald sat behind the driver's wheel, unable to hide his surprise. No doubt wary of any impeding fireworks between his brother and me.

"I gotta go. Remember you promised, Mrs. Swift." Jermaine stepped back inside the building.

"I hope you're not leaving on my account," he said with

an air of satisfaction.

As Bear walked passed, he made his thumb and forefinger into a gun and pretended to shoot at Maggie. He laughed as he held the door open for Lamar. I had to give Maggie credit; she didn't flinch. In fact, she appeared pretty angry.

"I guess you told Tania about us?" I said.

Lamar's smile widened. "How could I be a friend and withhold the truth? In fact, I'm here to give my support. Heard she had a rough day at one of her gigs." His sincerity didn't ring true, which made me suspicious.

"Considering the circumstances, why don't you find someone else to make your cake? I think Betty Crocker has an opening, or even this Duncan Hines guy."

His smile disappeared as he stepped toward me. "I paid in full." The emotion had drained from his voice. Though, he wore shades, I sensed his eyes bore into me. This was a man used to getting his own way, and his usual method seemed to be bullying.

"I'll give you your money back."

Lamar shook his head slowly, and his grin reappeared, but there wasn't much warmth behind it. "I always get what I pay for, Ms. Wilkes." Lamar leaned in close, his eyes locked on mine. "And I got you."

CHAPTER

19

Maggie and I spent much of the drive to the Blue Moon in a heated debate. We each had a point of contention: the first being her inexcusable promise to Jermaine to find Rovell's killer and the other, whether or not I'd been threatened by Lamar. There was no winning the Jermaine debate because Maggie refused to change her mind. She would do this with or without me. As for Lamar, I wasn't quite sure he had threatened me. I just thought he didn't like my suggestion of shoving the cake he'd ordered into some small, moist, dark hole. He seemed a little put out about my idea to plug any of his orifices. In all honesty, I wasn't referring to his mouth.

"You can't talk to men like him that way. They have no sense of humor," Maggie warned as we walked into the restaurant. I caught the smiles on Rocket and Allie's face and appreciated at least, they had a sense of humor. Rocket's smile widened at the sight of Bebe standing at a table in the back of the restaurant, talking to some familiar faces. Allie's smiled vanished because one of those faces belonged to her brother. He hadn't seen us arrive, so he didn't notice his sister stop and do an about-face, causing me to bump into her.

"I'm going to help Esperanza," she announced and headed for the front door. I said nothing about the shortcut through the kitchen because she would have had to pass her brother to get to the bakeshop. I shook my head, disappointed in her retreat. What really drained my smile was the sight of Bebe's lawyer, Ziemann.

"I made a record!" Rocket held up his CD to show to Bebe when we arrived at the table.

"Who would have thought RTM made kiddies music?" Ziemann said, snidely. Dressed in an impeccable charcoal gray suit, he made Lee sitting next to him, look like a slob. I gave the slob a quick kiss on the cheek in greeting, doing my best to ignore Ziemann's presence.

"Mr. Dunn said you went to talk to potential witnesses I haven't even interviewed yet." His manner remained aloof.

"Hello to you too." I glared down at him as he sipped his coffee.

Lee's eyes danced between us as if he was a referee in a title match that was about to go horribly wrong.

"They did it for Rocket, special." Maggie proudly smoothed out the top hair of her son's wayward locks. Rocket's brow furrowed because I didn't think he liked his music being referred to as kiddie.

"Because he's sweet and hasn't turned into a bitter, insecure, and vain man." I never took my eyes off of Ziemann.

Lee shifted in his seat, possibly to prevent Ziemann if he lunged for me.

"Insecure." Ziemann feigned hurt as he patted the spot over his heart.

"You know, unsure of oneself, lack of confidence, apprehensive." I ticked off the words as if each were a confirmation of my opinion of him, especially the last one. "Impotent."

"Oh, Christ," Maggie said beneath her breath.

Lee's amazed expression made me smile. I never tired of

that. Thankfully, Ziemann's response was interrupted by a declaration by Rocket.

"I'm hungry."

From the expression on his face, he seemed as if he wanted to go as far from another adult drama as possible. Bebe appeared the same.

"How about a hamburger with fries?" Bebe offered. "Afterward, we'll ask Esperanza if she might spare some chocolate chip cookies."

Rocket and Bebe turned to Maggie for approval.

"Okay, but behave and stay out of George's way. And only one cookie," she said before Bebe and Rocket escaped to the kitchen."

With Rocket out of earshot, I turned my complete attention on Ziemann, who seemed ready for me. "Why are you here?" I crossed my arms and glared at him.

"Because, my client isn't where he's supposed to be. He's working when he should be recuperating from a serious injury. So serious, the police can't question him." Ziemann's attention floated back to his coffee. He'd sipped with satisfaction and sighed. His imperious gaze drifted in my direction.

"Instead, he is pulling a sixty-hour work week, living in the suburbs and becoming the personal chef to a future pop star." Ziemann's condescending voice grated on my nerves.

"He couldn't stay at his house because Louis wants to kill him. And what's wrong with where I live?" an annoyed Maggie said as if Ziemann made the suburbs sound like a low-rent strip joint.

"Why can't you be happy I'm discussing this case with your boyfriend?" Ziemann said to me.

From the growing irritation on Lee's face, he didn't seem too happy to be included.

"It would help if you stay away from my case, stop

interviewing witnesses, and searching for this Cherry person. She's isn't a priority," Ziemann said in a patronizing tone, I often found in teachers, preachers and my sister.

"Why do you care if we find Cherry?" Maggie injected.

"You're muddying the waters. No one from the party even saw her except Dunn. The issue is Mr. Dunn's knife was found in the victim's back. Even he admitted she'd gone by the time Rovell was murdered."

"We think she was invited by someone at the party. Someone knew she was there," Maggie said.

"You think!" he mocked.

"Forget you." I waved him away, and turned to leave when he grabbed me by the forearm, much too forcefully. I winced.

"Let her go." Lee's voice flared up in warning.

Patrons of the nearby table took notice of us. A flustered Ziemann released me as if he hadn't realized what he had done. "I can't tell who is worse little Ms. Cupcake here, or the Weather Girl." His eyes danced between us. "I don't need any amateurs screwing up my case. My investigator wasted time trying to find out about the two bumbling detectives tramping all over his investigation. I told him not to squander his time," Ziemann said.

"You had them investigated?" An incensed Lee pushed up his glasses and glared at Ziemann.

"I know how protective you are of Ms. Cupcake here considering her delicate condition," Ziemann teased.

We all knew he hinted at my anxiety disorder. Considering I hadn't had an attack in months, I resented this being thrown in my face. From the scowl on Lee's face, he resented the inference, as well.

"You're an ass, Thad. This wasn't why you came here. You've talked to Bebe. Why don't you finish your coffee and leave?" Lee said.

Ziemann ignored him and turned to me. "How does a top ad exec go from million dollar accounts to a small cake shop in Queens? A tremendous step-down, I'd said," he continued, satisfied in his smugness. He eyed the now-seething Lee. "Like seeks like, I guess."

I didn't understand what he meant, but Lee seemed to, and his annoyance had turned to anger. Ziemann seemed unfazed by Lee's hostility. They acted less like old friends and more like adversaries. Maybe for lawyers, this meant friendship. I didn't know what to make of their relationship.

"Time to leave, Thad," Lee insisted. Ziemann remained seated.

"The thing about throwing stones, Mr. Ziemann, someone can always throw them back," Maggie interjected, breaking the silence, her voice soft and low.

Ziemann chuckled. Bad move.

Maggie's blue eyes went a little darker. "Give us some credit," she retorted.

"How are those community college classes coming? What was the last one, real estate, death planning for pets? My personal favorite had to be belly dancing." Ziemann wiggled his eyebrows in amusement.

"You know you're an idiot?" I said in defense of my friend's penchant for exploration.

"I don't like to say anything unpleasant about people." Maggie's jaws clenched.

"There's nothing you can say to me that my ex-wife, the New York press, and my mother haven't already said, sweetie." He laughed, but none of us joined him.

Maggie's face relaxed, and her bright blue eyes lingered on the lawyer. She cupped her elbow with one hand and tapped her lips with the other. She reminded me of one of those scientists who found an unknown creature that oozed and slithered their way into their path. You can't decide whether to step on them or put them in a jar for further study.

"I wondered why you'd take on Bebe's case. He's not your typical client, is he?" Maggie asked.

"It's called pro-bono work. Do you want me to explain the concept to you? I sure Nassau Community College is giving a class on the subject." Ziemann's mouth went into a lopsided smile.

"You'd be surprised what I know," Maggie said.

"Pray tell," he teased.

Maggie sighed. "You defend rock stars from paternity suits, politicians on bribery charges and organized crime figures from murder. The case you did last year with the embezzler was front-page news for weeks. Bebe's case wouldn't get you the press time at the local penny saver. Then I considered Lee. You two haven't seen each other in a while, yet one phone call from him and here you are. That must have been some call." Maggie turned to a silent Lee, who looked like a man who already knew the answers to her questions. He had the expression of a man who knew Maggie all too well. He sat back and watched the fireworks.

"You drive, don't you?" Her shift in the conversation caught the lawyer off guard for a moment.

He blinked, slightly bewildered. "What?"

"In the past, the celebrity pages in the news always said you loved fast cars. You like the Italian ones. I forget what they're called," Maggie continued.

"I can't help if small people are interested in my life." Ziemann smoothed his tie.

"Now you use a car service. Where are those Italian sport cars, those long, fast drives to the Hamptons? You haven't driven yourself in years."

She'd found a connection, and she hadn't told me. Again, keeping secret in the belief Lee would tell me eventually. She'd done the same with Bebe. Not too keen on her new philosophy, I planned on a long heart to heart about friendships and keeping secrets.

"You haven't driven yourself since an accident you had on the Garden State Parkway in New Jersey several years ago. It involved a very fast car, an Italian seventeen-year-old model, and an embankment. There was some confusion as to who was driving, considering both of you were under the influence." Maggie raised an eyebrow at him. Ziemann said nothing.

"As quickly as the stories appeared in the papers, they disappeared. All parties shutting down the press until the next big story took their interest. The model went back to the south of France to recover, quite comfortably and all was right with the world."

"You've made a lot of assumptions," Ziemann said, almost in warning.

Maggie sighed deep, content that she'd dug enough into Ziemann black hole of a soul. "At least mine is based on the public records, which include a blood alcohol report three times the normal limit." She cocked her head to the side, which almost made her appear childlike. There was nothing benign about Maggie's speculations, and we all knew it. If Ziemann didn't think much of Maggie's forays into Adult Continuing Education, she didn't think much of his poor choices either. Her dismissive tone said as much.

"You were in deep trouble. The girl was underage, drinking and in your company."

"She told me she was older," Ziemann said smugly.

"Yeah, that was plausible. Considering, you represented her model firm in a contract dispute with another modeling firm. I'm sure you knew more about the young girl than how she posed on the last issue of Seventeen Magazine." Maggie added.

"Do you have a point?" Ziemann tone went cool.

"Throughout the entire mess, that man stood by you." Maggie's eyes fell on Lee. "The press reported him as a colleague but he was your friend. Only a friend would help you maneuver around an underage model and her firm wanting to sue you for lost of income while she recovered. Lee helped you and you owed him."

The table went silent as Ziemann scrutinized the little redhead as if they were the only ones in the room.

"Now, I'm going to find my son and make sure he's only having one cookie with his meal." Maggie spun around and walked away.

Ziemann watched her go until she disappeared through the kitchen's double doors. "She has a perky little butt, don't you think?"

Lee shook his head in disgust.

"You kiss your mother with that mouth," I said.

"I try not to kiss my mother. She says it ruins her Botox. Please don't think that little revelation says anything about me, Ms. Cupcake," he said.

"It says you got smacked by a tiny redheaded amateur who wasn't even trying hard. So, do what you have to do and so will we."

"Even if your digging might make Mr. Dunn's trouble worse than it already is?"

"Then you'll be the brilliant lawyer Lee thinks you are. I'm sure the pound of flesh you owe him will cover it." I followed my friend into the kitchen; certain Ziemann's eyes were on me. I didn't think this time he'd ask Lee if my butt looked perky.

CHAPTER

20

Normally, when I go out of my way to offend someone, I try never to cross their path again. Regrettably, Lamar insisted I fill his cake order. Candace insisted I fill the order—considering she already deposited Lamar's money. My sister wasn't one to let money grow mold. Also, Maggie insisted I shouldn't refuse the job. She seemed afraid of the man's response if I once again told him to shove it where the sun never shined. Of course, I hadn't told Lee about my encounter with the man because he would add a dire warning of his own. Despite my resistance, I put on my best O So Sweet chef jacket, an extra touch of lipstick and a steel plated attitude.

For me to succeed at my goal, I needed support. I went to Maggie. Our equal distrust of the man might keep me out of trouble, or at least I hoped. Allie tagged along because she had nothing better planned for the evening, and the idea of being alone in the house with Lee terrified her. Her other option was a night out with Maggie's boss. I didn't trust Frank enough to do that. Though I was growing fond of Allie, I felt complicit in her avoidance of her brother and the issues that put her on a plane. Allie didn't want the drama of what a confrontation might bring, and I agreed, if not passively. Lee agreed with his usual silence. The only conflict he wanted was in the courtroom, and the baseball game he planned to watch. We were all gutless and in denial.

On the drive over to the Brooklyn venue, Maggie gave me the quick lowdown on Lamar and his business. "Things started when Lamar left the army. He had disciplinary issues. He'd been put in the army version of a jail a few times for minor infractions," Maggie said.

"I think it's called a brig," Allie chimed in. She'd been tight-lipped on most of our little escapades, but now she seemed almost gleeful when she got into the van. Searching for Cherry had become an adventure for her.

"He got out of the army and landed in Atlanta where he had family. He had a few scrapes with the law and even went to jail for a year on aggravated assault. He did a lot of entry-level jobs but found his niche in bodyguard work. Somehow, he got involved with the record industry down there. He got close to a prominent Atlanta rap artist and followed him to New York when the artist got signed to a leading company. Lamar stayed. I think he liked New York. Lamar hooked into a small management company, and did bodyguard work for them. I suspect he did a little more than that," Maggie said.

I maneuvered the cake shop's delivery van through the streets of Williamsburg, Brooklyn. An up and coming neighborhood filled with artists and trendy restaurants. A former industrialized area the place was now populated with converted warehouses. Lamar's venue was in one of these warehouses. His production music company Chaos 182 occupied two floors.

"What do you mean?" I asked.

"Tell me what you think?" she said with upraised brows. "The owner of the company decided to retire a year after Lamar showed up. Then Lamar brought him out, and the amount wasn't much."

"Maybe he was tired of the music business and wanted to move to Florida," I said.

Maggie shook her head. "The guy just turned thirty and ended up in California, starting a new company – minus Lamar."

This made me wonder how a bodyguard might buy out a business he'd only worked at for a year. Did Lamar have deep pockets, and convince the owner to sell? I thought of Tania. Could Lamar persuade her to give up her father's business? He wanted RTM in the worst way.

"What kind of name is Chaos 182 for a business?" Allie asked.

I also wondered where the name came from. I doubted that Lamar sat around with some tea and a thesaurus coming up with names for his business.

"In a few interviews, Lamar said 182 came from the house number he and his brother grew up in Atlanta and Chaos, because he liked the idea of bringing disorder to the establish music industry. He thought of himself as an outsider, I guess." Maggie shrugged, but I could tell she had something else on her mind. I cocked an eyebrow at her.

"Some people say it had to do with when Lamar worked at a club in Atlanta called Chaos. Someone died and Lamar left soon after to come to New York. Also, 182 is a penal code when two or more people plan to commit a crime. A rumor started that Lamar had a falling out with the person who died. They said he had him killed. The police couldn't hold Lamar because he had an airtight alibi."

"Would he be so blatant?" I asked.

When we pulled up to the converted warehouse that housed Chaos 182, an old feeling of dread and nerves came over me. A sense of apprehension, I sometimes get with a new job, but this felt worse. A worrisome Maggie took in the large building as if she might never come out again. Allie seemed oblivious of our unease. Sometimes, it was good to be clueless.

"Let's get in and out." I wanted this over with. I'd planned to speak to the event planner and set up the cake display then go back to the Blue Moon and put Lamar on the No Bake list indefinitely.

One of the valets instructed us to park in the back of the building by a loading dock. We maneuvered the cake into a small freight elevator, which took us to the main floor of a two-story open floor plan. While Maggie and I had the majority of the cake in two large boxes, Allie held the topper and some of the decorative pieces we needed to assemble. With the exception of the catering staff, Lamar and his entourage were nowhere in sight. The event planner, a harried thin woman name Maxim, showed us to a roped off area near a series of buffet style tables. Maxim wore a headset connected to some walkie-talkie at her belt. Crackled noises coming from the set interspersed with garble only she understood was a constant interruption as she instructed her crew. Black and white was the theme of the evening. Maggie, Allie and I stood out in a loud pink.

"Mr. Jones expects perfection," her high and trilling voice explained. Dressed as if she was trying out for the part for the mortician's assistant, the woman was perhaps on some chemically induced overload.

"The cake is perfect," I reassured her.

She shook her head, and I thought it might topple off her tiny little neck. Thin to the point of emaciated, if the woman turned sideways, she'd vanished.

"You're not dressed appropriately." She glared at our O So Sweet pink chef jackets and t-shirts.

"Excuse me?" I said.

"You're wearing...." Her face twisted in disgust. "Pink."

"Yes, it's pink."

The woman's face was devoid of color, along with the theme she'd chosen for the party. I didn't think she knew there were any other colors. "Mr. Jones wants a complete black and white party - totally." She gestured at herself and then at her crew, all dressed in black.

"I won't be around when the party starts, so what's the problem?"

Her eyes enlarged unnaturally, and her gray irises floated in a sea of white. Her head began to shake spastically, and I thought she might have a seizure. "You're supposed to serve. Mr. Jones insisted." The woman had a clipboard and flipped through it. The pages sounded like a bird trying to achieve lift. Obviously, unable to find what she wanted, she continued to flip until I placed her hand on her clipboard to stop her. From her shocked expression, it told me people didn't do that too often.

"That's not going to happen. Lamar wanted my cake. He's got my cake. I will set up and I will leave," I said slowly and clearly. Her head continued to shake.

"What makes you think we're supposed to serve?" Maggie said, hoping to get through our impasse.

"Mr. Jones insisted. You were to serve him and his guests and not in that." She pointed to my jacket again.

"Miss, whatever your name is, I'm going to set up the cake and leave. If Jones has a problem with that, then he can call me. So we're wasting time, your guests will be arriving soon and talking to me isn't going to change anything." I reassured with a tight smile. This only seemed to terrify her more.

"No, no, no," she ranted. Some static came over her headset, and she struggled to listen. Her eyes widened so much I thought they might pop out of her head and roll along the floor. They didn't.

"Time's a ticking." I tapped my wrist to emphasize the point, and with that, an unhappy Maxim dashed off.

"God, I wish I was like you." Allie's admiration touched me.

"One Odessa is enough," Maggie said as we pulled the cake pieces out of their boxes.

Allie set the topper and the other box down. "I mean, you don't let people push you around."

"Oh, they push her around," Maggie chimed in. I gave her a smug grin. "She has a tendency to push back."

"But, no one seems to tell you what to do," Allie said.

"People try to tell me what to do all the time. Just ask my sister. Hell, ask your brother."

"My brother?" Allie said with some doubt.

I nodded. "When we first got together, Lee had issues about my involvement with Maggie and McAvoy investigation. At first, we got into fights. Then I learned from Maggie here, I was doing it all wrong." I put an arm around my best friend.

"Don't blame me for anything." Maggie shrugged my hand off her small shoulders.

"I learned the reason why she and Roger have a happy marriage. You let them talk, listen thoughtfully, and make sure they understand you respect their opinion," I said with the utmost sincerity and hand over my heart. Allie listened attentively. Maggie rolled her eyes. "Then you do what you want," I added.

"There she is." Maxim screeching voice bellowed behind us.

I couldn't turn around because Maggie and I were maneuvering the base of the cake into the right position on the display table. Once placed, I turned to the sound of Maxim's six-inch heels stomping toward me. She pulled Gerald in her wake. He seemed about as happy as I was being at his brother's party.

"Ms. Wilkes." He said my name almost apologetically. He nodded politely to Maggie and Allie. "I'm sorry for the misunderstanding." His brother made me edgy, but I could take Gerald with my hands tied behind my back in the middle of a Macy's two-for-one sale.

"There's no misunderstanding."

"I'd made arrangements for the party and didn't realize my brother spoke with your lovely sister, Candace about the service arrangement. She didn't seem to have a problem with it."

I sighed at the mention of my sister's name. If Lamar spoke to her, I was sure money had exchanged hands. I didn't even need him to tell me, Lamar had called her to include the extra service. Something I normally didn't do. Most parties had their own catering staff. In all fairness, I hadn't explained my issues with Lamar to Candace so I couldn't blame her.

"I'm sure Ms. Maxim's staff can serve the cake," I said.

"It's just Maxim," the woman corrected. "I have just enough staff for the bar and the added security.

"My brother wants you. If you're not here..." His eyes darted away from me, and his anguish seemed genuine. "He can make things difficult, especially if he thinks he's paid for something or someone. It's best to give him what he wants," he said as if confessing something he shouldn't confess. "It's a lot easier to do what he says."

"I kinda have a problem with that." I cocked an eyebrow at him.

Beads of sweat appeared on his forehead. I knew I was making Gerald's life more difficult than it had to be. He seemed like a decent guy, despite his relations.

"Odessa, we'll do this and go," Maggie said.

If I refused to acknowledge the problems that might erupt

between Lamar and me, she did. "But I don't want to do it," I said firmly and sounding like a petulant child.

Maggie began unbuttoning the pink jacket. Allie stood behind her, unsure what to do.

"I don't like this." I protested and I unbuttoned my jacket, as well. Allie followed suit.

"Thank you so much," Gerald said and I was afraid he'd drop to his knees and kiss my feet. Even Maxim seemed relieved as she barked orders to her staff now that the impasse had passed. As if by magic, three black t-shirts appeared with the word STAFF silkscreened on them.

"I wouldn't be so quick to thank me, Gerald," I warned, but he seemed oblivious to this. He hadn't realized I have given him a reprieve from an impending catastrophe. Despite Lamar and Maxim's desires to have a totally black and white party, I saw red.

CHAPTER 21

For two hours, I handed out cake while losing my hearing from the ear-numbing music, losing my patience from the crude remarks from some of the guests, and losing my temper with Lamar. During the course of the evening, he stopped by the cake table several times. I made good cakes, but not that good. He reveled in Allie's almost catatonic fear as one young man dressed in low-riding jeans, a *'Kill the Man'* t-shirt and chrome plated teeth, sized her up as if she were something dipped in melted butter. To Maggie's credit, she didn't recoil when Bear commented that she looked like a doll. While an arrogant Lamar sported two scantily-clad women on each of his arms, as if they were accessories. They fawned all over him, like a third-rate Hugh Hefner. Maggie, Allie and I couldn't help but admire at the physical impossibility of the firmness of their enormous breasts, their plump oversized lips and their lack of clothing. Women's lib was officially dead. It had been beaten down by breast implants, collagen injections and the less was more theory when it came to women's clothing.

"I brought these ladies over for something sweet. I love giving my girls something sweet," Lamar cooed. The women giggled, and everything jiggled.

"You so right, baby," one on the left, said.

Lamar planted a kiss on her cheek. "If you're a good girl I'll give you some extra sweet later on." His lustful smile made my stomach shift in response. I groaned.

"What's your problem?" She glared at me.

"I'm here." I didn't miss the obvious pleasure Lamar seemed to get from my discomfort.

"She reminds me of those lunch ladies," the other woman snickered. Both women laughed. Lamar's smirked with pleasure at the women's critique.

"Hey, it's a living, and she could always eat cake." The other flicked a condescending hand in my direction. These were the kind of women who read Marie Antoinette's autobiography, skipped over the ending and highlighted her younger and dumber years.

I turned to Maggie; she shook her head in warning. She knew me too well. I was hot, tired, and I had a matching set of Barbie dolls acting as if they had a right to comment on my life. Hell, I don't even give Candace the privilege.

"Oh my, Maggie, it's the Harvard Debate Team," I said in mock awe.

Maggie said nothing.

"Hey, my ladies are bright." Lamar took offense.

"So are light bulbs but I wouldn't let them operate heavy machinery," I said.

"Is she insulting us?" One woman seemed uncertain. Antoinette probably had that same expression of total disbelief when she realized her French subjects didn't think much of her.

"Yeah baby, I think so," Lamar egged her on.

She disengaged herself from the music promoter to face me in all of her manicured fury. "At least I'm not some food service worker." She snapped her fingers.

Behind her, Lamar's smile widened. He'd love the idea of

two women fighting as if we were some bikini clad mud wrestlers and a show for his amusement. A little screaming, hair pulling and cake throwing would make his party.

I glowered at Lamar but turned my full attention to his rented bimbo. "One thousand four hundred dollars," I said.

The woman blinked. "What?" She turned to Lamar, who shared her confusion.

"He's paying me, one thousand four hundred dollars, including tax. All I have to do is serve cake, sweetheart." I put an emphasis on the word cake and smiled. Knowing, even if Bimbo One and Two didn't, I did my business standing up and fully clothed.

Lamar's brow furrowed, understanding my meaning perfectly. "Hey." The humor drained from his face.

I turned to Maggie. "I'm sure she's independently wealthy and loves his company and intellect."

Maggie shook her head and pleaded with her eyes for me to stop. I huffed at her. Lamar shoved away from the other woman, almost knocking her companion over, to stand in front of me. Grateful for the table between us, I put my best O So Sweet smile. Often used with irate brides or psychotic mother's of the groom,

"I don't pay for nobody," he growled at me.

I scanned the crowded space as people drank his liquor and ate his food. I wondered how many would stay if everything vanished. Money made the circus go round, and Lamar paid for everything. This observation was lost on him.

"Oh, I'm sorry," I said, feigning remorse. "Or is it charity work?" A vein on his neck pulsed as his face darkened with rage. I picked up a plate with a large slice of cake and offered it to him. "Eat up. Don't want to let your money go to waste," I said.

He flared his nostrils in response, snorted like an angry

bull ready to charge. I held my ground, equally annoyed at his attempts to intimidate me.

"Isn't that…" Allie broke the stalemate by pointing toward the other side of the open space where the bathrooms were located.

I reluctantly took my eyes off Lamar, and I followed her line of sight to a group of women entering the bathroom. Standing in the back of the line was Cherry, red hair and all, identified by the photographs I'd taken from Vesta's salon.

"No way." A disbelieving Maggie ran from behind the table and slipped passed Bear like a ninja. I followed on her heels.

"What the…" Lamar complained as he was no longer the focus of our attention and turned to find out what had distracted us. By then, Cherry had slipped into the bathroom.

"Odessa!" Allie squeaked to me. She stepped from behind the table to follow.

I stopped her. "No, stay here. Finish up. I'll be right back."

She seemed uncertain, but returned to her spot. Lamar called to me, but I ignored him. I caught up with Maggie at the bathroom door.

"She hasn't come out yet." Maggie pointed to a well-built man walking across the dance floor. He was dressed in a black t-shirt labeled security. He spoke into a walkie-talkie, and acted as if he were searching for someone.

"He's been on the floor working the crowd since she went into the bathroom," Maggie said as we let the guard stroll by us, and weaved in and out of the dancers on the dance floor. I had to agree with Maggie, that once again, Cherry had found a way into a party where she wasn't invited. This girl should work for the CIA.

"Where's Allie?" Maggie asked.

"I told her to stay put." I pointed to her across the floor. Lamar, Bear and a frightened Allie watched us. With a sense of urgency, we entered the bathroom. I heard Cherry before I saw her. She stood in front of a mirror above the sink, adjusting her bra and talking into a little red phone. Swinging from her wrist was a bejeweled bracelet with a little red camera hanging from it.

"Don't have a heart attack, I'll get your money," she said.

Maggie and I stood out of her line of sight.

"Maggie, go stand by the door and tell everyone the bathroom it's out of order for awhile," I said.

"What are you going to do?" Maggie probably thought I might dunk Cherry's head in a toilet considering my dangerous mood Lamar had instigated.

"Appeal to her better nature." I smiled. Her eyes held mistrust.

I waited until the last woman left the bathroom before I entered. Finally alone, I found a distracted Cherry still trying to convince someone she had their money. On the counter sat her oversized pocketbook, which rivaled the ones Maggie favored. It was big enough to carry the kitchen sink and probably a few other appliances. She searched through the bag, and a pair of stockings, a purple wig and flip-flops got dropped on the countertop.

"Hi Sherrilyn," I said.

The use of her given name made her whirl around. At the sight of my Maxim's staff t-shirt, she grew alarmed. "Do I know you?" She squinted at me.

I shook my head. "We have a mutual friend," I said guardedly. I'd seen her in a hundred photographs, but in person, she seemed older. She wore too much make-up and the permanent scorn of loathing marred her prettiness.

"Yeah who?" She disengaged the phone and dropped it in

the bag without a goodbye.

"Bebe Dunn." I waited for a reaction.

"You mean that busboy from that dingy restaurant?" Her lips curled into a sneer. I almost took offense at the restaurant remark. "He said you were at Linwood Rovell's party."

"Yeah, and he had a lot of nerve telling me to leave. Who the hell was he?"

"He said you argued."

"I had a right to be there," she complained.

"People thought Bebe fought with Mr. Rovell, but it was you."

When I said nothing more, Cherry shrugged indifferently.

"You know Mr. Rovell is dead," I said.

She dug in her bag for something. Did she hear me or was she ignoring me.

"Yeah." She pulled out eyeliner and worked on her already-exaggerated makeup. Afterward, she admired her reflection, snatched up the tiny camera that hung from her wrist, took a picture of her reflection in the mirror, and smiled. She turned to me and rolled off a few shots, blinding me with the flash. She wielded the thing like a damn weapon. My eyes took a moment to focus against the spots floating in the air.

"Who are you again?" She narrowed her gaze.

"Like I said, a friend of Bebe."

"Well I ain't." She snapped another picture of me. She began to shove things back into her bag, hinting our conversation had come to an end. She eyed the exit behind me. She wanted to leave. I needed her to stay, so I snatched one of the straps of the oversized handbag and yanked. She grabbed and pulled on the other.

"Lady, you better let go or somebody is gonna get hurt." Cherry wasn't the kind of girl to fight with jabbing metaphors and biting witticism. Despite the fact I had about six inches and maybe twenty pounds on her, she probably thought she could take me.

"I'm willing to compensate you for your trouble," I blurted.

She stopped and gave me a pensive smile, no doubt already counting the money in her head. "You mean money?" She sounded receptive.

I sighed in relief. "You are going to tell the police you were in Rovell's office arguing with Bebe."

"Really!" She sounded genuinely surprised.

"Yeah."

"How much?" she asked.

"How about a nice dinner at the Blue Moon?"

"How about a thousand."

"Are you nuts?" Did she think I would pay her to tell the truth?

"Two thousand or I'll tell the police I saw that busboy fighting with Rovell." She smiled and cocked an eyebrow.

Annoyed by my own stupidity, I cursed. "You expect me to pay you one thousand dollars to tell the truth, or two thousand not to lie?" I asked, indignantly.

"O!" An ashen-faced, wide-eyed Maggie burst into the bathroom. Considering I'd been suckered into bribing Cherry, how bad could her troubles be?

"What?"

"I can't find Allie. She's gone." Out of breath and slightly panicked, she grabbed me by the arm and pulled me toward the door.

"Who the hell are you?" Cherry asked, eyeing Maggie.

Cherry's question seemed secondary to my immediate problem. I'd told Allie to stay put. If I've lost Lee's sister in the middle of a crazy Hip Hop party in Brooklyn, he'd kill me, and I'd let him. I began to follow Maggie out the door when

Cherry called to me. "What about my money?"

I whirled back on her, barely keeping my fear about Allie in check. My anger seemed to radiate off my skin. She took an anxious step back as I approached. Inches from her face, I growled my response. "I'm going to find my friend, and you're going to stay right here. We're not done."

Cherry's bravado wavered a bit, and she blinked. For added insurance, I snatched up large handbag.

"Hey!" she yelled, getting some of her courage back.

I shoved the bag into Maggie's hands as she stood in the doorway. I held my finger up at Cherry in warning as she tried to get passed me. "You better be here when I get back, or I'll find a landfill in The Bronx to throw this."

"Bitch…" she said, but by then all my patience had vanished.

I used my height to crowd her personal space the same way Lamar had tried with me. "Yes I am," I said between clenched teeth, turned, and ran.

CHAPTER

22

I'd left Lee's sister in the middle of an insane asylum. In the short time we'd gone to speak to Cherry, the party had ballooned out of control and tripled in size. Somebody must have screamed free food on the Brooklyn-Queens Expressway, and invited anybody with a pulse. Cutting through the crowd of gyrating bodies, flashing lights, and music so loud my bones rattled. Maggie's red hair was the only way I could keep track of her through the dance floor as we made our way to the last place we'd seen Allie.

"Oh God," I yelled over the noise as we scanned the crowd in vain for her.

"We'll find her," Maggie reassured me.

We'd reached the empty cake station. Maggie hopped onto a chair to get a better view. She pointed to the event planner Maxim a few feet away. Despite the chaos, Maxim seemed competent and would know what was going on. I needed to find Allie before things totally got out of control.

"Maxim!" I had to yell over the music. "Where is the other woman who was with us?"

Her beleaguered expression told me the new influx of people had added more drama than she wanted. Allie was the last thing on her mind. The requests of her staff were a constant interruption. Under different circumstances, I'd empathize, but I had my own priorities.

When one of her staff talked about running low on liquor, I stepped between them because I no longer had the luxury of being diplomatic. "The blonde woman." I pointed to the empty cake station table. My proximity got her attention, and I made it clear I wouldn't move until she talked to me.

"She's a grownup. If your friend wants to make nice with Lamar, she's an adult," Maxim said. Possibly reading first, the confusion, the fear and then extreme anger on my face, her smugness vanished.

"She wouldn't go with him willingly," Maggie added.

Quick to comprehend our distress, Maxim pointed to stairs that led to the second floor of Chaos 182.

"What's up there," I said glaring at her. She hesitated.

"I think you better tell her," Maggie warned.

"Mr. Jones's office," Maxim squeaked.

We left Maxim to her assistants and pushed through a wall of people to the other side of the room. We stopped short at the sight of Gerald at the base of the stairs as if standing guard. I didn't know if Gerald's pensive expression had anything to do with Allie's abduction or the near riotous behavior of the party guests. I didn't care which. He was in my way.

I pulled Maggie to the side and pointed at Gerald. "I need him gone."

She thought a moment and nodded. She told me to wait as she pushed back through the crowd, her small body disappearing in a sea of dancing bodies. She said something to one of the security men and pointed at Gerald. The man gave her an acknowledging nod and headed for Gerald. Maggie made her way back to me. We watched Gerald and the security guy talk. Gerald's grim face turned to wide-eyed panic. He began to push through the massive crowd unapologetically and disappeared into the gyrating crowd of dancers.

"What did you say to him?" I asked.

"I told the guard to tell Gerald that Maxim complained the party was out of control, and she was about to pull her staff and leave.

I smiled. "No more staff, no liquor, music or security."

With Gerald handling Maxim, we bounded up the stairs to a darken reception space, illuminated only by strips of blue mood lighting at the baseboard. As the party roared on below, we caught muted voices from behind a large door.

"Maybe we should call the police?" Maggie whispered.

I didn't think they'd get here in time, but what would it hurt? Then I realized I'd left my phone in the van with my pocketbook. Maggie had done the same, thinking we would be in and out. I got a better idea when I remembered Maggie still had Cherry's handbag.

"Check inside?"

A reluctant Maggie found the small bejeweled phone I'd seen. She did a quick examination of it before encouraging me to continue.

"Why'd they want her?" Lamar's booming voice came from a closed office door. There was no response.

"Odessa!" Maggie whispered.

I turned to find her routing around in the large handbag for something else. Before I had a chance to ask why, Allie's high-pitched squeal of distress propelled me through the door. I found her being loomed over by Lamar and Bear. Her frightened bloodshot eyes locked on me in an instant.

"Odessa!" She tried to stand, but Bear's meaty hand shoved her back down.

"Get your hands off her, you damn dirty ape," I yelled, quoting Charleston Heston's famous lines from the movie

Planet of the Apes. Inwardly, I groaned knowing I spent too much time watching old movies with Lee. I dashed to Allie, who reeked of liquor. On the large desk sat an almost empty bottle of vodka.

I scanned the office decorated in a style in what I like to call testosterone chic: lots of leather and metal. Much of the room's illumination came from a four-foot long fish tank that took up center stage against the front of the room. Its sole occupant, a miniature shark, swam in its confined space. The dark beady eyes scanned the tank for a way out.

"Honey and I were having some drinks. You want to join us?" a gruff Lamar said. He took Allie by the chin and gave her head a little shake. The movement made Allie's eyes roll back.

"Stop that." I cursed and reached out to get Allie. Lamar's mitt-sized hand grabbed my wrist and pulled me away. I struggled to free myself but couldn't. Bear chuckled.

"Let go," I demanded.

He ignored me and gripped me harder. "Why are you trying to find Cherry?"

When I said nothing, he yanked me toward him. I fell hard into his chest as he wrapped a thick arm around me. He pressed me close and ground his hips against me in a provocative manner. I cringed at the contact. He gave me a tentative sniff that almost made me pee my pants. In an instant, my bravado had left the building. My mind broke the news to the rest of my body, that this maniac might actually hurt me.

Lamar grinned.

Once, George, the Blue Moon chef and ex-marine, told me when you show an ounce of fear, they've already won. He insisted you had to make your fear appear as anger. Of course, this was easy for George to say, he made Lamar seem like a fat kid with antisocial tendencies. I took a deep breath and tried to calm myself anyway. I channeled every angry thought I had; the day I got fired from my advertising job, when Davis dumped me, and when at eight, Candace destroyed my Easy Bake Oven. I put a scowl on my face.

"Is this how you'll ask Tania for the Mackies?" I watched his eyes narrow. He hadn't expected that. "Since you tried asking nicely and got nowhere. Is this how you'll persuade her?" His grip tightened on me, taking away my breath.

"I like my women with a little bite." He grinned.

"That explains those kennel bitches with the awful boob jobs," I snapped, and embraced my fleeting anger.

"All women are bitches to me, baby. As for Tania, she's her daddy's little girl, playing with the big boys. Rovell made RTM work and she ain't got it in her."

"I bet you asked him nicely for the Mackies too. I bet he said no." I struggled to get the words out as Lamar gripped tighter.

His eyes glistened with understanding. "You think I killed Rovell?" He laughed. "Hate to break the news to you, sweet thing, but I was on a party boat heading for Montauk that night. I have a boatload full of witnesses to prove it. Didn't get back into the city until the next evening. Someone did me a favor taking care of old Rovell for me."

I didn't have time to think about this revelation, because I couldn't take a deep breath.

"Now tell me why you want to speak to Cherry?" The playfulness vanished from his voice as his face set in a permanent scowl.

A loud thud interrupted any response I attempted to make. We turned to see Bear on the floor, his limbs in spasms, his face stuck in a position of terror and embarrassment. Maggie stood over him. It took me a moment to realize she had a stun gun in her hand. My confusion as to where she'd found one took a back seat to the crumpled body of Bear. Tinkerbell had laid out Goliath. The sight stopped Lamar from terrorizing me. I just stood with my mouth opened. Allie started to do this kind of hysterical giggle. I wanted to join her because nothing made sense at the moment.

"What the...." Lamar released me. I struggled to take my first deep breath.

Lamar's attention went to Bear and then toward Maggie. Before he took two steps, she'd reached down to Bear's prone body, opened his jacket and pulled out his gun. Lamar froze. I silently thanked Frank McAvoy, because she looked as if she knew what she was doing. She held the gun with both hands aimed at Lamar's chest. The impasse gave me a moment to gather my senses and pull an unsteady Allie to her feet.

"Now don't play..." Lamar said.

A drooling and semi-conscious Bear gazed up at Maggie in what appeared to be either adoration or psychopathic rage.

"This is a semi-automatic P12 Glock. It holds a casing of eight in the load and has a heavy trigger. The gun is popular with military police, and civil law enforcement," Maggie recited as if, she was explaining the proper way to remove grass stains from blue jeans.

"Let's go, Maggie." I tried to get an unsteady Allie out of the room.

As if on cue, her hands move over the gun, snapping pieces apart. Within a minute, she tossed the disassembled gun into the shark tank behind her. If my life hadn't been threatened by an oversized maniac I would have applauded. Instead, I followed Maggie as she ran passed me as if her pants were on fire.

We didn't stop running until we reached my pink van in the parking lot. By then Allie seemed able to walk under her own steam, but I didn't know for how long. I opened the side panel and she clamored inside on her hands and knees before she collapsed next to a stack of empty cake boxes. A minute later, Maggie and I sat in the front seat as I struggled to keep my hands from shaking. Running on the last of my adrenaline, I shoved the key into the ignition and started the van, ready to drive out of the lot like a criminal.

"Stop!"

I recognized the high pitch squeal as the voice of Cherry. In my side view mirror I caught sight of her running in six-inch heels. A few seconds later, two security guards burst through the door and gave chase. Obviously, she had worn out her invitation. I shifted gears, yanked the van in reverse, made an exaggerated U-turn, and pulled up alongside her. "Get in!" I stomped on the brakes. The tires squealed, Allie rolled and Maggie braced herself.

Despite her choice of shoes to escape in, Cherry jumped into the back of the van expertly. No doubt, this wasn't her first fast exit.

I made a sharp turn onto the street, the van’s tires screeching as we went. Not knowing if we were being followed, I made several turns into side streets until I got onto Kings Highway. I had to slow down. My hands shook too much to drive safely. A silent Maggie sat next to me in shock. Allie just moaned.

"You got my bag?" Cherry said. The pitch of her voice made my spleen ache.

A silent Maggie released the death grip she had on the oversized pocketbook and held it out to the ex-hairdresser.

"I think I'm going to be sick," Allie announced, weakly.

"Not on me." Cherry slid away from her.

I found a gas station on Nostrand Avenue and stopped. Allie crawled out of the van, stood against a chain link fence, and vomited. Her pale face, damp hair and tortured expression told me this wasn't on her bucket list of things she wanted to accomplish. I unclenched my grip from the wheel and got out. Maggie followed. Cherry watched us from the open side door. Allie dry heaved a couple more times. I sank to my knees and clutched them so they'd stop shaking, and Maggie mumbled.

Cherry took the time to use the van as her personal dressing room. She put on a pair of yellow leggings and some shabby, brown flat shoes she retrieved from her pocketbook. She snatched off the red wig and the oversized gold tone earring and shoved them into the bag along with the miniskirt she'd been wearing. She ripped open a few handy wipes and removed her make-up.

"I can't believe you pulled a gun on him," I said to Maggie. "I can't believe you pulled a gun on anybody."

Maggie's eyes widened as if the realization of how she had saved us finally hit her. She'd gone Dirty Harry on Lamar and his bodyguard without blinking an eye. "I had the safety on," she said as if that were an excuse.

"Who you pull a piece on?" Cherry seemed intrigued by the idea of Maggie threatening anyone.

"Mr. Jones."

Allie started to giggle again, a little star struck by Maggie's bravado. Maggie cringed as if she wasn't the bad ass in question.

"On Lamar, no shit!" Cherry still wore the small camera on her wrist, expertly flipped it into her palm and took a picture of us. Then she snapped another and laughed. A laugh so annoying Allie covered her ears. No doubt the sound made her liver want to sober up. The laughter focused me enough to listen to the questions about Cherry that were floating around my muddled head. A woman we've been searching for days, a woman, whose only reason for being, was to get paid and someone who knew Lamar Jones by his first name. For her to show up at Chaos 182 made me wonder and ask the question that bothered me.

"Why were you there?"

CHAPTER

23

After finding refuge at the gas station on Nostrand Ave at one o'clock in the morning, Cherry promptly told me to mind my business when I asked why she'd been at Lamar's party. When I wouldn't whip out my cash card and hand her one thousand dollars, she gathered her things, hailed a gypsy cab and drove off into the night without a thank you or goodbye. Maggie, Allie and I sat like Post Traumatic Stress poster pin-ups unable to stop her. Allie didn't know how. A shell-shocked Maggie hadn't come to terms with the fact she'd pulled a gun on someone. My anxiety disorder reminded me it hadn't gone away but lay dormant until terrorized by a self-important thug called Lamar.

When Allie and I finally made it home, I was grateful that a 7:00 a.m. meeting had forced Lee not to wait up for us. Considering the state I was in, I preferred any confrontation with him fortified with a solid ten hours sleep and my wits about me. That early in the morning, I only had enough sense to dump my future sister-in-law in her room.

Around ten a.m. the next day, I struggled out of bed and blindly made my way down to the kitchen to set up the coffee maker. While the coffee brewed, I checked on Allie. I found her sprawled beneath blankets like a dead person, but snoring louder than a 747 landing at Kennedy Airport. Content that she was still alive, I gently closed her door. Lamar had forced her to drink liquor in the hope she might tell him what we were up to with Cherry. I wondered if she still thought this was fun and exciting. I didn't. My confrontation with Lamar triggered a mild anxiety attack.

My brain couldn't cope with such reckless behavior. My mind replayed the events again and again, until my body just shut down from the overload of fear and panic. The medication just told my brain to shut the hell up and calm my silly self down. A little pill can put things into perspective.

While I mulled over the night's events, I dropped bread into the toaster, leaned against the kitchen counter, poured a cup of coffee and called Maggie. I hoped she had some ideas about what to do next about finding Cherry. I knew I didn't. Instead of Maggie, I got Bebe. He'd taken Ziemann's advice and stayed away from the Blue Moon.

"She went out after dropping Rocket off at a play date. She said she'd be back by noon," he said. In the background, I heard unfamiliar women's voices.

"Who's there with you?" I asked. Bebe sighed.

"Ms. Maggie's mother-in-law."

I stiffened at the thought of Lenora Swift, the ultraconservative, sphincter-challenged matron of the Swift family alone with Bebe. The idea put a knot in my stomach. I checked the kitchen clock and told him I was coming over. He seemed mildly relieved. I showered and changed quickly, left a note on the nightstand in Allie's room telling her where I was going, and instructing her to stay home and relax. I headed for Hicksville, Long Island.

Forty minutes later, I stomped up the path of Maggie's house. Mrs. Swift's late model Coupe de Ville sat in the driveway like Hades' chariot. Determined to protect Bebe from one of Mrs. Swift's slightly racist, incoherent dementia-producing tirades, I banged on the front door.

A moment later, Bebe answered wearing one of Maggie's Kiss the Cook aprons. The attire clashed with his jeans, head bandana and vintage Yankees t-shirt. He seemed both weary and relieved to see me. He gestured me to follow, which I did until I came upon the gaggle of blue-haired octogenarians occupying the living room playing cards. You would have thought they were playing high stakes poker the way they were shouting. Mrs. Swift's shrill voice could be heard over the others, complaining to another woman about something while waving a playing card in her face. Bebe and I continued into the kitchen unnoticed by anyone.

"Who the hell are they?" I pointed in the direction of the living room.

"That is Mrs. Swift's Cribbage Club," Bebe informed me.

"What are they doing here?"

"Mrs. Swift stopped by to pick up Rocket. I told her about his play date and Ms. Maggie leaving. Fifteen minutes after I hung up the phone, she comes driving up in that boat of hers, checks the place and then some nursing home clears out and ends up here."

"She's got some nerve. What does she think you're going to steal Roger's baseball card collection?"

Bebe just shrugged.

"Oh Bernard, we're out of lemonade," someone sweetly called out from the other room. As if on cue, Bebe opened the refrigerator and pulled out a large pitcher of pink lemonade. Suddenly, I realized the kitchen smelled fantastic. Platters of finger foods, small cakes and fruit tarts were everywhere.

"You've got to be serious." The idea of Mrs. Swift standing guard over Bebe as he served her friends pissed me off.

"No worries, Ms. O. It's all good. I offered to make food for them. Mrs. Swift doesn't think I'm a menace anymore, and I've had five offers to work as a personal chef. I agreed to do Mrs. Raymond's granddaughter's baby shower. I hope you don't mind. I said you'd do the cake." His lips crooked up in a semi-smile.

I was speechless. I'd come to rescue him, and he'd rescued himself. Bebe didn't need me to defend him against Lenora's harangues. All he had to do was shove food in her mouth.

I settled myself at the kitchen table, grabbed a plate and loaded up on smoked salmon with dill and cream cheese sandwiches to eat. Bebe returned, fixed me a plate of spinach quiche, salad and lemonade. While he served the blue hair brigade and we waited for Maggie, I caught him up on events.

A half an hour later, Maggie burst through the front door, more than likely expecting to find Bebe in handcuffs and her mother-in-law standing atop him waving the American flag and spouting the mission statement from the Tea Party manifesto. She'd seen the Coupe de Ville in the driveway too. What she found was the last of the Cribbage Club packing up to leave and the Sunny View Assisted Living Van pulling up to take some of the ladies back home. I sat eating a delicious raspberry tart while Bebe finished making doggie bags for a few of the ladies.

"Should I ask what this is about?" Maggie stood in the kitchen doorway waiting to pounce on someone. She shrugged off her large shoulder bag, deposited it on the kitchen table and plopped down in a seat next to me.

"It's all good." Bebe put the last of the dishes in Maggie's antiquated dishwasher.

"You missed all the fun. Bebe's a hit with Lenora's posse." I held out a glass of lemonade to her. She took it, slightly perplexed.

"Ms O, I'm going to help the ladies take the tables to the van." Bebe went to the living room.

"Where have you been?" I asked.

"Busy." She pulled out her laptop and powered it on.

"Where did you go?" I asked.

"To the mall." She began searching for files.

"Somebody had a sale," I mused.

She snorted and returned to the computer.

"I guess we're not going to talk about last night." I cocked an upraise eyebrow at her.

"Nothing happened last night." Her blue eyes blinked several times as if to wipe away the image of Bear sprawled on the ground. It took me a moment to accept her right to live in denial.

I nodded; denial looked impressive from where I stood.

I knew the idea of Bear's attempts at intimidation had annoyed her. Also, the intimidation went against everything she'd ever told her son about being bullied. Often the smallest one in his class, he had a tendency to be the one picked on. When harassed, she instructed him to find an adult and tell. For Rocket, this only worked with mommies and other adults. Out of the watchful eyes of grownups, children can be monsters. When one such bully, named Howie Manzo targeted my godson, he resolved the problem in his usual Rocket fashion; he put yogurt in Howie's sneakers during gym, added a ton of salt to his butter and jelly sandwich at lunch and my personal favorite, super glued his notebook. Rocket's mind games lasted until the boys' teacher found out and called each child's parents in to resolve the issues. The meeting ended with Rocket promising to stop terrorizing the former bully. Howie had been losing sleep over the harassment from his unknown assailant. Rocket's resolute, tenacious and wicked sense of payback genetically stemmed from his mother. Maggie would never admit this, of course. She rarely would since she lived in the land called Denial.

What she did want to talk about was something she had on her computer. Somehow, she'd managed to get a black and white surveillance video of the local mall the day of Tania's promotional event. I recognized Tania and the female artist I met at RTM, at a table signing autographs. A nice sized crowd had gathered around them. Suddenly out of nowhere, three young black men in hooded sweat tops, baseball caps and jeans pushed through the crowd. A moment later, mayhem ensued, with everyone running for cover.

"Where was security?" I asked.

"An altercation occurred out in the parking lot, and much of the security got pulled there." Her fingers glided along the keyboard. Another image came up with a view of the mall's parking lot area. Several uniformed security officers surrounded two cars. The same SUV Bear drove Louis to the precinct with.

"Bear," I said in disbelief.

"There's more." Her fingers danced along the keyboard, and another video came up of one of the hooded thugs purchasing something at a clothing store. He's seen talking to a pretty sales clerk for a long time.

"I found the store and talked to the girl. The guy was coming on to her pretty heavy. She wasn't impressed, so he tried harder. He said he worked for a famous music producer. She didn't believe him, so he gave her this card." Maggie slipped a tattered business card in front of me. The name Chaos 182 was embossed in gold letters.

"Lamar set up that attack at the mall," I said.

Maggie nodded.

"I went and talked to security. They felt pretty upset

about the incident. I told them my suspicions, and they helped me find the surveillance tapes for that day. If we can prove Lamar instigated the entire thing, they want to sue the pants off him. He caused a lot of damage and some customers got hurt." She smiled.

"What made you suspicious?"

"Think about it, O. Tania is struggling to keep her artists with RTM and this happens, some of her staff is MIA. Then Lamar shows up saying he'll fix everything."

"If he didn't have an alibi for Rovell's murder, this would be just another thing he pulled to get what he wants," I added.

"His people are starting riots and threatening Tania, why not something more?" Maggie raised an auburn eyebrow at me. "A boat in the middle of the ocean is a nice little alibi don't you think?"

"Would they commit murder for him?" I wondered for the first time. At worst, Lamar's crew seemed more like obedient thugs than cold bloody killers.

"We need to tell Tania. She has to know what Lamar is doing. He might try something worse if he hasn't already."

"We need to find Cherry to get Bebe out of trouble," I said. "After last night, we're no closer to finding her. Neither the police or Ziemann will wait."

This wasn't what she wanted to hear. She wanted to help Tania, Jermaine and all of Whoville, but we had to deal with one problem at a time, finding Cherry.

"We're back to Louis Mackie then," she said.

"Why?" I didn't hide my sense of apprehension.

"He knows her better than we do."

I couldn't argue with that. "How are we going to get Louis to talk to us?" I said, a little resigned to the fact I had to face him again.

"I'll get him to talk to you," Bebe said as he entered the

kitchen.

"You think that's a good idea?" I said.

His lips crooked into his smile as he leaned against Maggie's old laminated countertop, folded his arms and said, "No."

CHAPTER

24

The idea was ridiculous, ill planned and doomed to fail. First, Jermaine would convince Louis to meet him at the RTM studio, under some contrivance. Secondly, Bebe and Jermaine would persuade Louis to talk to us about Cherry. I remembered Louis's anger toward Bebe and even me for intervening at the precinct. Jermaine insisted his brother would stay in control. I didn't know him well enough to believe that. Bebe added his steadfast reassurance, and Maggie threw a hopeful plea to get me to agree. They all believed. I held on to my skepticism like a lifejacket because I was drowning in a sea of their optimism. Jermaine's deep belief that blood was thicker than water was all well and good, but I wanted to make sure he spoke metaphorically, and the blood wouldn't be real. Things could go wrong, and if they went wrong, they would go wrong badly. The memory of Louis sitting in Bear's car embracing the dark side played in my head, and no amount of convincing would erase the image.

After some time, Bebe and Maggie convinced me and we went to RTM. Thankfully, Tania had gone home for the day. To my surprise, Les let us inside. He volunteered to go along with Jermaine's plan. Unsure of how he had convinced the RTM engineer to help, I decided not to ask.

"Hey, where's Allie?" Les locked the door and guided us downstairs to the studio area.

"She has a cold and won't recover until she gets on a plane and lands in California to the loving arms of her husband," I said acerbically.

Les waited a beat before his lips hitched up into a broad grin. "Maybe I can bring her some chicken soup before she goes."

I thought, whatever Allie had, she needed to bottle and sell it at bowling alleys, Shriners conventions and 24-hour Laundromats.

Still with a grin on his face, we followed Les to the basement studio. He left Maggie and me in a darken control booth. Bebe and Jermaine stood inside the insulated sparsely lit isolation room adjacent to the control room.

"So what happens next?" Maggie asked. As if I had a clue.

We watched Jermaine and Bebe through the large control room window, their faces set in determination. I wondered how determined they would be when faced with an equally determined Louis. I understood sibling betrayal. Candace still maintained a friendship with my investment banker ex-boyfriend in the hopes he might come to his senses, divorce his wife, marry me and continued to give her free investment advice. It didn't compare to murder, but betrayal was betrayal, right?

We didn't have to wait long. The door to the isolation room swung open, and the looming body of Louis stood there, hand on the knob, talking over his shoulder to Les, behind him. When he spotted Bebe, every emotion drained from Louis' face but was quickly replaced with barely-contained rage.

The attack happened in a second. Louis pounced on Bebe, a feverish assault that numbed me into immobility. Louis grabbed Bebe around his midsection, nearly lifting him from the ground. Louis had more muscle and had several years of stored up anger and forced Bebe backward with ease. They crashed to the floor in a jumble of arms and legs.

Maggie and I burst out of the control room as if we could actually do something to break up the fight. Les made an attempt but Louis had thrown him off like an old coat. The poor engineer rolled head over ass right outside the room. Jermaine wrapped his arms around Louis in a vain attempt to stop his brother. He didn't even slow him down.

Louis punched Bebe hard in the stomach, doubling Bebe over. Another blow struck him in the ribs. The hit dazed him and sent Bebe stumbling backward, clutching his side. Maggie rushed to Bebe, even as I tried to warn her off. Unfortunately, Louis treated her as a minor impediment. He shoved her and sent her like a rag doll crashing into a wall. Louis got Jermaine off his back with an elbow to his gut and went after Bebe again. Entangled in some power cord, Bebe struggled to get up. As Louis reached for him, I grabbed his arm and held on for dear life. My efforts only gave Bebe time to get to his feet before Louis swung again. The momentum twisted me around and sent me crashing into Bebe. We landed in a heap, me on top.

I now lay between Louis and his objective: killing Bebe. The idea I was anyone's last line of defense didn't reassure me. I'd do anything for him, but I didn't want to be his body armor. Pumped on rage and adrenaline, Louis reached for me. I expected him to toss me like yesterday's trash, and closed my eyes in anticipation. Nothing happened. I bravely opened one eye and found Louis' attention fixed on someone.

Maggie stood there pointing Cherry's stun gun inches away from his broad back. Like two old gunslingers, each waited for the other to make a move. In all honesty, they were more like John Wayne and Little Bo Peep. Luckily, Bo had a fully charged stun gun.

"Louis," Maggie warned as he flinched in my direction.

I took the opportunity to scramble to my feet. "She'll do it." I didn't expect him to believe me; no one ever did when explaining Maggie's supernatural need to protect. Only a few things could switch Maggie into the Terminator. Don't mess with her family or friends. Maggie saw Bebe as both. He'd slept in her house, befriended her son and shared their meals. He was blood. Either Louis thought I'd been bluffing or believed he was fast enough to stop her. He wasn't. She pulled the trigger with the calm of a woman who'd done it before.

To be honest, Louis didn't go down like Bear; I guess he didn't have the weight. He crumpled. Jermaine gawked in horror as his brother fell as if boneless. Rubbing his backside, Les gave Maggie an appreciative smile.

"Well, that went really well." I threw up my hands in exasperation. "That was your plan, invite him over and wrestle." I glared at all them.

"I..." Jermaine began, but I put up a hand to stop him. I didn't want to hear the blood and family speech.

Jermaine seemed reluctant to have his brother restrained. I said I refused to deal with him otherwise. After struggling to get him seated on a chair, Maggie tied him with audio wire. The mother of a Cub Scout, Maggie had a knack for knots. Louis groaned, and his eyes fluttered open when she finished. We watched as he oriented himself and tried to make sense of the five people staring back at him. Being tied to a chair didn't improve his mood.

"Shit, you tazed me," he bellowed.

"That's no way to communicate, Louis," I said calmly.

Jermaine tried to intervene only to become the target of the next hail of profanity.

"I'm going to kill you bitch," Lamar growled at Maggie.

She stood wide-eyed and slightly perplexed. Didn't he understand she was trying to help him? I guess the part where she'd stunned him and wrapped him up like a Thanksgiving turkey threw him off her meaning.

"No you're not," I said. "Stop threatening people."

Louis stilled. He glowered at me as his chest heaved.

"Good," I said sweetly. Now we had an understanding. "We're going to have a conversation."

Louis responded with a sneer and turned away.

"Maggie!" I held out my hand for the stun gun. When she put it in my hand, Louis nearly jumped out of the chair.

"I'm listening." He tried to hop away in the chair.

"Better." I gestured Bebe to stand in front of Louis. Louis strained slightly against his bonds, clearly agitated by his closeness. "Bebe has something to say."

Bebe took a deep breath and began. "Jermaine invited me the night of your party." He kept his voice low and even. "We reconnected a couple of months before you got out. He said everything with you would be cool. I wasn't so sure, you still being mad at me for what happened with him from before."

I wondered if this had to do with the falling out Maggie mentioned. I noticed Jermaine seemed both regretful and miserable. Maggie said the falling out happened at the same time Bebe had been arrested for stealing a car when he was fifteen years old. The sous chef never spoke about the arrest, and I never pushed. I simply thought he wanted to put the past in the past. I didn't realize he was keeping a secret.

"You goddamn right, you messed with my baby brother. Damn right, I'm mad. Hell, I've messed shit up, but I made sure Jermaine stayed out of trouble, kept him away from the gangs and shit. You snatching the car was stupid. You wanted to take him with you was fucked up." Louis' angry words flew at Bebe.

"That's your story, but then there's the truth," Bebe said solemnly.

Then it dawned on me: Bebe and Jermaine's plan was to confess. As to what, I didn't know. Maybe something that would deflate the older Mackie's anger and rage over the death of his mentor and friend.

"I thought you always got into trouble because you made lousy choices even when you knew it was wrong. Like you getting close to Lamar and thinking he's your friend. He slips you a few dollars, lets you ride around in his car. That's not bad, just dumb," Jermaine accused.

"He saved me from shit when I was inside. He protected me, looked out for me. Wood didn't have the juice or the pull. Lamar understands," Louis spit back.

Jermaine dismissed him with a wave. "He ain't your friend, never will be. He wants RTM's business, and he wants you. With you, he thinks he gets me. He won't. He ain't my friend," Jermaine said.

"Wood's gone and Lamar can get us our deal. Tania ain't got the heart for it." Louis struggled against his restraints. I waved the gun at him and he stopped.

"Wood was family, and he's my friend." Jermaine pointed at Bebe.

"Bull shit. He almost got you arrested," Louis growled back.

"A friend warns you not to get into a stolen car because the asshole who stole it knows your older brother and thinks you're a badass too," Jermaine said his voice heavy with regret. "You get in because you don't want to be a punk. Or you're sick of being labeled the good one in the family, the one who never breaks the rules or has fun because he's got to hold the family honor, like some second generation immigrant. Luckily, he has a friend who gets in the car with him because he knows the idea is bad, but he wants to talk you out the stupid shit you're about to do. When the cops flashed us, we crashed the car and ran. When the friend gets snatched by the cops, he doesn't say a word about you being there. He doesn't tell anybody. That's a friend, Louis, you ass-hole," Jermaine said.

I digested Jermaine's revelation like a rock in my stomach and glared at Bebe, who stood like a statue as the truth came out. Had he sacrificed himself for Jermaine? Did Bebe protect him from his adolescent stupidity when Louis hadn't been around to do the job? Bebe had a younger sibling of his own, so he understood. Yet I didn't know who to be angry with, Bebe or Jermaine. The incident changed Bebe's life forever. Thankfully, a quick thinking judge from family court believed the first time offender might take advantage of a special youth work program. Bebe found his way to the Blue Moon, George, Candace and me, which changed his life and ours.

Bebe stood just behind Maggie and gave me a knowing expression. It took me a moment to understand. I nodded slightly to his unspoken truth. How many times had I followed her, and she followed me, without question? Friends did things for you when no one else would. Stopped you from a marrying the jerk of your dreams, or sat with you on an all night stakeout because your boss ate bad Thai food and couldn't finish a surveillance job. Despite your better judgment, there are times when you have to get into the damn car.

CHAPTER

25

Supposedly, what Bebe did to Jermaine had become neighborhood lore. However, it didn't come close to the truth. Bebe had taken on the role of the bad guy and did nothing to dispute anyone's version of the facts. In his defense, Jermaine kept the secret, terrified of disappointing the people who genuinely cared about him, his mother, a brother who wanted more for him, and the man who had taken on the role of father in his life, Linwood Rovell. Whether driven by guilt or maturity, eventually he told someone. The night at the party at RTM, when Linwood Rovell refused to let Bebe enter, Jermaine finally spoke up. He confessed to Rovell. Before he had a chance to tell anyone else, Rovell was dead and Bebe had been accused of his murder.

Louis seemed to contemplate the idea that Bebe hadn't almost derailed Jermaine's journey toward his role as the saintly son. The silent exchange between the Mackies played out before us like some Greek tragedy. Louis had always been the cautionary tale his mother used to keep Jermaine in line.

Don't be like Louis.

Or Bebe Dunn.

Confronted with the fact his brother happened to be human, he had an extreme desire to punch him, and told him so. He did sound contrite about demonizing Bebe and gave a grumbling apology to the sous chef. Bebe nodded his acceptance. After their tussle on the ground, I didn't think Bebe wanted a hug.

"The thing is, Louis, I told Wood about what happened with Bebe the night of the party. He sat us down and talked to us, and everything was cool. He said I should have manned up about it. How Bebe was a true friend and I did him wrong. Don't you remember how he told you to back down when you wanted to toss Bebe out? Wood knew," Jermaine said.

"He doesn't sound like a man who thought Bebe was a threat to your brother," Maggie said.

Still smarting from being zapped, Louis seemed wary of her. He'd probably have nightmares about little redheaded pixies and stun guns. Maggie wouldn't get any hugs from him either.

"We need to help Bebe," Jermaine demanded.

Louis gave him a dismissive sneer. Jermaine would be hug free for a while.

"Everyone saw the confrontation with Rovell when Bebe first arrived. The next day Rovell is dead, and the first thing out of anyone's mouth is about the argument. They skipped the part where everyone made up and played nicely. Rovell held no animosity toward Bebe," I said.

Louis didn't much like me either since I threatened to zap him as well. Hell, I didn't want a hug.

"I found Cherry in Mr. Rovell's office. News got out you was home, and she comes sniffing around. I didn't think you needed the drama, so I made her leave," Bebe said.

Louis did an imperceptible nod of gratitude.

"The police need to search for the real killer," Jermaine reiterated and pointed to Maggie and me. "I hired them to find out."

Louis barely managed to control his laughter, possibly

judging whether Jermaine had lost his mind.

"Trust me, they can," Bebe reassured.

"Yeah, right," Louis gave us an insincere smile and pulled at his restraints. "Could someone untie me?"

"Not before we finish what we had to say," I said, not minding that Louis had no faith in us. He wouldn't be the first or the last.

Maggie took the opportunity to retrieve her laptop. She powered on the computer. She stood in front of Louis and played the surveillance tape of the mall incident.

"He's familiar, right?" Jermaine pointed to the figure of the man talking to the salesgirl.

Louis drew closer to the screen, narrowed his eyes and sat back. "Jay. Jay Long from Fourteenth Street."

"He works for Lamar, part of his crew. They hang around his studio all the time," Jermaine said. "They went after Tania and Keisha at the gig."

"They scared them half to death and ruined the publicity event, which was the point. The distraction in the parking lot made what they did easier. Your friend Bear helped. We don't have to guess why," I said.

Louis couldn't keep his eyes off the small screen. The muscles around his mouth went tight as an expression I hadn't expected to witness grew on the young man's face; disappointment. Rovell's death must have devastated him and his brother's lies about Bebe and Lamar's duplicity made him question everything.

"They all hang out at the studio, Morris, Jay, Little Pete and the other guy over from Linden Blvd," Louis said in a hushed tone.

"You mean Stevie Harmon, Cherry's cousin?" Jermaine said.

"What?" I said.

"He said he wanted to help her...Tania." Louis' voice was barely audible.

I'd been betrayed once, and lied to by people I thought cared about me. It felt like a body blow. For the first time since I'd met Louis, I felt something other than dread—sympathy.

"Do you know how he got Chaos 182?" Maggie asked.

"He hooked up with an independent a few years ago and bought him out," Jermaine said.

Maggie shook her head. "Before Lamar started Chaos 182, the business belonged to a guy name Max Hoffman, under the name Hoffman Production. A business he began in college. He did well for a local promoter. Lamar comes along with an Atlanta artist as his bodyguard and somehow ingratiates himself with Hoffman. A year later, Hoffman is on the west coast building a new business and staying far away from New York. Now tell me how a bodyguard gets enough money to buy out Hoffman? Lamar barely made it out of high school and was almost kicked out of the service."

She waited for an answer, but none came.

"I called Hoffman and he wouldn't talk to me. He sounded like a guy, who thought California wasn't far enough from Lamar."

"I don't think Lamar wins people over with his charms and his handsome appearance. He likes bullying them to get what he wants. He has his sight set on RTM. Will you accept Lamar taking over Rovell's dream?" I asked.

Louis averted his gaze, found a stop on the floor and said nothing. He shook his head as if struggling with the truth. Lamar had used Louis' grief and, and pointed him straight at Bebe, distracting him from Tania, and his brother: the voices of reason. And then he'd offered himself as a replacement for Rovell.

"You okay?" Maggie placed a hand on Louis' shoulder.

He seemed to tense beneath her touch. His eye showed confusion and beneath that, his anger. Louis gave a slight nod, cleared his throat and steadied himself.

"Release me?" He tugged at his bindings.

When Maggie started to untie him, I stopped her.

"What?" Louis complained in frustration.

"Cherry," I said.

"What about the bitch?" Louis' eyes flared again.

"We're been trying to find her. Where would she be?" I asked.

"Do I have to be tied up to do this?" He pulled again at his restraints and glared up at me.

"No, but I like your undivided attention." I smiled.

"I haven't seen her since she left me at the gas station dealing with the cops. Never came around during the trial, never came to the jail to check if I were dead or alive. All I know is she never had a pot to piss in. She played me, and she left." Louis said.

"Doesn't she have any friends?" Maggie asked.

Louis' eyes went comically wide in disbelief. "Would you be her friend?"

Maggie and I said nothing.

"You said she had a cousin who worked for Lamar," Maggie said.

"The bastard hooked her up with me."

"When you were together, where did she live?" Maggie asked.

Louis shrugged. "We either hung out at her cousin's or found someplace. I never knew where she lived, didn't care. It wasn't love or anything. I'd give her a call and we hung out. Find a friend's house or something." He shrugged.

"She gots to be close to her cuz." Jermaine asked. "Didn't she live with his family for a time?"

Louis nodded. "Harmon's mom kicked her out for getting too friendly with her new boyfriend."

"Isn't Cherry a little old for you?" I said.

Louis simply smirked at me. "Like I said, she was willing and ain't ugly. Free candy is free candy."

Should I have been surprised that Louis had objectified Cherry into a breath mint? I guess his time with Lamar had been educational and not totally wasted.

"That's kinda of harsh," Maggie said.

"The day I got snagged by the police, Cherry sat in the car next to me. One moment, she's telling me how much she loves me and she's my girl. The next thing I know, she goes off to the bathroom and a half a breath later I got cuffs on me and she ain't nowhere to be found. Didn't see her at my trial or when I was sentenced. Never called or visited while I was locked up. So yeah, I'm a little harsh." Louis had gotten some of his anger back.

"So she wouldn't have come to the party to see you and ask for your forgiveness for running out," I pondered aloud.

"Unless she got stupid all of a sudden." Louis said. "Because if I had, I'd be back in jail." He pulled at his restraints and glowered. I guess Cherry remained a touchy subject, along with jail, his little brother's stupid choices and turning his back on Maggie.

Taking pity on him, Maggie reached around the back of the chair, yanked on a dangling cord and released him in one swift move. His eyes widened in surprised, possibly wondering what other super powers she had. She smiled warmly back. Louis attempted a smile but failed.

"I read the transcripts of your trial," Maggie said in a tone so casual it sounded like she was talking about the weather. "There wasn't very much to it. The owner of the car, a 'Naz-Boy' aka Kenneth Roy Clarkson, said he never lent it to you.

He met you at some party and when it was time to go, he found his keys gone. The cops stopped you because he reported it stolen."

Louis nodded. "He come out of Atlanta, trying to get some representation in New York. Met him at a party thrown by Steve. Me and Cherry been there the whole night. Naz got to talking and I told him about Wood. He seemed interested. I thought we was cool. Then Steve needed someone to make a run to get some more beer. Cherry showed up with someone's car keys and volunteered me. I didn't ask so I went." I shook my head. Louis' inability to use his common sense amazed me.

"You receive a light sentence because you had no other major priors," Maggie said.

"Wood's lawyer handled the whole thing," Jermaine said.

"Things went to shit real quick. Cherry was my only witness," Louis shook his head. "I just wanted it over."

Bebe and Louis' fate seemed somewhat similar. Both relied upon the most unreliable person I'd ever met to save them. If the apocalypse were to start tomorrow, Cherry would arrive before the Four Horsemen in a stolen car.

"Why ask about Louis' arrest?" Jermaine asked.

"Yeah, why?" Louis absently rubbed the spot where Maggie had shot him.

"Curious." Maggie shrugged.

I didn't buy her sudden dismissal of his question. Was Cherry randomly wreaking havoc with those around her or had her path been carefully planned? The idea floated in my mind until my phone interrupted me.

"Dessa, where are you?" Lee asked with a hint of impatience.

"Why?" I asked. I wasn't sure I wanted him to know.

"I need to talk to you and Maggie. Can you come by my office now?"

“This sounds serious,” I teased and tried to lighten the tone.

“It is.”

“Can you tell me what’s going on?”

There was a moment of silence when I heard a beep through the phone.

“No, Ms. Wilkes, I would like you and your little friend to come to Lee’s office right now,” Ziemann said. He'd put the call on speakerphone.

“Please, Dessa,” an exasperated Lee added.

I promised I would come, but a sense of apprehension formed in the pit of my stomach.

“Everything okay, Ms. O?” Bebe asked, possibly reading the concern on my face.

“Fine.” I lied.

CHAPTER

26

When I pushed through the doors of the law office I half expected to find Ziemann standing in front of a bunch of bedraggled village folk, with a torch in one hand and a noose in another. Instead, Maggie and I were greeted warmly by the receptionist. My unease didn't vanish. She instructed us to go to Lee's office. I thanked her, steeled myself and took the familiar route to Lee's office like some criminal on his way to his execution. When we passed a small conference room my sense of dread evaporated in an instant. The last person I'd expected to find sitting at the large oak table was Cherry Turnbull munching on a powdered donut.

"What the—" I stopped in the doorway. Maggie bumped into me and grumbled until she caught sight of Cherry.

An unconcerned Cherry added several spoonfuls of sugar to her coffee. Her oversized handbag—that probably held a heat seeking missile, handcuffs and a small attack dog sat on the table.

"What the hell are you doing here?" I stood across from her with my hands on my hips, a pose I considered my best when shocked and horrified.

"You took my gun. Someone's gonna pay for it." A long polished nail, covered in confectioner sugar pointed at me.

"What?" I didn't care about her stupid gun."What are you doing here?"

She made a sucking sound with her teeth and turned away in a demonstration of exaggerated indifference. The witch was ignoring me. Dumbfounded and outraged at her slight and her presence at Lee's law office, I did the only thing that worked to get her attention. I went for her handbag.

She grabbed the opposite hand strap. A tug of war ensued over the conference table. I gave a hard yank, which pulled her off her feet and onto the table.

"No you don't," she yelled as her short purple skirt inched up her legs, threatening to expose more of Cherry than I wanted to see. With one hand still on the bag strap, she tried to shove the skirt down. She lost her grip. This gave me some leeway to pull harder, forcing Cherry to let go. This sent the bag and me falling backward, and on my backside. The entire contents of the bag flew out. Maggie and I got hit with a barrage of flying objects. Something hard bounced off my forehead. I rubbed the spot and wondered what hit me. The culprit appeared to be an amber prescription bottle filled with several camera digital storage disks. Someone had handwritten the word *Payday* on the top. I scooped the bottle into my pants pocket. I stood up to find Cherry on all fours coming across the conference table like a pit bull. I stepped away.

"What are you, one of those kleptos or something? That's real crocodile," Cherry yelled at me.

One of the office's law clerks popped his head in to investigate the noise. "Everything okay in here?"

We glared at him like the witches from Macbeth, and he quickly popped out, no doubt to get reinforcements. I turned my attention back to Cherry. Her eyes locked on Maggie who hurriedly shoved things back into the handbag.

"I'll give you back your bag when you tell how the hell

you got here." I had my hands on my hips again.

"I don't have to tell you a goddamn thing, but it wasn't hard to figure out. I called that restaurant where he worked and told some fool I had information and they gave me his lawyer's name." She crouched on the table like some cat about to spring.

Cherry dressed in her Easter best, a purple two-piece suit cut a little too tight, and too short to be considered business attire. I guess this was Cherry's professional attire, and I had no doubt what profession she aimed for with it.

"I got a lawyer now, and I'm gonna sue your ass off for my stun gun," she shouted. "I'm going around unprotected because of you two." Maggie picked up a box of condoms and gingerly dumped it into the bag.

"My mistake. I didn't know you were working. You're giving an office discount," I said snidely, then remembered Lee worked here. "You better not be."

"Go to hell." She'd hitched up her skirt and started across the table when Lee and Ziemann showed up with the law clerk that slunk out of the room at the sight of Cherry, and me doing my best impression of Zena, warrior princess.

"What the hell is going on here?" Lee barked.

Ziemann went to get Cherry off the table, but she shrugged him off, getting down on her own.

"That bitch got my bag, and she owes me a new stun gun." She pointed at us.

Lee gave me an inquisitive glance.

"We need to calm down, Ms. Turnbull." Ziemann sounded a tad condescending.

Cherry sneered at him. "I want you to sue her."

"Give back her bag, Ms. Swift," Ziemann's tone had turned both impatient and imperious.

"Why is she here?" I asked.

"It's none of your business, right?" Cherry turned to Ziemann for conformation. He sighed deeply and closed his eyes. His expression of disappointment when he opened them again only confirmed my suspicions. He wanted us to go away.

"Ms. Wilkes…" Ziemann rubbed his temple with his thumb and forefinger.

"For Christ sakes, tell them and this will all be over with." An exasperated Lee stood next to me. I knew he had questions that wouldn't go away without a drawn-out explanation. I didn't have the time or the energy.

Ziemann groaned. "Ms. Turnbull will give the police a statement regarding the evening of Mr. Rovell's death. She will readily admit she argued with Mr. Dunn in Mr. Rovell's office and that Mr. Dunn later escorted her out of the premises—period. This being the argument everyone heard. "

This was terrific news, but I didn't trust it. I narrowed my gaze on Cherry as if she were a new life form discovered in a New York City sewage drain. This had to be studied and dissected before I confirm this was a good thing.

"Just like that?" I asked Lee because I didn't expect the truth from Cherry, and all I got from Ziemann was attitude. He cocked a critical eyebrow at Ziemann. After living with me for a while, he's perfected the move.

"Ms. Turnbull has some outstanding warrants against her, and Thad thinks it's a good idea to clear them up before she speaks to the police." His voice dripped with recrimination. "Thad has even offered Ms. Turnbull as few days at a hotel to gather herself before her statement."

"How long will that take?" Maggie still held the handbag, and took a step behind Lee and me, shielding herself from Cherry's lethal gaze.

"A few days, maybe a week," Lee said with some derision in his voice. He wasn't happy with this plan.

"Why don't you give a statement now and deal with your crap later?" I demanded.

Cherry snorted and shook her head. "Ain't doing nothing until my stuff is done."

In disbelief, I glared at Ziemann whose expression of indifference fueled my annoyance. He acted as if he was above it all. If he thought this was the best way of dealing with this, he'd lost his mind, and I told him so.

"You lost your mind," I said.

"I wouldn't have to do this if you hadn't tried to bribe Ms. Turnbull." An edge of irritation had crept into Ziemann's voice for the first time, shattering some of his unflappable facade.

"Bribe?" I exclaimed. "It was more like cab fare for her trouble. Only she wanted more."

"She said you offered her money so she would tell the police whatever you wanted," Ziemann said.

"She's a liar, a blackmailer, a thief." I struggled to find another word that didn't include cursing. "And she dresses badly."

To my surprise, Cherry took offense at the clothing remark. She smoothed down her skirt and straightened her jacket. "This is designer," she proclaimed.

I snorted. "Was he blind and had only two fingers?" I turned to Ziemann. "You're going to trust this woman to tell the police the truth after she gets what she wants?"

"Considering she is willing to tell them otherwise if I don't," Ziemann said tightly. "So if you don't mind, give back her pocketbook."

Cherry beamed triumphantly.

"Okay." Maggie stepped from behind her protective barrier of Lee and me. She held out the bag to Cherry, who yanked it away.

"Yeah, sorry." I went to leave, but Lee blocked my exit.

"Thad, would like you to stay away from Ms. Turnbull," he said with some warning.

"What about my stun gun?" Cherry blurted.

Lee's eyebrows furrowed.

"They're illegal you know." I tried to keep the tone conversational.

"You want to explain?" he said.

Should I explain how Maggie disarmed Bear to save Allie? No.

"Can I talk to you about it later at home?" I begged. Knowing Lee, this story would not go down well, considering it included his sister, a gun and a shark.

"Home?" Cherry's quizzical eyes danced between Lee and me.

"Ms. Wilkes is the fiancée of Mr. McKenzie," Ziemann said drolly.

Cherry cackled. "You got yourself a white boyfriend, and he's a lawyer. You must got money."

I seemed to have more value now that I was a person of substance by association. I inwardly groaned. From some unknown pocket, she whipped out a tiny blue camera and snapped a picture. Instinctively, Lee shut his eyes at the flash. I'd been prepared and turned away.

"She also owns her own cake shop," Ziemann added. I half expected Ziemann to tell her my net worth and pull out my bank statements. I scowled at the lawyer.

"Maybe you better go?" Lee said.

"Not before she promises to stay away from Ms. Turnbull," Ziemann said. "And provide restitution for her property." The restitution part sounded like an add-on and a dig.

"Let's go, O." Maggie stood by the conference room

door.

I read the urgency on her face. I could stay and argue with Ziemann, piss Lee off more and kill Cherry. Or I could just leave. I decided to leave.

Purposely, I turned my back to Cherry and Ziemann and faced Lee. From the displeasure on his face, he didn't like the role of circus master to the drama we threw at him. This was a man who enjoyed his peace of mind and his future wife, not in prison. He'd involved himself because of Bebe. So I didn't want to lie to him or make working with Ziemann worse.

I gave him a hug and whispered in his ear, "Please trust me?"

When I pulled away, the concern and doubt in his eyes possibly questioned my sanity and his patience. Yet he nodded in the way that he always did when he had total faith in me. Or at least when he believed I wouldn't break any city, state or federal laws.

"I'll talk to you at home," he said.

I took a deep breath and turned to Ziemann and Cherry, who glared at me impatiently.

"I promise, to the best of my ability to give Ms. Turnball what I owe her," I said stiffly.

"What about harassing her?" Ziemann said.

Keeping a straight face, I faced Cherry. "No problem." I gave them both a tight smile before hurrying from the conference room.

Ziemann called out to say something, but I was already out of the room with no intention of going back. When I got to Maggie, she pulled me out of the office to the small elevator that serviced the building.

"What did you steal?"

I didn't particularly liked her accusatory tone or the mommy voice she was using. I pulled out the prescription bottle and gave it a little shake. The SD memory disks rattled around. I thought of the beauty shop and Cherry's photographs that lined the mirror behind her work station. The boxes filled with photographs given to me by Vesta. I turned the bottle so Maggie could see the handwritten words.

Payday

CHAPTER

27

After leaving the law office, Maggie and I headed to my house. She scolded me all the way. Her issues were the theft of Cherry's memory disks. This came from a woman who stole a stun gun and used the thing not once but twice. If I felt any remorse about stealing from Cherry, that particular train hadn't quite arrived yet. I promised Maggie she'd be the first one I'd inform when that train pulled into the station. My bigger concern had to do with Cherry's storage disks. I hoped the theft was worth Ziemann adding burglary charges to the threats he hurled at me as we left.

At home, we found a pale and miserable Allie sitting at the kitchen table. I put on a pot of coffee and raided the cookie jar for all of us. I asked Maggie to set up her computer to view Cherry's storage disks. She hesitated, probably wondering if my shipment of remorse and guilt had arrived. It hadn't.

While I poured coffee, Maggie explained to Allie what had happened during the day. Despite her condition, Allie listened intently. Her fearful expression when I pulled her from Lamar's office had gone.

"Why did you steal these again?" Allie asked as she munched on a large chocolate chip cookie. Maggie had loaded up her computer with images from several disks.

"I wouldn't say I stole them," I said. "Anyway, the woman takes pictures like a damn photo journalist covering a war. These might tell us something and give us some leverage if she tries to renege on her deal with Ziemann."

Maggie's expression of recrimination gradually faded. Her little shoulders heaved in a big sigh of resignation as she boarded my guilt free train.

"I thought about…" She tapped her index finger on lip before she continued.

"About time you used your superpowers." I gleefully rubbed my hands together.

Allie said. "Superpowers?"

"Maggie thinks everyone has superpowers. She says mine is the ultimate reality check." I said "I come along and give you the reality check from hell to show you the stupidity of your ways."

Allie averted her eyes. I smiled, gratified my powers remained in full force. "Maggie's powers are of observation and deduction. She can find out who did it faster than figuring out how to get out ink stains from her husband's shirts."

Allie cocked an eyebrow at Maggie.

"Hairspray on the stain, washes it right out," Maggie said proudly.

An expectant Allie turned to me. I shrugged. "Mrs. Park." I said. This confused her. "Park's Dry Cleaner on Springfield Boulevard. Now can we get back to the point?"

"The answer had been staring us in the face before we even talked to Louis," Maggie said.

I made a circular motion with my finger for her to hurry up.

"The party Rovell gave and how Cherry got inside. Bebe had trouble getting in, how did she?" Maggie took a cookie and pointed at us.

I shrugged.

"I think Rovell invited Cherry. He got her in, and no one knew except Bebe, who ran into her in his office," Maggie explained.

"Why?" I asked.

"She had something he wanted." Maggie scrolled through as a series of photographs she'd loaded on to the computer.

"Louis?" Allie questioned.

I shook my head. "Louis remains a hot commodity. Rovell had him and Lamar wanted him. Then Rovell died."

"If I were Rovell and knew someone was trying to poach my talent, I'd be pretty pissed off. Then someone comes along and says, I've got something that might put a stop to that," Maggie said.

"Cherry?" Allie interjected.

Maggie nodded.

"At a price, of course," I said.

"What could Cherry possibly have that Rovell wanted?" Allie asked.

"What's one of the most annoying things about Cherry?" Maggie kept going through the images.

"She's still breathing," I said, not wanting to play twenty questions.

Maggie rolled her eyes.

"Taking pictures," Allie chimed in, proud of her contribution.

"You said it. She acts like a photojournalist, recording everything. She can't stop herself. Maybe she captured something powerful enough to get Rovell's interest," Maggie said.

I thought about Cherry, Rovell and Lamar with one common thread between them, Louis. "Rovell made no secret about still wanting to work with Louis. Then Lamar shows his hand by sniffing around the Mackies."

I doctored my coffee then Maggie, Allie, and I went through hundreds of pictures all afternoon. The most recent were of Cherry's time at Vesta. We recognized none of these people. Surprisingly, a photograph of Lamar's brother popped up a few times. His terrified expression indicated Cherry's candid snapshots had caught him off guard. A few from Lamar's party popped up, including one of me in the bathroom. We almost gave up hope when we found what we wanted on the sixth disk.

Maggie worked her magic and pulled up photographs from her online newspaper and database services. The moment Bebe got arrested, she read all the news articles on Rovell's murder, Louis' gun charge, and anything regarding Lamar. Many discussed Louis and other hip hop stars that had fallen into trouble. An interview with Lamar talked about the tragedy of Louis' talent going to waste in prison. He'd expressed his hope Louis would come out the stronger for the experience. His insincere words made me want to puke.

Maggie found the photograph we wanted, and gave Cherry unexpected praise. It took a devious mind to work this one up.

In the photograph, Lamar stood with a man outside his office shaking hands. In the foreground Lamar's very attractive receptionist at her desk, grinned into the camera. She held up a newspaper, opened to a photograph of a famous couple holding hands. At first it seemed Cherry had caught Lamar by accident in the background.

Maggie's fingers danced across the keyboard again, and she cropped out a headshot of Lamar's visitor. Then she pulled up a publicity photo of a young man who had given a statement to the police during Louis' gun arrest. "Our guy from Atlanta, Clarkson," she said as she cropped the archive photo and showed both images side by side. They were the same person.

"Lamar knew him," I said in astonishment.

"Even better." Maggie went back to Cherry's original photograph and highlighted the newspaper the receptionist held. She enlarged the date at the top. "Weeks before Louis' arrest, Lamar had the man in his office. Cherry caught the date and saw the receptionist's desk clock. She even got the time."

Cherry could give CIA operatives lessons in stealth and surveillance techniques.

"I read that Lamar told anyone who'd ask he'd never met Clarkson," Maggie said. "He did several interviews during and after the trial."

"Same story he probably told Louis." I shook my head at Lamar's deception.

"Cherry lost her opportunity when Rovell died. So she goes to Lamar for her payday," Maggie added.

"Wouldn't that be dangerous?" Allie asked.

"Maybe she thinks she's smarter than everyone," Maggie said.

Cherry had the tenacity of a New York City rat and was just as hard to kill. Somewhere, she sat in a hotel suite going through the room service and the minibar and thinking about her big payday.

"Won't she be mad you have these?" Allie said.

"Pissed," I said with a wide grin.

"She'll tell Ziemann or Lee," Allie continued.

My smile faded a bit, but not much. I shrugged.

"You don't seem too upset about Lee finding out," a surprised Allie said.

"It's like ripping off a bandage. Might hurt a little, but I'll survive."

"They'll fight and have makeup sex. Sometimes I think she does it on purpose," a prudish sounding Maggie said.

My grin widened at the prospect. "We don't call it makeup sex. We call it Tension Reduction Therapy, and I don't do it on purpose. You know how hard it is to get him mad."

"I couldn't do that." Allie shook her head in wonderment.

Maggie placed a hand on Allie's. "Good, don't pick up Odessa's bad habits."

"What? You and your husband don't fight?" I asked.

Allie's eyes widened and threatened to water up, but to her credit, she didn't cry. "Phil went to a conference in Scottsdale Arizona for a week. I thought I'd go with him but things changed. Other arrangements were made and we argued about it before he left." Allie played with the cookie.

"You don't like Scottsdale?" Maggie asked.

"Never been," she said.

"You want to tell us why you didn't go?" I prompted, hoping I could get to the bottom of Allie's impromptu visit.

Her lips quivered a bit. She took a bite of her cookie and fussed with the crumbs before she finally spoke. "I hate San Diego. I hate the country club, the new offices and my so-called new friends. I can't even be a dental hygienist anymore," she confessed in one breath.

"Phil is a good oral surgeon, and when an office in Orange County wanted him to join their medical practice, Phil couldn't believe they wanted him. They have rich clientele, and they specialize in cosmetic surgery. The old surgeon got brought up on malpractice charges and is fixing teeth in a minimal security prison," Allie said. "Phil said yes without talking to me. He always wanted a bigger practice, but I thought we were happy where we were in San Bernardino. I helped out in the office because he loved working with me. At the new place, no wives work there. They have assistants with gigantic boobs doing everything. I don't think they pay those girls, just give them free surgery or something."

"So, what did you do with your days?" Maggie asked.

Allie's lip quivered again. "Someone from the office gave him a membership to the country club. He told me to make friends. I tried. They acted like a pack of wolves. Then Phil suggested I volunteer for a committee, and I did. Everything went wrong after that." Allie straightened her shoulders. "Before long they dumped the entire thing on me and laughed about it behind my back. I overheard them one day saying horrible things about my clothes and how I cut my hair. The worst part is they said Phil needed a new and improved wife. One woman said Phil would be her special summer project to find him someone more suitable. I thought it had to be a joke. I wasn't sure. I'm still not." She sounded wounded.

"What does Phil say about all this?" I asked.

A disheartened Allie shrugged. "He thinks they're teasing, and I should try harder to make friends."

"Husbands can be a little clueless sometimes." Maggie's husband still thought she just answered phones and did a little light filing at McAvoy Investigation.

"So you came to New York to find the new and improved you?" I said.

Allie shrugged.

"That explains Frank."

"Frank's sweet," she said.

"Bunnies are sweet, old ladies with blue hair are sweet, but Frank is a lousy poker player, with flat feet and a receding hair line," I said.

"You hadn't planned any of this?" Maggie questioned.

"Phil told me about the conference in Scottsdale. He said no one planned to take their spouses. I was extremely disappointed. I thought it would be fantastic to get away, but I stayed home and worked on the club's committee for the summer gala. Until Jenny Holder said she thought the shade of green I picked for the paper umbrella reminded her of the color of vomit. That's the same woman who thought Phil needed a new wife. She told me to buy different ones immediately. I was the chairperson, and she treated me like a go-fer. She even gave me a sample to take with me in case I got confused." Allie huffed.

"What did you do?" Maggie asked.

"I got in my car, drove to a party store and sat in the parking lot and cried for about an hour. Then I went to the airport and came here. I needed to see my brother." Allie bite into her cookie and blinked back tears.

I sighed with relief that my future sister-in-law with her funny voices, self-esteem problem, and a clueless husband, wasn't wanted in twelve states. "I guess they're getting those umbrellas when hell freezes over," I said.

Allie's lips twisted in a crooked grin when the realization hit her. "I guess."

CHAPTER
28

Maggie needed to get home. She had a husband, a son and a dog to manage. Besides, we couldn't make any decision about what to do about the photograph of Lamar. The picture had considerable ramifications. Not only could it open an investigation vindicating Louis from his gun charges, the photograph might give the police another suspect in Rovell's murder—Lamar. Despite what he said about his alibi, Lamar had enough pull to get someone else to do his dirty work. His alibi, of being in a boat miles away, was too perfect.

Maggie and I agreed we needed a little more than Lamar making friends with the guy from Atlanta. We also had Cherry to deal with. Sooner or later, the absence of the picture might put a crimp in her plans. It wouldn't take a rocket scientist to figure out how the disks came up missing. My enemy list grew in leaps and bounds. The uncertainty formed a worrisome pit in my stomach as I sat in the kitchen with Allie. She sat patiently waiting as if I had a next move. I didn't have any next move. I'd run out of next moves.

"I think we should bake," I announced. I needed to erase my uneasiness, and the only way I knew to do this was to bake.

"Excuse me?" She seemed terrified of the idea. "I don't bake."

"That's okay because I do and we need to make something." I rubbed my hands together like a mad scientist. I pulled out some aprons and handed one to a resistant Allie. Her face held a mixture of confusion and terror; you would have thought I'd asked her to perform brain surgery. I wanted this to be fun for her, so I plugged in my iPod playlist, hooked up the speakers, and selected some retro R & B music of my mother's favorites. My memories of my mother and baking were interconnected forever, more than Christmases and birthdays. Sometimes I could still remember her dancing in the kitchen to the sound of Gladys Knight and the Pips.

"You're going to make one of your brother's favorite cakes," I said.

The panic grew in her eyes. "I can't."

I nodded, and tied the apron around her waist. "I bet those women at the country club never baked a Black Forest Cake in their lives. They're too worried about the color of some damn paper umbrellas. You can't love paper umbrellas, but a cake, made with love is a joy, sweetheart." I said.

"You have to help me?" Her concern faded a bit.

"Of course, that's what families do." It sounded cliché, but I meant every word. In time, Allie would become my sister-in-law, but I wanted to be her friend.

She took a deep breath. "Where do we begin?"

I handed her a large measuring cup and scoop for sugar. "In the beginning, there was sugar," I said reverently and held out the large canister.

For two and half hours, I coached Allie into making her first ever Black Forest Cake. Motown's greatest hits played in the background as we sifted, measured, creamed and baked. In the end, Allie's cake wasn't pretty but tasted fantastic. Though she looked as if she'd gone toe to toe with the Pillsbury Dough Boy and lost, she was smiling.

"I think Phil would like this." She held up her creation lovingly.

"He'd better, or I know a perfect place for the paper umbrellas," I said.

Martha and the Vandellas' *Dancing in the Street* played. I swung my hips to the rhythm and danced. Allie had watched tentatively for a while before I grabbed her by the hand to join me. She abandoned herself to the music and let go. We laughed and swayed with the smell of chocolate in the air.

***

Lee arrived home as we set up for dinner. His disheveled and somewhat haggard expression told me an afternoon with Cherry and Ziemann had sucked the life force out of him. I had a strong desire to run him a hot bath, put on his favorite recording of Charlie Parker and hand him a bottle of ice cold beer. However, I couldn't put off this confrontation with his sister. The bath, beer and the music would have to wait.

Lee stood in the kitchen doorway transfixed by the sight of his sister tossing salad for dinner and humming the Temptation's tune *Papa was a Rolling Stone.* I grinned and held out my arms to him. He walked into the hug like a man uncertain of his fate. I wanted to reassure him the kitchen was safe to enter, no more emotional meltdown or dashes to hide. I peeled off his jacket, helped him with his tie and sat him down at the table. He said nothing, to confuse by the change of temperature in the room.

"Everything okay?" he asked as I finished setting the table for dinner and sat down to join him.

"Everything is good." I passed him the salad bowl. We filled our plates in communicable silence. Before Lee had taken his first bite, I stopped him. "I want to say grace before dinner."

His expression of mortification almost made me laugh.

Not the most traditional in regards to the religious aspect of my life, the idea of me saying a prayer before any meal signaled to him that something had to be wrong, if I had to call on God. Thanksgiving, Christmas, and Easter were months away, and nobody had recently died. A conspiratorial Allie bowed her head, and I caught the hint of a smile. Lee eyes stayed fixed on me for a long time. Impatient, I glared back until his head dipped.

"God, please accept our praise and bless our food. Grace, health, and strength to us afford." I waited a beat before I continued. "Also, bless Allie for finding her way to us, and may her brother be tolerant of her recent behavior. She loves and trusts him and hopes he understands she can no longer impose upon his hospitality and will be booking a flight to California in the morning."

Lee's mouth opened but nothing came out. I continued.

"Also, dear Lord, we are grateful Allie is okay, her marriage is fine, and her relationship with her brother will be fine when they have a long talk after this wonderful meal. Amen."

"Amen," a beaming Allie chirped.

An astonished Lee followed with an uneasy amen. The guardedness he'd arrived with had begun to depart, replaced with a smile he aimed at his sister.

"I made dessert," Allie announced proudly to her brother.

An hour later, over cake and coffee, Allie had a conversation with Lee. She talked about the move to San Diego, the country club and the women who ruled it. She told him how she sat in the shopping parking lot and cried like a baby. She'd run to her brother for solace only to find him stern and unsupportive. Lee listened intently, then apologized and called Phil a jerk for being equally unaware of her distress. Family unity was restored, much to my delight. Allie got him to promise to bring me to California. She wanted to introduce me to the ladies at Lake Shore Golf and Tennis Country Club. He thought it was a damn brilliant idea.

Lee spent much of the evening talking to his sister, but later joined me in the bedroom. He stretched his lean body across our king sized bed and he watched me strip out of my clothing; the frustration he'd shown earlier had faded. He no longer believed he had to commit his sister to a mental hospital or send her to a marriage counselor. Dressed in well-worn jeans and faded shirt, Lee the lawyer had vanished as well. His dark stubble added to the scruffy charm that had always endeared him to me. His languid mood shone on the half-smile he wore as he took off his glasses to clean on his t-shirt. He'd replaced them to get a better view as I slipped off my shirt. I often teased him on his preoccupation of watching me undress.

"When Allie was sixteen, she ran away with this boy named Harry Mitchem." He repositioned himself on a stack of pillows. "He told her some crap about being in love with her or something, and she went with him. Twenty-four hours later, she calls from the New York Port Authority saying Harry dumped her at the train station when she wouldn't sleep with him. He said she'd have to make her own way home. Our mom had passed away, and Dad was away on a business trip. He'd left us home alone before, but I knew he would never trust us after this. I borrowed my friend's brother's old beat up Dodge Dart. I was fifteen, nothing but a learner's permit.

"Terrified I'd be stopped by the police, I drove like someone's grandmother, but I made it. On the way to get her, I thought the worst. When I arrived, I yelled at her for half a minute, because I was too grateful she hadn't been hurt. I didn't speak to her the whole trip back." Lee folded his hands across his chest and sighed. "By the time, we got home, it had to be three in the morning, and my dad was due back that night. I slept most of the day, found Allie in the kitchen making peanut butter and jelly sandwiches for me. Dad was none the wiser. She was so thankful, I couldn't stay angry."

"Did she love this guy?" I slipped out of my jeans.

Lee shook his head. "No. She wanted some adventure and Henry was the easiest way to get it. I've been dealing with her momentary need for escapade since I was ten."

"She's a dental hygienist, who shops bargain basement and whose highlight is finding paper umbrellas. I don't blame her for wanting a little adventure." I slipped into one of Lee's old college t-shirts and joined him in bed.

"Between wanting to join the circus, starring on Broadway, and jumping out of an airplane, the most normal thing she ever did was marry Phil. I thought she'd settle herself down by now. I guess not." He said.

"You have a thing against adventure."

He shook his head. "How can you say that? I live with you, Dessa." He gave me a lecherous smile and pulled me close.

"I hope you act that way when I'm eighty."

"I have an excellent memory." His hand went under my t-shirt.

"What if your memory goes?" I covered my hand over his, stopping his exploration.

He grumbled but thought on the subject and smiled. "In that case, I'll think I'm sleeping with a different woman every night." He freed his hand to continue his raconteur.

For the next hour, I kept Lee's hands, as well as other parts of his anatomy, busy. Though recent events had put us off our usual habits, Lee treated our return to intimacy as if there had been some long famine we'd survived.

"You know you won't be able to do that when you're

eighty," I said some time later as we lay in bed, and I tried to catch my breath and my senses. The t-shirt hung from one of the bedposts, half the bedding was on the floor and Lee lay sprawled next to me like a dead man. When he said nothing, I turned to face him. His eyes were closed, his breath deep, but steady. I gave him a jab in the ribs. He barely flinched.

"Did you hear me?" I said. He nodded. I gave him another jab, annoyed at his lack of response.

"Please, don't do that. Or I'll have to poke you back."

I smiled at the idea but realized, as he lay there motionless, there wasn't a likelihood of this happening. I sighed as my mind wound down and waited for him to recover.

"I like Allie," I said to make conversation. He acknowledged this with an agreeable grunt. "Since you two are getting along, I think she should stay a few days and really visit."

He opened one eye and turned to me. "Don't you think she should go home to Phil?"

"A few days will do, I think."

This time he fully turned to me. Even in the dark, I could make out his usual questioning if not mistrusting expression. "A few days for what?" He sounded alert.

"To reconnect with you and get her feet beneath her," I said.

"She should go home."

Without his glasses and his hair mussed, he always seemed younger to me. Not the stern hard charging defense lawyer who put fear in the heart of the prosecution. Also, it was hard to take him serious when he was naked.

"What are you afraid of if she stays?"

"Nothing." He placed a hand on my hip. I promptly removed it. I wanted his full attention. Obviously frustrated by my lack of response he groaned. "I don't want her distracted by...."

"Who? Me? Frank?" I said.

He groaned louder, and I knew I'd hit the nail on the head. Still concerned with Frank's attention to his sister, thank God he didn't know about Les' lustful advances.

"Don't worry about Frank. Anyway, he was good for her," I said.

"What!"

"He made her feel good. He complimented her. Gave her attention. No wonder she likes him. She needs to feel okay about herself," I said.

"He wants to sleep with my married sister," he argued.

I laughed at the absurdity of the idea. "Allie loves her husband, she just likes Frank's company. Anyway, he has more of a chance sleeping with me, than Allie."

"That's not funny," he huffed.

"For heaven sakes." I took his hand and put it back on my hip. "You have more important things to think about."

His fretted brow eased, and a smile returned to his face. "I did promise you a poke."

CHAPTER

29

The early morning phone call from George woke me from a deep sleep. I arrived at my bakeshop to the sight of the yellow police tape stretched across the store's large window or least where a window used to be. Lee stood next to me, solemn and serious, dressed in the clothes we'd rushed into when we got the call. Allie had insisted on coming. She said little, perhaps too surprised by my almost-catatonic state. Broken glass lay strewn at my feet, the beautiful hand painted name of my shop broken into a thousand pieces.

George and a few kitchen workers had arrived on the scene first and called the police. By the time Candace and I arrived, a report had been made. Candace was quick to call a glazer, who she must have on speed dial because he'd started taking measurements for the window already. A sign painter would be called later to redo the name. In a couple of hours, any evidence of the assault would be gone. On the outside, I was happy things were dealt with so fast, but inside the trauma lingered.

In all honesty, I'd never planned on having my own cake shop. The Blue Moon belonged to the family. When I worked in advertising, I'd always worked for other people. O So Sweet Cake Shop was the first thing that was all mines. Now someone had thrown a brick through the window shattering everything. I didn't realize I was crying until Lee pulled me into a tight hug. He'd mistaken my tears for anguish instead of barely controlled anger. Not in my wildest dreams did I think this was some malicious act by a random stranger. Nothing had been taken from the shop. This had been personal. I stayed in Lee's arms, taking in his warmth because my current emotions left me cold. Allie walked in the shop and started to clean up, leaving Lee and me alone.

"You're alright," Lee reassured.

"I know," I lied. I wasn't right by a long shot. My mood went south at the sight of Maddox and Russo walking toward us. Lee must have sensed my body tense because he released me and turned to see the men approach. He took a protective stance in front of me, which I appreciated but didn't need. Considering the state I was in, no one was safe.

"Ms. Wilkes, somebody doesn't like you," Maddox surveyed the mess, giving only the pretense of caring.

"Making friends again." Russo seemed amused by his own humor.

"You are?" Lee said.

"We're homicide detectives on the Rovell investigation," Maddox said. "You are?"

Lee seemed undecided how to answer. Was he my fiancé or lawyer? "Lee McKenzie," he said finally. Russo's eyebrows went up as if he expected more. Lee said nothing else.

"Why are you here?" I asked.

"We were in the neighborhood and got the call." Maddox pointed to the broken glass. "Where's Dunn?"

"Why?" Lee asked.

"He's asking Ms. Wilkes here," an ill-tempered Russo interjected.

"Why?" I repeated in a truculent tone.

"Just wondering. We figured if there was trouble, Dunn might be close by," Russo said.

"That's an enormous assumption, detective," Lee said.

"You sound like a lawyer," Russo said as if he tasted something nasty. Dressed in jeans and old college t-shirt, unshaven and with finger-combed hair, Lee looked anything but lawyerly.

Lee cocked his head and narrowed his gaze on them. "I am."

"He must be the boyfriend." Maddox turned to me.

"Right now, I'm the lawyer wondering what this is about. So, unless you caught the perpetrator who did this or have plans to track him down and bring him to justice, I'll remain the lawyer."

Russo made a face and Maddox just shook his head. "I'd be careful, Romeo, because what did that other guy call her? Cupcake! Yeah, Miss. Cupcake here is protective of our Mr. Dunn. I don't think you could handle the competition." Russo grinned.

From the expression on Lee's face, I didn't know whether he wanted to laugh or hit him. Before he had a chance to respond, I stepped in front of him. "What are you trolling for, evidence?"

Lee's hand went on my forearm and gave a gentle squeeze.

"You and Dunn might have had a disagreement, and this is how he expresses himself," Russo said.

I threw up my hands. "A meter maid with one eye with a cold has a better chance at solving this case than the two of you,"

Lee groaned.

"Did you think someone else besides Bebe might have

killed Rovell? Or does a new suspect need to be unconscious at the scene? Christ, you probably give him a ticket for littering."

Russo's face reddened. Maddox remained calm. They were like the Yin and Yang of cops.

"You have someone in mind?" he asked.

I thought about the photograph of Lamar but said nothing. What proof was that?

"With Bebe out of the equation, who do you have?" Lee asked.

"Nobody," Russo barked. "Everybody liked Rovell."

"Not everybody," I said.

Maddox eyes narrowed. "Not everybody, like who?"

I said nothing, because I really had nothing.

"Somebody didn't because he's dead," Lee said.

"Funny you should say that, because yesterday afternoon, I went to speak to his daughter Tania and that crew at RTM. She's had a change of heart about your boy. Everyone there seemed to. You talked to her, didn't you? They mentioned they had a visit from you and the redhead," Maddox said.

I'd imagined Jermaine and Louis had a conversation with Tania and convinced her of Bebe's innocence. Convincing Tania would be easy compared to the detectives. She didn't have to share a brain.

"Everything all right here?" a familiar voice said. Candace stomped out of the Blue Moon toward us.

I grinned. Wisely, Lee took a step behind me.

"You are?" Russo asked.

"Her sister," Candace barked.

"We're conducting an investigation here," Maddox said.

"Of a broken window?" My sister's tone was masterfully incredulous. "I talked to the police. Speak to me."

"No. Of a murder," an inpatient Russo said.

Candace's eyes narrowed. "Whose murder?"

Russo groaned.

"Excuse me Ms...Ms..." Maddox tried to interrupt, but Candace stared him down. My sister didn't have the ability to turn men to stone, but came pretty close.

"I don't see a dead body, do you? Unless he's invisible," Candace folded her arms across her chest and waited for an answer.

"It's the Rovell murder, and we're just asking questions—" Maddox began.

Candace dismissed him with an upraised hand. "Aren't you supposed to be doing something here?" she barked at Lee.

"You seemed to be doing fine." His lips lifted in a slight smile.

Candace sneered at him and then focused her attention back to Maddox and Russo. "I serve about six judges at my restaurant almost every day. Judge Braswell is sitting inside trying to have a relaxing breakfast. I think I should interrupt him to ask if this isn't considered harassment or something. What do you think?"

"Maybe Judge Ramirez might be better," Lee suggested.

Surprisingly, Candace seemed to agree.

"Listen Ms...Ms...." Maddox struggled to call her something.

"Ms. Wilkes and I don't appreciate you bothering my sister or disrupting my business. So why don't you take your little investigation someplace else, because half my customers are watching." We all turned to several curious faces staring back at us through the large plate windows.

"Or I will find Judge Ramirez—who, I might add, is a federal judge—and get him to explain the pertinent points of harassing the public. The public, who pays your salary and will talk to your superiors," Candace snapped.

Russo flinched, and Maddox just closed his eyes and

shook his head.

"Listen lady, I can get the food inspectors down here so fast..." Russo threatened.

I thought I heard my sister growl, in that low audible sound of complete annoyance I'd grown accustom to growing up with her. "Don't waste the call. He eats here every Thursday. Sits in that table and orders the seafood platter." She pointed to a table by the window.

Russo blinked. Maddox put a hand on his partner's shoulder. At least he recognized they'd picked the wrong place to interrogate me. Russo, visibly deflated. "This isn't over," Russo said before Maddox led him away.

"Is it ever," Lee said beneath his breath. He directed this to me.

"Thanks Candy," I said.

She sighed, shook her head and gave Lee a withering sneer. "You were no help."

"You scared them a lot more than I did," he said good-naturedly.

She huffed before leaving.

With Maddox and Russo gone, our attention went back to the glazer replacing the window. Still, Maddox's question replayed in my head. Did I know of another suspect besides Bebe? To say I did would invite more trouble than I already had with Lamar. Would he stoop so low as to get someone to throw a brick through my window? What would he do if he knew I pointed the police in his direction? Before I did that, I needed to make sure my accusation would stick, and Lamar could complain about our relationship in prison. I had another nagging thought. What if it weren't Lamar? I turned to Lee.

"Where's Cherry?" I asked.

"Why?"

"We didn't exactly part friends," I said.

"So!" He stared at the broken window. "She wouldn't...."

"This is a woman who's holding Bebe's life hostage. So I kind of believe she's capable of anything."

For over fifteen minutes, we debated or, should I say, argued over me contacting Cherry. Lee reminded me of my promise to Ziemann. I said I didn't care. If she threw a brick through my window, all bets were off. Lee said he'd talk to Ziemann, and Ziemann would talk to Cherry about it.

"You think she's going to tell him the truth?" I laughed.

"She's got some pretty serious warrants against her. Thad's the only decent lawyer who'd take her case for free. So yes, I think she'd tell him the truth."

I shook my head at him. Everyone underestimated this woman, but I wasn't going to argue the point anymore.

When Esperanza showed up, she, Allie, and I took the rest of the morning to clean up the shop. Lee stayed around until the glazer finished, but had to get to the office. I said I'd manage and told him to go. I knew he didn't want to leave me alone, but I reminded him George and Candace were only a scream away. He didn't find the screaming part funny, maybe because I wasn't laughing when I said it.

By late afternoon, we got the shop running again. I called Maggie after the first break I had. I told her what happened. She thought Lamar was the most likely culprit. I said Cherry was my pick. She'd spent the morning doing research on Lamar's short music industry career. He had a nasty reputation for dirty fighting and underhanded deals. The shady acquisition of his music company was one of the most public of many questionable acts. Only recently has he tried to rid himself of his bad boy persona. I laughed at the idea. For that to work, he'd had to die and come back as a goldfish.

"I need to find Cherry," I said.

There was a long pause, and I prayed Maggie wasn't

communing with her inner saint. I needed the investigator.

"Give me a half an hour and I'll get back to you." She disconnected. Thirteen minutes later, Maggie found Cherry at the airport Marriot on the ninth floor under Sherrilyn Turnbull. While working with Frank, Maggie learned how to hunt wayward husbands faster than Hollywood paparazzi.

"What are you going to do?" she asked.

"Have a little talk with our Ms. Cherry," I said, not hiding my anger. I still couldn't shake the image of the shop's shattered window. Despite Maggie's belief that Lamar might have sent one of his thugs, my bet was set on Cherry. This kind of vindictive act reeked of her.

"I better go with you."

"Why?"

"Because!"

"I just want to talk to her." I lied. A moment of silence hung between us. I could tell she was gearing up for something.

"Because the last time you were this angry you threatened to put a hit out on your ex-boyfriend."

"I wasn't serious," This was another lie of course. I even checked the yellow pages.

"I'm going with you," she insisted.

"Whatever," I said, thinking that if I did kill Cherry, Maggie would at least help me bury the body.

CHAPTER

30

By the time we reached the hotel by Kennedy Airport, my anger hadn't abated. My sense of violation and more importantly, the fact that Sherrilyn 'Cherry' Turnbull continued to walk the earth annoyed me even more. My reactions might have seemed disproportionate, especially the part about killing her. I get that way when people mess with my stuff. To be fair, I'd taken her bag, not once but twice. Each time, I'd returned the bag in the same condition. Could she say the same? Considering her state of finances, I didn't expect her to repair the damages. She'd probably claimed the entire thing was my fault for pissing her off. Either way, Ms. Cherry and I were going to have a reckoning and give a new meaning to the words Cherry Pop!

Allie insisted on coming with Maggie and me. She seemed eager to play her brother's role as the voice of reason and calm, or she had a healthy sense of fear when it came to Cherry. I didn't like Cherry, Maggie didn't trust her, but Cherry terrified Allie. Cherry's lack of boundaries, propriety and respect for others both amazed and frightened my future sister-in-law. A woman capable of anything, Cherry did as she pleased. If Allie thought changing her hair color and buying new clothes was a reckless act, she only had to take a page from Cherry's book, to realize how bland her life actually was.

By the time we entered the hotel lobby, Maggie and Allie had me somewhat calmed me down, but not much. Maggie's hopeful blue eyes pleaded with me to keep my composure. I took a deep breath and thought about what might happen if I gave Cherry more than a piece of my mind.

"She'd go to Ziemann and threaten to sue me again," I reasoned and shrugged.

"She might throw a brick at something else." Maggie pointed to my head. I huffed at the idea. "You need to be reasonable."

"I'll be as reasonable as a brick through the window." I pressed the elevator call button.

"You think she'll get physical?" A worrisome Allie looked around furtively at the spacious hotel lobby and the unsuspecting guests.

"Why don't you wait in the car," I suggested.

Allie shook her head. "No, I want to help." She followed us into the elevator. Inwardly, I smiled—in for a penny in for a pound.

On the ninth floor, I braced myself for the confrontation. Though my anger had dissipated somewhat, I had enough to deal with Cherry. The sight of a hotel's cleaning cart by Cherry's open room door deflated me a bit. I stepped in to find the maid, standing in a room that looked as if a family of monkeys lived there. Our entry startled the maid, and she let out a small yelp. Young and Hispanic, she had a slight build and a pretty face now ruined by her expression of panic.

"Sorry." I held up my hands in apology.

"What happened?" Maggie asked. To get further into the room we stepped over clothes and shoes.

"Mess, a mess," she said in accented English.

"The woman who was here, Ms. Turnbull, where is she?"

I gestured around the room.

"Que?" she said. Then she mumbled something in Spanish.

I didn't speak Spanish. None of us did.

Maggie threw up her hands. "This is getting us nowhere."

Cherry was gone.

"Why don't you call Esperanza?" Allie said.

I gave her a quick grin. "I knew your brother wasn't the only smart one in the family." I pulled out my cell phone and dialed the cake shop. Esperanza picked up after the first ring. I put her on speaker phone and told her our situation. Quick as always, Esperanza acted as an interpreter as I asked the maids some questions. The story didn't take long.

About twenty minutes prior to our arrival, Cherry had two visitors to her room. The maid described them as young, black and dressed in baseball caps and hoodies. She'd been cleaning the room next door when she heard them argue, but understood little, except the woman kept on repeating the same thing over and over.

I don't have it.

When the noise stopped, she peeked out of the room and saw the men and the woman enter the elevator. The woman didn't seem happy. After they left, she checked it and saw the mess.

"Oh my," Maggie said.

"They kidnapped her?" a shocked Allie said.

"She walked out under her own steam. She might have known them. One of them might be her cousin," I said, but I wasn't sure. Cherry probably thought she could talk her way out of trouble. She did have a gift for it.

"What were they searching for?" Allie surveyed the room. Items were strewn everywhere, clothes had been pulled out of dressers, and every pocket was out turned.

"Something small." Maggie examined some of Cherry's toiletries.

We rummaged around the room, not quite sure what we expected to find. Maggie picked up one of Cherry's tiny cameras. She popped open the back and shook her head. "The memory card is missing," she announced.

I shrugged. "So?"

"The disks you took. They came here to get it." She pointed a finger at me and shook it.

Unfortunately for Cherry, she no longer had the disk in her possession. I did. I felt a pang of guilt. I wished a lot of things for her, like introducing her to natural fiber, hiding her make-up case, and a year in obedience training. To be threatened by Lamar wasn't one of them. The most I'd do would be a stern warning and a finger in her face. Lamar might take the finger, literally.

"This is bad, O." Maggie shook her head.

"Should we call the police?" Allie suggested.

I almost laughed at the idea and thankfully Maggie kept her mouth shut.

"And tell them what?" I said. "Cherry willingly left the hotel with a guy who might be her cousin. If she wanted to get away from them all she had to do was walk through the lobby, and scream her damn head off. I would."

"What about Ziemann?" Allie asked.

"God, please don't involve him," I said.

"This isn't good is it?" Allie's worried expression grew.

"I don't know what's more dangerous, knowing where she is or not knowing," Maggie added.

We stood around, unsure of what to do. Even the maid seemed contemplative in our shared concerns. What if she told Lamar? How would he react? A ring tone from the television show, *Law and Order* played and rocked us from our stupor.

The sound came from beneath the bed. Maggie went to her knees, rooted around, and pulled out Cherry's bedazzled cell phone. We read the display.

"Ziemann," said a wide-eyed Maggie.

"Perfect." I threw up my hands in frustration. I didn't want to be the one to tell him Bebe's only witness had just been kidnapped, or worse, gone to the other side. We let the phone ring until it stopped. The phone rang again. Ziemann was persistent.

"What do we do?" Maggie asked.

I didn't have an answer. After a while, Ziemann might show up. I didn't want to be around when he did. Before I voiced my concerns, Allie grabbed the phone and connected the call.

"You know what time it is!" she exclaimed in the best imitation of Cherry I'd ever heard. She did Cherry better than Cherry, loud, bad-tempered and irritable. The maid's mouth dropped open. Maggie blinked as if she didn't trust her own sight.

"I ain't got time for that now. I'll do it tomorrow," Allie continued. "I'll call you when I'm ready." Without a goodbye, she disconnected the call. A hysterical laugh escaped from me. A bold move made by someone, not known for bold moves.

"You have mad skills," I said, giving her an affectionate hug.

"How did you do that?" Maggie asked, peering into Allie's mouth as if she expected Cherry to pop out.

"You...sound like that lady." The maid pointed at Allie.

"At the catering, when she was in the van with us. She wouldn't shut up," Allie said.

I barely remembered. I guess Cherry made an impression on her.

"Amazing," Maggie said, still in disbelief. A bashful Allie

smiled.

"Okay, Ziemann's on hold for a while. What do we do about Cherry and Lamar?" I said. No one had a clue. "How about we get the hell out of here?"

All members of the Hunt for Cherry Committee raised their hand. We thanked the maid and suggested she close the door and wait for Cherry's return. We took Cherry's cell phone, just in case.

At first, I suggested Maggie's office, but she feared Frank might show up, and she didn't want to explain all of us standing around like scared rabbits, especially Allie. Maggie and I were capable of lying to the rotund detective, but I didn't think Allie had the nerve, despite her verbal skills. Maggie suggested we go to her house in Hicksville. If Cherry talked to Lamar about us, he would go to the restaurant to retrieve the disks and me. She didn't have a clue about Maggie… at least I hoped.

An hour later, we were entrenched in Maggie's kitchen. Along the way, we picked up Rocket from his play date. Maggie fixed him a quick snack and herded him outside in the backyard to play laser tag with the dog. This game consisted of Mr. McGregor waddling around the yard being chased by Rocket with a toy ray gun with a laser sight. No doubt, this training would come in handy when Rocket joined the Special Forces, his current occupational dream. Last week, he wanted to be a circus clown.

"Why would you think she'd tell Lamar about you?" Allie asked.

"She's not stupid," I said.

"I'm sure right now, she's blaming you for everything," Maggie said.

I laughed nervously. "She'd be right."

"What are we going to do?" Allie's eyes locked on mine.

"I'm more concern with what Lamar might do."

Cherry's phone that sat on the table between us like a bomb. She picked it up and worked the keys. I guess if your friend's life was at stake, personal privacy would go out the window. I was so proud of Maggie at that moment.

"She called Chaos 182 early yesterday. Around one o'clock in the afternoon, before we went to Boyer's office. She called the place a lot," she said.

"She's trying to make a deal with him," I said. "When she found out she no longer had the storage disks, I'm sure she stopped calling."

Maggie checked the log again and confirmed the calls stopped late last night. Several calls weren't returned.

"What are you going to do?" Allie asked.

"In all honesty O, we can't give the disks to her. They're evidence to clear Louis and maybe give the police another suspect besides Bebe." She was annoyingly right, as always.

I took Cherry's golden ticket, and she had nothing to barter. If something were to happen to her, I'd be responsible. Crap. I hated being responsible for someone I truly disliked.

"It's just a picture, right?" Allie asked. "Why can't you make a copy?"

Maggie and I turned to her slowly, impressed by her simple solution. The photograph had value, not the disk. Maggie had a copy on her computer. I could give them what they wanted and still have a photograph.

"Allie, you're brilliant." I went over to her and gave her a hug. My ringing cell phone interrupted our celebration.

"Odessa, where are you?" My sister's terse voice rattled in my ear. I wondered if another brick had gone through my window.

"Why?" I asked.

"Because that crazy Cherry girl is here waiting for you and

she won't leave until you come. She's ruining everyone's appetite," she barked.

"Is she alone?" I asked, considering she'd just been kidnapped. Did she get hungry along the way and stop off for a bite?

"There are more of them." My sister sounded as if she might have to call the exterminator.

"There's only her. Thankfully, God only made one." I promised I'd be there as soon as possible. When I told the girls about Cherry's reappearance, Allie summed everything in one sentence.

"That can't be good."

CHAPTER 31

At the Blue Moon, I found Cherry at a window seat working her way through a plate of ribs as if they might leave her an additional twenty on the table for her services. An unappetizing cocktail of a reddish substance sat half-empty and surrounded by three cherry stems laid out like dead soldiers. Obviously, not her first drink of the day. In between bites of ribs, she'd sip the drink through a straw as if it were Kool-Aid. Dressed in her usual inappropriate best, she wore a tight crimson and white striped t-shirt, blue Capri pants with stars, and four-inch red patent leather heels. I didn't know whether to gawk at her bad choice of clothing, or salute her for her patriotism. I also wondered how she might maneuver in those heels with four cocktails under her belt.

"Where's my stuff!" she growled.

Nearby patrons turned in our direction. Their expression of annoyance matched my own. I pulled out a seat and sat opposite her. I laced my hands together and placed them on the table in the hope this would stop me from wanting to strangle her.

"You threw a brick through my window," I accused.

She laughed and licked her lips of wayward barbeque sauce. A man at a nearby table seemed transfixed, no doubt wishing he was a piece of rib smothered in George's secret sauce.

"Says who?" she said with a sneer.

I sneered back. This woman had disregarded her friendships, cheated, blackmailed and vandalized her way through life without impunities. Did she think she could do what she did to me and walk away? The hell to the no with that.

"Says me." Her pocketbook was on the seat next to her. Did she have another brick?

"Just give me what I want and I'll go away."

I laughed at her offer. I'd have a better chance of ridding myself of a yeast infection. "And if I don't?"

"Something worse if you don't." She nodded to a parked car across the street. I'd recognized Lamar's SUV. Also, I noticed the two men wearing hoodies standing just outside the front door. Even at that distance, I caught the family resemblance of Cherry's cousin Stevie Harmon. My eyes drifted back to the SUV. As if on cue, the tinted window rolled down. Bear's menacing expression glared back at me. I gave him a little wave. I suspected someone had to have given her a lift, considering she'd left her broomstick at the hotel.

"You crazy, pissing him off," Cherry said as if she were giving me sage advice. She licked her fingers and drained the rest of her drink. She eyed the bartender and did a little wave. Trevor gave her a half smile that died once his eyes fell on me. He returned to cleaning glasses and ignored Cherry's interest in another drink. I returned my attention to her.

"You've made a deal with him, didn't you? Though riding with the devil doesn't seem to bother your appetite." I said, eyeing her ravage plate. Being evil must give her a mighty appetite.

"I told him, you'd show up, and I was right." She seemed

quite proud of herself.

I shook my head, disappointed in the woman's shortsightedness. Maybe, I'd given her too much credit. "You know Cherry. I thought you were a smart woman. You played Ziemann pretty well. But messing with Lamar and that ape is stupid."

"I don't need advice from you. I just want my stuff, so I can go." She surveyed the restaurant as if she were a mouse trying to avoid a trap. My eyes followed her line of sight to the emergency exit by the bathrooms in the back.

"I wouldn't try it if I were you," I said.

She did her sneering thing again. She had the sneering and smugness down to perfection. "Well, I ain't you. I want my shit." Her raised voice drew my sister's attention as well as half the restaurant.

An irate Candace stomped to our table. "I thought you were taking care of this!"

"I am." I shooed her away.

She wouldn't go.

"I ain't no this." Cherry glared up at my sister. "You better watch who you talking to." Candace glared down at her the same way God might have done to the inhabitants of Sodom and Gomorrah. Cherry was about to get smite, Old Testament style. Candace put a hand on her hips and cocked her head to the side. This was the international danger sign of an angry black woman. Even Eskimos in Alaska knew this sign. Suddenly, Candace snapped her fingers. Out of nowhere, a waitress appeared like magic.

"She's done." Candace snatched up the plate before a complaint came out of Cherry's mouth. My sister handed the dish to the waitress, who disappeared as quickly as she'd arrived. Candace glared at me for a hot minute, possibly forgetting we were related. "Finish this."

"You can't—" Cherry stopped abruptly as Candace's golden eyes bore into her. I'd never seen her so angry. This said a lot about her hidden affection for Bebe. She knew who this woman was.

"I got this, Candace," I reassured, trying to prevent my sister's transforming into the female version of the Hulk. She turned to me, the anger still flushing her face. I matched it with my own determination. "Maggie and I got this."

She took a deep inhalation, possibly to clear out the brimstone in her lungs before she walked away to greet an arriving dinner party.

"She don't know who she's talking to," Cherry said beneath her breath, and out of earshot of my older sister. Just when I thought the girl was stupid, she showed some sense.

"You don't want to mess with her or me. So no more bricks through the window," I said.

Cherry huffed and touched the space where her plate used to be. "Give me my stuff, so I can get out of here." Cherry held out her hand.

I shook my head. I turned to see an impatient Bear standing outside his SUV. I gestured to him to join us. I had to repeat the request several times to convince him to come into the restaurant.

"What are you doing?" a nervous Cherry protested as Bear crossed the street. Candace made a face at him as he passed and came to our table.

Sometimes, I forgot how formidable he was, and I struggled to keep my nerves in check. He hovered over our table and scowled at us both. When I offered him a chair, he refused.

"Listen Bear, I don't care what agreement you have with her. That's between the two of you. I'm willing to give back the memory disk on one condition."

"You're in no position to tell me about conditions. I haven't forgotten what you and that little redheaded witch did to me," he almost growled.

"Come on, Bear, let bygones be bygones," I mocked, knowing the man had no sense of humor and a gun under his jacket.

"Give it to me now, or else."

I cocked an eyebrow at him. "Or else what? This isn't some back alley or Chaos 182. You're in the middle of a restaurant—my restaurant. You would go directly to jail without passing Go and collecting your two hundred dollars." Bear's face contorted in confusion. I guess Bear never played Monopoly on family game night. Despite that, his eyes scanned the surrounding dining room, realizing I was right. A group of uniformed court officers sat two tables away from us having a meal. I recognized them and waved. Officer Martinez, from the night court waved back.

"What do you want?" he said between clenched teeth.

I turned to Cherry and smiled. "What I always wanted: the truth. Cherry goes to the detectives handling Rovell's case. She makes her statement about Bebe and I give her back the disk. Cherry will be out of my life, and you and she can make babies for all I care," I said.

"Give the disk to me and I'll make sure she goes," he demanded.

I shook my head. "Is stupid written on my forehead? I trust you even less than her." I gave him my best eye roll.

"Hey," Cherry protested.

"Shut up," Bear said as he contemplated my idea. Cherry almost bit her tongue wanting to talk.

"The minute she's done, she's yours," I said.

Bear grinned at Cherry. She noticeably recoiled.

"How long will this take?" he questioned.

I held up a finger, pulled out my cell phone and dialed a number I'd taken from Cherry's phone. "Hi Ziemann," I said with my best happy voice. "Cherry wants to make her statement to the police, right now."

Cherry went back to sneering at me. Her time with room service had come to an end.

"Right now, this minute. In fact, we're on our way to the precinct. Trust me, this isn't a joke."

Ziemann didn't seem pleased to hear from me and even less because I had his personal cell phone number. He asked how I'd gotten Cherry to make her statement so fast; I said I didn't have the time to explain. If this were to happen, it had to happen now. Reluctantly, he agreed to meet us at the precinct. I disengaged the call and gave a Bear and Cherry a satisfying grin they didn't appreciate. We all stood up and headed for the door. Candace said something rude, but mercifully, Cherry and Bear didn't respond.

Outside, Bear insisted he'd take me to the precinct. I politely explained I wouldn’t get into a car with him if he were the last train from hell. One kidnap victim was enough. I told him to take Cherry, guaranteeing she would show up. Bear ordered her into the back seat of the SUV. She balked until her cousin and the other man, pushed her inside. Don't you just love family?

"You think you're so smart," Bear said as we watched his minions handled Cherry. I said nothing. I promised Maggie I wouldn't provoke him.

"Tell that redhead we're going to meet again." He scowled.

"After today, I hope not," I said. I wanted to believe this, but from the expression on Bear's face, this thing between us was far from done. "I think your biggest problem is dealing with Cherry. My advice is hiding your wallet."

Bear snorted. "I'll deal with her."

I didn't like the way he said that and hated to think Cherry might end up in some landfill in New Jersey. But then this was Cherry we were talking about, not some naïve schoolgirl. Before the day ended, she'd have his wallet, gold teeth and the rings on his fingers. So, I held my tongue. Moments later, Maggie, Allie, Rocket, and the dog pulled up in Maggie's minivan from around the corner. I hopped in the front seat, somewhat pleased with myself.

Maggie's idea of using Cherry's need to retrieve the disk as motivation for her to clear Bebe's name worked perfectly. The woman just needed an incentive to go to the police right away, instead of dragging it out for her own personal gain and access to a free minibar. The fact that Bear helped us do it was the icing on the cake.

If Lamar sent Bear to get the incriminating evidence, he should have warned the bodyguard to read the fine print on his contract. Never trust a redhead with good intention, or an annoyed black woman who believed revenge should be biblical in scale and never pin your hopes to a self-serving witch.

Somebody say Amen!

CHAPTER

32

Impeccably dressed in a dark tailored suit, Ziemann arrived at the Queens' precinct in his usual fashion, in a chauffeured Town Car. Cherry, Maggie and I acted like his fan club when we ran up to him. A modern day version of a screeching Greek chorus, we jockeyed for position, each wanting to have our say. Mr. McGregor seemed to be the only one not impressed with Ziemann's presence. Tethered to a leash held by Maggie, he eyed an intriguing patch of grass that promised a bathroom break after sitting in the car for so long. Allie and Rocket had been regulated to the nearby McDonalds for Happy Meals. Bear's imposing presence unnerved Allie too much for her to hang around. He sat in the huge SUV like a vulture waiting for something to die.

Ziemann stood in the center of all this estrogen brouhaha somewhat perplexed by it all. He demanded to know about Cherry's sudden change of heart, possibly suspicious of her intent, considering his last conversation with her. He wanted some answers. Cherry had none and grew annoyed with each question. Maggie and I stood silent, not wanting to illuminate their confusion by introducing Allie into the mix since she had been the one to tell Ziemann to cool his heels. He already thought we were meddlesome amateurs. Ziemann put an end to his questions when he pressed his thumb and forefinger to the bridge of his nose. He'd had enough.

"Maddox and his partner are waiting for us," Ziemann snapped. He gestured to Cherry to enter the precinct. She aimed a resentful expression in our direction as she stepped passed us.

A tight face Ziemann sighed deeply. "Stay here," he commanded as if we were Mr. McGregor.

At first, I took offense to this but dropped my complaint. Maggie and I didn't always bring out the best in the two New York City detectives.

"They still hadn't gotten over your last visit," Ziemann said.

"What did they say?" Maggie asked.

"Their exact words were, are those crazy women coming with you?" he said.

"We found evidence they ignored, and we're the bad guys?" I complained.

Ziemann laughed. "I'm sure they appreciate you clarifying their shortcomings. Do you always feel the need to castrate the men around you?"

"What?" I felt a little offended.

Maggie's eyes widened.

"If the stakes weren't so high, I'd let you give them all vasectomies, but I need them on my side for the time being. So please, stay here." His condescending tone set my lips in a thin line.

"If that's the case, I wouldn't stand too close to me." My gaze went down to his crotch. This only made him laugh.

"I wonder why Mackenzie hasn't strangled you yet. He's acquired a kind of selective ignorance, hasn't he? Who would have thought?" His knowing tone lay heavy with sarcasm.

"I'm not talking to you about Lee." I crossed my arms

defensively.

"But we've talked about you." He waggled a finger at me.

I couldn't hide my surprise. "He would never do that." My hands went to my hips making that universal sign, again.

Ziemann ignored the combative stance.

"I bet Lee told you we worked in Manhattan at the same law office, just after law school, before I went to the dark side." Ziemann's smile broadened. "But did he say I was the best man at his wedding?"

This made me swallow my own spit, and I almost choked.

"I don't believe you," I accused.

His smile widened. "Why would I lie? I could tell you what the bride wore, a lovely cream satin gown with tiny little roses. She was stunning."

"You knew Julia," I managed to say, still in shock about how close the two men were.

"I introduced them." He hitched his lips into a crooked smile before he turned and entered the precinct.

"I think he's growing on me." Maggie confessed.

"Oh Christ, you've drunk the man's Kool-Aid too." I cursed.

Maggie gave me a dismissive wave as she walked the dog to a nearby bench.

"So they used to be friends, it's not like they're related. You won't pass on any Ziemann genes if you have kids." She took a seat and pulled out a laptop from her saddlebag style pocketbook. "Beside, Lee divorced Julia, so much for introduction."

Considering my first introduction to Lee had been Maggie's oversize handbag striking his head. At our next encounter, he slimed me with a key lime pie. She was right, so much for introductions.

If what Ziemann said was true, that was all I needed was

someone else comparing me to Julia. A lawyer, now living in Washington D.C., their amicable divorce has left her a fond memory for Lee. He regretted the marriage hadn't worked out and taken much of the responsibility for its demise. From what little I knew, there was some suspect behavior on Julia's part, but Lee remained steadfast, it was his fault. I tried to make Julia a dead subject but people from Lee's past kept reminding me she wasn't. Julia and I were the Yin and Yang of Lee's romantic choices. Blond, petite and demure, Julia would give Grace Kelly a run for her money. I didn't have a Nordic petit bone in my body and the best thing I can say about being demure is that I can spell it. I tried not to think about it and concentrated on the problem at hand. "You're right, he's the least of our problems, girlfriend." I nodded in the direction of Bear's SUV. He'd been sitting there since he brought Cherry.

Maggie shrugged. "He's a bully," she said as if that defined who he was, and maybe it did. She powered on the laptop. Mr. McGregor sat in a ball by her feet dozing.

"A bully with a gun and anger issues."

"He had anger issues before we met him."

"Maggie, you tasered him, and he dropped like a rock. I think he peed in his pants. Then you disassembled his gun like some Girl Scout Green Beret, you talk about me emasculating someone for laughs and giggles, you do it and don't even realize what you've done."

Her brow arched. "What did you want me to do? He gave me no choice."

She was right of course. She'd save Allie from Lamar. As always, I had no plan, and she had come to the rescue. "We'll stay out of his way," I said, not believing this was a solution. If Bear wanted, he could chase us down like a mad dog, to get his due, he could.

We waited, and Maggie typed away on her laptop. Bear

glowered at Maggie, reiterating their unfinished business. Maggie continued to ignore him. I don't know how she did it. Maybe it was Ziemann's so-called selective ignorance. Obviously, something I hadn't quite mastered. Whether she acknowledged him on not, Maggie was firmly planted on his radar. I think his obsession had something to do with being rendered unconscious by a woman who weighed less than his size twelve shoes.

Right before my nerves got the better of me, Ziemann and Cherry emerged from the precinct. Ziemann's relaxed expression told me all had gone well. Cherry's face said something different. She appeared with her wig sat slightly askew. Her makeup needed a total redo and a fine sheen clung to her skin. She took a deep breath as if she'd been locked up in a small room with two New York Detectives and not much air. Someone had slipped her a sizeable humble pill. An image of Detective Russo, a rubber hose and bright lights came to mind, and the thought made me smile.

"Where is my shit?" she croaked.

"Is it done?" I asked Ziemann.

Ziemann nodded. "Maddox was coming around anyway, but Cherry's statement pushed him. Bebe had no motive to kill Rovell. Besides, the evidence was weak. Rovell's daughter would only reiterate that fact. They'll go back to the witnesses to confirm Dunn had no conflict with Rovell."

"Where's my shit," she demanded. Again, I ignored her.

"Detective Russo didn't appreciate Ms. Turnbull's delay in coming forward. I had to convince him not to press obstruction charges against her." Ziemann sighed.

"Are you going to give—" Cherry yelled before I stopped her with a well-placed finger in her face. She recoiled. Russo had made her a jumpy wreck—thank you, Detective.

"Interrupt me one more time and I'll give your shit to the

Vin Diesel wannabe across the street," I said.

Cherry huffed but shut up. An intrigued Ziemann's eyes darted about at the women before him and then at the parked SUV across the street. "Should I know what's going on?" he asked.

"No," Maggie said, but plastered a quick smile on her face. "You were saying?" Her misdirection didn't fool anybody.

"There isn't much left to say, except Maddox wants to talk to Bebe again about what he saw when he returned to the RTM."

"Could this be a trap to get him to confess something?" I asked.

Ziemann shook his head. "I'll be there. They're only interested in the time period after the party, in the parking lot before his attack. I'm sure Bebe told you what happened when you pumped him for information," Ziemann said smugly.

Maggie and I tried to act contrite, but we couldn't hold it. "So it's truly done," a relieved Maggie said.

Ziemann nodded. "He's safe. I think the police are rethinking their evidence."

"Good." I turned to Cherry's whose tight-lipped expression seemed barely contained. "Then we're done." I pulled the prescription bottle from my jeans pocket and tossed it to her. She caught it like some starving man after a crumb.

"Happy?" I said.

This time she ignored me. In her head, I'm sure she was spending her money on a new fashion challenged wardrobe. Her happiness wouldn't last long. Inside Maggie's handbag was a copy of the photograph of Lamar with the man from Atlanta, along with a note. We couldn't be certain if Cherry's statement would go over with the detectives. Maggie and I debated as to when to give this to the police. I wanted to wait. She didn't. The compromise was the outcome of Cherry's interview with

Maddox and Russo. While Maggie wanted to hand over the picture right afterward, I resisted for obvious reasons. One being that Lamar will eventually find out who gave the photograph to them. The man wasn't stupid.

"You gonna call me, right!" an excited Cherry announced to Ziemann.

He had to lean away because she had invaded what little personal space we all had huddled together. He sighed and patted Cherry on the shoulder. I'm sure he said silently to himself, down girl, down.

"I'm the attorney of record for an outstanding warrant for Ms. Turnbull. I promised I would complete her case before I left," Ziemann said in a reassuring tone.

I didn't realize I had my mouth open until he placed his index finger beneath my chin and closed it. I smacked his hand away. "You're not leaving?" I complained.

"Sorry Ms. Cupcake, not quite yet. When I make a promise, I try to keep it."

"Yeah, that's right." Cherry huffed.

"Don't you have your soul to sell or something?" I said to her.

"I think you should go, Cherry." Maggie gestured to the prescription bottle in her hand. "That has an expiration date of about twenty-four hours."

"What do you mean?" Cherry demanded.

"Did you think we wouldn't make a copy?" I said, putting on my best happy face.

"Why?" Her anxious face returned, but her eyes darted to Bear and the SUV.

I feigned confusion and put a finger to my lips. "I don't know, maybe Detective Russo, or the Daily News… or how about Entertainment Tonight? Hip hop producer bribing a witness in Louis Mackie's gun charge case. My advice to you is to get the money and run. I heard Minnesota is nice in the summer."

She clutched the little bottle and began to breathe heavy. I'm sure every brain cell in her head was working over time figuring out the angles and how much time she had.

"Bitch." She pushed passed me, almost knocking me down. She dashed across the street nearly getting sideswiped by approaching patrol car. A dumbstruck Ziemann watched as Cherry dove into the backseat of the SUV before the automobile peeled away.

"What did you do to my client?" Ziemann asked.

"We gave her what she wanted," a somber Maggie said, her eyes still lingering down the street where Bear's SUV disappeared.

"What was that?"

"Her payday," I said.

CHAPTER

33

The quiet lasted for only a few days. We'd gone back to living our lives, before the proverbial crap hit the fan. To the dismay of Rocket and his Grandmother's Cribbage Club, Bebe returned to work and moved out of the Swift house. Maggie was back arguing with Frank about work and his preoccupation with Allie, and getting to third base. Before she returned to California, Allie helped out in the cake shop. I even had the opportunity to talk to her clueless husband when she called him from his conference. He hoped we'd meet soon and was glad his wife had a chance to visit with her brother. He mentioned something about a call from the country club and umbrellas, but he couldn't make sense of it. Allie told him not to worry. Good Girl!

On a day I'd set aside to teach Allie how to bake a lemon cream pie, a particular piece of crap walked through the front door of my bakeshop. To say I was happy to see Ziemann would be an understatement. His revelation about his friendship with Lee had my head trying to sort that one out. My opinion about him hadn't changed. He stood as a reminder of Lee's past, a time even Lee wasn't too fond of remembering. Yet his rekindled friendship with Ziemann seemed to overshadow his doubt.

With his insistence of remaining Cherry's lawyer, Ziemann hadn't returned to his Manhattan law office and clearly, they didn't miss him. In view of his patronizing and pompous personality, I'm not surprised. A Ziemann-free zone would be considered a holiday. He'd taken over an office next to Lee's, placed his feet on the desk and settled in. At first, Ziemann's presence in the small Queens Law office was a disrupting force. Before I knew it, Lee, Boyer and Ziemann were sitting at the Blue Moon over lunch laughing their heads off. Did everyone drink the man's Kool-Aid? Appreciative as I was he'd helped the Blue Moon sous chef out of a jam, I wanted Ziemann gone. When Lee asked if I'd join Ziemann and him for dinner, I begged off. I said I had something urgent to do. Disappointed, Lee took Ziemann to his favorite sports bar for a quick bite. While Ziemann and my future husband had hot wings and beer, I hid out at Maggie's house and had dinner of macaroni and cheese and frankfurter slices. Oh the good times.

She said I was being ridiculous. "You can't avoid him," she said.

I knew I was being childish but Ziemann brought that out in me. Did I think he would try to disrupt my relationship with Lee, I didn't know. The jury was still out on that one. Besides teasing me, he'd never said anything negative to Lee about me. I kept my doubts.

"Yes, I can. It's easy. He walks into a room and I walk out."

So, when Ziemann entered the shop the following day, my Spidery sense kicked into overdrive. Also, I couldn't leave; it was my shop. He hadn't dropped by to say hello and have some cake. He wanted something. When Esperanza directed him toward the workshop, he barely acknowledged her presence.

In the work area, Allie stood across a steel prep table

from me carefully separating egg whites and yolks. Her anxiety to do everything perfectly made teaching her how to bake harder than enriching uranium. She cracked eggs as if the shells contained nitroglycerine, measured the sugar as if it were gold, and treated the mixer as if it might explode. Busy with my own work, Ziemann approached me with my hands covered in powder sugar. I'd been wrestling with a large piece of pale yellow fondant. Ziemann's glowering presence messed with my mojo. He surveyed the area as if he were an alien just landing on earth. He didn't care too much for its inhabitants or the environment. Fearful to touch anything or have anything touch him. Allie gave him a quick smile he didn't return. She went back to cracking eggs and tried to be invisible.

"We need to talk," he snapped.

"About what?" I asked.

"Ms. Turnbull, of course. Is there somewhere we could be alone?" His eyes cut to Allie, who seemed to shrink away in Ziemann's presence. Possibly a little self-conscious that she'd fool the lawyer with her impersonation of Cherry.

"Here's fine," I said.

He crossed his arms and said nothing, possibly waiting for me to ask Allie to leave. I didn't. He sighed.

"Maybe I should..." Allie began, but I shook my head.

"You were saying?" I said.

"She's missing. She was supposed to be in court yesterday afternoon, and she didn't show." His brow furrowed.

"How does this involve me?" I said with some irritation of my own. Of all the people I wanted to talk about, Cherry wasn't one of them. "I'm not her keeper."

"Be that as it may, she called yesterday afternoon, saying she'd be there. She has no reason to skip out of this court date. Things were set with the judge."

"I repeat, how does this affect me?" I asked.

"You don't understand, do you? She'd have to be dead or dying to miss this court appearance." His voice hitched in annoyance.

Allie stopped cracking eggs, and Esperanza who had just walked into the work area froze in place.

"You think I did something to her?" I said incredulously.

He took a step toward me, taking away any personal space I had. His ire slipped off him like waves, all his charm and affability had vanished. I never suspected he cared about Cherry. Her legal issues had been secondary to Bebe's. Now he had some burning desire to set right her wrongs and play the knight in shining armor. Maybe Cherry had Kool-Aid of her own.

"I don't know where she is. Stop treating me like I'm a criminal."

"You're the reason she's gone." He leaned into me. I had to bend away from him just to get some space. "Don't think I didn't catch your conversation about taking the money and running at the precinct the other day. Something was going on. You're going to tell me, and you're going to find her."

I pushed him away, not remembering my hands were covered in confectioner sugar. A perfect powdery handprint waved at me when he took a step back and realized what I had done. He stared at the offending spot on his immaculate suit and then glared at me. I guessed powdered sugar doesn't go well with imported Italian wool.

Allie squeaked. Esperanza picked up an empty tray and headed toward the front of the shop, no doubt to put imaginary cookies in the display case.

"Sorry," I said.

He took out a handkerchief to clean himself and swiped angrily at the offending spot. No doubt he was thinking of me."You will be if you don't locate Ms. Turnbull for me."

Again with the threats. Ugh!

"Listen Ziemann, I'm not responsible for your client. You and the warden at Rikers can claim responsibility for that woman. You say she disappeared on you, I say good riddance."

His smile faded. "She is still my client. When a judge says I have to produce Ms. Turnbull in court, they don't want excuses. Ms. Turnbull doesn't hold our courts in high regard and feels she can deal with her legal trouble only when it suits her. She's missed her court date a few times and this time the judge isn't happy. I don't like unhappy judges. They make me unhappy."

"Why don't you get your hotshot investigator? Why bother with me?"

"He's tried. You know her better and found her once."

I laughed. "She found me is closer to the truth. Besides, why should I help you?"

Obviously this wasn't what he wanted to hear because he was in my face again, all puffy with irritation. He reminded me of a peacock on steroids. "In the time I've spent with Ms Turnbull, she can be a bit chatty. I especially like the story where your little redheaded friend tasered some bodyguard and pulled a gun on someone. Or your escape in pink cake shop van. She even showed me a photo of the aftermath. I made a copy. Wasn't that Lee's sister with you," he said smugly.

I remembered the flash of Cherry's camera as Allie, Maggie and I lay sprawled at the gas station, like some refugees after our disastrous encounter with Lamar.

"I wondered if Lee heard the story." He gave a half shrug and placed his handkerchief neatly into his breast suit pocket.

I'd just returned peace in my house and he wanted to disrupt it with his Cherry issues. How would I explain Allie being interrogated by Lamar, me stealing a woman's bag while Maggie pulled a gun on someone? In what setting might I even bring this up—over a bowl of cereal at breakfast? Short of telling him I'd joined the circus as the knife thrower's assistant, this wouldn't go down well. I wondered if Ziemann could fit in my large commercial oven. Crap. I sighed beneath my breath.

"Well, Ms. Cupcake. What will it be?"

"Well." My mind scrambled for a solution. Over time, Lee would understand why we did what we did at Lamar's, but the initial blowback would have the man sulking for days. He'd complain about having honest communication between the two of us. I'd sulk for a day or two before we both came to our senses and apologized. If I had a week to kill and an asbestos suit to deal with his death rays looks, I might be able to tackle the evitable emotional roller coaster with Lee, but not with Allie in the mix. Brother and sister were at a good place and Ziemann threatened to push them out of it.

I took a deep breath and cursed Ziemann. "Fine, I'll search for her." I shook my head, disappointed he played me so easily. "What are you defending her for anyway?"

Ziemann said nothing until I told him the information might help me find her sooner. This changed his mind. "A bench warrant out for a minor offense." He sounded much too casual. Ziemann wouldn't spend his money chasing Cherry over something minor.

"How minor an offense?" I pushed.

"She missed a court appearance."

"For what?" I didn't want to play twenty questions with Ziemann.

"Is it important?" Obviously, Ziemann didn't want to play.

"Your minor offense might turn into a major one if you don't produce Cherry. You gave the judge your word, which means more to you than me right now. I wonder how much it will be worth it to you if you don't have Miss Sunshine in his court on time and happy to be there."

I must have hit a nerve because he relented.

"She sold counterfeit media to an undercover officer."

"Counterfeit what? And don't say media. That could mean anything." I finally lost my patience with the haughty lawyer.

"Selling counterfeit music CDs to an undercover cop," he said.

"She's her own little crime spree, isn't she?"

Ziemann huffed at me. "When will you start?" His imperious tone returned much to my annoyance. Then I thought of the only thing that would tap it down a bit.

"You're going to pay Maggie for her services," I said with a smile.

"Why?" He seemed shocked.

"McAvoy Investigation would love a high-priced attorney on its books." I widened my smile.

"She's a secretary," he mocked.

"She can find a clue in the rain," I retorted, alluding to the evidence she deduced about Bebe in the parking lot of RTM.

A reticent Ziemann sighed. "What if her boss doesn't want the case?"

I laughed. "Wave a nickel in his face, he'll be happy." I waggled my eyebrows at him. If I had to deal with Cherry again, at least Maggie would get a payday.

"How much?"

I stopped my eyebrows waggling. Was he negotiating with me? How much was his reputation worth? "How much do you pay your investigator?"

"He's licensed," he shot back.

"Has he found Cherry?" I cocked my head to the side.

Ziemann made a sucking sound with his teeth. "Same rate, but you got twenty-four hours."

I held out my powered hand to shake. He didn't take it.

CHAPTER

34

With Ziemann in line, Maggie paid, and Allie reassured Lee wouldn't find out about our little escapade at Lamar's until she'd landed in California, Maggie and I had to find Cherry. I called Maggie and told her about the arrangement. She seemed pleased. She didn't think Frank would be. Preoccupied with his love life, Frank didn't want to chase down wayward husbands. She had to force him out of the door to follow up on a divorce case sent to her by Boyer. Frank had to find out if Mrs. Morella's husband was playing house with the counter girl at the local Baskin Robbins Ice Cream Store. Mrs. Morella suspected something when she noticed her freezer almost full with seventeen of Baskin Robbins' famous twenty-eight flavors. Considering, Mrs. Morella was diabetic and Mr. Morella lactose intolerant, she knew something had to be wrong. With Frank chasing after Mr. Morella, he wouldn't get in Maggie's way when she went after Cherry.

Around two o'clock, Maggie showed up at the shop, and we headed out to Boyer's law offices. Allie tagged along because she wanted to give Lee a taste of the pie she learned how to make. She was quite proud of herself. The slowest pie made in the history of the world, but time was irrelevant. Also, I enjoyed teaching Allie. When she didn't stress about life's little trials and tribulations, she was funny and easygoing. She forgot about the snotty women at the country club, her husband's misdirected ambition and even her brother's sometimes superior attitude. Baking therapy should be recognized by the American Psychological Association.

At the office, we found Lee finishing up with one of his clients. When Allie presented her brother with the pie, he seemed touched by the gesture. He made a fuss over her efforts, and I was pleased they were close again. Maggie and I excused ourselves, stating we had to ask Ziemann something about Bebe. Lee's eyes narrow slightly before returning his attention to his sister's baking masterpiece.

Maggie and I entered Ziemann's temporary office without knocking. Sitting at his desk with his feet up and on the phone, our arrival surprised him. He almost fell backwards, but caught himself in time and glowered at us. "Have you ever heard of knocking?"

I leaned over the desk and rapped my knuckles twice. "Does it go something like this?"

"Funny," he said snidely before disengaging the call.

Without asking, we took a seat and waited. He got up, slipped on his suit jacket, readjusted his tie and smoothed his brows before he finally took a seat.

I moaned. I knew sixteen-year-old girls who primped less than him.

"Can we make this quick?" I said, aware of the time constraint he'd put on us. Also, I didn't think Allie could keep her brother distracted for too long.

"You're on the clock, aren't you?" His lips curled in an impish smile. Now that we were under his employ, he seemed much too satisfied.

"When was the last time you spoke to Cherry?" Maggie asked.

"Around one o'clock on Tuesday. She was supposed..."

Ziemann's was interrupted by his office door abruptly opening. Maggie and I turned to find Lee standing in the doorway with Allie behind him holding her pie. I guess her ability to distract her brother fell short.

Crap!

"Hey Lee," I said.

His cautious expression had shifted into something less pleasant than before. He walked in and took a seat next to me, crossed his legs, interlaced his hands on his lap, and glared at Ziemann.

"Something wrong, Lee?" Maggie gave him a weak smile.

"Allie just told me an interesting story."

Allie's guilt-ridden expression and her sudden interest in her shoes said everything.

"About what?" My voice cracked.

"We started with her kidnapping, moved on to someone forcing her to drink liquor against her will so they could pump her for information about you two." Lee wagged a finger between Maggie and me. "That's not even the best part." He cut his eyes toward Maggie. "The part I love was when Maggie disarmed a three hundred pound bodyguard with a taser and pulled a gun. I'm sure Roger was upset when you told him." Lee said as if he couldn't wait to tell him.

Then he turned his hazel eyes on me. He was so close, I saw the greenish specks in his irises through his glasses.

"Can I explain?"

"Allie explained." He took my hand and squeezed. "I think we should spend our time talking about communication and trust issues, don't you?" When a man tells you he wants to sit down and talk to you about communication and trust issues, you are either in an alternate universe or you're in real trouble. I swallowed hard hoping the lump in my throat wouldn't choke me.

Ziemann seemed to be working on a lump of his own, obviously not pleased with Lee's arrival. With the truth out, he couldn't force me to do anything. Ziemann scowled at me as if I were the source of his impotence.

"Thad, you're still a manipulative asshole." Lee's eyes darkened on Ziemann. "You try that crap again with Odessa, and you and I will have a problem." Lee spoke calmly, but I knew he was anything but calm.

Ziemann offered up a playful smile. "Fine." He shrugged his shoulders and turned to me. "Will you still find Ms. Turnbull for me?"

I thought for a moment. "Yeah, for a big fat check."

"I said I'd pay the usual rate."

"I hear Judge Braswell doesn't like his bench warrant ignored. One lawyer almost got thrown in jail for contempt because his client was fifteen minutes late."

Lee wore a sly grin.

"I'm sure the ladies will find Turnbull." Ziemann didn't seem to certain. Lee's smile grew.

"We'll find her," I reassured. Though I didn't know why I was certain we could.

"Now that we're all friends, can we get back to my question?" Maggie asked. "When was the last time Cherry spoke to you?"

"Around one o'clock. I wanted to make sure she gave herself enough time to get back."

"Back from where? Isn't she still at the hotel?" Maggie asked.

Ziemann shook his head. "She said something about her hair and nails."

"She wouldn't do something that stupid," Maggie said.

"Why not? You see how she dresses. I'm sure stupid fits her fine." I pulled out my cell phone. I dialed the number to

Divine Diva Hair Salon. The phone rang, and someone picked up.

"Hello, Divine Diva. How may I help you?" a chirpy Vesta said.

"Hi Vesta, have you seen Cherry. Has she been around?"

"Your girl decided to give me some hair?" she said as if she didn't know what Maggie's problem was.

"Well, she's considering," I avoided Maggie's gaze.

"No, haven't seen the girl, not at all," she said, too quickly.

If that were the truth, I'd kiss Ziemann on the lips. "Well, okay. Don't forget to call me if she shows." I kept my tone upbeat.

"She's lying?" Maggie asked, and I nodded.

"Does this woman know where Turnbull is?" a confused but hopeful Ziemann asked.

"Yeah. Which means one of two things: one, Cherry paid her the money she owes and they've made up. Second, Cherry has promised to pay her the money she owes, and that fool Vesta believes her and they have made up."

This seemed to confuse both Lee and Ziemann.

"Which means?" Lee asked.

"She's hiding Cherry who is avoiding someone. Most likely Lamar," I said.

"Why him?" Lee asked.

Ziemann glowered at Maggie and me. He remembered our warning to Cherry after she'd given her statement to the police. I guess he wondered if I would reveal this to Lee and test my willingness to be honest and open. I sighed and told Lee about the photograph of Lamar and Cherry's involvement. His brows lifted a few times in surprise but he said nothing. When I was done, he nodded. No fireworks, shock of reproach, or even an expression of disappointment. He simply wanted to know. Ziemann seemed the only one shocked… at Lee's restraint.

Then a thought occurred to me, everybody has superpowers. I got up and cornered poor Allie against the wall while a baffled Lee and Ziemann watched. Maggie must have come to the same conclusion because she joined me.

"I need you to be Cherry," I said.

"I can't." She shook her head. Now she had to think about it. She had a serious case of stage fright. You would have thought we'd asked her to show them her lacey underwear.

"Just a few words." I'd pushed Allie passed her comfort zone. She'd been set upon by an intense, towering black woman and a persistent red headed elf.

"What are you asking Allie to do?" Lee asked, a little worried we were treating his sister like a criminal.

"Be Cherry."

"What!" Ziemann chortled. He couldn't believe I would ask a white woman, with confidence issues, to pretend to be the most bodacious black woman he'd ever met. He needed illumination.

"When Cherry told you to take a flying leap the other day, who do you think you were talking to?" I said with a satisfying grin.

Ziemann's eyes narrowed. Lee gawked at his sister for half a beat and burst out laughing.

"That was you?" Ziemann turned to Allie.

"Sorry," Allie squeaked.

"No wonder Turnbull thought I'd lost my mind when I asked her about it." Ziemann slapped his forehead.

"Still doing voices, I see." Lee's lips lifted in a smile.

"You didn't mind when they got you out of detention," I said. While teaching Allie to bake, she regaled me with stories about growing up with her brother. "She used to imitate your mom, right?" I said.

Lee feigned betrayal for half a minute before smirking.

"I hate to break up this family lovefest, but can we get back to the point… where you pretended to be my client?" Ziemann interrupted.

"Get over it, Ziemann." I snapped my finger at him.

"Allie, it's like doing the voices with Rocket. You remember how fun it was?" A smiling Maggie took the pie away from Allie and placed the dessert on the desk. She clasped Allie's hands. Maggie went as soft as butter. Men, women and small dogs were unable to resist her sincere gaze. If Maggie had been Darth Vader, Luke would have gone to the Dark Side skipping all the way.

"What you have is a talent, a rare gift. Don't hide it away," Maggie said.

A spark glimmered in Allie's eyes. "I always wanted to do voice work, you know for animation and commercials or maybe some acting. I even took an adult class at the community college."

"You did?" Lee said.

"Sounds silly, right?" Allies cheeks reddened.

"No. Some of us take a while to figure out what we want. Nobody is judging you here." I was getting caught up in the moment and Maggie's powers of persuasion. With the exception of Ziemann, everyone in the room had taken a detour to another life and some roads led through community college.

"Christ," Ziemann moaned, the sugar level too high for his taste. All of us glared at him.

"Shut up, Thad," Lee commanded.

"Be Cherry," I chanted. "Be Cherry."

Allie surveyed the room and locked eyes with her brother. To his credit, he shrugged and smiled at her. "Be Cherry," he said, even though he had no idea what that meant.

"Okay. What do I say?"

CHAPTER

35

Before I left the law office, I promised Lee we would have a long conversation about communication when he got home. He even suggested making a night of it, with a home cooked meal, a good bottle of wine, and some heavy petting on the couch. Since I had to, once again, chase Cherry, I said he'd have to cook dinner and ditch his sister for the night. Having someone who was able to mimic every sound you made in the same house could put a girl off her game. We compromised with Lee picking up something at the Blue Moon, and a promise I'd handle Allie. He grinned wickedly at the idea and never asked what I might do with his sister. Either he trusted me to take care of her, or he was too occupied with the idea of wrestling me on the couch and didn't care—maybe a little of both.

After promising Ziemann for the tenth time we'd have Cherry at the court, Allie, Maggie and I drove to Brooklyn and Vesta's beauty salon. We parked a block away. With the shop in full view, we sat and waited. Allie preoccupied herself with one of Rocket's toys he'd left in the car: the tiny laser gun he'd used to torment the family dog. Every now and then, she'd shoot off a beam of light inside the car. Grateful the switch for the irritating space-age sound effect had been turned off. Every time I brought up the notions of her pretending to be Cherry, an illuminated red dot danced nervously around in the car's interior.

"Relax," Maggie reassured.

I nodded my own encouragement and handed her my cell phone. Her hand shook a little as she took one deep breath, closed her eyes and searched for her inner Cherry. It was kind of like embracing your inner bitch. When she was sure she had it, she called Vesta. "Hey!" Her brow furrowed. As expected, her impression of Cherry was dead on. "You'll get the rest of your money... I said I will, dammit."

Watching the transformation as Allie embodied Cherry was a revelation. She didn't just imitate the voice of the ex-hairdresser she personified the lady's irreverent spirit. I realized maybe for the first time, that Allie was a brilliant actress. The woman had talent. The idea of her spending her life as a dental assistant, or even planning an event with paper umbrellas at the local country club bothered me.

"Now listen up, my lawyer is gonna call. He wants me to sign papers. I gave him your number in case he had to get a hold of me. I don't want to talk to him, you understand. He might put the police on me. I told him the only thing I'd do was sign them papers."

An angry Vesta shouted through the receiver. She wanted nothing to do with the police and she'd enough of Cherry's drama.

"I will...I will. He's gonna send some papers to you, and I need you to bring them over. Once I got my stuff, I'm gone. Yes, dammit, you will get your money," Allie reassured the irate woman.

This seemed to calm Vesta. In typical Cherry fashion, and without saying thank you, Allie hung up. Maggie and I applauded. Allie smiled back, relieved her performance had ended. We had little time to congratulate her when a small courier service van pulled up in front of the salon. I'd made arrangements prior to leaving Lee and Ziemann to utilize the office's courier service with fake papers.

The courier walked into the salon and interrupted an already-irritated Vesta washing a client's hair. Without tipping the courier, she palmed off the customer to her assistant, grabbed her handbag and dashed out the door, leaving a disappointed driver, a yelling client, and a put-upon assistant.

Vesta hopped into a late model electric blue Honda, the color so bright you could have seen the thing from space. With a missing hubcap, a few dents on one side and a bumper that seemed to hold on by sheer will, there would be no confusing the car with anyone else's blue Honda.

Maggie pulled out into the late afternoon traffic. Vesta drove like a woman on a mission, a mission, to get Cherry out of her life. I felt guilty about deceiving her. I liked Vesta. Unfortunately, she'd picked the wrong person as a friend. Being friends with Cherry might cost you bits of flesh and the contents of your wallet.

"What are we going to do when we find her?" Allie asked.

"Yeah O, what are we going to do?" Maggie was doing her best to keep up with Vesta, who broke the Brooklyn land speed record. Unfamiliar with the streets, it took all Maggie's efforts to keep up. I held my breath and tightened my seatbelt.

I didn't have a plan to deal with Cherry. Short of yelling at her, I was clueless. However, the fact that she was on the run with her blackmail money, gave me some ideas. A minute later, I knew what I had to do. "We need to get the money Lamar gave her. She'd follow that around like a dog with a bone," I announced. We had stopped at a large intersection; two cars back from Vesta and waited for the light to change.

Maggie gave me her full attention. "How do we do that?"

"Between, you, me, and Allie, we can take her."

Allie and Maggie seemed uncertain

"What about Vesta? She probably could take all of us," Maggie said.

Vesta might be a problem. When she found out Cherry wasn't leaving, she wouldn't be happy. When she found out we'd deceived her happiness would drop to a whole new level. How would I convince her to stay out of it? I contemplated this for a moment while Maggie drove. Her face went tight with intent, her blue eyes focused on the road. She'd tied back her hair into a long ponytail, a kick-ass Tinkerbelle chasing down her prey. My attention went back to the thick ponytail.

"Do you have some scissors?" I kept my tone conversational. She pointed to her handbag, said she had a small pair in her make-up bag and asked Allie to pull them from a pink pouch. Allie put down the toy gun and dug through the bag. To my surprise, she held up Cherry's stun gun and frowned.

"You still have this?" I took the gun from Allie. Maggie cocked an eyebrow upward.

"Should I leave the thing around for Rocket, or even Roger, to find? I don't think so."

I shuddered at the idea of any of the Swift men with access to this. Rocket would zap one of the neighbor kids to see how it worked and Roger would stun himself stupid trying to get it away from him. In truth, I suspected the little redhead liked the idea of carrying the gun. Often the smallest person in the room, the thing had become her great equalizer. I put the gun back into the bag and took the small pair of nail trimming scissors from Allie.

I waited for the stoplight to turn green and for Maggie to follow Vesta again. When her focus was on her task, I mumbled a prayer she wouldn't kill me, leaned over and snipped off four inches of her red locks. She jerked, and veered into oncoming traffic before righting the car. With one hand on the wheel, she clutched her ponytail.

"You cut my hair?"

"Watch out!" Allie pointed to a car that had stopped short.

Maggie slammed on the brakes, shooting us violently forward. My seatbelt saved me from crashing through the windshield, but I remained trapped in the car with an irate redhead.

"Have you lost your mind!" she screamed, trying to find out where I'd cut, her face flushed with anger.

"Sorry honey, but it will grow back, and Vesta would kill for this," I said.

"She's turning," Allie interrupted.

Vesta took a sharp right down a residential block. Maggie's hands clutched the wheel as she seethed. If it weren't for the honking of the horns behind us, I didn't think she'd move. Thankfully, she took off after Vesta. Every now and then, her narrow eyes cut at me as her chest heaved in anger.

"Maggie..." I began, but her cold blue eyes shut me down.

"How would you like it if I zapped you?" She sounded as if she might enjoy it.

"I'm so sorry, I owe you big time. I thought this was the only thing that might get Vesta's attention."

Maggie shook her head and kept her eyes on the busy Brooklyn traffic. We drove in silence for at least another ten minutes. Maggie refused to speak to me. Vesta parked in front of a small, pale blue clapboard house with a tiny front lawn in need of serious care and surrounded by a small chain link fence, obviously there to protect the lawn in case any grass showed up. She wore flip-flops and the large pink apron she'd forgotten to take off when she left the salon. She stomped up the cement pathway to the house.

"What do we do?" an uncertain Allie asked as Maggie parked across the street.

The question seemed reasonable, but I didn't have an answer. "The money has to be in her handbag. We grab the bag, and we're good." I didn't know if this were true or not, but it was a start.

"Yeah, we're perfect," Maggie grumbled as we got out of the car. She slammed the door, expressing her displeasure.

I shook my head, knowing this would only get worse. Either she got over being pissed at me and forgave me, or burned through it like some supernova. This particular mad seemed the pyrotechnic type. I had to run to catch up as she dashed across the street. Allie followed, keeping a healthy distance.

Vesta had rushed through the front without closing it. Shouting voices emanated from the back of the house. Vesta went on and on about their nonexistent phone conversation. Cherry kept saying she was crazy.

At first, Maggie wanted to charge in, still driven by her annoyance with me. I held her back and pushed the door open slowly. We stepped into a tiny living room cluttered with boxes and junk. Preoccupied with calling each other names, the women never heard us. The house appeared abandoned, except for a long stained couch, several stacked boxes and large black trash bags scattered about the room. Cherry must have been sleeping on the grungy thing because a blanket and pillows sat folded at one end. She'd made herself at home. A cheap plastic lamp sat on the floor next to a folding table that held some costume jewelry and leftover Chinese food and a Diet Coke.

Allie saw it first and pointed to Cherry's pocketbook hidden behind the couch. I snatched the bag. A wad of money peeked out from the corner of the envelope. Crisp one-hundred dollar bills stacked together like Monopoly money. There had to be at least ten thousand dollars. My smile widened at the idea, I was about to punch a hole into Cherry's golden parachute.

CHAPTER

36

Breaking and entering not being one of my strong suits, I cursed when my foot knocked over a stack of CD cases lying around the living room like an obstacle course. It took all our efforts to maneuver around the junk. The sound of the crash stopped the voices in the kitchen.

With a large wad of money in my hand, I dumped Cherry's handbag onto the floor and shoved the bills into Maggie's shoulder bag. Her lips pressed tightly together and she pointed an angry finger at me. I'd just made her a target of a crazy woman. I mouthed a silent sorry. She rolled her eyes in disgust.

Vesta stepped into the living room to see us staring back at her. Our guilty expressions didn't help. "What the—"

Cherry pushed passed her and spied her pocketbook on the floor. She wore a long blonde wig beneath a pink bandana. The scarf matched her tight-fitting jogging suit. Unlike most athletic suits, you don't expect to wear them with four-inch red patent leather heels, but Cherry did.

Adding up the situation quickly, Cherry's screwed her face into a venomous glare. Her eyes danced between Allie, Maggie, me, and her bag, which lay open, and empty.

"Give me my money." She pointed a finger at me.

"You're always taking my shit. Where's my money?"

"What the hell is going on here?" Vesta stepped away from Cherry and the bonfire of her growing rage. She held the open envelope the courier had delivered. I'm sure the blank pieces of paper added to her confusion.

"We followed you," I said to Vesta, but never took my eyes off Cherry.

Poised to pounce on someone, she seemed undecided as to which of us had offended her the most. When her eyes landed on me, I held my breath.

"You said you didn't know where Cherry was," Maggie said.

A contrite Vesta just shrugged.

"Give me my money," Cherry repeated.

"That's what I've been saying," Vesta said to Cherry.

Cherry waved her away. She took two steps, reached beneath the couch and came out a baseball bat. We all took a collective step back.

"Cherry, put that damn thing down," Vesta stepped in front of her former employee. Cherry pushed passed Vesta to get to the source of troubles. I ran.

I had a list of shortcomings. I can't sing worth a damn, or do the backstroke when swimming. I have flat feet, allergies, and I'm terrified of snakes. Thankfully, I wasn't slow.

Cherry gave me an edge in her four-inch heels. She ran like a drunken turtle as she chased me around the room threatening to break every bone in my body. Everyone screaming their heads off amplified the craziness of the situation. Of course, no one seemed brave enough to try to get the bat away from her.

"I want my goddamn money!" She batted at a tower of boxes I stood behind. Hundreds of CD jewel cases crashed to the ground.

"Ziemann sent us. You have to be at the courthouse at—" Maggie said.

Cherry pointed the bat at her. Maggie found a stack of boxes of her own to stand behind. Vesta remained by the kitchen door, Allie by the front; both were ready to bolt.

"Just promise you'll show up at court tomorrow and you'll get your money back," I said, but Cherry was beyond listening. She'd gone rabid. She cursed and foamed at the mouth. I knew I was in trouble when she kicked off her shoes. We did another go-around through the tower of boxes when she trapped me behind a stack. With her shoes off and more maneuverability, she had me.

"Cherry, I wouldn't do that," Vesta warned, but who was listening to her? I didn't know if she was trying to protect me or not be a witness to my murder.

Allie screamed as a wild-eyed Cherry stepped toward me with an upraised bat.

"Who's laughing now, bitch?" She grinned. Then without warning, her mouth twisted, her body did a spastic dance and she dropped like a doll. She let out a little yelp and fell face down onto a pile of trash bags. Behind her, Maggie stood with her finger on the trigger of the stun gun.

I took a deep breath of relief. "You are my hero," I said to her as I stood up. She glowered at me, still mad at the hair thing. Not only had I cut her hair, but once again, she had to come to my rescue by stunning someone stupid.

"You killed her!" Vesta cried.

"She's just sleeping." Maggie bent to roll over a dozing Cherry, who began to mumble. "She's breathing fine."

Vesta came closer. "You women are crazy." She pulled out her cell phone. "I'm calling the cops."

"You don't want to do that, Vesta." I stood up. She huffed and started to dial. "You won't get your money." She stopped punching numbers.

"What did she owe you again?" Maggie drew out the envelope of money.

"Five fifty-three ninety-eight." Vesta perused the neglected house and possibly wondered if she should charge anyone for this hovel. She shrugged. "Maybe another two hundred."

Maggie handed me the money, and I counted out an even thousand. Vesta's eyes opened in surprise and delight. She snatched the money.

"An extra five hundred for stress and aggravation," I said, and Vesta's smile broadened.

"You got that right. She said she wouldn't have the money for a couple of days, the liar. Told her she could stay at my Gran's house while she's visiting family. I come into all this junk. Girl more trouble than she worth." Vesta counted the money gleefully and shoved the wad into her bra. "Should still call the cops on you. You can't go around tasering people." She sounded a little self-righteous. This came from a woman who hid a blackmailer, con artist and extraordinarily bad hairdresser. Vesta stopped her complaining when I waved a lock of Maggie's hair in front of her.

Her eyes widened even as she grinned. "For me?" Vesta snatched the lock of hair.

You would have thought it was Christmas. Maggie seethed. I accompanied Vesta to her car, content with her money, a sample of Maggie's hair and Cherry out of her life.

"Tell Cherry she better be gone by tomorrow and take that crap with her." She drove off.

I returned inside the house to find Maggie and Allie had positioned a dazed Cherry on the couch. Maggie took the extra precaution to tie Cherry's hands and feet with a pair of her stockings. Her expertise in hog-tying people grew. Allie adjusted her wig so she didn't look deranged. We waited a moment, hoping she'd wake up. She didn't.

Maggie took the lull in the chaos to address her issues with me. "You cut my hair." She stood with her arms crossed

"You would have said no," I said in my own defense, which was no defense at all. "I'm sorry, really I am."

"Vesta seems happy," Allie interrupted. She was right, of course. A happy Vesta had left, Cherry sat tied snugly, and all was right with the world.

"Rocket's Little League has a fundraiser next week, and you're going to donate three hundred cupcakes for the cause," Maggie said.

I flinched at the amount. However, it was a small price to pay to get back on her good side.

"In the team colors," she added. "And not the mini ones, the large ones you sell at the shop."

"Okay, I swear." I crossed my heart and decided to tell Esperanza the good news later.

"Boy, she has a lot of CDs here." Allie searched through a box of CDs. While Maggie stood guard over the snoring Cherry, I joined Allie. She was right; there were hundreds. I pulled a few out to examine. Most were urban street music and hip hop, and a lot of artists I recognized.

"Maggie, come here." I held up one of the cases.

Leaving Cherry to her nap, she joined us. "These must be the counterfeit CDs she'd got arrested for."

"Hundreds of them," Allie said.

We opened other bags and boxes and found more.

"This is a little deeper than a minor offense," I said.

Maggie grabbed a handful of the CDs and put them into her bag. "If they're copies, they're pretty good."

She was right. These CDs had been professionally manufactured. Before we had a chance to get into what it might mean Cherry started making noises. We retied the bags and went back to her. It took her a moment to regain her senses and the twelve-alarm anger she had going. She started cursing again until Maggie waved the stun gun at her.

"Here's how this works, Cherry." I used a tone I reserved for belligerent brides who expected doves and fireworks to explode out of their wedding cakes. "You show up to the court on time, dressed like an adult, and finish your case with Ziemann. If you behave, I have no doubt he'll get you off on a misdemeanor, considering all this." I waved to the CDs behind me.

"You have a full-fledged operation here," Maggie added.

"I don't care, Ziemann will be happy, and so will I," I said.

"I can't show up," Cherry said, barely covering her anger.

"We'll make sure Lamar doesn't find you," Maggie assured.

Cherry remained doubtful.

"Call Ziemann, make the arrangement, and he'll have a car waiting for you to go to the courthouse. Deal with this and you get your money back," I said.

"Untie me." She pulled at her bonds and gave us all the evil eye.

"Agreed Cherry?" I demanded.

She huffed and contemplated her options. "Okay, but when will I get my money?"

"When your court appearance is over, the money's yours," I said.

"Something else," Maggie interjected. "Did Rovell invite you to his office the night he died?"

Cherry's eyes widened. I could tell she was calculating what the answer might cost her or what she could receive for divulging any.

"Do you want all your money back," I threatened, "because I could flush some of it down the toilet."

"You can't—" She stopped, possibly realizing I would do it. "Yeah, he did."

"What about Bebe?" I asked.

"I didn't see nothing. When that fool ass threw me out, I was mad. My feet hurt, and I didn't talk to Rovell. Bebe had no right. So I went back. Found him on the ground, almost dead. Didn't know what to do. Started raining, so I left and caught a cab."

She'd left an injured Bebe and did nothing. I wanted to zap her again.

"Why didn't you tell this to the police?" Maggie said.

"What was in it for her?" I accused, not waiting for her to answer. "Who attacked Bebe?"

She shook her head and pulled against her restraints. "I don't know. Let me go!"

I had no sympathy for her. She was like a feral cat you couldn't housebreak.

"Bebe could have died," Maggie snapped.

"Well, he didn't, did he?" She huffed.

"Screw this," I cursed. "We should leave her here, call Lamar and let him deal with her."

"I bet he didn't like seeing the photo you took of him," Maggie said.

"Somebody put the damn thing on the internet," she accused.

Maggie's lips hitched in a slight smile. I knew she'd given a copy to the detectives, and in between laundry loads, she downloaded copies to several gossip websites.

"Yeah, I bet he'd love to see you," I said.

"You wouldn't... You don't know what he's like." Her eyes suddenly widen with alarm, showing true fear for the first time.

The truth was I did know what he was like. I had the sore wrist to prove it.

CHAPTER

37

Later that evening, Lee sat on the couch watching the New York Mets lose and ignoring me. The plan of snuggling and deep conversation hadn't gone as expected. Despite Maggie and my recent success at locating Cherry, he didn't find my solution to getting Allie out of the house reasonable. In fact, he asked if I'd lost my mind. I said I hadn't when I made arrangements for her to take in a dinner and a Broadway show. Lee didn't like the escort I'd chosen—Frank. Despite my assurance that he wouldn't do anything irresponsible, my words fell on deaf ears. I explained my threat of Frank's death and dismemberment, and Maggie's promises never to do his laundry again, if he tried anything. Lee didn't care.

While Allie went to enjoy her night, she left her sullen and mistrusting brother with me. Lee and I picked over our dinner in hostile silence. I swore, sometimes the man acted like a twelve-year-old. Our evening of intimacy turned into him watching a lousy baseball game just to spite me. Every attempt to elicit conversation from him rewarded me with grunts and mumbles. As a last resort, I pulled out my only weapon.

"Okay, stay here and act like someone stole your bike. I'm going to bed." I stood in front of the television, hands on my hips, to get his full attention. He sat there, silent, stewing his juices and being ridiculous.

"I will be naked," I informed him. "This offer is valid for the next fifteen minutes. Otherwise, I withdraw my offer and sleep the sleep of the dead."

Lee's resolved lasted eight minutes. He appeared in the bedroom just as I stepped out of my jeans. He hesitated a moment, refusing to acknowledge his weakness.

"Baseball game over?" I asked in a casual tone.

"No." He began undressing, and then stopped, probably frustrated by his easy manipulation.

"You want to finish watching the game?" I smiled at him as I lowered myself into bed.

"No." His curt response coincided with yanking off his t-shirt.

"Do you want to talk about your sister?"

"No." He took off his socks, aimed them toward the hamper and missed. He pulled off the rest of his clothes with equal frustration before slipping in next to me, begrudgingly letting go of his annoyance.

"You want to tell me how you and Ziemann know each other?" I continued.

He made a grumbling sound and rolled on top of me, propped himself up on his elbows and groaned. "Unless you're giving me instructions like, more to the left, faster or slow down. I don't want to talk. Not about Allie and Frank, and I damn sure don't want to talk about Thad." He slipped a hand between us and found a spot that made me forget about any more questions.

"Do you want me to stop?" he asked.

"No!"

***

Early the next morning, Maggie came by to pick me up to meet Ziemann at the courthouse. On the way there, we talked about her conversation with Tania Coffey. She'd called her after Cherry made her statement to the police. It started awkwardly at first, but Maggie was determined to reconnect with Rovell's daughter. Just like Jermaine, she wanted to find the truth about Rovell's death. She thought Tania needed closure before she could move on.

I agreed. I liked Tania and wanted the best for her, which included running her father's business. Lamar didn't think she was capable, but I did.

"She's okay?" I asked.

A solemn Maggie nodded.

"If Lamar would leave her alone, she'd have a good chance at succeeding. She loves her job and the people she works with. She doesn't know what she'd do without RTM," she said.

At the Queens County Courthouse, we found Cherry complaining to her stoic lawyer. Dressed in an austere dark blue dress and matching shoes, she could have passed as a prison matron. Her short brown wig didn't distract from the simple make-up of tinted lip-gloss and mascara. Her restraint revealed a pretty woman approaching her thirties with dignity. This illusion ended the moment Cherry saw us approach, and scowled.

"Good morning to you too," I snipped.

"You got my money?" she barked, her illusion of refinement vanishing in an instant. This Cherry I recognized.

"Should I know what's going on?" Ziemann interjected without much interest. Maggie shook her head, and he dropped it. He told Cherry to go inside the courtroom and wait.

"You always bring out the best in my client," he mused, once Cherry went inside.

"Her best side is face down in handcuffs," I replied.

Ziemann gave me a lopsided grin. "You, Ms. Cupcake are a treat," he said.

"You, Mr. Ziemann, are a pain," I said.

He laughed and threw me a smile before he went inside the courtroom. Maggie and I followed, finding seats in the last row with the rest of the early morning spectators. The hour hadn't slowed the pace set by the judge, a compact man of around sixty with thinning gray hair, and the grace of a New York traffic cop in rush hour. I understood Ziemann's concern as the judge admonished, browbeat and reprimanded those in his courtroom. His impatience kept the cases flowing and justice only slightly appeased.

A half an hour into the proceedings, an unwanted guest arrived. Dressed in a dark suit and sunglasses, Bear looked like a pallbearer for a South American despot's funeral. He sat behind the defense table. Cherry's reaction when she turned and saw him, ranked up there with finding an alien trying on her grandmother's underwear: first, shock, then horror and finally fear. She said something to Ziemann, who turned to locate the source of her dread. That's when his expression soured as well. Then the idiot turned to us, pulling Bear's attention to the back row.

"Oh crap," Maggie said beneath her breath as Bear took off his glasses for a better view.

"He doesn't like us, especially you," I said with some concern. Bear had acquired an unhealthy interest in my friend.

"I'm starting to realize that," she said.

"Did you call them?"

"Yes. They said they'll be here." She returned her attention to the proceedings. I tried too, but Bear's imposing presence was hard to ignore.

"Did you bring the stun gun?" I felt a little defenseless.

"Are you crazy, into a courthouse?" she said between

clenched teeth. Then I remembered we had to pass through security and so did the bodyguard. This eased my mind a bit, but not by much. The only thing he could threaten us with was his scowl. Besides scaring babies and small dogs, I felt safe.

We waited patiently as Cherry's case came up. Expertly, Ziemann handled the witnesses, the police and even Cherry. He painted her as a naive woman and a victim of her own poor judgment and trusting nature. I sat awestruck as he'd described Mother Theresa in an off-the-rack dress and matronly shoes. Ziemann had the prosecution's witness so turned around, he became unsure if Cherry had sold him fake CDs or donated them to charity. Cherry played the role of the innocent to the hilt and walked off after her testimony acting like a victim. Lee had been right; Ziemann was brilliant. He could talk the Devil out of his matches.

To no one's surprise, the judge admonished the D.A. for bringing such a flimsy case to his court. I'd imagined Ziemann smiling as his record remained intact, and wouldn't' be thrown in jail for contempt. This left me the only one in the world who found the lawyer contemptuous. The judge dismissed the case and called the next one. Everyone seemed relieved, except for Cherry. Her eyes went back to Bear.

My attention remained on the closed courtroom door. I prayed the cavalry would show up, but it didn't. Ziemann and Cherry vacated the defense desk as the bailiff called the next case. Cherry stepped in behind Ziemann, using him as a human shield. When what she was doing registered with him, he hesitated.

"This may not go well," Maggie said as we both stood up to meet them.

Ziemann's anxiety grew as Cherry prodded him toward the exit. Bear got up and made his way to the center aisle. He had to get passed several unhappy spectators who were annoyed they had to make room for the massive man. His exit caused a commotion and drew the attention of the judge, who whispered something to a nearby bailiff. When someone inadvertently stepped on someone's foot, things got loud. Two court officers appeared at Bear's bench, possibly to calm everyone down. We took the opportunity to leave.

Before we got through the door, Cherry demanded her money. She wanted some distance between her and Bear. I ignored her rant as the Cavalry appeared. Detectives Russo and Maddox walked over to us. Cherry tensed at the sight of them, and Maggie sighed in relief. Ziemann just acted confused.

Unbeknownst to anyone, the detectives had been Cherry's exit strategy. After leaving her hideout, we contacted them and explained that she would be at the courthouse. If they were interested in talking to her about what she might have witnessed after she returned to RTM the night of the murder, it would be the best time. We were sure they'd like to hear the details she had left out in her first statement. They begrudgingly thanked us.

"Is this your handiwork, Ms. Wilkes?" Ziemann asked.

"You may thank me for this," I said as a red-faced Bear burst through the courtroom door. He zeroed in on us like a heat-seeking missile. In reality, he focused on Cherry. We stood behind Ziemann, who viewed the man coming toward him for what he was, a threat.

He turned to the two clueless detectives. "You wanted to speak to my client, Russo?" He shoved Cherry into the detective's arms. Cherry complained a bit, but sized up the dilemma and kept her mouth shut.

"Yeah, we got a few questions," Maddox said.

"Can we do it someplace else?" Cherry pleaded.

Russo gave Bear a long stare as he approached. He pushed his jacket aside to reveal the detective badge clipped to his waistband. Bear ignored the move. The testosterone level went up a couple of degrees as the men squared off. I half expected them to whip out their manly parts and call for an umpire and a ruler.

Ziemann broke the stalemate, not willing to whip out anything. "Why don't we go to the precinct now?"

Despite the good idea, everyone seemed frozen in place as Bear invaded our small circle. His flushed face and narrowing eyes bored down on Cherry, who shrank away. "I see you got out of your troubles," Bear said.

She stood behind Russo and said nothing.

"I'm here to give you a message from your cousin. Seems he hurt himself at work, and he wondered if you could come visit him. He's at Kings County Hospital." Bear's expression was neither compassionate nor sincere.

Cherry slipped further behind Russo. "I'm busy right now." Her voice trembled. Not surprising, considering a three-hundred pound gorilla was delivering his condolences.

"We'll take her," Russo said with a warning of his own.

For the first time, Bear seemed to acknowledge the detective's presence. He offered up a hard smile. "You do that." He nodded and stepped back. Before he left, he turned his gaze on Maggie. I froze. "Haven't forgotten you," he said, his tone low and menacing.

A stoic Maggie didn't back down. She seemed so minuscule compared to his large bulky frame.

Once, we talked over coffee, she'd said Bear was a bully—like the kids at Rocket's school who picked on the weaker kids and tormented them to cover up their own inadequacies. The way she stared back at him, I wondered if she'd confirmed his inner bully because his outer one was taken up a lot of space and most of the air.

"How's your reading coming? Learning a lot?" He

sneered at her.

He was referring to the gun book Maggie had been reading when they first met. She gave an imperceptible raise of a thin auburn brow as she contemplated the question. "Recently, I'm been reading about the vulnerable points on the human body," she said studiously as if explaining something to a fellow academic.

Bear seemed bewildered.

"I believe there are five good points, maybe less than that. Most would think the clavicle, or the hyoid bone. That might take more force than someone my size could handle, don't you think?"

Bear seemed to have a hard time keeping up with the conversation and subject matter.

"I prefer the anterior nasal spine. It hurts like hell when struck, even lightly." She pointed her small fingers in an area beneath Bear's nose. He flinched as if he expected her to hit him there. The big man's reaction surprised us, and Russo might have snickered. A thin sheen of sweat adorned Bear's brow. He stepped back, saying nothing. He gave Maggie one last perplexed look before turning away.

"What the hell was that about?" Russo said.

I sighed with relief and wrapped and arm around my friend. "Reading something new?" I said containing my emotions.

She nodded. "The other book was due, and I didn't want a late fee. The library can be a pain about things like that. I found something more entertaining." She shrugged her shoulders.

I smiled. "Those damn library fees."

CHAPTER

38

The news broke big the next day about Lamar. I sat on my workbench at O So Sweet spray painting yellow sugar orchids when Maggie called. She'd spent much of her day at the office researching Chaos 182 when she heard the news. The buildup from the internet stories Maggie had dropped pushed the momentum into a white hot fervor. Many had questions about Lamar's involvement with the primary witness in Louis' gun charge case. Rumors turned into speculations, and then accusations. As expected, everyone gave their opinion, from a country and western superstar, to the guy who sold pretzels on the street—none were flattering.

Someone tracked down Max Hoffman and asked him a few probing questions about his former employee. Soon, the true nature of Lamar's patterns of intimidation seeped out like toxic waste. One entertainment news reporter made the unfortunate mistake of ambushing Lamar at his office, and asking about the charges. A flustered but angry Lamar refused to answer. Bear did, he stepped in like a linebacker and shoved the reporter into a large, thorny bush.

"This might reopen Louis Mackie's case," Maggie sounded hopeful. As expected, she wanted a happy ending for the Mackies. Still determined to find out who killed Linwood Rovell, she wanted to keep her promise to Jermaine. Not keen on the idea of involving ourselves in a murder investigation, I didn't encourage her.

"What time do you have to pick up Allie?" She changed the subject abruptly, giving me mental whiplash in the process.

I'd dropped Allie off at RTM earlier in the afternoon. Les had invited her to do some voice work for him. In exchange, he'd make a demo tape for her that she could shop around to agents. I suspected he wanted some alone time with her to check the status of her cold. I didn't worry about leaving Allie alone with the semi-lecherous Les because I'd gotten Jermaine's reassurance the engineer would keep his hands to himself and on the control panel. Oblivious of Les' interest, Allie jumped at the opportunity. She seemed intent on a new experience. Not many women from her country club could boast studio time with up and coming music stars.

"In about a half hour. I thought we would have a lovely dinner together at the Blue Moon before she goes home. She's leaving in a few days, and anyway, Lee is out with Ziemann, bonding or something," I said.

"You okay with Lee reconnecting with Ziemann?" she asked, no doubt sensing my unease.

I wasn't a fan of Ziemann. His sudden reappearance in Lee's life bothered me a little. He embodied Lee's past. A past, Lee admittedly walked away from because it made him unhappy. Bebe's case had given the two men a reason to reconnect.

"I don't know yet," I said.

"Well, keep an open mind. I don't think Ziemann is all that bad. A little full of himself," she said.

I said nothing. I refused to drink the man's Kool-Aid.

"Come on O," she implored.

"I have to go. I don't want to be late or Les might get ideas," I said, as an excuse to drop the subject. I gave a quick goodbye and began cleaning up my work area. After I had finished, I gave Allie a call.

"Hey..."

"Odessa, thank God it's you. You better get here." Her voice had a nervous quiver.

"What's wrong?"

"That man Lamar is here." She spoke in a hushed tone. "I'm down in the studio. Les told me to stay here. They're yelling."

"What?"

"Lamar is saying horrible things about Tania and her father. Odessa, please come."

"Where's Tania?" I asked.

"She left a half an hour before they came. I think she's home."

"They who?"

"His brother and the bodyguard, I can't remember his name. Oh yes, and that Cherry woman."

"Cherry!" I said with surprise. I thought Maddox and Russo had tied her up, in a little room with no food or water. Cherry on the loose was worrisome.

"What do I do?" an anxious Allie asked.

I told her to stay put, and I promised to get to her as soon as possible.

Why did Lamar go to RTM? Did he want to make one last plea to the Mackies, or tell a new set of lies to Tania? Or did he want revenge on the people who'd refused him?

When Maggie sent copies of the photograph of Lamar to the news services and blogs, I did a happy dance. We sat back as his life and business exploded. We'd lit the fuse to the dynamite gleefully. I pulled off my apron, annoyed once again that my future sister-in-law found herself in the middle of a mess of my making.

I called Maggie.

"Do you think he's dangerous?" she asked.

I nearly laughed at the question. Did I think snakes were dangerous, open cans of gasoline or colorblind fashion designers were dangerous? Hell yes, I said.

"I'll meet you there," she said. .

The worst-case-scenario movie played in my head again, with Allie in a supportive role. I tried to remain calm as I drove to the RTM building in the late afternoon. I forced myself to concentrate on my driving, because my nerves were finding purchase. I struggled to ease my breathing as I clutched the driving wheel and maneuvered through the Queens' neighborhood. I had horrible thoughts of Lamar hurting Allie. Bear wasn't the only bully in the bunch.

When I arrived, I parked a block away, keeping my pink van out of sight. I sat and waited for Maggie. Lamar's gleaming SUV sat out in front, like an intrusive middle finger. I wanted to rush inside, but stayed put. Too many bad scenarios were running through my head and I needed the voice of reason and calm. By the time, Maggie arrived the sun had begun to set, and the streetlights had come on. The coming dark added to my dread as her minivan cruised slowly passed the RTM building, before heading in my direction.

"You okay?" she asked as she stepped out to greet me.

I didn't respond right away, because the sight of her attire pulled me up short—all black, like some pint-sized ninja, her red hair covered in a baseball cap, and a small black nylon knapsack hung from her back.

"What are you wearing?"

She perused her outfit and shrugged. "They say wear dark clothes if you're doing surveillance at night." She pointed her chin at me.

I pointed mine back at her. "They who?" I asked

indignantly.

"Larsen Peterman's book on investigative techniques."

I sighed. Another damn book. If Mr. Peterman knew the trouble he caused, he'd stop writing. Then I realized what I had on. Even with the approaching darkness, my light colored shirt and pants reflected the streetlights. There was nothing stealthy about me. Compared to Maggie, I stood out like a lighthouse. I sighed in resignation. Maybe I needed to read one of Maggie's books, because I was going about this all wrong.

"Whatever!" I headed toward RTM. I took two steps, but Maggie grabbed me by the arm and herded me toward the side of the building and the back. I questioned why.

"Do you want to walk in on Lamar?" she asked in a hushed voice.

"Not really." From what I gathered from Allie and her terrified state, Lamar sounded a little crazed. He wouldn't be happy to see Maggie or I walk through the door. If Bear saw Maggie dressed as she was, he might piss his pants.

"I called Tania before I came, told her what happened. She's ready to run over here, but I told her to hold up. Maybe it's nothing but Lamar blowing off steam," Maggie said.

"What if he's blowing off more than steam?"

"Let's hope not. The main reason I called her was to ask about another way inside, besides the front and back doors." Maggie pointed to the opposite side of the building as we entered the empty parking lot. "The place use to be an old furniture store, with a loading bay and storage area. Her father had the loading dock bricked up to increase his storage room. He recently put in a security door with access to the outside. In fact, Tania just put a new combination on the door."

We walked along the back of the building. Les' truck sat parked fifty feet beyond the RTM's back exit, a heavy security door lay nestled discreetly against the wall. The door had a small keypad. Maggie punched numbers into the keypad. The door clicked open.

"Tania just gave you the access code?" I said.

"Yes."

People's willingness to trust Maggie with almost anything always amazed me. If I'd asked for the keys someone's business, they'd tell me no and have the cops on speed dial.

Before we stepped into the darkness, Maggie shrugged off the bag and opened it. She pulled out a tiny round, flat object and twisted off the top. The smell of something waxy hit my nose. She held out the bag for me to hold before she began applying the contents—a black matted makeup—on her face. I stood dumbstruck as she covered her face. When she finished her alabaster skin was covered in black. She could have been Al Jolson's kid sister. She held out the make up to me, but I shook my head too astonished to talk.

When my voice came back, I spoke. "Larsen Peterman?" I questioned, and she nodded. God help me, my best friend has morphed into Rambo—or Rambette.

"I need to blend in," she said her tone serious and genuine. I let it go because you do not interview crazy.

"You don't happen to have a seven-inch serrated knife on you?" I asked warily.

Her brow furrowed as she shook her head. I knew she still carried the stun gun, I recognized the outline of it through the bag. She'd grown fond of the thing, maybe too fond of it. It had become her great equalizer. How could I explain how my sweet natured friend, mother to my godson, den mother, and wife had reinvented herself into a one-woman assault team, with camouflage gear and a stun gun? In equal disbelief, I was willing to follow her into a building to save my future sister-in-law from a pissed off music producer. I couldn't make this up.

The sound of an approaching car interrupted my reverie on the question of Maggie's and my sanity. We dashed inside the dark storage room and peered through the slightly opened door. A late model dark car pulled into the lot and parked. Rap music reverberated from their sound system, disturbing the quiet of the neighborhood. The door opened, and Louis emerged from the passenger side. Two other men came out of the car and quickly flanked him. I recognized one of them from the surveillance tapes from the mall, Cherry's cousin, Stevie Harmon. From Louis's expression, he hadn't come of his own free will. Harmon gave Louis a hard shove when he didn't walk fast enough. Louis glowered and cursed. Harmon laughed maliciously and cursed back. I imagined what incentive they used to coerce him to come; his brother.

I briefly thought of Allie in the middle of this mix, and stopped breathing. Lamar, Louis, Cherry and poor Allie in the same room together terrified me.

"Oh Christ," I exclaimed as the three men disappeared through the back door.

We stepped out when the door closed behind them.

"That's not good," Maggie said.

"I can't stay here with Allie inside." I exclaimed.

Maggie nodded in understanding. I'd brought Allie to this crazy party, willing participant or not. I didn't know if I was being brave or stupid, but I knew I had to go in alone. With Maggie dressed like some Navy Seal groupie, I didn't want to add any more confusion.

"Give me a minute to find out what's going on. Come in through the storage room. If things get crazy, call the police." I said.

Maggie nodded. As ridiculous as she was in her camouflage, I trusted that face to save me.

"Be careful, I'll think of something," she reassured.

If things went south, whatever that something might be, I hoped it included the rest of Maggie's Seal Team. Before I left, I stopped with an odd thought nagging me. "You said Tania changed the combination?" The question seemed out of place, but I needed to know.

Maggie nodded. "She said Detective Maddox suggested she changed all the locks. She finally got around to it when Les complained some things around the place were coming up missing. Why?"

I pointed to the keypad. "Someone got into this building somehow. The other doors are keyed with regular locks, but this one has a keypad. Just like Tania did for you, Rovell gave the number to someone, he trusted."

"I don't think he had to trust them. Tania said the keypad can be changed manually. She could change the code tomorrow if she wanted. Linwood might have done the same thing, but someone killed him."

I didn't have to ask, but I did. "Who would he give the code to?"

Maggie's lips quirked up in a smile, knowing the answer, as well. "Cherry," we both said.

CHAPTER

39

I pushed opened the front door to RTM to find the reception area empty. I heard Lamar before I saw him. A large decorative wall panel blocked his line of sight, but I could see between the spaces of the panels. Lamar had corralled everyone like sheep in the lounge area. What choice did they have? Bear sat on a stool with his back against the wall thumbing through a magazine, as if, he were the gate keeper to hell and it were any other day his boss went nuts. I could just make out Gerald's left shoulder as he stood next to Harmon. Lamar paced before his captive audience like a caged animal, his right hand shoved deep into his jacket pocket.

"Now your brother's here, we're gonna settle this," Lamar yelled.

The stairs to the basement studio were four feet away, in clear sight of everyone. I couldn't reach them without being seen. Allie would have to remain where she was, at least until Lamar and Company left.

"You're gonna understand what the hell I did for you," Lamar's voice boomed.

"You didn't do shit for me," Louis cursed back.

"I kept you alive in prison. I can make you a star."

To my surprise Louis laughed. "You put me in prison,

you asshole, and you can't do nothing for me."

Lamar's face twisted in anger. "That photo is a lie, and she's here to prove it." Lamar turned his attention to Cherry, who sat cowering in a chair.

"Like I'd believe anything she said," Louis said.

Cherry mumbled something in protest, but no one cared.

"You killed Wood," Jermaine accused. The accusation made the room go silent for a long time.

"I did not kill him," Lamar declared. "I got an alibi, just asked the cops. I spent hours with those bastards and they cleared me. I don't care what nobody says. If they say otherwise, they better say it to my face."

"Bullshit," Louis said.

"He's right, the police questioned him, contacted his witnesses," Gerald said. "He was at a party on a boat. He left from Pier 62 near 23rd street at eleven p.m. The boat docked in Montauk nearly three hours later and didn't return until late afternoon. He didn't kill Wood."

"Don't make you innocent," Jermaine said. Not impressed by the news, Jermaine's eyes went to Bear. He'd come after Cherry and threatened Maggie and me. Was murder the next logical step or was this how guys expressed themselves.

Then the shouting began again.

"Who the hell are you?" someone said from behind me.

I nearly jumped out of my skin. One of the men who'd brought Louis stood by the open bathroom door zipping up his pants. When I said nothing, he came over and shoved me into the lounge area with hands I was certain he hadn't washed.

Lamar swirled on me; his dark skin glistened with sweat. I caught the distinct whiff of something alcoholic. Obviously, he'd been fortifying himself. When he whipped out his hand

and pointed his cell phone at me, I yelped. Relieved that the only thing he was packing was his speed dial; thankful he wasn't armed, I took a breath. Then realized his weapon of choice was the silent man next to him. Bear sneered at me before returning to his magazine.

"What the hell are you doing here?" Lamar said.

"Why don't we all calm down." Gerald walked over, placing himself between Lamar and me. I appreciated the gesture, but I didn't think Gerald could stop his brother if he wanted to get at me. Gerald couldn't stop a mood change.

"Shut up, Gerry." Lamar shoved his brother hard, causing the smaller man to stumble away from me, and fall.

Gerald tried to hide his embarrassment with a weak smile but failed as he struggled to get up. "Please, bro, don't do this, you know I can fix this. I can."

"I'm gonna fix this my damn self. All this talk got us nowhere." Lamar glared at his brother. Gerald got up, resignation etched on his face, as if he'd gone a few rounds with his brother before they'd arrived.

"Her and that redheaded bitch are to blame." Lamar turned on me.

"Got that right," Cherry chimed in.

Dressed in her usual flamboyant clothing, the black and blue mark on her cheek she tried to cover with makeup matched nicely. Obviously, Lamar helped her change her mind about the validity of the photograph. I glowered back at her. I had no sympathy for her predicament. My concern stayed on Louis, Jermaine and Les. From their expressions, they held equal concern for me because Bear was giving me a dangerous look.

"Where is she?" Bear demanded.

"Who?" I asked.

"The redheaded bitch," Cherry interjected.

"Home baking cookies." This was no time to irritate anyone, but he made teasing him too easy. He was like an elephant afraid of a mouse—a mouse with a stun gun and a working knowledge on how to break bones.

"Check the building," Bear commanded to Harmon.

I inwardly kicked myself for goading him. The two men got up and began a thorough search of the building. They pulled a screaming Allie up the stairs ten minutes later.

"Hey, get your hands off of her," I yelled. Gerald blocked me from going to Allie.

"Don't make it worse." His pathetic eyes pleaded with me.

I scoffed at him in disgust, annoyed with his lack of a spine. I pushed passed him, went over to the man holding Allie much too tight and glared at him. "Let her go." My teeth clenched in anger. He grinned at me, unapologetic, and yanked hard on Allie's arm. She squealed. She tried to be brave but failed.

I thought I blinked first. I wasn't sure. Maybe I'd had one of those out of body experiences. I did see Allie's terrified face staring back at me. Harmon had the same wide unsympathetic eyes of his cousin. Certain, their family motto, had to be *Destruction Above All Else.*

I grabbed his fleece jacket and kneed him hard in the groin. His eyes spread wide, his brown irises floated in a sea of white. As he bent over to clutch his damaged man parts, I lifted my knee, connecting with his face. The crack of bone was clear and distinctive. He stumbled back, toppled over and curled into a ball. The action happened so fast no one reacted except Allie, who scampered behind me.

"Whoa! No she didn't." Louis laughed.

Jermaine gasped and covered his mouth in disbelief. Les just shook his head. Louis turned to Lamar defiant. "I ain't working for you, and I ain't signing shit."

"Bitch, someone needs to hurt you." Harmon's cohort thug stomped toward me and gripped me by my hair. He snapped my head back and grabbed me by the throat.

Allie jumped on his back, covering his face with her hands. In the struggle, he had to release me to regain his balance.

"Let me slap her." Cherry got up from her seat.

"Stop this." Gerald pulled Allie free. He pointed at Cherry in warning to stop. Surprisingly, she obeyed.

"Do something!" A frustrated Lamar glared at Bear. The brawny man lumbered up from his seat, came over to Allie and me, grabbed us by the forearms and shoved us onto the couch next to Les and Jermaine like rag dolls.

Then, the lights went out.

Allie screamed again, piercing my eardrums. Lamar cursed and shouted at a fumbling Gerald as they collided. I held tight to Allie. My eyes adjusted slowly to the weak streetlight coming from the large storefront windows. I could make out shapes but not much more. What truly caught my attention was the dancing red dot that played across the wall and bodies in the room. Watching the thing made me dizzy.

"What is...?" I began to say when my phone vibrated in my pocket. Squashed between Les and Allie, the damn thing was hard to reach. Maggie's imaged flashed on the small screen. I engaged the phone.

"Play along," Maggie said.

Play along with what? I had a sinking feeling. Could Maggie be that crazy?

"Bear," Maggie's voice spoke from the darkness. "Don't

move." It took me a moment to realize the little illuminated dot now rested on Bear's chest, just above his heart. He hadn't seen it, too preoccupied with the chaos in the room.

"What is that?" Gerald's finger pointed at the dot. Then everyone scrambled away from Bear as if he had the cooties.

I tried not to search the darken room in fear of giving away Maggie's whereabouts. She'd been right about her clothing; I couldn't find her.

"Thank you," Maggie said in her familiar authoritative Mommy tone. A tone she'd used with the out-of-control eight years old at Rocket's last party at the local Chuck E. Cheese, on Frank when his unprofessional behavior had tweaked her last nerve and with me, when I've put my moral compass in my back pocket.

Bear remained still.

"What the hell is going on?" Lamar bellowed.

"Bear, did you know the 9x19 mm Parabellum cartridge was designed by Georg Luger? An extremely popular cartridge with law enforcement and used by at least 55% of the police in the U.S. Works nicely with the LC9. The trigger guard mounted laser has an ambidextrous switch."

Bear stood like a statue.

"She's crazy. She gonna shoot him." Cherry's high-pitched squeal was worse than a bullet to the brain, and heightened the tension of the room.

"Shut up," Bear barked. "Everyone shut the hell up."

Everybody did.

"Thank you," Maggie spoke calmly. "Could you instruct the two men with you to remove any weapons they may have." The two men didn't move, but the little dot did, from Bear's heart to his forehead.

"I ain't giving up nothing," Harmon's companion

announced. Before he was able to say anything else, Bear whipped out his gun and pointed it at him.

I thought I had wet my pants a bit.

"Bear, what you doing, man?" Lamar said in disbelief.

"I ain't dying for no fool." Bear aimed the weapon level at one of the men's heads.

"Do what she says," Gerald yelled at the man.

Harmon grumbled and pulled out a large, shiny gun and placed it on the table. The other man followed as Gerald glowered at him.

"Odessa, could you gather them up?" Maggie asked politely.

I hesitated for a moment, not believing what was happening, but I didn't want my hesitation to signal I didn't believe Maggie wasn't armed and dangerous. I hopped off the couch and picked up the guns.

"Now, your turn, Bear. My finger is getting tired." A hint of impatience laced her voice.

"I told you not to piss her off," I said, standing an arm's length from the bodyguard.

A reluctant Bear sneered at me but held the gun out by the handle first. I took the gun and smiled. I almost became delirious with the idea that Maggie had just unarmed three men. Holding a hysterical giggle back, I placed the weapons in the large trash receptacle in the kitchenette. This wasn't the time to lose my mind.

"These women are crazy." Cherry crouched behind one of the sofas.

"Thank you so much, Bear." Maggie said, sweetly.

Without a word, Bear smoothed out his suit lapels, straightened his shirt collar, took a deep inhalation and gave a slight nod to Lamar. His eyes scanned the room briefly, before turning and heading for the front door.

“Where the hell do you think you’re going?” Lamar reached for him, but Bear pushed him aside with one meaty hand. Bear had had enough.

"What kind of bullshit is this?" Lamar screamed at his former bodyguard.

Silent, stoic, but resolute Bear gave the room one last sneer before leaving out the front door. As the door closed behind him, the sound of sirens filled the air.

“What the...” Lamar said as flashing lights danced along the walls. Within minutes, several police cars pulled up in front of the building. Suddenly, the lights went back on. We shielded our eyes from the brightness.

Possibly not keen on dealing with the police, Lamar’s group scrambled toward the back door. It did little good. Maddox and Russo charged in with uniform officers with hands on their guns. Maddox told everybody to freeze. Everybody froze. Allie, Les, Jermaine and Louis remained seated. I stood very still. Russo corralled the fleeing group back to the lounge. They grumbled their innocence as Maddox encouraged them to take a seat.

“Anybody wants to explain Conan the Barbarian sitting in a squad car, asking for a lawyer?” An exasperated Maddox scanned the room. He had to be speaking about Bear. The bodyguard decided to sever his relationship with Lamar. Then Maddox made a face when his eyes locked on something behind me. I turned to see a black face Maggie sitting atop the reception desk with her legs crossed and her hand held above her head.

“I think I can,” she said smiling at him.

Maddox stood with his mouth open and speechless.

CHAPTER

40

When frustrated and told something untruthful, Lee had a tendency to get loud. Detective Russo told Lee he couldn't talk to me, mistake number one. Then he told him, he had to leave, or he would arrest him, mistake numbers two and three. The only thing that stopped him from mistake number four had been his partner, ending Russo's continuing efforts to put his foot in his mouth. To be fair to the detectives, they hadn't expected two lawyers to show up at a crime scene five minutes after the police. Maggie's urgent phone call to Lee had interrupted his dinner with Ziemann. Their arrival added another level of headache for Maddox and Russo.

"Is it all off?" Maggie's face was flushed from scrubbing off the black makeup.

"Yeah." I grabbed her chin and tilted her head back and forth to make sure. "Where did you get that stuff?"

"When Rocket was a pirate last Halloween." She'd taken off the baseball cap and combed her hair. The fairy ninja was gone.

"Things seemed to have calmed down." Her attention went to the men standing outside.

"Russo's an asshole," I said, still annoyed with the detective's refusal to let Lee talk to me. All of us had been held prisoner in the lounge area, waiting for the detectives to sort the situation out.

When peace had been achieved outside, Lee, Ziemann and the detectives entered. I sighed in relief, wanting to close down this circus, take Allie home and go to bed.

"Are you alright?" Lee pulled me into a hug. The tightness of the embrace told me how worried he'd been. I could barely breathe.

"Now give your sister one," I said when he released me. I aimed him toward an awaiting Allie, who squeezed him even tighter.

"Ms. Cupcake, you are never dull." Ziemann sidled close to me, as silent as a snake.

"Bite me," I sneered and took a step away. He laughed.

"Now, can we figure out who broke the law?" Maddox rubbed his temple.

"Somebody's going to jail tonight." A pleased Russo said. He held up several evidence bags containing the guns I'd stashed in the trash.

"I want to call our lawyer," Gerald stood up to say.

Maddox gave him a dismissive gesture. "Why don't you find out if you need one first?" Maddox pointed to a seat. A reluctant Gerald sat.

"I think I'll take a seat for this one too." A smirking Ziemann found a seat as far from Cherry as possible. When he first arrived, she'd announced he was her lawyer. Ziemann was quick to correct her. Their business had concluded at her trial, his current role, was that of spectator only. Cherry protested. She had confused Ziemann's representation of her as a lifetime arrangement. Russo shut her up with a warning of arrest for being a public nuisance.

"I missed dinner for this, so someone better make sense," a weary Maddox complained.

The room exploded with a cacophony of voices trying to explain what had happened. This deluge of noise lasted for half a minute until Maddox told everyone to shut up. He scanned the room until his gaze landed on me, and pointed.

"Why me?" I didn't want to be singled out in a room where half the people wanted to hurt me.

"Because, you Ms. Wilkes, have a way with words, and will get to the point before breakfast."

"What am I, the human version of Cliff Notes?" I complained.

Maddox smiled and nodded. I turned to Lee, questioning whether this was wise. He shrugged. "Did you break any laws?" He gave me a crooked smile. He always asked me this question. I proudly said no.

"Fine." I got up, smoothed out my shirt and stood in the middle of the circle of people, who didn't appear happy to be there.

"Lamar came to force the Mackies into signing a contract with his company. He brought Cherry here to convince Louis her photograph of Lamar bribing the witness was a fake. Louis wasn't buying it and refused the offer. Lamar wouldn't accept Louis' refusal," I said.

"That's a damn lie," Lamar cursed.

I sensed his rage below the surface of his words. "Then Allie and I were assaulted by him." I pointed to Harmon, who was being treated by an EMS technician. A thick bandage decorated his nose, and an ice bag rested on his crotch.

"She broke my nose and kicked me in the nuts." He winced.

"If I had time to plant my feet better, I would have cracked them," I snapped. Groans emanated from several of the men in the room. Lee shook his head, warning me to stay on point. "Sorry. Where was I?" I took a deep breath to gather myself.

"Assaulted," Maddox added. A bemused Russo took notes.

"Yeah, right." I took a deep breath and continued. "Anyway, Bear here started manhandling us too. I didn't believe anyone was going to leave until Lamar convinced Louis and Jermaine to sign with his company."

"Lamar sent these assholes to get me and said they had my brother. I better do what he said or else." Louis glared at a dispassionate Lamar, who sat like a stone no longer speaking.

"This is all speculation. They could have left at anytime," Gerald protested. No one believed this, of course, but I guessed he had to say something.

"We weren't the only ones with guns," Harmon said. Everyone turned to Maggie.

"She had one. I thought she would kill us." Gerald pointed to her. Without the make-up and the cap, she appeared as meek as a mouse.

"You Mrs. Swift?" a curious Maddox asked. I thought the detective might giggle at the idea.

"She aimed right at my head." An angry Bear pointed to spot on his forehead as if anyone might confuse the spot with his foot.

"You mean this?" Maggie's little nylon bag lay at her feet. She opened the drawstring and pulled out Rocket's toy space pistol. She pulled the trigger, and a red beam came out along with a tinny blast sound. She aimed the beam at Bear, who almost jumped out of his seat. All eyes danced between Maggie and Bear, whose expression of confusion morphed into embarrassment. The big man slumped back in his seat, a casualty of the battle of wits he'd been having with a Hicksville housewife. A battle he'd lost.

"All warfare is based on deception. You should read *The*

Art of War," she informed politely.

"Lady, are you crazy?" An incensed Russo snatched the gun away from her.

"You actually read *The Art of War*?" Ziemann sat relaxed on one of the couches, taking in everything.

"Okay, whatever. So, let me get this straight. We had kidnapping, possible illegal weapons, not including the toy and assault. Anything else?" Maddox scanned the faces in the room. No one said anything until Maggie raised her hand slowly. Maddox made a noise deep in his throat and sighed. "Yes, Mrs. Swift."

"What about the murder?" she said meekly.

"Maggie, are you talking about, Rovell's murder?" Lee asked.

She nodded. Her mention of Rovell's death brought the nagging feeling back.

The murder had always been central. Rovell's death remained the 800-pound gorilla in the room. Now Maggie had asked it to take a seat in a place filled with suspects. I went to Maggie and yanked her out of her seat.

"Can you excuse us for a moment?" I held up a finger to Maddox. I gave him little time to respond as I took Maggie out of the circle of people and headed toward the small bathroom behind the receptionist desk.

"Where are you going?" Maddox caught up to us and blocked our way.

"To the bathroom," I said. Maddox didn't hide his skepticism brow furrowed. "I need help with my bra strap." I couldn't think of anything else. When in doubt, fall back on feminine garment failure.

Maddox didn't buy it. He followed.

"Can you give us a few minutes?" I begged.

"Why would I?" he grumbled.

"We need to work things out about Rovell's murderer," Maggie sounded almost apologetic.

"You mind telling me what the hell is going on?" Russo said, coming up behind us.

"The ladies think they might know who killed Rovell," Maddox said, with a pinched expression.

Reading Russo's face was hard because he had only two facial expressions, angry and clueless. "Can't do any worse than us." He shrugged. Surprised by his acquiescence, I reevaluated my opinion of him.

"I'm sure it's Miss Plum with the candlestick," he added.

As quickly as it came, my high opinion of him left like a deer in hunting season. I started to say something, but Maddox raised his hands. "Enough! Follow me."

We fell in behind the detective as he made his way to Rovell's old office. We weren't enthusiastic about entering a former murder scene, but Maddox didn't want to be overheard. He switched on the desk lamp and crossed his arms. "Well?"

Aware, this had been the room Rovell had died in, I huddled close to Maggie.

"Lamar said he had an alibi for the night of the murder?" Maggie asked.

Maddox nodded. "Even his bodyguard was spotted on the boat."

"Is Bebe still a suspect?" Maggie added.

Maddox shook his head. "No, he was at the wrong place at the wrong time. Somebody wiped prints off the knife. I don't think Mr. Dunn would kill someone, wipe the prints and then hang around for several hours waiting for the cops to find him. That leaves the people next door. Lamar might not have been around, but he's got a few soldiers willing to kidnap and do his dirty work."

"Exactly." Maggie pointed her index finger at the detective.

"Are you saying you know who killed Rovell?" Russo said.

Maggie's blue eyes narrowed at the question. "We know why he was killed."

"We might know how," I added.

"Do you know who?" Maddox sounded interested.

At the sound of high heels on linoleum we stepped outside the office and found a contrite Cherry standing in the narrow hallway, caught in the act of tiptoeing.

"I needed the bathroom," she said.

"Christ." Maddox yelled someone's name. A moment later, a female officer showed up. "Take her to the bathroom and afterwards make sure she finds her seat."

A reluctant Cherry teetered on her heels to the bathroom, with the officer close behind.

"That woman has more moves than a Cirque Du Soliel acrobat," I said, knowing her ruse to go to the bathroom was to eavesdrop.

Maddox shrugged. "She's a wannabe, a little past her prime to be a video vixen, but she's still trying. She makes a little money selling knockoffs to the unsuspecting, does some hair at cut-rate prices, maybe sells more than her charm to a guy with a free dollar or two, but she doesn't strike me as a murderer. From what you said about the photograph, Rovell was her golden ticket. She needed him alive. So I don't see it," Maddox said.

"I'm not saying she murdered him," I said with exasperation. "I'm saying she's the kind of thief who'd break into your house, steal your grandmother's pearls, and leave the door wide open so the neighborhood maniac can kill you in your sleep."

CHAPTER

41

Exposing Rovell's killer meant we had to get the truth from someone who treated the truth like a social disease. Once again, Cherry held the key but wouldn't give up her golden goose without compensation. I deduced two things from being around the woman. The world may not revolve around her, but she was the only one on the planet she cared about. Secondly, when push came to shove, she would play the best odds in her favor. The truth had become nothing more than a bargaining tool for her. Nothing Maggie and I could offer would induce her to talk. However, I knew someone who did have something she wanted, her freedom. She needed Ziemann. Maddox had threatened to charge her, Lamar and his crew for extortion, false imprisonment and kidnapping, despite the bruises on her face.

"Come on," I begged.

An incredulous Ziemann huffed at me as if I'd asked him to prostitute himself. To get Rovell's killer, Maddox agreed reluctantly to let me convince Ziemann to help coerce Cherry.

"I've had enough of Ms. Cherry. Would you like to check the hotel bill I've been saddled with?" He leaned against Rovell's desk, arms crossed and seemingly resistant to the idea of coming to Cherry's aide.

"Stop whining, Thad. You spent most of our dinner complaining about the CEOs you have to defend, who have done a lot worse and sworn their innocence," Lee admonished, obviously enjoying Ziemann's anguish.

Ziemann responded with a mischievous grin. "Okay, as long as I'm invited to the wedding."

"No," I snapped. He only asked for the invitation to piss me off. I turned to Lee for support. He gave a noncommittal shrug.

"You can sit him at Candace and Aunt Renne's table," he said with an impish grin of his own. I smiled at the thought. My opinionated sister would put him six feet under, and my eighty-year-old ultra-conservative Southern Baptist aunt would close the lid. By the time I threw the bouquet, his ears would be burning, and his soul would be saved. I invited Ziemann to my wedding. With everyone in agreement, we returned to our motley crew of suspects.

"You can't hold us against our will. Either let us go or let me call our lawyer," Gerald insisted. A hostile and uncommunicative Lamar sat, hands clenched and seething.

"Soon." Maddox waved him down and gave me an imperceptible nod.

I set my sights on Cherry. "Cherry, Ziemann is going to take you back as a client, under one condition." I stood before her, with my arms crossed.

"Which is?" She said warily.

"The night Rovell died—I need the truth."

"I don't know nothing about him dying." She shook her head to emphasize the point.

I didn't let this deter me. "You insisted on a meeting to talk about the photo, to make a deal, am I right? He gave you the security door pass code. He didn't want anyone seeing you arrive, especially Louis. He was aware of how he felt about you and didn't want a scene at the party." I prompted. Cherry said nothing but kept her eyes on her cousin. He glared back in warning. She turned away, unwilling to face him.

"I understand why you went to Rovell. He seemed like a decent guy. He would have paid you and sent you on your way. Things went wrong when Bebe showed up and kicked you out before you had a chance to make your deal. Then Rovell was murdered," I continued.

Cherry touched her bruised cheek, possibly realizing for the first time she'd played this game way above her pay grade.

"With Rovell gone, you were left with only one other option, the Joneses. God knows why they didn't put you six feet under, but you got your payday and you ran like a rabbit. How in the hell did you maneuver your way around that?" I said, giving her slight praise. "Afterward, either your cousin found you, or you called him, but he showed up at Vesta's house. You let him unload some counterfeit CDs there—taken from Chaos 182, no doubt. Did you promise him some of the money you'd gotten from the blackmail? Either way, he didn't tell Lamar where you were. You would have gotten away with it until Maggie and I showed up."

"No one believes this shit," Harmon cursed.

From the growl that emanated from Lamar, I bet he believed it. Maybe he didn't appreciate Harmon's family's tendencies toward duplicity and moonlighting.

"How else could Cherry get her hands on those CDs if not from you? You're one of Lamar's inner circle," I said.

Harmon shook his head and scoffed at me.

"Now that Cherry is in a truth telling mood, I wonder what she'd say if I asked her about Louis' arrest?" Cherry's eyes flared up at me, but settled on Ziemann, who gave her an imperceptible nod. His eyes said the truth would set her free, at least from this bunch. She sighed deeply. In for a penny, in for a pound I always said.

"Stevie told me to put the gun under Louis's seat first chance I got. When the police came, I ran." Her voice strained at the truth.

"You always run," I said with heavy accusation.

"Bitch, you're dead," Harmon snapped. So much for family ties.

"Are you threatening her? Sounded like a threat, didn't it?" Maddox's His tone sounded almost playful.

"Yeah," Russo chimed in gleefully.

"You're in this deep," I said to Harmon.

"I ain't killed no one," he insisted.

"I didn't think you did, but that night, you told someone how Cherry got into RTM and why, because your cousin tells you everything." I turned back to Cherry. "What time did you tell him about meeting with Rovell?"

"Stevie called me when I was in Rovell's office. Rovell was busy with the party, people were leaving, and he told me to wait. Maybe around twelve, a little after," Cherry said.

"Being a loyal employee, Stevie told his boss about the photograph, the meeting and the access codes, didn't he? Even he understood it would be a mess if it got out. He also didn't want Lamar to think he had anything to do with Cherry's latest scheme," Maggie said.

"You called Lamar, but he was stuck on a boat somewhere with Bear. You talked to the next best thing." I turned my attention fully on Gerald. He sat next to his brother, a small man in a big man's shadow. Lamar was doing his best impersonation of a prisoner of war. Gerald hadn't quite mastered the facade as a thin sheen decorated his face.

"This got me thinking about you, Gerald." I cocked my head to side contemplating how I'd misjudged him so easily. He'd been so overshadowed by his brother I'd missed the clues. Had Gerald been more than his slight build and meek exterior? Was he more dangerous than Bear or even his brother?

"If the photograph got out, the backlash would be damaging to Chaos 182. The company was already bleeding money." Maggie stood in front of the younger Jones. "Your brother dealt with the problem by finding talent, even forcing them if he had too, like the Mackies. You were more subtle by selling and exporting counterfeit music on the side from that brand new studio. The music gave you an influx of cash, but not enough the way your brother went through it. He had an expensive lifestyle, didn't he?"

"I—" Gerald stopped and turned to his brother for support. Lamar told him to shut up.

"I wondered how Lamar could accomplish so much in such a short time. He barely graduated high school, nearly thrown out of the army and already had a stint in prison." Lamar's dark eyes locked on me, daring me to continue.

"He had the street smarts, the presence to bully his way to the top, but he didn't get there alone. While everyone gravitated toward Lamar, no one noticed you as you worked behind the scenes, fixing everything. You were masterful. I first saw you in action at the party and should have guessed then. Lamar walked around with the pretty girls, flashy jewelry, nice clothes, but you were the wizard behind the curtain. Everyone deferred to you when your brother wasn't around. I should have recognized there was more to you than being your brother's go-fer. Now I wondered who actually pushed for me to be there at the party, you or him."

A telling hint gleamed on Gerald's face, and I knew. What was the best way to find out what we knew about Cherry than on his own turf? I could kick myself.

"You stole other people's music and concocted a scheme

to send an innocent man to prison, so you could manipulate him to sign with you. You tried to destroy RTM and Tania just to get to the Mackies. I guess murder seemed like the next step," I said.

"This is stupid. I couldn't hurt anyone. I liked Rovell." Gerald shook his head as if the words wouldn't fit.

Maggie stood next to me, head cocked to the side, coming to some final insight about him. She'd misjudged him as well. She'd expected such behavior from men like Lamar and even Bear, not the mild mannered Gerald. "You might have. Maybe he liked you. Something Tania said once, about her father never turning his back on Lamar. I think that's true. But you, anyone would turn their backs to you Gerald. Maybe, alone in Rovell's office he did. At first, I thought it might have been an accident. You got into an argument and Rovell wouldn't listen. But you planned this," Maggie said, with some surprise.

"You need to shut up," Lamar warned.

"No, I think she's doing fine." Maddox said.

"Once you found out what Cherry was going to do, and you couldn't stop her in time, you went to RTM to deal with Rovell. The Mackies were in reach, and this would lose them for you," she said.

"Your brother wasn't around to do the dirty work, so you did the deed yourself," I added.

Gerald's eyes stayed fixed to the ground as he shook his head. Maggie walked over to Maddox. "Bebe stood by the back door waiting for Rovell. He wouldn't leave without his knives. Gerald couldn't wait. He also didn't need witnesses to what he was about to do. Attacking Bebe was necessary. The fact you killed Rovell with Bebe's knives was a lucky coincidence and helped muddle the investigation."

Maggie turned her blue eyes on Gerald. "Rovell didn't think you were a threat. You were the quiet one, never been arrested, college educated and soft spoken. Bebe became the perfect scapegoat when you found out who he was. You aimed Louis at him and tried to turn Tania against him."

Gerald's expression went blank; his hands remained clutched together tightly as if holding everything inside. I noticed a slight tremor in his leg. He needed one more push.

"What about your alibi for the night Rovell died?" I asked.

Gerald's intelligent eyes peered up at me, for an instant, they resembled his brother's – ominous and dangerous. "I don't have to answer you." Gerald's mouth twisted in a weak smile he couldn't hold.

"You didn't go on the boat trip with your brother. I bet you dropped him and Bear off at the pier in Manhattan and then got the call from Harmon telling you what his cousin was up to. You had to do something. New York City is a city of bridges and the quickest way from the Manhattan Pier was over one of the Queens-bound bridges. The fastest would be over the ones with tolls. I bet you have an EZ-Pass because you're efficient and practical, and I remembered seeing one of those pass holders in the windshield of your car when I drove here tonight." Maggie said.

Gerald averted his eyes. This got Maddox's full attention. He walked over to his partner and whispered something in his ear. Russo stepped away from the small group to make a phone call. While his partner busied himself, Maddox stood in front of Gerald and Lamar Jones, his large arms crossed, his face severe with resolution.

"Do you have an alibi?" he asked Gerald. Gerald's eyes fell on his brother bowed his head. Lamar said nothing.

"We're going to the station. Call a lawyer when you get there." Maddox gestured to two officers who'd been standing behind the brothers. He asked them to stand. Lamar rose reluctantly. Gerald remained seated and had to be pulled up.

"You have nothing," he finally said to Maddox, but his voice held no conviction. He didn't have his brother's bravado or confidence to talk his way out of things. In a dark room, behind closed doors, he could have figured things out. But in the light of day, the younger Jones had nothing.

"Right now, I'm asking a judge for a warrant to search your place of business, home, phone, credit card statements and EZ-Pass records. Trust me, I'll find something. I can start with kidnapping, blackmail and assault and work my way to murder," Maddox said.

"You don't say nothing to nobody," Lamar said as police cuffed him. They escorted him out as he continued to yell. I wondered how long his kingly edict would last under the weight of the charges Maddox and Russo planned to level on Lamar's crew. Russo gleefully rubbed his hands at the thought of it.

"Do you think any of this will stick?" I asked Maddox. They led Cherry away next. Ziemann followed.

"If half of what you said was true, I'll make it stick." Maddox scratched his head. "Once we cleared Lamar's alibi, we never once thought of his brother." He sounded annoyed at his own shortsightedness. A solemn Gerald walked past, hands cuffed behind him, his eyes not making contact with anyone.

"Sometimes the devil is an accountant" I sighed.

CHAPTER

42

A few days after the incident at RTM, I sat across a somewhat penitent Cherry. Dressed in an orange inmate jumper, no make-up, wig, impossibly high-heels, or faked polished nails, she seemed ordinary. Somehow, she'd convinced Ziemann to arrange a meeting with me. I refused at first. With Bebe free and clear and the Joneses locked up, I had no need to communicate with the woman. Being the persistent irritant that she was, Cherry promised to drop the countersuit she'd threatened to charge Maggie and me from our encounter at Vesta's house. Considering, she'd been the one chasing me with a bat, I didn't think her case had merit, but went anyway just to get the meeting over with once and for all.

"First, I want to apologize for everything I did," she said. "What I did was wrong, and I should be held accountable for my actions. I was misguided and led astray by people who didn't have my best interest at heart."

I stared at her through the three-inch Plexiglas, rendered speechless by this new incarnation of Cherry. Who knew Riker's Island Prison had a brain transplant program.

"Zee said I should make amends with people I've wronged," she continued as if she'd been reading her words from a script.

I raised an eyebrow at her. "All the people?" I hoped she planned to start with the beginning of the New York City phone book and work her way through.

"I've already talked to Bebe." She sounded pleased with this Herculean effort. "He didn't say much, but he seemed okay."

This surprised me. Not because, Bebe would say much, he wouldn't. The world might end tomorrow, and he'd barely manage a goodbye. What surprised me was that he hadn't refused her request. To be fair, I hadn't either.

"Anyone else you talked to?" I asked out of curiosity. I wonder who else had come along on Cherry's trail of contrition.

"Vesta stopped by." She frowned slightly. "Didn't offer me my job back, but she might."

"How about the Mackies?"

Cherry turned away and shrank back into her hard plastic chair. Her face slackened. The orange jumpsuit, a size too large, enveloped her. The tight, neat cornrows capped her head and snaked down her back, like a child. All she needed was ribbons to complete the image of the most helpless creature in the universe. A weaker person might have fallen for this little show, but not me. I waited until she made an attempt at gathering herself.

"They won't return my phone calls," she said as her bottom lip trembled. "I told them, I would help get Louis clear of those charges."

I veiled my amazement and annoyance as Cherry disconnected once again from reality. She'd helped put Louis in prison, or had she forgotten that? A simple I'm sorry wouldn't do, at least not for me. If I knew anything about Louis, Cherry would have to give more than words to get back into his good graces. She would have to save a busload of children with life-threatening diseases, and then join a convent.

"I'm not surprised, but can you blame them?" I said, hoping to get some reality back into the conversation. Her eyes widen in comprehension or lack of it.

"I'm trying to tell them I'm sorry," she insisted her tone a tad belligerent.

I sighed deeply and grew impatient. Cherry must be working out a new twelve-step program for morally compromised human beings. She missed a few steps.

"Okay, I'm here, you said you're sorry. I guess that's it." I got up from my chair.

"No wait," she said almost in alarm. She waved at me to sit. I felt uneasy in the confined space, other prisoners and their visitors and guards noticed us, me in particular, so I sat.

"What else do you want?" I crossed my arms and tried to contain my impatience.

Maggie would have been more forgiving. She would have seen Cherry doing her sad girl routine and fell for it. Thankfully, I left her waiting for me at the Blue Moon.

"I need a favor," she said.

"I hope it's not for a character reference or a witness for the defense."

Cherry almost laughed. "When hell freezes over," she retorted. We smiled in agreement.

"Then what?" I asked.

"The money… you know…" She leaned forward and spoke in a conspiratorial tone.

"You mean the blackmail money." I purposely raised my voice, to Cherry's consternation.

"Hey, that's my money, I worked hard for it."

My incredulity didn't faze her. "You lied and cheated for it, and you barely broke a sweat."

"Still mine," she huffed defiantly. So much for contrition.

"I need it. Ziemann thinks he can get me out on bail."

I groaned at the idea of having her run loose, but she did have a point. The Joneses weren't going to claim the money. They were too busy getting their own heads out of the noose. I didn't want the money and gave her a thoughtful gaze. "Tell me how you got it. Why didn't they just bury your butt in a landfill? Last I saw, you were in the backseat of Bear's car, not terribly happy being there."

Her lips quirked up in a smile, and she seemed pleased with herself. "Easy. After we left you, first chance I got, I waited for a red light, jumped out of the car and took off. I was near a subway, took the first train going anywhere." She shrugged.

"Amazing." Astonished at her bravado, I had to smile.

"Once I got free, I made my deal. Gerald paid me. I said I was leaving town anyway. I needed to get far, far away."

"To where?" I wasn't curious as to where Cherry might end up, I just wanted to make sure I never visit that particular part of the world.

"Atlantic City."

I shook my head and sighed. Did she think New Jersey was in Europe?

"What about your cousin?"

"Told him already. He can't help me, he's locked up anyway. So is Lamar and Gerald. Nobody can do anything to me now. Once I'm out, I'm gone."

I sighed inwardly at Cherry's ill-constructed plan but said nothing. I no longer cared what she did.

"So you gonna get me my money?"

I pondered her request and decided why not. I had one stipulation though. "I'm taking out for damages to my window." I stood up. Her brows furrowed in anger. "I'm also taking some to replace Bebe's phone you stole and the money he had in his wallet. When you came back to RTM you took it, so don't deny it."

She huffed. "You can't prove that," she yelled catching the eye of the attending guard.

"You were the only thief at the scene. First of all, the phone was a birthday gift from my sister, and Bebe had just gotten paid. Somebody went through his pockets when he was unconscious. He arrived at the hospital with nothing. You mugged him. No reason for Gerald to take it, or anyone else." I didn't need Maggie to figure that one out for me. The instant Cherry said she'd gone back to RTM after Bebe had kicked her out explained everything. She'd gotten her own payback on him.

"You can't do that."

I smiled at her, leaned forward and tapped on the Plexiglas with my index finger. "Sue me." I turned and walked away.

She yelled something, but I didn't hear or care. Cherry should thank me; I might have sent Candace to deal with her.

I drove back to the Blue Moon with mixed feelings. Cherry had gotten herself in a situation of her own making. She allowed people to manipulate her at the cost of others. Her moral center was east of hell and left of damnation. What would Cherry do if I gave her back her ill-gotten gains? If she were smart, she should skip Jersey and try for the Hawaiian Islands for some distance. Try to become a better hairdresser and find a steady job. Get a houseplant and see if she could maintain a relationship. Instead, I imagined her on the boardwalks of Atlantic City searching for an easy mark.

Could I blame her for a heightened sense of self-protection? Not really. I'd blamed her insensitivity to the havoc she caused to those in her proximity. Ziemann wanted to make her sympathetic to the people who might decide her faith.

Once again, Cherry would have to find a busload of sick children and join a convent on Mars to change my mind.

I left my thoughts of Cherry fade away when I walked inside the Blue Moon. Much of the lunch crowd had thinned and I found Maggie sitting at a far table with Rocket at her side. He'd finished the last of his lunch and was working his way through a milk shake.

"Where does he put all of it?" I commented as I took a seat. Maggie gave her son an appreciative pat on the head.

"Hey Auntie O," he said, his mouth full of fries he'd stuffed into his mouth.

"Thanks for the cupcakes?" Maggie said.

"Can I go see Bebe?" Rocket shoved the last of his fries into his mouth before hopping off his chair.

"Sure, but stay out of George's way," she said. Maggie's instruction seemed wasted on Rocket as he dashed through the dining room as if his pants were on fire.

"How did your visit go?" Maggie asked, watching her son dash through the kitchen's double.

"She wanted something, of course." I told her about the money.

She wasn't surprised. "Prison can't be easy for her," Maggie lamented.

I huffed. "Yeah, orange isn't her color. Compared to the rest of them, Cherry got off light. We can thank Ziemann for that. He'll probably get her bail."

"He's good." She knew my truce with Ziemann remained fragile. Though he'd returned to his Manhattan law firm, Cherry's case and his renewed relationship with Lee kept him in my life. How could I forget that he was invited to my wedding? Ziemann wouldn't let me. He already told me he had plans for Lee's bachelor's party.

"Maybe Gerald and Lamar should have hired him." I

didn't think any lawyer could get the Joneses out of their current situation. They'd found themselves mired in a mess of litigation and bad press that made the Salem witch trials seem mild. The D.A. office was on them like a bad rash. Besides the murder charge against Gerald, the Joneses were saddled with federal charges of counterfeiting, kidnapping, tax evasion and a host of other major crimes. Maddox and Russo had devastated Gerald's alibi. His EZ-Pass records showed he had crossed the Tri-borough Bridge into Queens an hour before the murder. Footage from security cameras gotten from his high-rise apartment building had Gerald returning two hours later in a disheveled state. What put the nail in the Joneses' coffin was the lack of loyalty their employees displayed. Once threatened with serious charges of their own, Harmon and his pal turned on Lamar and Gerald like the flip side of a B album. I felt no sympathy for any of them.

The biggest surprise came from Bear, A.K.A. Jasper Johansson. It turned out Bear had his own lawyer on retainer, who had him released from custody within 48 hours. Maggie found out he'd only worked for the Joneses two months before Rovell's death. Bear's presence was more for show than the actual protection of Lamar or Gerald. Along with the pretty girls, Rolexes, and fancy cars, Bear had been just another accessory. Cleared of the charges, Bear vanished into the wind.

"Lee thinks it will be years before Lamar gets out if the federal charges hold," I said.

"I can't believe Gerald thought killing Rovell was the answer to anything," Maggie said.

"If he got away with it, maybe. They would have pulled Louis in, and Jermaine would've gone, as well, despite what he said. He's too close to his brother to abandon him to the likes of Lamar. Tania might have held out for awhile but for how long until something bad happened?"

Maggie nodded. "Who do you think was worse, Lamar or Gerald?"

I could tell she had pondered the question. I had as well, but only briefly, a dangerous man was a dangerous man no matter how he seemed. It took me a while to figure out how dangerous Gerald truly was. Soft spoken, he blended into the background of his brother bigger-than-life personality like an old rug. In retrospect, he'd orchestrated Louis' arrest, subsequently stymieing Linwood Rovell's plans for the Mackies. He'd undermined Tania at every turn, not only with the attack at the publicity appearance, but with her missing staff, who'd been scared off by Lamar's thugs. Though outmaneuvered by Cherry, he'd dealt with her temporarily by paying her off. I wondered how long she would have lasted, given time.

His brother didn't fare any better. He'd liked intimidating and ridiculing people. Lamar acted like a blunt instrument in comparison to Gerald's subtle yet deadly maneuvers.

"Wouldn't want to meet either one of them in a dark alley."

CHAPTER

43

The smell of vanilla filled my nostrils as the last of the cupcakes came out of the oven. Esperanza sat in her favorite spot icing ones that were already cooled. Her quick, deft hands spread blue icing methodically. Each oversized cupcake would be topped with a yellow sugar canary, Rocket's team's mascot. Blue and yellow, were Rocket's team colors, as promised. The unhurried practice of preparing the treats seemed a far cry from the turmoil of clearing Bebe and finding out who murdered Linwood Rovell. The aftermath still lingered with all concerned. I'd had misgivings about getting involved with finding out the truth. Maggie had been determined, like a pint-sized pit bull. As always, she surprised me with her deductive talent, intuition and inner belief she could find the truth. I needed a little more faith… and my own stun gun.

As days turned to weeks, life floated back to normal. Bebe cooked, George commanded, Candace bossed and I baked. Maggie took on more cases, and Frank complained. Lee lost himself in his work and me. Allie had gone back to California and the loving arms of her husband, a little blonder, a little tougher and a lot wiser. She told the ladies at the country club to take their green umbrellas and stick them into an orifice of their choosing. Good one, Allie. She'd sent out the demo tapes

Les had made and got herself an agent. News of the Mackies signing a two-record deal with a major recording label came as little surprise. Good one, Tania. These stress-free days were interrupted only with the news of the continuing troubles of the Joneses and their legal issues. Lee arrived at lunchtime at the shop to give me the latest.

"The Feds have taken over the case against Lamar." He plopped on a stool across from me as I worked on boxing up the last of Rocket's cupcakes. Maggie would arrive soon to pick them up.

"I thought you said he was taking a plea deal." I started a new box as Esperanza put down another tray of finished cupcakes.

"Those were local charges. Gerald's arrest just opened a can of worms. There were a lot of things going on at Chaos 182, most of them not legal. The arrest gave everyone who'd been done wrong the chance to turn on the brothers. Also, Gerald fronted several side ventures; the federal government wants their cut and their pound of flesh." He eyed one of the cupcakes. When he reached for one, I slapped his hand away.

"These are for charity."

He pouted. This garnered no sympathy from me. Then he pulled out his wallet, handed me a twenty-dollar bill and took a cupcake. He made a show of peeling off the paper cup, removing the sugar bird and taking a bite. He rolled his eyes in delight and which made me envy the cupcake. When he regained his senses, I told him Maggie would arrive soon.

"Has she forgiven you for lying to Bear about her being a C.I.A. operative?"

I shrugged. "I was thinking more F.B.I. than super spy. Either way, Bear fell for it. Anyway, she's not so innocent. She used my little lie to her advantage. She had the man questioning his manhood after the stunt with Rocket's toy.

When I told George about it, he said Maggie got into his head, like a little redheaded worm."

"She can do that. She's in Ziemann's head. He wouldn't admit it, but he was impressed with both of you—slightly confused, but impressed." He finished off the last of the cupcake and licked his fingers of icing.

"About Ziemann." I said, a little hesitant to bring the lawyer's name up. His smile faltered a bit but remained. I'd never asked about their relationship before, too distracted with Bebe's problems and finding a resolution. Now, Ziemann had reentered Lee's life, I'd become intrigued. I still thought he was a pompous, obnoxious jerk, but he was also Lee's friend. This gave him a few brownie points, but not many.

"What's to say? We started off in the same place and ended somewhere else," he said.

"Is it as simple as that?" I asked.

Lee's mouth crooked up in a smile. "Ziemann is never simple, but we were close once. He did something I didn't like, and our friendship suffered for it. I won't go into what happened right now, but it was serious enough. I'll tell you, I will," he said, his tone turning somber.

Now, I regretted bringing up the subject. We lingered in silence for a while letting the gloom settle until I slid another cupcake toward him.

"Two for one sale," I said, and he happily took the dessert.

"Thad said something funny about you the other day." His eyes were playful again and full of mischief.

"I can't see Ziemann saying anything amusing about me, except imagining a piano falling on my head."

Lee laughed. "He said, if you'd been around when our friendship imploded, you would have gone after him with a vengeance and sent Maggie to finish him off."

I liked the idea of going Old Testament on Ziemann. What I didn't care for was the implication that whatever happened between them, Lee had been hurt by it.

"You've forgiven him, haven't you?" I finally understood why their relationship had thawed. Lee gave me a slight nod. I wouldn't ask him about what happen, I'd save the discussion for a more intimate place, not my cake shop and Esperanza a few feet away.

"It took some time," he admitted.

"Maybe this time he won't be so stupid, and if he is, I will bury his butt in the backyard, have a picnic over his still warm body and invite all his enemies," I said with a straight face.

"I can't wait to tell him." Lee grinned.

He kept me company as I finished off the last of the cupcakes. Maggie walked in fifteen minutes later to pick them up. Dressed in the team jersey, jeans and sneakers, her hair done in a high ponytail, she could have been any mom trying to raise money for her son's Little League team. If only the public knew. She'd come to the aid of a friend and slain men twice her size. Even on days, I felt more like her sidekick than friend, I felt blessed to be in her company: Maggie Swift, Community College graduate and person extraordinaire.

She hugged Lee and dropped her pocketbook and a large plastic bag on my work table. Imprinted on the bag was a slogan from the Hicksville Library, touting the benefits of reading to your children. Obviously, Maggie had stopped at the library before she arrived. She eyed one of the cupcakes and I slid one over to her.

"Business must be good," Lee said. "Boyer said he gave you another case."

"Against every effort made by Frank, yes." She smiled broadly, but quickly lost her smile. "He made me get rid of Cherry's stun gun." She took a bite of the cupcake and grin.

Finally, I was forgiven.

"Probably afraid you'd use it on him if he got out of line again," I said.

"Send him my regards," Lee said.

"Since he no longer wants to sleep with your sister, you two are all buddy-buddy again," I said. "Yes." He smiled.

"That's good, Frank needs all the normal friends he can get," I said.

"O, this is so good, the kids will love it." She licked bits of frosting off her fingers. "Speaking of kids, where's Bebe?"

"Where else would he be?" I nodded in the directions of the Blue Moon's kitchen.

"I'm going to say hello." Her ponytail bounced as if it had a life of its own as she walked away and disappeared through the access door that led to the restaurant's kitchen.

"Bebe's a lucky kid," Lee said. "He's got two moms now."

I smiled at the notion of Benjamin Bernard Dunn having Maggie as a fill-in mom. I was content with remaining his nosey but loving auntie.

"What is this woman reading?" Lee peered into the plastic bag and pulled out one of the books to show me the cover: *How to Locate Anyone, Anytime and Anywhere: An Investigator Guide to the Missing.* Most of the other books had to do with investigating techniques, a few by Lars Putterman. I shrugged. What could I say? Who was I to get in the way of anyone's dream? If Maggie's dream was to become the best private investigator in the world, so be it. I dared anyone to say anything to the contrary. Lee was about to say something when the front doorbell chimed, announcing a customer.

"I'll get it." Esperanza dusted off her hands and went to greet them. She came back a moment later with a scowl on her face. The answers to her uncharacteristic behavior strode in behind her. Ziemann entered the small workshop with his usual demeanor of annoyance. He approached us cautiously, as if he'd stepped into a place filled with landmines. As always, he wore a finely tailored suit, which didn't belong in my workshop.

"What is he doing here?" I turned an accusing eye at Lee. He shrugged and professed his innocence. When Ziemann stood before us, haughty and arrogant, I raised an eyebrow at him, cautious of his presence. He mirrored the movement, as if to say no one had more indignation than he.

"Slumming again?" I said in a chilly tone.

"Where's your other half?" He scanned the place. I pointed to Lee who wore a lopsided grin. "He's your better half. I'm talking about the other half of your brain. I saw her walk in here."

My eyes narrowed on him, unsure of whether I should take offense or not.

"He's talking about Maggie," Lee explained, accepting his role of interpreter. He understood I had trouble understanding his pompous friend.

"I know." I huffed. "What's up with Cherry?"

Ziemann's exasperation and impatience with me reminded me of all the reasons why he annoyed me. He acted as if everyone had read from the book of Thaddeus Ziemann and could easily interpret every nuisance, gesture and fart the man made.

"I called the office, which was closed, and then her house." Ziemann sighed deeply. "I got her son."

"You mean Rocket. Roger's her husband."

"I obviously spoke to a child. Who names their child Rocket?" He sounded nonplussed.

"It's a nickname," I sneered at him. "Who names their child Thaddeus?"

"My mother," he said.

"Exactly." I pointed at him.

Lee chuckled. "Why are you here, Thad?"

"I have a job I need done," Ziemann said.

"You need a cake," I asked, knowing he didn't. The man wouldn't trust me to bake anything for him in fear I'd poison him.

"Don't be absurd." He complained.

"What's this about, Thad?" Lee prompted, clearly hoping to keep the conversation civil. I didn't have much hope for it.

"What is it always about? I need Ms. Cup—" He stopped himself, took a deep breath and smiled at me. A smile that reminded me of a hyena before it tore its prey apart. "I want Ms. Wilkes and Mrs. Swift to find someone for me."

I blinked a few times, letting the moments pass as I connected the dots in my head that led to an annoying conclusion. I took in Ziemann's strained expression, knowing there had been a reason for it. I'd convinced him to do something he swore he'd never do, represent Cherry again. Now, in the process of defending her against counterfeiting charges, extortion and other assorted high crimes and misdemeanors, the self-serving, manipulative, lying, scheming thief, former hairdresser and worst friend had disappeared on him again.

"Please don't tell me this has something to do with Cherry?" I groaned.

"You think I'm here for the stimulating conversation?"

"I don't know, Ziemann. You haven't been here five minutes, and I'm already stimulated. I have a strong need to throw something chocolate at you," I warned.

Ziemann took a step back.

"Don't worry Thad, she wouldn't waste the chocolate," Lee assured.

"Not the imported chocolate, of course." I said.

Ziemann seemed unsure of how serious I was. Lee was right; I wouldn't waste my good chocolate on him.

"What do you want?" I begged, hoping to get the man out of my shop.

"I need to find Cherry Turnbull."

"Don't you have an investigator?"

"He can't find her, and we've been through this." His tone grew impatient.

"What's going on with Cherry?" Lee asked.

"She'd been out on bail for a week, checking in regularly. I got a call from one of the federal prosecutors wanting to talk to her. I made the mistake of telling her this, and now she's gone." Ziemann straightened his tie and smoothed his lapel, an action I'd begun to recognize as a nervous tick.

Lee noticed, smiled and turned to me. The cool and unflappable Ziemann was as normal as the rest of us mortals. This hinted there was more to the man than his overpriced suits. Something Lee knew and I had begun to learn.

"Well?" Lee said.

I sighed deeply and spied Ziemann glaring back at me. I came around the table, pulled up a stool and patted it. "Sit, Thad."

He hesitated briefly, taking out a handkerchief and dusting off the flour seat before dropping onto it.

"Give me twenty dollars."

"What?"

"Twenty!" I repeated.

He reluctantly pulled a bill out of a fine calfskin wallet. I slid a cupcake to him. He acted as if he didn't recognize that it belonged to any known food group.

"I think she wants you to eat it," an amused Lee told him.

"Why?" Ziemann asked.

"This is about trust. I want to trust you, so eat the damn cupcake. You eat the cupcake and I can trust you."

Ziemann took a reluctant bite of the cupcake and seemed mildly delighted by the taste.

"Triple rate," I said.

Ziemann's eyes widened and he almost choked. Lee gave him a few slaps on the back before Ziemann righted himself. "That's ridiculous. I need to find her, not put a hit out on her."

"Killing her might be easier and cheaper," I said.

Ziemann went tight around the eyes but quickly relaxed. "Odessa." He said my name with a familiarity that didn't quite work. He hadn't gotten used to the idea we could be civil to each other.

"Ms. Cupcake and the Weathergirl work for double, the rest is for pain and suffering when dealing with that woman." I managed to say it with a straight face.

Lee muffled a laugh as Ziemann gritted his teeth. "Where is the Weather Girl?" he asked in a forced insouciance, already conceding to me.

"Talking with Bebe. Why don't you go and tell her the good news?" I waved a hand in the direction of the kitchen.

Ziemann took a slight offense at the dismissal but stood without comment and smoothed out his suit. He turned and went in search of the other half of my brain, and taking his cupcake with him.

"Why'd you do that?" Lee asked.

"Do what?"

"George is probably already annoyed with Maggie in his kitchen fawning over Bebe. With Thad in there, you're asking for trouble."

I smiled at the idea. George wouldn't stop yelling until Ziemann left the borough of Queens. "Yeah. I know."

"You're cruel." He grinned appreciatively.

“Yeah, but you love me anyway.”

"I do.” His grin widened and it made me feel like a cupcake with blue butter cream frosting.

"So you think you can find Cherry?"

I shrugged, thankful, that Atlantic City wasn't in Europe. I suspected she'd gone there. I'd resigned myself to the awful truth I'd be chasing Cherry once again.

"Yeah, I do." I was getting good at it.

Made in the USA
Columbia, SC
09 April 2022

58754358R00191